D0101591

Vowed

While writing her debut novel, *Banished*, Liz de Jager fostered her love of YA and genre fiction by developing the popular *My Favourite Books* review blog. This ran for seven years and enabled her to gain a unique insight into the publishing industry. She grew up in South Africa and now lives and works in the UK with her husband Mark. *Vowed* is her second novel.

You can find out more about Liz here:
www.lizdejager.co.uk

Or follow her on Twitter:
@LizUK

Also by Liz de Jager

Banished

LIZ DE JAGER

Vowed

The Blackhart Legacy: Book Two

TOR

First published 2014 by Tor
an imprint of Pan Macmillan, a division of Macmillan Publishers Limited
Pan Macmillan, 20 New Wharf Road, London N1 9RR
Basingstoke and Oxford
Associated companies throughout the world
www.panmacmillan.com

ISBN 978-1-4472-4767-8

1 3 5 7 9 8 6 4 2

A CIP catalogue record for this book is available from the British Library.

Typeset by Palimpsest Book Production Ltd, Falkirk, Stirlingshire
Printed and bound by CPI Group (UK) Ltd, Croydon, CR0 4YY

This book is dedicated to fellow storytellers and writers everywhere, in particular authors such as Charles de Lint, Terri Windling, Ellen Kushner, Ellen Datlow, Holly Black, Emma Bull, Diana Wynne Jones, Neil Gaiman, Mike Carey, Guillermo del Toro and Bill Willingham, to name but a very few. The future truly does belong to the storytellers.

Acknowledgements

This book would not have been possible without the superior tea-making abilities of my husband Mark, and his endless patience as I whined piteously about plot and character arc and fighting styles. A girl could not have a better partner.

My two steadfast beta readers and friends – Sarah Bryars and Jenni Nock – are invaluable assets. They kick my butt and I love them for it. Thanks for supporting Kit, Dante and Aiden throughout *Vowed*. I also really appreciate their helping me make sense of so many things; they kept me on the level when I spent too much time navel-gazing and flailing.

The past few months have been a steep learning curve and my editor Bella Pagan has been by my side through it all, helping and guiding me. She hasn't just helped with writing *Vowed* but has also had some great thoughts about what else we can do within the Blackhart world. She's amazing and I'm so grateful to her, Julie Crisp and Team Tor for their support.

My agent, Juliet Mushens, is an extraordinary young woman. Her dedication and belief in my work has been unquestioning and unwavering from day one. Having her fight on my side has been a revelation and an honour. I am truly proud to be part of Team Mushens.

I've been very lucky to have received a great deal of support from my friends at SCBWI BI. I've also had wonderful encouragement from a swathe of bloggers, the UKYA community and fellow writers across all age groups and genres. It is an overwhelming experience being published for the first time, but it really does help that others are there to guide you with advice from their own first-hand experiences. I will forever be grateful to Kim Curran, Lou Morgan, Non Pratt, Tanya Byrne and Zoe Marriott for keeping me sane and making me laugh.

These acknowledgements could go on for pages and pages, but I think I'll stop here for now. More than anything, to any aspiring writers reading this (I love acknowledgements, used to read them all the time and still do): just don't give up. Your journey is yours alone and never ever measure yourself against another person's success because that way lies insanity. Do things at your own pace and realize it's not a race! And remember to have fun because this is what it's all about.

Come away, O human child!
To the waters and the wild
With a faery, hand in hand,
For the world's more full of weeping
than you can understand.

W.B. Yeats, The Stolen Child

Chapter One

Several Days Earlier

The boy sat up in his bed, his bedclothes pooled around his waist. The darkness in the room was absolute yet he had seen a shadow pass by the window outside. Which should not be possible.

From somewhere he could hear music, which wasn't that unusual, but this music wasn't the usual kind you'd hear on the estate, where drum and bass and angry rap music ruled. It was fainter, sweeter; the harder he listened for it, the more it felt as if it was slipping away.

His room was at the back of the flat, overlooking the play area with its broken swings, where no one really played any more. The flat he shared with his mum and older brother was six storeys up and usually he could sit at his desk before bedtime and watch the lights of London in the distance.

He'd never seen anything go past the window before, especially not at two in the morning. With no trees nearby, and none that grew as high as six storeys, he couldn't even cling to his first thought – that he'd glimpsed a tree moving in front of his window.

The flat lay in hushed silence around him. He slipped

out of bed, his easy stealth a testament to the many times he'd needed to get up in the past without waking anyone. He didn't pull on his slippers, instead crossing the floor in his bare feet, his toes curling upwards at the cold touch of the threadbare carpet. Pushing against the desk beneath the window, he leaned forward until he could see out.

The little play area lay deserted. Deep shadows clung to the areas where the poor lighting couldn't reach. The usual mob of hoodied kids who hung out at the end of the park weren't there either, probably doing mischief in the nearby underpass, terrorizing whoever was stupid enough to venture that way at this time of night.

The boy was about to pull back, still intrigued by the music he could hear so faintly at the edge of his hearing, when something caught his attention. He pressed his cheek against the cold glass of the window and peered sideways, along the side of the block of flats. All the lights were off and so it was hard to see, but there was definitely something there, something that made his breath hitch in his throat.

There was something hanging off the side of the building a few windows away. He couldn't quite make it out, but the creature looked nimble and was dressed in a coat that hung around it like torn wings.

The boy felt fear creep up his spine on soft kitten paws. He stood frozen, watching it press closer to the building, impossibly shifting through a solid wall and disappearing into the room where he knew another boy, Arvind, slept. He would be tucked up in bed, fast asleep and utterly unaware of the monster trying to get into his room.

The watching boy opened his mouth to scream, to warn someone – anyone – but his throat constricted and a sound

2

like a soft mewl came from him. He shut his eyes and drew a deep breath to try and shake the terror. He knew he had to do something.

With an effort greater than he could ever have thought possible, he raised his hand and formed a fist. He thumped it against the window. It hardly made any noise. He hit it again, harder this time. The sound was dull and muffled and he wondered if it would be enough to distract the thing and startle it to fly off into the night.

He did not expect the thing to turn so swiftly or move with such incredible speed; suddenly the creature was right there in front of him, its face pressed against the window, peering in at him.

Monster and boy stared at one another for what seemed an eternity. The boy moved first, stumbling backwards into the chair and knocking over his wastepaper basket, scattering balled-up pieces of paper and secret sweet wrappers across his floor. A part of his mind told him that his mum would be annoyed at the noise and the mess, but another part of his mind, the part that was trying to help him survive, told him to run.

He turned to leap for the half-open doorway but some-thing held him fast. He turned back to free himself. As he reached out to grab at the grey-skinned hand, with its strange pearlescent nails gripping his arm in a death grip, he real-ized that the creature wasn't actually trying to get into his room. It was trying to pull *him* through the wall. And possibly kill him.

That did it. The thought that this monster was trying to steal him away to eat him released the boy from his fear. Adrenalin spiked through him and he threw back his head and screamed at the top of his lungs. He didn't care that he would be waking his mum, who was working the early shift, or that his brother was studying for his exams and needed sleep. He screamed in terror and annoyance; as he did so, he was pulled backwards and fell down hard, his bum hitting the floor with a loud thwack. The carpet rucked his T-shirt up, burning his back as he was methodically hauled towards the wall. He scrabbled around, clawing at the carpet, trying to catch hold of something to prevent himself from being pulled out into the night. His questing fingers found his spiked football shoe lying halfway underneath his bed. He grabbed it and spun around, using the spikes to hit the creature's oddly papery skin.

The thing snarled at him through the window, revealing a range of small white teeth that tapered to sharp points. It spat at the window, and the spittle sizzled where it hit the glass. The monster increased its pull on the boy's arm and the boy fought, hitting the arm, scoring the skin with the spikes.

The monster tilted its head and focused on something behind the boy, cocking its head, listening. Then it pulled harder, using more force, and the boy was yanked upwards, several feet off the floor, the creature now gripping his T-shirt. The boy heard the noise of someone behind him and called out, but the cry was cut short as he was slammed into the wall – once, then twice, with violent force – before being dropped to the floor.

The boy collapsed, unconscious and bleeding, just as his bedroom light flared on.

As the older boy rushed into the room he let out a shout of his own, peripherally aware of the sound of far-off music, something sweet and soft, like a lullaby, and of *something* hunched outside the window.

His gaze skittered away from the shadow and the impossibility of someone crouching there. He dropped to his knees next to his little brother, pushing his fingers to his neck, feeling for a pulse.

Chapter Two

'My lady?'

I bare my teeth at Strach, Petur's youngest son, and growl at him in warning, but he brushes my behaviour away with a grin. He clearly hasn't forgotten me telling him not to call me that. Or any of the random titles King Aelfric bestowed on me, long months ago now, as I lay recovering from a multitude of cuts and breaks in the Citadel.

'What?' I ask him. 'And don't call me "my lady" again, under pain of severe death.'

Strach's handsome face goes carefully neutral as he reports. 'The team is in position.'

As he settles down next to me on his stomach I'm pretty sure I hear him say 'my lady' again and I decide to make him walk home from tonight's raid. He props himself on his elbows, bringing the binoculars to his eyes.

I turn my attention back to the two warehouses below. They look unremarkable and lie on the outskirts of a mostly residential South London suburb.

The warehouses are supposedly empty and the owners are deciding what to do with them. There are bids to rezone them and sell them to property developers. All very interesting – if it's your kind of thing. And it definitely isn't mine.

It's all background I found out when I moved into the neighbourhood to keep an eye on these buildings a few weeks ago.

They've fallen into ruin pretty quickly after a few months of being empty, but we now suspect they are home to a group of Fae who are selling a drug called 'Glow'. There are traces of the stuff all around the premises and it's a nasty mix of hallucinates and something else as yet unknown. Kyle's been working with someone we know at a research facility to try and figure out the drug's components, but I'm not holding out much hope – not if the stuff we're looking for comes from the Otherwhere.

The Fae High King of Alba, Aelfric, had an epic-scale fit when he found out that Glow had a link to the Otherwhere. His own investigations had shown it was someone from the Seelie King's Court peddling the stuff in clubs in London and around the Midlands. And after meeting with the Sun King and his Seelie advisers, when the Seelie King professed his innocence . . . things got a bit heated.

Glow is a nightmare cocktail which seems perfect for clubbers. Similar to ecstasy, the stuff makes you alert and hyper-aware of sound and colour, giving you a high that lasts for far longer than MDMA ever did. But the stuff is also far more potent and addictive than any other drug on the market. It's far more fatal too. Someone's baby sister, a girl of thirteen, popped some and is currently lying comatose in a private clinic. The doctors are unable to determine if she'll make it. If she does, they're unsure if there'll be permanent brain damage or not. And she's not the only one. Two clubbers got hold of some Glow and dropped into spasms on the dance floor, dying within minutes of ingesting the stuff. The police are at a loss because no one can find any dealers, and users just babble about pretty fairies giving them Glow to use. For free.

It's strong and crazy, and it's taken the clubbing scene by storm.

Aelfric, once he was unable to locate the Fae culprits, called in the Blackhart family. Despite being the most junior member, I was handed the job as no one else was around to take it on. The assignment came with a small team of Fae, made up of his grandson, Strachan, and a further three Fae who have been courteous to a fault in my presence, but coldly aloof. Feeling outnumbered, I had called in Aiden Garrett, who was more than happy to play guard-wolf for me on this.

'How long do you want to wait?' Strach asks me, offering me the binocs. I shake my head: I can see fine without them.

'Until they show up,' I tell him. 'It's early still, not even midnight yet. Besides, it's Halloween. What better time to walk among humans wearing their real faces without having to worry about glamour?'

Strach grimaces and I notice him touch his ear self-consciously. He lost the tip of it in the battle at Lake Baikal – against Eadric's forces who had been hell-bent on bringing back the Elder Gods. The damage to his ear was hardly noticeable but he covered it up, using a faint glamour to make it appear to have the sought-after Sidhe tip. It was a status thing and I didn't understand it.

He shifts next to me, trying to get comfortable on the roof, and I frown at him irritably. I hate sharing overwatch with anyone, especially someone who can't seem to sit still for longer than three seconds.

'Where's Aiden?' he asks after about thirty seconds of silence.

I suppress a sigh and point. He sights down the line of my arm. Aiden's curled up in wolf form in the darkest shadow of the furthest warehouse. I can easily see him using my sight but Strach takes a bit longer using the binocs.

'How do you do that?' he asks me and I smirk at him.

'Magic,' I whisper back.

He snorts and we lie silently side by side watching the empty square of concrete before the two warehouses, which form a T-shape. After a few moments Strach rummages in his bag and hands me a choc chip cookie that I take without comment and munch, relishing the sticky sweetness of it. A few months ago I would have eaten the entire bag of cookies, because the hunger my magic generated would have demanded it. Keeping vigil like this would have required an entire bag full of eats: using my sight while also using magic to create a protective layer of warmth. I would have needed a week's rest too to recover from abusing my magic, but these days my magic comes more easily and takes far less of a toll than it did in the past.

Something happened while I was in the Otherwhere, fighting tooth and nail against Istvan and Olga as they tried to complete a ritual to bring back the Elder Gods. I was exposed to powerful magics: a crazy ritual on an island humming with latent ancient magic, and I was drenched in a tide of power that spilled from Olga when I decapitated her. My own magic, sluggish and tired, pulled the new power inside, content and sated for the first time since I discovered my ability.

It took a long while to get used to how fast my magic now comes to my bidding. I no longer see it as a separate thing I consciously think about using. It's just there, doing what I want it to do. I spent time with Aelfric's sorcerers as I lay recovering from my own wounds and they reluctantly taught me how to tap into the well of magic within me. I also learned how, if it's ever exhausted, to draw on the natural energies of the world around me. They urged me to go to them for proper training, but being in Alba, especially the Royal Citadel, hurt too much. I couldn't think of being there without thinking about Thorn.

The High King of Alba's youngest son entered my life in a mess of blood and tangled truths and I found myself intrigued by him and the madness that surrounded us. A part of me wonders where he is and what he's doing almost every time I'm not busy with something else.

I find myself moping around, remembering how he laughed and tried to be polite to everyone and mostly how he hated Aiden making fun of him. More than anything, I remember him saying goodbye to me. I remember how utterly broken I felt as the door closed behind him, leaving me standing alone and hurt in a beautiful room overlooking the gardens of the Citadel.

Much later, when his mother came to talk to me, she took one look at my face and held me as if I was breaking. Maybe I was. I hated her so much right then. I wanted to push her away and shout and scream at her, but then I saw how deeply she was affected by her son leaving too and I felt vile and selfish, which made me sob even more.

She sat with me until the sun set, speaking to me about the decision to send Thorn away. How, in their wildest dreams and in her nightmares, they did not expect the duty of the guardianship to fall to one of their sons. The guardian prophecy was an ancient one, one fulfilled over time by various noble Sidhe houses. The tradition had fallen by the wayside and for the past four or five hundred years no guardian had been sent to watch over the worlds, because the prophecies never spoke of invasion. The Fae set great stock by their prophecies, seers and sorcerers.

I felt angry, but not just for me. I genuinely thought Thorn had been betrayed by his entire family and I wanted nothing to do with them. She left, pressing a kiss to my forehead, with a promise to send me Megan, but I had kept quiet, sitting rigidly on the bed, staring at her as she shut the door behind her. She left a small item behind, and I curled my fingers around it. I knew what it was without looking. Thorn's ring.

Megan, Marc and Kyle stormed the room, bringing with them laughter, hugs, tears and gossip. I listened, feeling hollow, holding on to the ring. When they left I opened my hand and looked at the plain gold band. It was far too big for me but I slid it onto my ring finger on my right hand and closed my fist over it. A small vibration startled me and I opened my hand to find that it had resized itself, now looking as if it had been made for me.

'. . . not even listening,' Strach says in my ear, his breath tickling my cheek.

'What?' I say, jerking back, annoyed that I had let myself wander around my memories while on a job.

'Morika is on her way.'

I blink at him and frown.

'So soon?'

'It's after three in the morning, Kit.'

I pretend not to hear the reprimand in his voice. I lost three hours thinking morbid thoughts rather than paying attention to the job at hand. 'Who is she bringing with her?'

'Three others. And a human.'

I nod. I tug the dog whistle out of my pocket and give three short blows on it. Aiden's head comes up and looks in my direction, but he doesn't leave the shadows. I can see the blue of his eyes clearly in the darkness and I hold up my left hand, showing him four fingers, then close it in a fist, then show him one finger. Four Fae, one human.

He swings his head away and sits up.

'Aiden's ready.'

'We have the team on standby.'

I flash Strach a grin. 'Are you ready?'

'Absolutely.'

I stand up and stretch, getting the kinks out of my back and legs.

'Let's do it.'

I step off the roof and drop to the ground, bending my legs to absorb the impact, my coat swirling around my legs; I feel so Batman right then. With my drawn sword and Strach on my left, a comforting presence with his twin fighting knives and long braid, we slip between the buildings towards the warehouse forming the cross-bar of the T. Behind us other shadows skim the night and fall in behind us. Not a single footstep sounds on the concrete and we ghost into the unlocked warehouse just as Morika walks in with her group. My escort fades into the background to circle them without a sound and I step forward into a beam of light slanting through the broken warehouse roofing.

Morika's head comes up and I see her nostrils flare as she catches my scent. The three Fae behind her stop in confusion when they see me, but the human just keeps on walking, his head bent while his thumbs work the keypad of his mobile phone, oblivious to any threat.

I stand quietly, just watching them, trying to figure out what they will do. I think Morika will fight, but I don't know whether the human will or what the three Fae will decide to do.

The human notices his Fae friends staring at something and looks up from texting. His jaw drops open in surprise.

'Hey,' he says. 'This is private property. You can't be here.'

I shrug. 'You don't own this property. You're not allowed to be here either.'

He blusters and looks at his friends but Morika steps forward. She has a tall shepherd's crook in one hand. It completes her Swiss farm-maid look. She taps the staff on the floor and it grows by another four foot, becoming a lance, bearing her house crest on the blade. She tosses her cap off into the shadows and a pair of ram's horns sprout from her brow. Her thick auburn hair cascades down her back and her eyes glint in the dark as she faces me, her gaze dropping to the softly glowing piece of antler hanging around my neck.

'Blackhart,' she says, sounding annoyed. 'You are interrupting a serious business transaction.'

'What I'm interrupting is a drug deal,' I reply. 'I'm stopping you from selling more Glow to this stupid man. Dealing drugs is illegal in both worlds, Morika. Did you think no one would notice human teenagers dying in clubs? And from drugs rumoured to come from fairies themselves?'

Her answer is to leap forward and swing the lance at me. I don't move and the lance slams to a halt inches away from my face as it shudders into the wall of magic that surrounds her. She's walked into the circle I'd drawn earlier, into which I'd then spent most of the day pouring my magic.

A bolt of energy sizzles along the haft of the lance and she lets out a yelp of frustration as it burns her hands; it drops to the floor with a clatter.

It's not necessary, because she can't go anywhere, but I still point my sword at her. Behind her, Strach and the rest of our team have surrounded her small group of cronies. Aiden has a giant wolf paw resting on the chest of the human – he tried to run the moment Morika grew a full set of ram's horns before his eyes.

'Morika, Lady of the House of the Ram, by the authority of the High King of Alba and by the trust placed in the House of Blackhart, you are sentenced to return to the Seelie Court. There you will face punishment in accordance to the treaties signed by the Summer King. Your crimes are numerous and show a disregard for the lives of those who inhabit both the mortal world and Alba. The creation and selling of hallucinogenic substances is a major offence in both worlds and for this alone you are sentenced to be taken back to face a jury of your peers. You will have a chance to plead your case, but we will submit the consequences of your deeds in this world to the judge. Your trial is set to start in seven days' time.'

Morika's beautiful face twists with anger. 'Your time will come, Blackhart.' She swears loudly, slamming her hands into the wall of magic keeping her trapped. 'Do you hear me, girl? I will hurt you so badly the next time we meet; your precious family won't even recognize you.'

I watch her rage for a few seconds, wondering if I'll ever get over the shock of being disliked by the Fae I send back to the Otherwhere. My cousins shrug it off, wearing the threats against them like badges of honour. Me? I keep an eye on the shadows all the time. It makes for uneasy trips to the shops.

Once Morika's threats peter out and she's glowering at me venomously, I spin on my heel, sheathe my sword and nod to Strach. He takes out the token from the Seelie King's chamberlain, Zane, and snaps it between his fingers. I walk out into the night and breathe the night air. Behind me I hear the team secure the three Fae and prepare to transport them back to Alba. The small token will open a portal for long enough to send them all into the arms of Counsellor Zane and his guards, ready for sentencing. The human is stripped of his wallet and the Fae hit him with a memory spell, making sure he won't remember anything that went down in the warehouse.

I pocket the wallet and join up with Aiden, who's waiting for me by the gates, still in wolf form. He falls in beside me as we walk through the gates into the night surrounding the quiet suburb.

'I don't know about you, but I need sleep.'

In answer he nudges my hand with his head and I curl my fingers into the ruff around his neck for a moment, taking strength from his presence. Aiden lopes off and I take my time walking back to the van. By the time I get there he's back in human form and dressed in jeans and a hoodie, his concession to the colder weather.

He wordlessly hands me a mug of coffee from the thermos in the back of the van and I wrap myself around the black stuff, drinking it in.

'You sure you want to finish up as planned?' Aiden asks as he sits next to me in the open door of the van.

'The instructions were clear,' I tell him. 'We signed the contract.'

'The Spooks are gonna have a fit when they realize what went down here and they weren't involved.'

I shrug and push my own doubts aside. Her Majesty's Department of Supernatural Defence and Investigation, or the HMDSDI, more popularly known to us as the Spook Squad, have been unable to make head or tail of the Glow case. I think I know more about the supernatural world than they do, and that's not saying much.

'Strach and his team know what they're doing. We're dropping the human in the West End. None of this will bounce back on us.'

Aiden grumbles under his breath but I take comfort that I'm following Uncle Andrew's orders to a T. We all know what happens when I go off script.

We don't have long to wait. Strach and two of his team turn up with the unconscious glamoured human, the others escorting Morika and her cronies back to the Otherwhere. They take a moment to each give me a slightly formal nod and an odd little half-bow of the head before leaving the human on the floor between them. I'm dropping them near Hyde Park, where they've arranged for the forester Crow to wait and take them back to the Citadel.

As we drive off, the sky behind us is lit by an explosion that rocks the quiet neighbourhood. Destroying the warehouse is symbolic and messy but necessary. It sends a message to whoever is running Glow in the Frontier that the Blackharts don't play around. I watch the flames reach for the sky in the van's wing mirror before I point its nose north, back towards the ramshackle house I share with my cousins while Blackhart Manor is being rebuilt.

* * *

16

Fire at Disused Warehouse in Catford Brought Under Control

About forty fire-fighters have tackled a fire that has destroyed the roof and part of two warehouses in the London suburb of Catford last night.

Emergency teams were called to the warehouses, near the bus garage, just after 3:30 GMT.

London Fire and Rescue Service said the roof of the two-storey derelict warehouses had been completely destroyed. There are no reported injuries.

Six fire engines, two height vehicles and a command support unit were at the incident.

News report extract from an ongoing investigation
into suspected GLOW raid by the Blackharts,
filed in HMDSDI HQ, November 2016

Chapter Three

I walk into the house just before dawn and find Kyle waiting up for me. I notice, not for the first time, that his shoulders have widened in the last few months, pulling tightly at his T-shirt. He's in desperate need of a haircut too and in danger of looking like a hipster with it falling into his eyes all the time. I resist the urge to tuck it away and instead watch him curiously as he goes about making me breakfast.

We make light conversation but I get the impression that something else is going on with him. I tell him how the job went down and he points to my paperwork waiting on the table in the dining room. I go in and sit down as he busies himself in the kitchen.

This is how I know something is up.

Kyle's not the food-making type. With our brownie Mrs Evans in Devon while the Manor is being rebuilt, holding court and looking after the builders who are living on the site, we are left to our own devices in North London. Kyle tends to order food in and is very bad at making anything apart from toast, but even then you have to lie and say you like it burned. I eye the scrambled eggs and toast he puts in front of me with suspicion but sit down to dig in anyway.

'What's going on?' I ask him after my first cautious bite.

I watch him with narrowed eyes as he moves his computer screens around so he can look at me. The dining room is the operational heart of the Blackharts at the moment. It's a bit cramped but then the house is a fraction of the size of the Manor in Devon, and until it's rebuilt, we're living here, on top of one another in a narrow tall house with weird little nooks and crannies. 'You're making me nervous.'

'It's because I'm nervous. Suola's been in touch.'

I almost choke on my bit of unburned toast and rubbery egg. 'Really?'

'Yes. She sent one of her messenger hobs along with a message. She wants to see you. In person.'

I open my mouth to say something but my mind is completely blank. I shut it again and chew on the bite of food. Suola is the Queen of the Fae Unseelie Court and I've been in her presence peripherally on one or two occasions. I've even done work for her, returning Unseelie faeries who've transgressed either human or Fae law, here in what the Fae call the Frontier. I've never actually had a face-to-face meeting with her. She always uses intermediaries and usually those go straight to Kyle's dad, my uncle Andrew.

'Okay,' I say. 'Do you have any idea what it's about?'

'It's a job – that much the hob messenger confirmed. But other than that, I have no idea.'

'When is the meeting?'

'Tonight. Midnight. At Milton's.'

I try not to think that it sounds like a bad noir movie title. 'Does your dad know she wants to talk to me?'

Kyle nods, adjusting his chair slightly to compensate for moving the row of computer screens. His wide eyes watch me warily.

'Yes, he knows. He wants to talk to you later, daytime.'

What Kyle means is that, with his dad in New York seven hours behind us, I must wait till later today to call him.

'Okay. Should I be worried?'

'I don't think so. The hob didn't look more nervous than usual. He delivered his message, I fed him some cake and off he went again.'

'As easy as that.' *Nothing* is ever as easy as that.

Kyle nods and I shovel the last bit of egg into my mouth. 'Thanks for breakfast. I'm going to try and get some sleep.'

He waves at me as I head upstairs to the top floor of the house. My room's not big but it's cosy and has a great view out over the rooftops. I strip down and have a quick shower before crawling into bed. I set my alarm to wake me up at midday, which should give me around six hours' sleep. That will leave me time to chat to Uncle Andrew and get my paperwork underway for Aunt Letitia, the family's record keeper.

The paperwork used to be the bane of my existence but my Latin and Greek are coming along quite well, thank you very much, and I no longer have to rely so heavily on Kyle to help me write them up.

I make sure my sword's leaned up against the wall next to the bed before I pull my covers over my head, blocking out the rising sun, and I drift off into a light slumber as people outside in the mundane world wake up to go to work.

I'm in an unfamiliar place, walking along a damp corridor. The roof above my head is broken and torn away, allowing me glimpses of a midnight-blue sky. The building feels old, with crumbling stone walls in some places that are over-grown with ivy and lichen.

It's also far warmer than London, where I know my body is lying asleep.

I look down at myself and I'm relieved to see that even in my dreams I'm armed with my sword. I jiggle it loose from its scabbard to make sure it will slide out when I need it. I'm dressed in a pair of denim shorts, socks and hiking boots. My tank-top is damp with sweat and I've got a khaki scarf around my neck.

I look like a cross between Lara Croft and the guy from Uncharted. I'm even wearing a hat, which is so wrong it makes me itch even more. I toss it aside. Dream-me can't dress, I decide.

There's nothing about the scenery here that's remotely familiar. I can't tell where I am, only that I feel compelled to keep on moving. I stalk the passages, going from one abandoned and crumbling room to the next, catching glimpses of high ceilings, faded tapestries that fall to dust under my touch onto broken tiled floors.

I can't shake the feeling that I'm being watched or rather that someone is aware of my presence here, in this dream place. They're not happy with me being here, but at the same time, they are very curious about me.

I ghost along wide passages, ducking cobwebs, my feet lifting motes of dust to swirl in the heavy silence. The whole place makes me feel sad, oppressed, but I keep moving, working my way further into the enormous building. The arched windows show me views of a ruined city lying at the base of the palace I'm exploring. The city, too, seems derelict and empty of people, with long winding roads and whitewashed buildings with red roofs. It almost looks as if it could be Tuscany, except that I've never seen a forest that stretches from one horizon to the next in Tuscany.

I come to a room, far larger than the rest, with a cavalcade of high ornate columns decorated with hand-sculpted vines and leaves. I hesitate, taking in the once grand room that's fallen into decay. There is debris on the floor, bits of rock and concrete that have fallen from the roof. I look up and notice the remains of the beautifully painted ceiling, where a flock of sheep graze in a meadow. A revel of Fae creatures take up the rest of the domed expanse. The room is so large the corners are hidden in thick shadow.

A heavy sound draws me forward – something is shifting in that Stygian darkness, darkness that should be lit by the sun streaming through the windows.

'Hello?' I call, my voice surprisingly loud. It's thrown back at me, echoing around the room and columns. I listen to the echo go on for an age; it sounds like a hundred voices whispering 'hello'. It fades to soft whispers before it comes hurtling back at me. My own voice, louder still than before, like a steam-engine screaming before it hits a tunnel. The sound is so awful that I press my hands to my ears and spin around the room but there is no one else here. Nothing else.

Just me and the dust motes and a blanketing quiet.

The feeling that someone's watching me is heavier now. My sight's kicked in without my conscious thought and my magic hums happily within me, telling me it'll be easy enough to call on it. It can jump to my fingers or rise through my skin to burn anything that comes too close. I take a cautious step towards the shadows and rear back when I hear something move.

It sounds heavy, metal scraping against stone, and it comes from somewhere in the far darkness.

Curious now, and scared, I creep forward, slowly drawing my sword free of its scabbard. I haven't gone five metres when there's the sound of running footsteps to my left and they're coming closer, fast.

I draw myself up, positioning my sword into a high guard: that way I can either strike or defend against who-ever is coming towards me, keeping the point steady.

A young man dressed in leather armour, carrying a battered sword, stumbles into the room. Shoulder-length dusty blond hair spills over his face, obscuring his features. He doesn't notice me but throws a wild look over his shoulder at his pursuers. Now I can hear them too. Heavy feet and the sound of a pack of dogs baying.

The young man comes to a halt a few feet in front of me. He brushes his hair out of his face. When he turns his head, he sees me, and his dark grey-blue eyes widen in shocked surprise.

'Kit?' he gasps, reaching for me with a hand that's covered in cuts and bruises.

'Thorn.' I move towards him on instinct but the people hunting him burst through the doorway behind him and there's no chance to talk.

He grabs my wrist and we turn to run towards the dark-ness that seems to be receding even as we approach it. I throw a wild look over my shoulder and confused images of a pack of lean, muscular dogs crowd my mind. They are flooding the room, and I catch glimpses of long muzzles and flashing teeth. Behind them come their handlers, a group of wild men in furs and patched leather, their faces as feral as the dogs they handle.

We near the line in the floor where the shadows start and I spin around, hating that I'm running away from a fight. Thorn curses but turns next to me and brings his sword up in a two-handed ready stance.

I grin fiercely at him and I'm rewarded with a wry look. The two of us against the hounds and their handlers? No contest. I almost laugh at this because this is a dream, but my heart is pounding and adrenalin courses through my body – getting ready to fight by Thorn's side again.

The wild Fae seem surprised to see me standing beside Thorn, our backs to the shadows, our weapons drawn. There's only a moment's hesitation before they charge towards us, the dogs' claws scrabbling to find purchase on the tiled floor beneath their feet.

'Run,' Thorn shouts at me, pushing me backwards, into the shadows. 'You have to help her.'

I try to argue and demand who I should help, but he stands his ground as the dogs race closer.

I open my mouth to protest, to tell him I can fight and that him fighting all of them is a really bad idea when my alarm buzzes in my ear and my eyes blink open.

I push upright, my hands shaking and my heart thundering in my ears. I blindly reach for my alarm, turning it off. The sun is high. I'm in my room, in my bed, and there is no sign of Thorn, the dogs or whatever was hiding in the corners of that dark room.

It takes some time for my breathing to return to normal and when I slide out of bed my knees are shaking. I toss my bedding aside and let out a yelp as my sword tumbles out from where it had become tangled in my duvet, narrowly missing my unprotected toes.

Chapter Four

The house is quiet when I go downstairs. Kyle's not at his bank of computers and I find a little note from him telling me he's gone out, but it doesn't say where.

Lunch is a grilled cheese toastie and a cup of super-strong filter coffee. I only allow myself to think about the dream and its implication when I sit down on the couch.

My dreams about Thorn are always framed by snapshots from the island or the Manor. They are usually more like remembering-what-happened dreams than anything new.

Today's dream felt hyper-real. As if, if I had been hurt in that dream, I would have woken up with that wound in real life, in my bed. I lean forward and touch the small of my back where Thorn's hand propelled me away from him and the dogs. I can still feel the warmth of the contact right there.

I finish my lunch and do a quick wash-up of the dishes and pack them away before I sit down on the stairs and reach for the landline plugged in there. I dial Uncle Andrew's number and it rings after a few seconds of making the transatlantic connection.

'Kit?' he answers. The sound of his voice in my ear makes me smile.

'Hey, Uncle Andrew,' I say. 'How are you?'

He barks a laugh. His voice sounds exactly the way he looks. Big and gruff, Uncle Andrew has the craggy good looks of an action movie star. The first time we ever met, after my nan's death, he pulled me into the longest hug imaginable and told me that I was back where I belonged, with all the family.

'Oh, you know how things always are, Kit. On the brink of something or other.'

I sit up, alarm bells ringing. 'Do you need help?'

'No, no. Not at all. We've got it handled here.' There's the sound of movement in the background and I picture him at his desk in his brownstone in Brooklyn. I've only visited once but I fell in love with its quirky charm. 'Now, Kyle tells me Suola wants to see you personally. Do you have any idea why?'

'No, sir.' Calling him 'sir' started as a joke; now I can't seem to stop and I don't really mind. It occasionally annoys him but he'll get over it, I'm sure. 'It's come as a surprise to me too.'

'Huh.' More noises that sound like a mug being stirred. 'Well, just be careful. Don't promise anything, don't sign anything, accept the job if you think you can handle it. Don't eat anything she gives you unless she revokes whatever spells have been placed on it. Remember your lessons in etiquette. Then call me and tell me what the job is.'

'Okay.' I nod even though he can't see me.

'Before you go, Kit. The Sun King's been in touch to pass on his thanks for taking care of the Glow issue.'

'Yeah, about that, Uncle Andrew. We blew up the warehouse and we sent everyone back to the Otherwhere to be dealt with, but I don't think it's the last we'll see of Glow on the streets.'

'What makes you say that?'

'Think about it. If I were making illegal drugs I wouldn't *just* set it up in one location. Or have one set of distributors either. It makes no sense.'

'I'm not comfortable with you sounding quite this know-ledgeable about drugs,' Andrew rumbles in my ear. 'But I take your point. You think there are others out there selling the stuff?'

Now I'm glad he can't see me because I've adopted Megan's favourite gesture of rolling her eyes. 'Yes, for sure.'

'Huh. Okay then, well, I'll get Kyle on it and let's see what we can turn up by putting our feelers out. In the meantime, find out what Suola wants and then call me.'

'Will do.'

We hang up and I stay sitting on the stairs for a few seconds longer, wondering what to do next. It looks to be an amazing sunny autumn day outside and I feel stuffy and closed up. I've not had a decent workout for some time, mostly because the local gym caters more to teeny tiny people in skimpy outfits who are out to pull rather than actually working up a sweat. I reach for the phone again and ring Aiden's mobile number.

He answers with a grunt.

'Thisbetterbegood.'

'Geez, you sound charming.'

'Uch, don't ask. After you dropped me off I had to run errands for my dad. I got home like an hour ago.'

'Oh.' I almost feel guilty. 'So you don't want to go for a run, then.'

27

'I don't know. It depends. How short will your shorts be?'

'Oh gods, Aiden, shut up.'

He chuckles. 'Give me forty minutes.'

I hang up and run back upstairs to my room to get changed into my running gear. Contrary to what my cousins may think, Aiden and I have become really good mates over the past few months. I back him up on the occasional job and he does the same for me. There is no romantic interest. I think Aiden's a good guy and we've got the whole banter thing going on, which is fun because Kyle is rubbish at being social, and I hardly see Megan and Marc any more. Besides, Aiden likes dancing and so do I. No better way to come down after a job than flinging yourself around on a dance floor like a crazy person and forgetting about monsters.

Aiden is sweet and sexy but he is maddening and I'm not his type. Firstly, I'm not a tall, leggy, well-endowed blonde or a male model who's graced music videos or the cover of fashion magazines. I have zero sexytimes experience and from the state I've seen him in after a heavy weekend, he likes his girls, and occasionally his boys, older and, well, how to put this delicately – *wild*.

To be fair, I'm not sure I have a type. And even as I think it, I know I'm lying. My traitorous eyes slide to the sketchpad propped up next to my wardrobe. I know that if I flick through a few pages I'll find Thorn's face there.

I did the sketches after I recovered enough from everything that went down on the island. It was a way for me to make sense of what happened and to figure it all out. Sketching things also helped when I couldn't sleep. It was like exorcising some of the worst bits. Let me tell you how it screws with your head, having vivid dreams like that all the time and little to no sleep for weeks on end.

I'd been a wreck for a long time after I came back from the Otherwhere. My cousins tiptoed around me, their eyes dark with worry. In an attempt to tire me out, Jamie made sure I exercised and ran obstacle courses until I couldn't move. I did paperwork and helped Kyle research whatever needed researching for the others. And, slowly but surely, things started going back to normal again. I could fall asleep for longer than half an hour and not wake up screaming or crying. Mostly there was crying, and ugly crying at that, but it started getting better, eventually. But it took a long time.

I still feel a bit strung out, a bit weird, not all quite there. On the days I feel peculiar like that, I make sure to put on my extra sparkly Kit face and I have discovered that by pretending I'm okay, most of the time I *am* okay.

My thoughts wander back to Thorn and the waking-dream I've had. I sit on the bed and grip my sword as if it is a talisman of some sort. If I was honest, I'd say that I don't know quite how I feel about Thorn, mostly because we never had the chance to figure it out.

We spent a lot of time together and things just kept happening and we kept fighting and running and trying to stay ahead of the game, so our relationship started off strange and it stayed strange. Even so, I can't stop thinking about him, or the way he would casually touch my arm or hand and I'd feel as if I was on fire.

I fall back against my bed and groan loudly. I'm definitely in danger of winning the prize for most navel-gazing monster-fighting teenage girl in the world of monster-fighting teenage girls. But I can't deny that I miss him like crazy.

I'll be out and about, going to the shops with Megan or hanging out with Aiden at a nightclub and I'll see a tall blond guy and my heart stutters and my stomach flips. Of course it isn't Thorn, but just for that very brief *second* it could be.

Another thing I know is that I've never thought about a guy this much before in my life. We shared one incredible kiss and I'm pretty sure it's spoiled me for all others. This definitely sucks because he's not even remotely close by to lock my lips on and I'm not sure if I'll see him again, ever. Possibly never, if the prophecy his father's so fond of is to be believed.

The doorbell jerks me out of my reverie. I grab my phone – still the same battered one with its broken screen that seems not to be affected by my weird magic – and pocket it. I've got a small punching knife that fits between my fore and middle fingers and I slide that into my shorts pocket. I'm not as armed as I'd like, but running with a fighting knife and my sword in a public park will probably get me locked up.

I thunder down the stairs, yelling at Aiden to stop ringing the doorbell. I pull the door open and stand back in surprise when it's not Aiden standing there, but someone I don't recognize at all.

I have an impression of an immaculate suit, wide shoulders, long legs and a pair of shiny shoes, but what draws my attention most is the arresting dark eyes behind frameless glasses that survey me as if I'm an interesting science experiment. Framed by silky long lashes, the eyes are set in a ridiculously attractive face with hints of a mix of Asian and

Western descent. This manboy's genetics do him all the favours because he is a piece of art.

'Yes? Can I help?' I ask, drawing myself up to my full height, squaring my shoulders and lifting my chin. Ready to do battle.

'Are you Kit Blackhart?' His voice is deep and my traitorous knees tremble just a tiny bit. A voice to match the face and build. Megan, if she was here, would be excited; she likes tall, dark and mysterious.

'Who's asking?' I counter, not to be coy, but to make sure I have time to check him for anything magical, including glamour, but he comes up clean and I'm a little disappointed.

'I'm from HMDSDI.' There is a tiny pause as he lets that sink in. 'My name is Dante Alexander.'

I have a real-life member of the government's Spook Squad loitering on my doorstep. I school my face into a cool mask.

'Then you know who I am,' I tell him. 'I hear you have files upon files about the Blackharts.'

He doesn't look awkward or embarrassed by my words; instead he just nods.

'You're right, of course. I was just trying to be friendly, not start off on the wrong foot.'

'I don't think we've got much to say to one another,' I tell him, my hand reaching behind me for the doorknob. 'The Blackharts never consult with your agency and we never ever talk to you.'

He sighs lightly and squints at me and, I admit, it's cute. But I've seen cuter.

'I thought you might be the exception.' He dips a hand into his pocket and my own hand goes into my shorts pocket, the small punching blade slipping between my fingers, but all he brings out is a small white card the size of a bankcard. 'My contact information,' he says, holding it out towards me.

I don't take the business card from him and his hand hangs in the air between us in no-man's-land for a fraction longer than necessary. He's making a point that I'm being rude and I'm making one back that I really don't care.

'I'll leave it right here then, shall I?' he says, placing it carefully on the top step where I'm standing, right next to my trainers. He has to bend down to do it and I'm aware that he takes his time to straighten again, getting an eyeful of my legs in my running shorts.

If he thinks he's embarrassing me, he's failing miserably. I'm comfortable with my build, having been in training in martial arts, boxing and ballet dancing all my life. You pretty much learn to disregard people checking you out, because within minutes of meeting a new instructor or team mate their hands will be all over your body. It doesn't mean anything unless you let it.

By the time he's upright I've lost all goodwill towards him and my gaze is colder than the icy tundra in winter. He doesn't seem phased by it and offers me an attractive smile, showing neat white teeth. His perfectness is starting to annoy me and my allergies towards neat and tidy rise up in my chest.

'I think you should go now,' I tell him.

Over his shoulder I recognize Aiden's lean form heading my way along the pavement. He misses a beat in his stride when he sees me in the doorway talking to someone wearing a suit. Alarm crosses his face, he lengthens his stride, but I wave at him and smile to show it's okay.

Mr Spook turns his head and spots Aiden jogging towards us.

'A friend of yours?' he asks me.

'You know he is,' I counter. 'You should go now.'

He watches me implacably for a few seconds longer, his eyes resting on my face. 'We'll see one another again,' he says.

'I look forward to it.' The false tone in my voice makes him laugh before he turns around and exits through the gate. He passes Aiden who gives him the stink eye and an obvious sniff that's very wolf-like. To give the Spook his due, his walk remains easy and unconcerned but I notice how there's a slight tightening of his shoulders, just in case of an attack. He gives Aiden a brief smile and nod before moving along and getting into a black Lexus.

Aiden pauses by the gate and watches the car pull out and drive smoothly along the road before indicating to join the main road again.

'And that?' he asks me, his voice holding a lot of growl.

'That was a friendly Spook who decided to come and introduce himself to me.' I step back indoors and hold the door open. 'Come on, I just need to leave a note for Kyle, then we can go.'

'Why was he here?' Aiden asks, bending down to pick up the business card before following me into the kitchen. 'Dante Alexander. Huh, Junior Agent with Her Majesty's Department of Supernatural Defence and Intervention.'

'Doesn't trip off the tongue, does it?' I look up from the notepad on the fridge. 'What?'

'Did he threaten you or anything?' Aiden's eyes are very dark, the irises blown wide, and his expression seems more tense than it should be.

'No, why do you ask?'

He shrugs. 'You smell weird. You look . . . off.'

Do I? I'm not a vain girl but being told by a friend that you smell funny and look crappy does tend to put a dampener on your spirits.

'I'm okay, just tired. Had weird dreams. Are we going running or are we talking?'

'Will you buy me lunch afterwards?' he counters, dropping the business card on the counter.

'It's not a date, Aiden. You can buy yourself lunch.'

He grimaces and points a finger at me accusingly. 'You have a bad attitude, Kit Blackhart. Has anyone ever told you that?'

'Never from where they're lying on their backs after I've punched them,' I reply. 'Less procrastination, more running.' I walk past him to the front door. 'After you.'

Otherwhere, the Tower at the End of the World

Thorn relished the complete absence of sound as he continued his descent into the chambers below the tower. The silence was a balm, settling over his frayed nerves, focusing his mind for his training ahead.

His destination lay at the end of an ornate stone passageway with tall curved ceilings and elegant arches. The chamber he was heading for was unremarkable, except that it was carved from crystal. It was also old, perhaps even older than the Sundering itself. But it still wasn't very impressive, not compared to the large tower stretched above ground.

As before, a deep sense of homecoming surrounded Thorn

within moments of arriving in the crystal room. He leaned into the warmth of the space, letting himself be pulled deeper into the room by the unseen winds that greeted him within. As usual, they guided him to the middle of the chamber.

A now familiar presence appeared just behind his right shoulder, a steadying influence. There was a brief touch against the nape of his neck and he tilted his head up to stare into the reflected colours of the crystals above him.

He stilled his breathing, steadied his heart and listened intently to the silence. The sound, when it came, was soft and clear, a small sharp sound as if from a brass tuning fork.

The room dissolved around him and he became part of the hurricane of sound that rippled from that single bell-like note. His magic surged inside him in answer to the sound, and he was wrapped in the resonance. Thorn relished the way the reverberations affected him, propelling his senses higher, heightening them until it was almost painful. The onslaught of sound allowed his consciousness to soar free from the chamber and the tower, even though breaching the tower's protective barriers wasn't without pain.

He lost track of time, sunk within the harmony of sound and a thousand visions until he found a discordant note that jostled him from his contemplative reverie. When he pursued the note that jarred against his attuned senses, he was unsurprised to find Aelfric was the source.

Thorn hesitated only briefly before pushing the vision into clearer focus, aware that time was fluid in this room. One of his hardest tasks was figuring out what time his visions were set in: whether past, future or now.

Thorn's father Aelfric was talking to someone via the ornately embellished mirror in his study. He was dressed in formal court clothes, his leonine hair swept back from his chiselled features, the embroidered collar of his coat tucked high, emphasizing the firm line of his jaw. The colours he wore were dark, which meant it was winter. Aelfric was always conscious of which Court held sway in the Otherwhere, dressing to acknowledge each in turn.

There was an initial reluctance to spy on his father but Thorn let it pass as he tightened his concentration.

'. . . be ready, Odalis?'

'He is stubborn, your majesty. It is taking longer than expected to win him over.' The woman's features in the mirror weren't clear but her self-important tone was unmistakable.

'I'm starting to think I chose the wrong tutor.'

'Feel free to replace me, your majesty. I will of course bow to your superior choice.'

Aelfric huffed at that. 'Odalis, all I am asking from you is a report on how my son's abilities are progressing.'

'And I am telling you, your majesty, that his abilities are not what we expected. He has taken to his training remarkably well. He spends days in the chamber, and when he comes out he vibrates with such power. It's even obvious to some of the servants, even if they have no magic. He often proceeds to lock himself in his room, refusing to talk to me or anyone else on these occasions. He makes the servants uncomfortable and they mutter that the storms that lash the tower are his doing.'

'Superstitious twaddle.' Aelfric dismissed the thought with an impatient growl.

'If you say so, your highness.' Her voice indicated that she wasn't entirely sure that the servants were wrong.

'I need him to be ready by Midwinter. See to it that the

Guardian of the Realms does not lose his mind and sense of self in the meantime. I do not want to present a drooling idiot to my closest allies.'

Thorn pulled back from the conversation, feeling revulsion. It was not the first time that he'd seen things that left him feeling sullied. Yet, hearing his father speak about him so coldly, as if he were a mere pawn in his schemes, brought home how little Aelfric cared for him.

Thorn allowed himself to fall back into the songlines, burrowing deep within the magic, letting it flow over him. They soothed him, carrying away all negative thoughts and feelings of impotent anger.

Odalis pushed open the door to her charge's room. The room was bathed in the harvest moon's golden light, but in spite of all the light, the room held darkness, drawn by the prince's dreams. She stood for a moment, breathing in the cool night air before moving to the side of the bed.

Thorn lay tangled in his bedclothes, a frown drawing his brows together. *Even in sleep he wrestles with his destiny.* The thought came to her and she pushed it firmly aside. She watched him silently for a few more moments, noting with interest how faded he seemed: partly there, partly in the dream realm.

How long has this been happening? What has drawn him into the realm of dreams so utterly that he leaves himself open to attack in this way?

'It is time to wake, boy.' Her voice was barely a whisper in the darkness.

He came awake instantly, the knife from beneath his pillow held firmly in his hand, the cutting edge a hair's breadth from the delicate skin of her throat.

'Odalis?' He blinked at her in surprise, taking in the slowly receding darkness, the full moon, the impossible hour and, even more impossibly, her presence, unchallenged by any guard, in his room.

He did not move the knife from her throat, which was as it should be. She kept her face passive, waiting for him to assess her and decide if she ranked as a threat at this time. The knife eventually dropped to his side and she gave a small nod.

'None other. Get dressed. We have training to do.'

She left the room as silently as she had entered, prodding the sleeping guard with a finger. He snorted in his sleep before jerking upright.

'He's awake. See him to the top floor.'

The guard looked ashamed to be caught napping but managed to muster the appropriate small salute.

'Yes, Lady Firesky.'

Odalis barely refrained from sending a bolt of energy searing into the imbecile. She could have been an assassin who, impossible as the thought may be, might have gained access to the tower to kill both its occupants.

She resolved to speak with Aelfric and have the current guards replaced with a more experienced group. It would not do to have their plans come apart before they had even begun.

Chapter Five

I drop to the ground beneath some trees in the park and lie on my back, gasping for air. Aiden collapses next to me and lifts his T-shirt to wipe his face. Two girls jog past and almost get whiplash from looking at his bared abs before they stumble into one another, right themselves and then jog on, laughing.

'You are a menace to society,' I inform him, in case he didn't know.

He pretends innocence but I shake my head, wearing my disapproving face.

'It's not my fault I'm this devastating.'

'Devastatingly *boring*,' I say. 'What do you talk about when you hang out with girls who don't know who you are? Don't you ever, you know, want to tell just one of them: "Hey, I'm a werewolf and I fight monsters"?'

He looks at me in surprise. 'I do know how to talk to girls, you know. Normal girls too.' When I roll my eyes at the 'normal girls' jibe he nudges me. 'Okay, so maybe some of them are a bit intense but none of them has tried to feed me to an ogre or anything.'

'Well, that was a mistake. You annoyed me. I did tell

you I was sorry afterwards.' It was true. He at least had to give me points for honesty.

Now that I've had a decent run – and running with Aiden is never just a light jog, it always turns competitive and full on – I feel more comfortable, looser limbed.

I accept the water bottle he holds out to me and take a long swig before handing it back. Aiden takes a gulp and splashes water onto his face and over his head, spraying me with water when he shakes himself. I shove him away from me in distaste and he just laughs.

'What are you doing tonight? Fancy hanging out at Milton's?' I ask. The place is one of our favourite clubs. The music is good, the venue itself is decent enough, but what makes it special is that it's run by an Infernal called Miron. The club is a neutral zone. Everyone in the super-natural community can go and hang out there, no questions asked. The dance floor is usually occupied by the younger paranormals while the upper mezzanine with its quiet booths and private rooms for hire, is where the older crowd go. It's a known haunt for doing business deals and maybe just relaxing, taking in the ambiance.

Interestingly, a lot of humans go to Milton's and there's yet to be any kind of incident. It really is a showcase of how things could be, if humans knew about the supernatural creatures that shared their space and didn't have an issue with it.

'It depends on what my dad wants me to do later today,' Aiden says. 'There's a wolf conclave coming up and he's got his hands full arranging things.'

'Cool. Suola said she'd like to meet me at around midnight, so I'll head out there possibly at about nine. We could grab dinner before at Lucy's? Then go and dance till it's time to meet her.'

Aiden sits up and pulls me up too so we face one another. His expression is very serious and his eyes have gone dark.

'She wants to see you? Alone?'

'Yes.'

'Any idea why?'

I shrug and pluck at the grass blades at my feet. 'Nope.'

'Are you worried?'

I grimace at him and he holds up his hands in apology.

'I am worried, of course. I mean, she's, you know . . .'

'A Fae queen.' His voice is low and I'm aware we're sitting in an in-between place. The shadows beneath the tree can easily carry our conversation to her. She's a Fae queen, one of the most powerful in Alba. Suola is only slightly less powerful than the high king himself and just as powerful as the Sun King. In fact, I realize with a start, we're heading into her time of year. Now that summer's come to a close and autumn's appeared, Suola's reign will be the stronger. The Sun King is governed by spring and summer and shares an uneasy alliance with her for autumn, but once the nights draw in and we head into winter, we're at Suola's mercy.

'Do you think that's why the Spook came to visit? They found out that she wants to see you in person?'

I look at Aiden in surprise. I haven't even considered that.

'It doesn't really make any sense. What would they know that we don't know? I mean, the hob that came by didn't know why she wanted to see me. How could the Spook Squad know?'

We sit and ponder the weirdness of the whole situation for a few seconds until I grow bored and stagger upright.

'Come on. Let's get back. I'm starving. You can buy me a burger.'

Aiden grimaces at my prodding but lets me haul him upright eventually and we set off towards the high street and its range of restaurants.

I nod at the doorman as I walk up to the front of Milton's. There's a queue of around thirty people waiting to get in. They're a mixture of human and paranormals but everyone looks human. Glamour is a requirement of the club and it's strictly enforced by Miron's security team. The only ones allowed to drop the glamour are the waiting staff and the bartender, if they so choose, and then it's understood that they tell human customers that they are actors, wearing make-up and prosthetics. No one has reason to disbelieve them and it gives Milton's an even cooler vibe if humans think models and actors hang out there.

The doorman, one of Miron's hand-picked security types, gives me a slow nod. The guy is as wide as the door he's standing in front of and almost as tall.

'Lady Blackhart. Good to see you again. Business or pleasure tonight?' His voice rumbles in his chest. He uses the title that annoys me so much, but sometimes you have to pick your fights. He's a big guy, and I'm not dressed for a fight, so I smile sweetly.

'A bit of both, Rorke. If Aiden arrives, get him to find me?'

He nods as he turns to lift the rope blocking the entrance for me.

'I'll tell him you're here when I see him,' he promises. 'Have a good evening. Try not to get into trouble.'

I pretend to look wounded at the admonishment but he

gives me an 'I've warned you' look that tells me he's serious, so I keep my mouth shut and walk confidently into the yawning darkness of the building. Behind me I hear voices raised in argument because he's let through someone who didn't queue up. Then he rumbles something and the voices of dissent disappear.

I pay a tenner and hold my wrist out to Cindy and she stamps Milton's UV club stamp on it. Cindy's a pretty girl, with delicate features and big eyes. She wears her faerie wings visible to the naked eye and is surprisingly strong for someone so fragile-looking. She keeps hold of my wrist so that the ink can dry.

'You carrying?' she asks me.

'Not tonight,' I say. 'Well, nothing big anyway. Just my knife.'

Cindy rolls her eyes. 'Kit. A *knife*?'

I look towards the doorway and bend down to slide it out of my boot. 'See? It's only small.'

'Your idea of small and my idea of small are not the same. But it's fine. Just keep it sheathed, okay? Try not to stab anyone accidentally like the last time.'

'I did say it was an accident. So did she.'

She just looks at me. 'I can make you lock it up.'

I sigh and nod. Gently removing my wrist from her grip, I head deeper into the building. I push through the sound-proof doors and the full blast of the pounding music hits me full in the face. The place is heaving with a capacity crowd.

I stand to the side for a few seconds, just checking things out. There's a higher percentage of humans than para-normals present tonight, which is how Miron prefers it. The humans, although they are never fully aware of it, tend to sense when they aren't the majority in the room and mishaps start happening all over the place. I've seen it in the past and had to run interference on nights like that. I also realize I'm referring to my own species as human and not including myself. I know it's weird, believe me, but now that I've lived almost two years with magic and the Otherwhere in my life I can't help but see myself as only marginally human.

The barman spots me and lifts a hand in greeting as he shakes a cocktail and pours it over ice for two girls. Philippe is one of the most astonishingly gorgeous creatures I have ever met. He is also a centaur and a devotee of Bacchus, the god of wine and revelry. The guy is dangerous to be around and knows more about alcohol and how to mix it into concoctions than any other person I've ever come across – even my faraway Uncle Richard who runs a bar in the Caribbean.

Without breaking stride, he tosses me a bottle of water that I catch without a problem. I twist off the cap and take a long deep drink before walking onto the dance floor. The music welcomes me like a long-lost daughter and I find a group of girls I recognize from other nights and wordlessly join them.

The DJ is one of the best Miron's had in here for ages and he knows how to play the crowd. We dance and throw ourselves around with abandon and, by the time my bottled water's finished, my loose cotton blouse is damp with sweat. I push off the floor and head towards the ladies' when someone steps in my way. I eddy around him, but he moves the same way.

I look up in annoyance and close my mouth in surprise as I recognize the Spook from earlier today. Only now he's dressed in jeans and a black T-shirt that shows off well-muscled arms and an interesting tribal-type tattoo peeking from beneath the sleeve. He's not wearing his glasses and I get the full impact of his dark eyes.

'Are you following me?' I demand, pitching my voice so he can hear me above the music. 'If you are, I can ask for you to be thrown out.'

A black brow arches in surprise. 'No, I'm not following you. I'm here to have some fun before going on to a meeting.'

'Really?'

'Maybe you're following me?'

I open my mouth to deny it when he smiles and I forget to be annoyed with him for just a second or two. Then I scowl at him, giving him a patented Kit dismissal.

'No. I have better things to do with my life than follow you,' I tell him, moving past him. 'Just stay out of my way, okay? I don't want anything to do with you.'

'Fine by me,' he replies, watching me thoughtfully. 'But I do think you'll find that we'll be seeing more of one another than you might like.'

I shake my head at him in disbelief before walking into the ladies' where I rinse my hands and make use of the facilities. I check my make-up to make sure I don't have panda eyes before heading back out again. I make my way to the bar and pay for my bottled water and get another.

Philippe beckons me closer and I lean over the bar towards him.

'That guy you were speaking with earlier? He's been asking about you.' I follow his gaze and see the Spook standing near the dance floor, watching the dancers.

'What did he want to know?'

'How often you come here. If you come here alone. Stuff

like that.' Philippe's most recently from the Bronx and sounds like a TV gangster on a good day but tonight he just sounds dangerous and protective. 'You want me to get Rorke?'

'No, it's fine. I can handle him.'

'He's older and bigger than you,' Philippe says, sounding genuinely concerned.

'The bigger they are, the harder they fall,' I intone, quoting Jamie. I pick up my bottle of water. 'Thanks for this. What time is it?'

He checks his watch. 'Just gone eleven.' Then his eyes go wide. 'You're seeing *her*, aren't you?'

'Yep.'

He swears something and it doesn't sound American at all, rather it sounds Greek. 'Do you want anything stronger?' he asks me. 'On the house.'

'No. Tonight I'm not drinking. I need all my wits about me.' I say the last bit with some dryness and he laughs because he knows I never drink alcohol.

'Fine then, but just say the word.'

I drift back through the crowd and find my dancing partners. A few guys have joined in but as usual they have no clue how to move and do their best to hit on the girls as they throw themselves around. The girls soon enough close their circle and we're once more a small clique on the floor, bouncing to the music.

Chapter Six

The DJ blends one dance track seamlessly into the next and I'm pretty sure he's a magician because I've not felt this enthusiastic on a dance floor in ages. I move to the rhythm of the beat and relish the feel of the bass line as it trembles through me, firing my blood and increasing my heartbeat. Some of the tracks I recognize, others are completely new to me. The friends I'm with move around me, but none of them leaves for very long.

We're a small tribe within the greater horde of bodies and it feels good to be part of something yet completely anonymous. I finish my second water and head back to Philippe to get another one. He passes it to me amid serving other customers and I head back without even thinking of taking a break.

I join the circle again and see that the Spook's on the dance floor. The girls seem taken with him, flashing him appreciative smiles and welcoming nods. He returns the smiles but, unlike every other guy who tried to break into the circle, he doesn't attempt to pair up with a girl of his choice. Instead he stays with the group and dances with us. And, annoyingly, his moves aren't bad. He's light on his feet and he knows how to laugh at himself when he fumbles the rhythm.

He catches me watching him a few times and winks at me. I flush and look away but refuse to move off the floor. Not until my time's up and I have to go and talk to Suola.

Even this far onto the floor we sense the disruption at the entrance. I look over, thankful for my height, and spot a group of people just coming in. It's a large group and the way the crowd shifts from them tells me that whoever they are, they're a big deal.

It has to be Suola and she's early and drawing attention. The supernatural creatures present seem frozen in place, shock and awe registering on many faces. Those who bow to the Queen of the Unseelie Court drop into curtsies and do that weird thing that freaks me out: they bare their necks to her. Girls with long hair scoop their hair away from their necks and incline their heads, men tug at their collars. They are utterly submissive in her presence.

She's past, swept by her retainers up the restricted-access stairs and into the private meeting rooms beyond on the mezzanine floor. If she's seen anyone she recognizes, none was acknowledged, but I suspect she knows exactly who was present and how fast each one was to bow.

None of the humans present seems to have noticed anything amiss and I turn back towards the dance floor. The Spook – what was his name? Dante? – for the first time looks a little nonplussed, but when he catches my eye he gives me a small tight smile.

Was Aiden right? Is his presence here something to do with Suola wanting to see me? What is the mysterious meeting he is attending this late at night? Suola, as far as our files tell us, never deals with humans, not directly, at least.

At ten to midnight I edge my way off the dance floor and as I do so I'm aware of Dante following me. I ignore him and go to the ladies' once more. I press some tissues to my face, getting rid of most of my perspiration. My mascara and eye shadow haven't run too badly and I repair both as much as I can. From my back pocket I slip out my compact and also slick some lippy across my mouth.

As suspected, Dante's waiting at the bottom of the stairs. He smiles when he sees me.

'Hi, again,' he says brightly, projecting so he can be heard over the music.

I scowl at him. 'You don't listen, do you? I told you to leave me alone.'

He shrugs. 'And I keep telling you we'll be seeing one another again and you just ignore me.' He gestures to the stairs. 'Shall we?'

The security standing at the gate doesn't look like much. There are two of them and they look like twins. A boy and a girl, maybe in their early twenties. Whipcord slender, both of them seem to vibrate with leashed energy. They are definitely not human and whatever they are is highly strung. I keep my hands in sight at all times because I don't like the idea of taking them on. They are all sharp edges and fast movements.

'I'm Kit Blackhart,' I tell them. Dante introduces himself and they nod, clearly having been told that we would be coming, and unhook the rope for us. As I pass them a light frisson of magic brushes the nape of my neck. The spell would be an alarm, alerting the guards if anyone tries to pass by pretending to be someone they're not.

I sweep past Dante and jog up the stairs. The mezzanine floor is where Miron has his VIPs. There are a few booths occupied and I see the flash of money changing hands as we walk past. I keep my eyes facing forward, because up here plausible deniability is a way of life. Dante is less successful when it comes to not seeing.

'Is that really . . . ?'

'An angel drinking infernal blood? That's what it looks like to me.'

He pales under his natural tan and stretches his legs to keep pace with me. We come to a halt before an anonymous black door flanked by two Unseelie Fae. It takes me a second or two to decide that they are both female. Their beauty is perfectly androgynous and they are similarly dressed in form-fitting black cat-suits, complete with little ears. I have the feeling that the restless tails they each sport do not come with the suits but are part of them.

'Names?' Catwoman on the right asks us.

We dutifully answer her. The one on the left swings the door open for us and stands aside to let us enter.

The room's large and comfortably appointed and looks like someone's party room. There are large plush couches, a TV on the wall and a sound system in case you wanted your own music rather than the tunes being spun downstairs.

I notice the man first, mostly because I've heard so much about him and anticipated seeing him in Suola's presence.

Suola's Beast is of average height and maybe a bit on the slender side. He's dressed in a dinner suit, the edges of his tie loose, the collar open. He looks for all the world like a slightly bored businessman pouring himself a drink after a hard day negotiating mergers in an office somewhere. The scariest thing about the Unseelie Queen's torturer is how utterly mundane he looks, how middle aged and depressingly normal.

Next my gaze finds Suola herself. Tonight she's dressed in black, of course. It's a stunning cocktail dress and she's paired it with antique jet beads that shimmer when she moves. She's talking to a young woman and, even though she's on the far side of the room, it's difficult to not stare at her.

She is one of the most devastatingly beautiful people I have ever seen. Her skin shines in the dim light of the room. Her hair is perfectly coiffed into an elaborate updo and I'm pretty sure that the wrap that keeps it in place is in fact a live snake.

When she looks over at us, I drown in the emerald green of her eyes. I feel myself smiling at her in a stupid way and I sway towards her, like a moth to a flame. Next to me Dante seems equally affected and we move in unison towards her.

'Are they not lovely?' Her voice is modulated and vibrant, holding amusement. She's talking to the young woman by her side. 'Just look at them. So earnest.'

'Your majesty,' I say, doing a curtsy Uncle Andrew would be proud of, even if it is spoiled by the fact that I'm wearing skinny jeans and biker boots.

Dante does a small formal bow from the waist and smiles at her. He looks utterly smitten, the fool.

The young woman with the queen moves towards us and gestures to the comfortable sofas.

'Feel free to sit down. Can I get you anything to drink? Or eat, perhaps?'

I shake my head and move to stand by one of the couches. 'No, thank you, I'm fine.' I stay standing, watching Suola carefully. Etiquette demands that we stay standing until she decides to sit. She notices my hesitation and inclines her head before carefully sitting down in one of the single armchairs.

'A glass of water, please,' Dante says, smiling at the woman before sitting down next to me.

It immediately annoys me because there are other couches he could have chosen. He's not very near but close enough to be in my way if something happens. I shoot him a venomous glance before settling back.

'I must thank you both for coming here,' Suola says, smiling at us benignly, her gaze flickering between us both. 'You've worked for me in the past, individually, through your organizations. I've decided that the next matter would benefit from both your expertise, but I want you to be the ones to choose to accept the task.'

The young woman passes Dante his glass of water and he places it on the table next to him, but doesn't take a sip. Clever boy. Another rule: if the noble in the room isn't eating or drinking, you don't either. A part of me is impressed with him knowing the correct etiquette. But another part of me wonders about Dante having worked for Suola in the past, or rather, having the HMDSDI investigate things on her behalf. We had been under the impression that she never deals with human authorities. I tuck the titbit away to mention to Uncle Andrew later.

'I've taken the liberty of preparing files for you with all the information you may need. The crux of the matter is this: someone is stealing children in South London and it's affecting the goodwill in the area. I have businesses that are reporting a downturn and the – how do I put this delicately – the *energy* is damaging to those of my people who frequent the area. I want you to find out who is responsible for taking these children, find out if they are alive, and if they are, restore them to their families. If they are not, I want you to hunt down these child thieves and send them to my Beast for . . .' She smiles and her teeth seem very sharp and white against the vibrant red of her lips. 'For interrogation.'

Not too unusual so far, as jobs went. I take the file the Fae holds out to me before she moves on to pass one to Dante. We flick the files open at the same time. There are photos, police reports and newspaper articles clipped into the file. The files aren't very thick and I feel sad that the disappearance of a handful of children isn't bigger news.

'Have your people heard anything about the disappearances?' I ask her. 'Are there rumours about the thief being human or paranormal? Anything concrete?'

'They have asked around and they have a name.' This comes from the Beast. He moves from behind the small bar and walks towards us. The polished black cane that supports his weight surprises me. 'The children in the area have taken to calling him the Ragged Man.' He moves and takes a seat opposite us, stretching one leg out in front of him. He sees my gaze directed to it and smiles wryly. 'Old age. Not as sprightly as I once was.'

I smile back, close-lipped, and look back at Suola. She's watching her Beast with a look of great consideration and for a second it looks as if she pities him, but then her gaze turns back to us.

'Do you have any further questions?'

'Why have you asked to see us personally?' Dante asks. 'It's flattering, your majesty, but we are both very young. Inexperienced.'

Hey, I want to shout at him, *speak for yourself. I may*

be young but my experience is pretty impressive. Instead I find my scowl deepening when I look at him. Suola sees this and gives a low laugh.

'I think you've just offended your partner, Mr Alexander. It's a valid question, although an impertinent one, assuming that I don't know what I'm doing.' She trails off meaningfully and takes obvious delight in the blush creeping up his neck. 'I am joking. I decided to come to you directly because of the age of the children involved. The community is distrustful of government officials. It is easier to have two young people, such as yourselves, investigating the disappearances, asking questions. You are more likely to get answers.' She stands up and we both immediately follow suit, like puppets on a string. 'Also, I wanted to meet you in person. I have heard glowing reports from your superiors and thought it was time to see who you were. And I am not remotely disappointed.'

The smile she directs at us makes me dizzy. I beam back at her and feel so happy just being around her, that I consider asking her for a permanent position, but I'm interrupted by the Beast moving, attempting to stand up, but dropping back onto the couch with a groan. I step forward, bracing my arm, and help him stand. He leans against me and I feel the solidity of his mass beneath his beautifully cut jacket.

'Thank you, my dear. You do an old man a service.'

Up close I realize he is older than I thought but no less attractive for it, for an older man, that is. His eyes, a rich hazel, twinkle down at me and I smile back.

'Always happy to help the elderly and infirm,' I joke and he laughs, pulling away from me so he can straighten himself to his full height.

'You flatter us, your majesty.' Dante's moved towards

the door, assuming the interview is over. He has his file in his hand and I grab mine where I dropped it on the couch. 'Thank you for the opportunity. Do we have the chance to discuss the case with one another?'

I open my mouth to explain that the Blackharts and Spooks never ever work a case together but the Beast fumbles his stick. I catch it before it hits the ground and hand it back to him. It happens quickly, but by the time I'm ready to raise my argument, the moment's passed and Suola stands by the door, her hand resting on the handle.

'I expect your answers by dawn,' she says. 'I will send Melusine for your answer. Be at the *Cutty Sark* pier by dawn, regardless of your answer.' She turns away but swings around a moment later. 'Oh, and one more thing: I want you both. If either one of you decides against taking this on, the other cannot continue it alone. Is that clear?'

Chapter Seven

The night air is cool against my skin as we step out of the club. I push my fringe back and take a deep breath to clear my mind before turning to look at Dante.

'How did you know?' I ask him. 'How did you know that I would be at tonight's meeting too?' No one told me that the meeting would be about partnering up on the same case, so who told him?

Dante's expression is a bit smug. 'I have my sources.'

'You could have warned me.' I scowl at an inoffensive rubbish bin and just about refrain from kicking it. I hate having stuff kept from me.

I realize a few metres down the road that he's been herding me away from the club without my noticing. I stop and frown at him.

'I don't want to work with you.'

He shrugs. 'Then we tell Melusine when we see her in Greenwich at dawn in a few hours.'

I bare my teeth at him in frustration, a bad habit I've picked up from Aiden. 'You are irritating.'

'Suola seemed to like me well enough.'

Argh! Was he that dumb?

'I think what we need to do is to get you sober and we

can talk about the kids going missing.' He moves past me and beckons me to follow him. 'There's an all-night cafe around the corner that I know of. They do great coffee.'

'Why would you think I've been drinking?' I ask him, annoyed by the assumption but tempted by 'great coffee'.

'I watched you down three bottles of whatever that barman gave you. Either you are far more hard core than anyone I've ever met or your metabolism is screwed up.'

I start laughing and it stops him in his tracks. He turns around and frowns at me.

'What did I say that's so funny?'

'You! You think I've been drinking? I wish I could let you go on believing that. It would do wonders for my street cred but, no, the stuff I was "downing" was bottled holy water.'

'You're lying.'

I shrug as I catch up with him. 'Believe whatever you like.'

He falls in next to me and I try not to notice how his stride matches mine. The night air is warm and breathless and I push irritably at my fringe, which has grown just a tiny bit longer than is comfortable.

'Where is this amazing coffee shop?' I ask him.

'Just there.' I turn to look and I swear I've never seen this place before – or if I had, it's never made much of an impression. It looks like a normal all-day-breakfast caff: the sort that makes its money from white van drivers stopping in for giant mugs of tea and artery-clogging breakfasts.

'Lead on,' I say and follow him across the road. The place is brightly lit and we choose seats by the window. The waitress, with a name badge reading *Hilary*, takes our orders for drinks and saunters off. We're the only people in here.

Dante places his folder on the table between us, his long fingers with their neatly trimmed nails tapping a rhythm on the cover. 'I think we should take on this case.'

'Why?' I counter. 'Why do you think that? Why isn't she talking to our respective' – I do air quotes – '*organizations* about it directly? Let them decide?'

'I think her curiosity has got the better of her. She wanted to meet us, like she said. I've worked on two jobs for her now and seem to have impressed her. I'm sure that whatever it is you've done has impressed her too.'

My lip curls. *Whatever I've done?* The way he spoke made it sound as if maybe I had tracked down some of her favourite chocolates. I bite back a retort and refuse to be lured into talking about any of the Blackhart jobs we've done for Suola – or anyone of the others, for that matter.

'Your drinks,' Hilary the waitress says, putting the mugs down in front of us. My coffee looks and smells like poison and I sigh in relief. 'If you want anything else, just shout. I'm at the back, just over there.' She points to the counter where there's a small desk set up before she moves off again.

'It's a big deal that she came here in person, right?' Dante asks me as he stirs far too much sugar into his milky tea. 'I think we should feel flattered.'

'It's as big as the Pope coming to your church for a service,' I say. 'I choose to be scared. There's something else that's going on, another game altogether, and we don't know what it is.' The coffee is strong and bitter and it hits the spot perfectly.

'So that's why you're not even going to look at the file?'

'Five children have been taken from their homes during the night. No sign of an intruder. No one caught on the CCTV cameras around the estate, no one woke up, no eyewitnesses, nothing. The children are all under eight years of age.'

He looks at me in surprise. 'You've heard of this before?'

'No. It's what I read in the file when she gave it to us.'

'You have an eidetic memory?'

'No.' How do I explain my magic? What I see, I SEE completely? 'I just have a good head for facts.'

He grunts and opens the file, turning it sideways so we can both see it, ignoring the fact that I was also provided with a file.

He flips through the pages as I watch, occasionally sipping my coffee. There is something . . . something. It hits me and I pull the file closer. I feel my curiosity being piqued when I look at the dates the children were taken.

'You seeing something?'

'Maybe.' I get up out of my chair. 'I need to talk to my uncle.'

He stays seated as I leave the cafe. I stand outside to call Uncle Andrew's number.

'Kit?' Uncle Andrew rumbles. 'Are you all right?'

'I'm fine, sir. I've just come out of the meeting with her majesty *and* I have all my limbs.'

His chuckle makes me smile. 'What did she want?'

'She wants us to investigate the disappearances of some children in South London. Brixton.'

'I think she's just had the file sent through. Hold on.' There are a few moments of silence but I hear him hitting the keyboard. 'I count five.'

'Exactly. All in the past two years. Notice the dates.'

There's a small pause. 'You thinking ritual?'

'Could be.' I look over my shoulder and watch Dante

chatting to the waitress, pointing at the menu. 'She's also wanting me to work with a Spook. I'm with him now. We're talking about the job.'

'Absolutely not. Walk away.'

'Why?'

'Because I tell you to. They are dangerous, Kit. They toy with things they know very little about.'

'Jamie told me my dad was a Spook. I don't think he meant to. It just came out.'

'That idiot.' Uncle Andrew exhales heavily. 'I'm sorry, Kit. There's so much that you don't know about your mum and dad. I promise you, come Christmas, we'll sit down and have a proper long talk about it.'

'Is that why you don't want to work with the Spook Squad? Because of my dad?'

'Partly, but there are other reasons as well, Kit. They are part of the government and the government is never quite comfortable with things it's unable to contain and predict.'

'These kids, Uncle Andrew. They need someone to look out for them, figure out where they've gone to, who's taking them, you know?'

'So investigate it. But by yourself.'

'Suola said she wants us both working on the case. And if the one doesn't want to do it, the other can't investigate either.'

'That makes things difficult.'

I sigh and rub the curve of my eyebrow. 'I know. Nothing can stop me from investigating this on my own.'

'Actually, Suola can. If you turn down this investigation and she gives it to someone else, you are bound by our laws to walk away from it. If you investigate, there will be repercussions.'

'So I'm stuck either way.'

'When do you give her your answer?'

'Dawn. It's a few hours away.'

'What's the Spook saying about this?'

I look back to where Dante's now watching me through the shop window. He waves at me and I turn my back on him, just in case he can read lips.

'He seems keen. Actually, he came by yesterday already, at home, to introduce himself. He knew that Suola had invited me to a meeting, I realized that tonight when I saw him.'

'What's he like?'

'Young. Maybe Marc and Megan's age.'

'What do you think of him?'

'I think he's cheeky.' My sigh is irritable. 'I don't know anything about him, at all. But I get the impression he knows a lot about me and us, as a family.'

'Let me do some sleuthing on my side. I'll call you.'

I turn and go back into the cafe.

'I took the liberty of ordering some pancakes,' Dante says as I slide back into the booth. 'If you don't want them, that's fine.'

'I can eat,' I reply and put my phone down on the table next to me so I can drink more coffee.

'What did your uncle say?'

'He's going to call back. He's not keen for us to work together either.'

'You Blackharts are stubborn.'

I spread my hands wide. 'Never pretended otherwise.'

'You are pretty confident for someone your age.' Dante narrows his eyes at me. 'How old are you anyway? Sixteen?'

'Seventeen.' I hate telling people how old I am. It makes me feel exposed, as if I'm lacking because I'm not older.

He whistles. 'Wow. You can legally drive.'

I open my mouth to ask him why he was suddenly being a dick, then Hilary turns up with plates laden with pancakes and crispy bacon and maple syrup. She leaves the plates with us and comes back with two more mugs.

'Looks like you kids need this,' she says, smiling not unkindly at me, before heading back to her small table.

'You're being a complete pain,' I tell him, choosing not swear.

'I've been told I excel at being a pain.' He bends his dark head over the pancakes and takes a whiff. 'These are really good, by the way.'

'You come here often, then?'

'At least once a week.'

'You're lying.'

'Okay, maybe I was told by another colleague that these are good.'

'What other colleague?'

Dante raises his fork and waves it between us. 'Uh huh. If real questions are being asked, you have to play along.'

I hesitate only for a second. 'Fine.'

The look he gives me is one of triumph. I decide I really hate him.

Chapter Eight

'I'll go first. How is it that you're out on a school night?'

His question is designed to annoy. 'I have private tuition. Both my cousin Kyle and I do.' I chew my pancakes and bacon and have to admit that they're good. 'My turn now. How old are you?'

'Twenty. I'll be twenty-one in December. Why does your family dislike the HMDSDI so much? We're doing the same job.'

'You work for the government, doing its dirty jobs when there are things that your local police forces can't handle. You are an interested outside party. The Blackharts work closely with the leaders of the Otherwhere and police their denizens in the Frontier. We try to prevent bad things from happening.' I raise my eyebrows at him. 'Now me. You're really young to be a Spook. How does that work?'

'I was sixteen when I came across my first supernatural creature. It was after a mate's party and we were all pretty wasted, staggering to the nearest Tube station. I looked up this alleyway we were passing and saw these two guys fighting. One guy was huge, the other was normal sized. I went to help and got an eyeful of something with claws and teeth.' Dante pauses for a second so he can take a sip of his tea. 'I was instantly sober. I know a bit of martial arts so I laid into the thing and it gave the other guy the chance to get his taser out. Afterwards he handed me his business card and told me to call him when I finished school. And I did. I've been with the agency for two years now.'

'You Saw the creature?' I'm sure he can hear the different tone I use to inflect in the word 'Saw' and he understands what I mean.

'Yes.' He looks thoughtful. 'I was pretty drunk at the time and apparently alcohol allows some people to See creatures like the Fae.'

'That is extreme but true.' I've read books about stuff like this in the past, when someone stumbling home after a night at the local free house would see fairies dancing on a local hill. They'd investigate and disappear, maybe reappearing twenty years down the line, oblivious that any time had passed at all.

Dante nods and watches me as I mop up the last bit of syrup with a slice of pancake. I don't know where to start trying to figure out more about this guy.

'So, you don't have true Sight?'

He shakes his head. 'The story goes that when I was little I used to have a lot of imaginary friends and I would know things were about to happen before they occured. My friends freaked out on me when it became obvious I *knew stuff* no one else did. I was brought up in a monastery school until I was seven, and the priests had one of their deliverance priests pray over me. He asked for my *gifts* to be taken from me until I was old enough to understand how they worked and not hurt anyone with them.'

This was heavy stuff: a mixture of theology and weird-ness that I didn't fully comprehend myself. But, as far as I understood, the true Sight is usually hereditary – something I and the Blackharts share. But if it's not understood by the parents, the kid often gets shipped off to visit psychiatrists. There, normality is forced on the poor child, along with a suitcase of drugs to prevent them from ever being remotely normal. A lot of parents talk about imaginary friends in hushed tones and sometimes even, as in Dante's case, priests are called in to perform exorcisms if things get completely out of hand.

'Can either of your parents See?'

The look Dante levels at me tells me he knows I'm fishing. 'I don't know who my real parents are. I'm adopted.'

'Wow.' I grimace. 'Sorry, that must have been hard for you.'

Dante's expression is frosty, and he looks me over as if I've just suggested his family might be cannibals. 'No, not really. The family that adopted me is the only family I need. My mum and dad are decent people and my sister . . . anyway, they were fine and are a great family. I couldn't have been happier.'

His expression warms as he talks of his loved ones and, just like that, Dante becomes human and likeable. I suspect it's what he planned all along because he sits back a bit and smirks at me as if he just stole all the cream.

'Can I point out that we've been having an actual conversation for five minutes at least and you've not told me you dislike me once?' he says after a few seconds, finishing his tea.

'It's still early,' I tell him. 'Don't get ahead of yourself.'

I grab my file and open it up. 'They're all from the same estate. That's unusual by itself.'

'You want to go there now?' Dante asks, digging in his

pocket for his wallet. 'It's not far. The traffic shouldn't be an issue.'

'Yeah. Let's go see what we can See.'

Dante pays up and I leave the tip for Hilary. She waves us off and clears our plates as we head into the night.

'I've got my bike here,' I tell him as we near where he's parked his Lexus. 'Wait for me.'

I walk the short distance between my bike and his car and undo the light glamour I threw over it, concealing my leather jacket and helmet. I shrug my jacket on and adjust my fringe before sliding the helmet on.

I gun the bike's engine; it answers a deep wuff beneath me and a thrill crawls up my spine the way it usually does when I get on it. Dante's in the driver's seat when I pull up next to him.

'Nice bike,' he tells me. 'Those pipes definitely aren't legal.'

'Loud pipes save lives,' I answer by rote and smile at him. 'Let's go.'

I slam my visor down and pull out into the minimal traffic, keeping to the speed limit and riding sensibly for a change so that he can keep up with me in his Lexus.

It's one of my favourite things, riding at night. There's something primitive about it that I like. Just me and the darkness out on the road. Even in the cities you can sometimes feel it. That you're being watched and whatever's watching you isn't benign or human.

Dante overtakes me as we near Brixton and gestures out of the window, indicating that I should follow him. I tuck myself behind him at a safe distance and cruise along until we pull off the main roads and take a series of side roads. Small businesses are shuttered and there's an air of melancholy about the place. Graffiti tags are thrown up but none of them looks familiar.

We eventually come to a halt in front of a large seventies-built concrete block, flanked by two more blocks slightly lower than the main one. Even the occasional bit of lighting makes the place look tired and in desperate need of a lot of money to tidy it up or, failing that, complete demolition to enable a fresh start. The three buildings form a horseshoe shape and in the middle is a patch of miserable-looking grass, with a sign that reads 'NO BALL GAMES' leaning crankily to the side.

I still the engine and get off the bike, pulling my helmet off.

'This is it,' Dante says as he gets out of his car and folds his arms on the roof, looking at the three blocks of flats. 'It doesn't look like much.'

This, if I didn't know better, is the trigger for the screaming to start.

Chapter Nine

As we speed towards the noise, I'm gratified to notice that although we are the same height, I'm the faster runner. Dante is only a step behind me when we round the corner of the central block. We are suddenly facing the banshee as she lifts her head from her hands and lets out another ear-achingly loud wail. She's in the process of floating upwards when she sees us but holds out her hand to us to stop us from interrupting her mid-wail. Dante makes as if to run at her but I grip his wrist and shake my head.

The banshee's doing her job; interrupting her would mean she would lose track of her passenger, and that could be potentially disastrous for them both.

'What is that?' Dante asks, shifting uneasily. He's wearing silver knuckledusters engraved with sigils that look like angelic script. My magic pings unhappily and I take a step back. Using angelic script on a banshee is like using a nuclear bomb to stop a peaceful sit-in demonstration by unarmed elderly hippies.

'A banshee. She's a portent of death.'

'No shit,' he says, sounding shocked. 'What's it doing here?'

'When she's done, we can talk to her. Ask her. Maybe she knows something about the kids who've gone missing.'

'How is no one awake with her howling like that?'

'Whoever she's here for can hear her. The average human can't. The frequencies the banshees operate on aren't usually audible to them.' I watch him thoughtfully for a second. 'And if you're wondering, I'm not counting you as an average human.'

'Huh. Thanks, I think.' He nods. 'You explain stuff well.'

'Thank you.'

I turn to watch the banshee just as she drops her arms to her sides and floats back down to the ground. At the same time she transforms from ethereal frightening wailing woman to a pretty twenty-something brunette with large eyes and a smiling mouth.

'Ah, an actual Blackhart. And you've brought a friend?' She's suddenly very close to Dante, really in his face, but he stands his ground and doesn't flinch when she takes a deep whiff of him. 'He doesn't smell of your blood, Kit. Who is he?'

'He's a Spook,' I say and watch her recoil as if she's just stepped in fox droppings. She's at my side in a flash.

'And you're *talking* to it?' Her voice rose incredulously. 'Does Andrew know?'

'He knows.'

'Oh.' She deflates a little and I grin, knowing she was hoping to get some gossip to hold over me so that I had to do her favours. 'That sucks.'

'What are you doing here?' I ask her. Female banshees just love talking about their jobs.

'There's a descendant of the MacDougal clan that lives here. I'm tied to their family so I've come to sing him home.'

'Is he dead, now?' Dante asks, unable to keep out of the conversation.

'No. I have three more visits to do before he dies.' She frowns at him and then at me. 'What are you doing here?'

'Have you seen anyone here that doesn't belong?' I counter. 'Children have gone missing from this estate in the past and we're thinking of investigating.'

She crosses her arms over her chest. 'And what's in it for me, if I answer questions?'

My hand slips into my jeans pocket and I draw out a single white pearl, not too large, maybe the size of my little fingernail.

'I'm happy to part with this *if* what you tell us is worthwhile.'

The banshee flutters. I see her real form overlay her corporeal body and I try not to flinch. Next to me Dante mutters under his breath but he stands his ground and, to my surprise, he moves closer to me, as if he's actually thinking of backing me up in case things go south.

'There is something here,' she says, her voice low. 'I've sensed it in the past when I've come to check on my charge, and each time I felt that it had grown stronger.' She sighs dramatically. 'I'd like to call it a ghost, but it isn't that. It is something different. Something that is pretty old. Older than me, certainly.'

I frown and look around, taking in the derelict little garden and play area. 'Has it ever tried to make a move against you?' I ask her.

'No. It watches and seethes. It feels angry sometimes too. As if it's annoyed I'm in its territory perhaps.' She reaches out a hand to me. 'Give me the pearl.'

'I'm not done yet,' I say vehemently.

'How often have you been here?' Dante asks her.

The banshee stares off into the night, gathering her thoughts before answering.

'I have come here for the past six years, in human time, at least twice a year, if not more, to check on him. Then I go away because nothing in his immediate future showed me that he would die.'

'And you saw the *creature* each time?'

She nods mutely, her attention focused on my hand holding the pearl.

'Have you ever spoken to it?' I ask her and her gaze meets mine reluctantly.

'I am not in the habit of hanging around conversing with things that are likely to do me harm, Blackhart.' Her tone and gaze as she flicks a look over Dante is rather pointed.

'Is it male or female?' Dante seems unfazed by her regard and I can't help but feel a little impressed by his attitude.

She shrugs elegantly. 'I don't know. Look, Blackhart, I have places to be and litanies to sing. I don't know who or what this thing is that you're seeking on the estate. But I know it's here often and I know it makes things unpleasant for me and *others* who have to work in the area. I suggest you look to the history of this place.' She shows me her teeth in a small sharp smile. 'I wish I knew more, Blackhart, but I do not. Now keep your word and give me my reward.'

I open my hand and turn my palm upwards so that she can grab the pearl without touching my skin, but even so the coldness that makes up her presence sends shivers down my spine and I sag a little as a bit of my life force is taken in the exchange.

'Good luck,' she says, turning on her heel and walking off towards the back of the estate where a row of trees separates the grounds from another set of low buildings. As we watch she fades slowly away until there is no sign of her at all.

'That,' Dante says, with a half-laugh that has a touch of nerves to it, 'was both creepy and cool.'

'That cost me a very expensive pearl,' I point out, grimacing. 'Dammit.'

'I think that the only way to make sure you get paid for it is to take on the job, don't you think?'

I narrow my eyes at Dante as I start moving back towards the front of the buildings where we've left our transport parked.

'Don't push it,' I tell him. 'Let's see what else we can find first.'

The group of teens hanging around my bike look as if they are up to no good. I leave Dante behind as I stride towards them, pulling myself to my full height, shoulders back and chin raised.

'If you don't get off my bike,' I tell them conversationally, 'I'll have to make you.'

A tall boy with short dreads looks over at me, his mouth open and smiling. 'We're just looking, right? This is a smooth ride.'

I look at the Ducati and think that maybe I should have come here in Dante's Lexus instead. But then it would have meant I was reliant on him for a ride home or to the nearest Tube station at least and I'm not keen on that either.

'She's a bit of a handful,' I say to him and walk closer. A girl's straddling the bike but her feet don't even touch the ground. She shoots me a venomous look as I near. 'Off my bike, please.' I keep my voice cool and measured because I don't really know how to deal with them. There are five of them, and the way they are aware of one another, spatially and physically, tells me they're a tight group of friends. Dread Boy is fast and he pulls the girl off the seat with one arm around her waist. He swings her to the side and holds a finger out to her when she opens her mouth to protest.

'No. Not a word.' He turns to his friends, who look awkward as they're not sure what to do now that they've been caught tampering with my bike. Their indecision comes as a surprise, but I wear my most stoic and unimpressed face as I watch them watch me and Dante.

'There, all yours.' He waves a hand. 'No harm done.'

For a second I think that's going to be that, but two of them surge towards me and I react instinctively, reaching down whip-fast for the knife in my boot. The sight of the blade reversed against the black of my jacket as I drop into a ready stance shocks them enough that they stop their advance.

Then one boy holds out his hand and shows me he's got my helmet.

'I just wanted to give this back, innit?' he says, his voice annoyed, rather than scared. 'Geez, woman. You need to chill.'

I point the knife at him. 'Put it on the seat. Then step back.'

I feel like a complete idiot. Aiden, had he been here, would be laughing his ass off and joking about how I can handle a banshee and all kinds of monsters from the Otherwhere – but a group of South London youths had me on edge, making bad decisions and acting like a crazy person.

'What are you and Captain Tattoo doing here, on our block?' Dread Boy asks me.

For a moment I think about lying but then I decide that it's not necessary. These are the kids Suola wants us to speak to. I look over my shoulder at Dante and motion him forward.

'This is Dante. I'm Kit. We're investigating the little kids going missing from the estate.'

If I had grown another head and done the can-can, I don't think they could've looked more surprised.

Dread Boy frowns a bit but it's the boy who had hold of my helmet who speaks up. He's got strange hazel-coloured eyes that are easy to see in the dim light. Not an unattractive face either; he just maybe needed to eat a bit more.

'So you guys're cops then?'

'Don't be stupid, Marvin, how can they be cops? She's like our age, right?'

'The dude, though, he looks old enough and uptight enough to be a copper.'

'Have you ever seen cops who look like this?'

'Could be undercover, right? Like in *Jump Street*.'

Everyone turns to look at the last one who spoke. Even in the bad lighting I can see the boy, no older than fourteen, flush.

'You watch too many old TV shows, bruv. Seriously.'

'Shut up. It was a movie, man.'

There's some shoving and pushing and I try not to grin because this is what it felt like dealing with my younger cousins.

'Just because we're young doesn't mean we don't know what we're doing,' Dante puts in. 'I work for a government agency and Kit is, well – how do I put this? Freelance? She's used to dealing with monsters and things.'

I watch the implication of what Dante's just said sink

in. The realization that we are playing open cards with them both impresses and scares them. And the fact that he quite seriously mentioned monsters has thrown them off kilter too.

'Monsters?' This is the girl. She's moving forward. 'Like things that have teeth and claws and things?'

'Exactly like that.'

'You joking, bruv? Because this isn't the place to joke about anything like that.' Dread Boy's expression is serious as he faces us and although he's showing a calm demeanour right now, as a fellow-pretender I spot how he holds himself a little bit too tightly, how his hands are clenched. Here is someone showing the world a facade of being okay, of holding it together, when really the world's a far bigger and uglier place than anyone ever told us.

'I don't lie,' Dante says evenly and calmly.

The group share a look. Not just your average *WTF is going on here* look but a look that says, *WTF they're telling the truth and we know it.*

'Have you guys seen anything that shouldn't—' I break off and wonder what to say. 'I mean that looks monstrous?'

They all talk at once but it's the girl's voice I hear clearest. Dante tries to shush them and points at the girl.

'You talk.'

'Like, a few nights ago, right? There's all this noise and my mum's so angry because she needs to sleep cos she's working the early shift. So we go over to check it out, right? Someone tried to break into this little kid's room. And he's only little, you know? Four or something.'

'Did anyone see who did it?' I ask them.

'His brother saw it.' This is Dread Boy. 'Like, he proper saw the thing trying to pull his brother out of the room.'

'Did he get a good look at who did this?'

'No. The thing was on the other side of the wall, hanging outside the window.'

Not what I was expecting to hear. I blink slowly and look at Dante, who looks equally taken aback.

'Which block did this happen in?' I ask them.

They point en masse to the middle block.

'Do you know about any of the other disappearances?' I ask them, my gaze resting on Dread Boy, whose face looks suddenly frail and very young.

'I've not lived here long enough,' the girl says. 'But my auntie, she knows about them all. Has scrapbooks about it and everything.'

The other kids don't really say much, except to nod and shuffle and look at their feet.

'What is your name?' I ask the girl. 'I'm Kit.'

'My name is Diane.' She holds out her hand and I'm impressed by the amount of jewellery on her wrist and fingers. If she hit anyone with it, they would be scarred for life. I shake her hand – after moving the knife into my other hand.

'Diane, do you think we can maybe get to speak to your auntie?' Dante holds out his business card to her and she accepts it, casting an eye over the printed front, as if she's used to being given business cards by government agents in the small hours of the morning.

'Not tonight,' she replies resolutely, a bit annoyed, as if we're dim, asking to speak to anyone at this time of night. 'She's asleep. Look at the time. It's only bad people out this time of night.'

I laugh. I can't help it. The tension clinging to all of us

evaporates a bit and they laugh too, suddenly just kids and not frightening at all.

'Like us, yeah?' says the boy called Marvin. He gets a few high-fives and slaps on the shoulder.

I slide my knife back into my boot and straighten up. 'Sorry about that,' I tell them. 'Not used to dealing with young people.'

'We could tell. Besides, no one brings knives to gunfights any more,' Dread Boy says, nodding towards an anonymous car sitting a distance away. I look over and ice shivers down my spine. The windows are too dark for me to see through but I sense the regard of whoever's in there and it's not friendly.

'Who's that?' Dante asks, turning back towards the boy. 'The local dealer?'

Dread Boy lifts his hands and shoulders in innocence and steps back. 'I don't know nothing,' he says, affecting a bad accent and slang. 'Don't go hating on a brother who's just out with his mates.'

This has everyone in stitches again but I no longer feel comfortable or safe.

'The little kid who almost got taken. Do you know his parents? Is there a way we can get in there to talk to him and his brother, do you think?'

'Why do you care?' The question comes from the one boy who's not spoken yet. His voice is soft and his eyes are serious.

I sense Dante leaving this for me to answer and I panic a bit, wondering how to make them believe that we're genuine, that we actually do care about these kids.

'Because I believe in monsters. I know that the fairy tales about creatures hunting small children in forests are real.

Only the forests have given away to big cities and the children are a bit wiser but so are the monsters that hunt them. I also know that sometimes what you imagine lurks beneath your bed or in your wardrobe is real. That if you miss that exact step on your carpet, when the moon shines through the window, that the thing waiting in the shadows really will get you.' I watch Dread Boy as I talk. 'That weird hollow feeling in the small of your back when you go to the loo at night, or when you run through the underpass and you know something is reaching for you? That's because whatever is lurking there is real and it's my family's job to find them and kick them to pieces.'

They're all wary now and I wonder if I overdid it. I possibly have, but they must understand that I am telling the truth here and that if anyone understands about things that go bump in the night, I do.

'You asked,' I end defensively, heaving a sigh. I really hope Dante pulls something out of his hat to convince these kids. I'm hyper-aware of each of them and how they're just so very quiet, as if they're waiting for something.

'I believe you.' The girl's voice is bright and fervent. 'You're not lying.'

There are murmurs of assent from all of them. I catch Dante's eye briefly and he gives me a light nod, conveying his approval.

'We'll get something sorted for you guys,' Dread Boy says. 'I'm Chem. This pretty girl is Diane. Marvin you know. That's Jamal and this guy here,' he says, pulling the quiet boy closer. 'This is Clifford. But we call him the Brain.'

We shake hands with them all and I like how their grips are firm, their nods friendlier than before.

'We'll call you tomorrow, about setting things up for you

to meet and talk to some people.' I hand Chem my business card. It's just my name and mobile number. I pass one to Diane too.

'Thanks,' I tell them, meaning it with all my heart. 'You guys are ace.'

After a few moments of awkwardness between us all and a few 'byes' they turn and wander away, leaving us standing alone by the Ducati.

Dante heaves a sigh and rubs his hands over his face. He looks tired and more than just a bit on edge.

'That was interesting.' His smile isn't really a smile, more like a grimace. 'Looks like we're taking on the case.'

'Yeah, against my better judgement.'

I swing my leg over the bike and pull my helmet on.

'Let's get to Greenwich,' I say. 'There's a place I know that's open twenty-four seven.'

Otherwhere, the Tower at the End of the World

Thorn entered the large room at the top of the tower. He could see the sky through the large windows; the moon hung pregnant in the night sky, the luminous stars almost within reach. He paused for a moment, looking up at the firmament, before turning to where Odalis stood behind her desk.

She wasn't very tall but had an enormous presence; one that made him feel small in comparison. She vibrated with quiet power, her movements assured and measured as she leafed through the large tome resting on the desk.

'Darkness surrounds the tower,' she said, her voice

betraying her annoyance. 'We have spoken about this several times, Thorn.'

He suppressed a sigh of irritation. 'I saw from my balcony.'

'What draws you to dream of the darkness the way you do?'

'Are you really asking me this? When you know what I faced, what I fought?'

'I ask because this is something new you dream of, not your uncle's attempt to bring the Old Gods back.' She rubbed her thumb and forefinger together under her nose, as if crushing mint leaves before inhaling the scent. 'The dream smells different.'

Thorn walked past the desk and looked at the map on the wall. The map represented the human world, the Frontier, and the Fae realm of the Otherwhere. It also showed the strange in-between realm known as the Veil.

The Veil stretched between the Frontier and the Otherwhere, and it was here that humans sometimes found themselves when drunk or high on drugs. It was the place where dreams are made manifest, the place where monsters seep between the cracks and carry dreamers away like the nightmares of old.

'I don't know who's in my dreams.'

'So it is a *who* and not a *what*?'

Thorn turned to look at her in surprise. 'Yes, I suppose I dream of someone.'

'The girl?'

Thorn didn't pretend not to know whom she meant. 'I dream of her every night. She is with me when I wake, when I eat, when I study.' His smile was tight and maybe a bit unpleasant. 'My father insisted I forget her, but it isn't easy.'

'It has been less than a year,' Odalis said, looking up from the book before her. 'It is understandable that your feelings for this human girl are still conflicted. You will forget, in time.'

'You didn't wake me up to talk about Kit Blackhart, Odalis, or to reprimand me for dreaming the darkness,' Thorn said, keeping the edge in his voice. 'I thought we were due to have a lesson.'

In answer Odalis threw her hands in the air and the table hurtled towards him at a stunning speed. Thorn turned the table aside with a grunt and, as he straightened, a searing bolt of pain streaked past his ribs, knocking the breath out of him.

Odalis stood over him as he lay gasping for breath, her face a cool mask.

'All warfare is based on distraction,' Odalis said. 'This is something you need to remember. Say "I understand" to show me you heard me.'

'I understand, Lady Firesky.'

'Good. Now stand up and defend yourself or you die.'

Chapter Ten

Greenwich has to be one of my favourite places in and around London. There's the old Naval College, the Observatory, the craft markets and eateries. There's also the little-known Museum for Maritime Fae, which is the place to go to when you're researching anything to do with sea folk and lore. It's also where you get the skinny on the events behind the big events in our (human) maritime history.

I park in front of George's, opposite the main Greenwich market, and pull together a bit of glamour to conceal the bike so that I don't have to lug my leather jacket and helmet with me. I'm ahead of Dante by a few minutes, so I choose one of the larger couches near the window and sit with my back against the wall – that way I can see the door and who's passing by outside.

Greenwich is busy for this time of the morning but then London seems to be becoming more and more the twenty-four-hour city, like New York, Cairo and Paris, if you know where to look, that is. I order a frappuccino for myself and a black tea for Dante. As I came in I spotted the fresh croissants being taken from the oven in the back and I ask for a few of those too.

By the time Dante walks in, our croissants and drinks are on the table. He sits down with a sigh.

'You do the no-sleeping thing a lot?' he asks me, crumbling a croissant between his fingers, before dipping it in his tea. He ignores the face I pull and pops the soaked pastry in his mouth with all the evidence of someone who enjoys it. Gross. Also weird.

'Yep. That's why coffee is your best friend. And when it's not coffee, or really strong tea, it's energy drinks and energy bars.'

He taps his head. 'So noted. It must be hell on your boyfriend, knowing you're always out and about.'

I grin at him and a bit of me feels flattered that he's cautiously fishing. 'I don't have a boyfriend,' I tell him. 'How about you?'

A light flush spreads across his cheeks and tints the tips of his ears pink. 'Ah. Not so subtle, am I? No, I don't have a boyfriend. Or a girlfriend, for that matter. I just don't have the time because of work and studying . . .'

'So why did you assume I had one?'

'The boy, the big guy that came up earlier today, no, yesterday, when we were talking. Isn't he your boyfriend?'

I roll my eyes and laugh because he's genuinely pretending he doesn't know who Aiden is. 'No, definitely not. That's Aiden Garrett. We're just really good mates.'

'With benefits?' He raises his eyebrows questioningly and this time it's my turn to flush.

'What? No! Geez, what's wrong with you?' I can't help but pull a face. 'No. Just no.'

'He looked as if he wanted to punch my lights out, that's why I'm asking. Guys don't usually act like that unless, you know, they fancy the girl.'

I wave my hand in the air between us to show how ridiculous it was. 'Aiden's a mate. He's very protective of me and my family.'

Dante watches me for a few seconds and I pretend not to notice. Instead I sip my frappe and stuff my face with a warm croissant. I'm not entirely sure how it's happened or when exactly I decided to investigate the missing kids with Dante, but I know my family's going to have a combined Richter scale 9 fit when they find out. With that in mind I dig out my phone just as it starts ringing in my hand.

'Freaky,' Dante comments at the synchronicity of my movement and the phone deciding to ring.

'It happens all the time,' I tell him. 'You get used to it.'

I excuse myself and go and stand outside with my back to the window, facing the closed-up market on the other side of the street.

'What have you been doing?' Uncle Andrew asks me without even waiting for me to say hello. 'I hear you've taken on the job. I've counted the hours and I don't see that it's dawn in Greenwich yet.'

I scowl into the dark, wondering how he even knew I had decided to take on the job.

'How did you know?' I ask eventually.

'You spoke the words at night, Kit. Of course Suola would be eager to pass that on to me. You know how she is.'

I try and stifle a full body shiver. How could I have been so careless? The Unseelie Queen's domain reaches further than most. Suola will be aware of everything I say or do at night, in the darkest of shadows, especially if the job I'm on is under her sanction.

'Shit.'

'Exactly.' Uncle Andrew doesn't bother to reprimand me the way Jamie would have for swearing. Instead he sighs heavily and I can feel disappointment radiating from him, even across the many thousands of miles separating us. 'So now you're working with the Spooks. I suppose I shouldn't be surprised. You are your mother's daughter, after all.'

'What do you mean by that?' My tone is sharp and, right then, I don't really care. I'm owed so many explanations about my life that I'm prepared to get into trouble to get answers.

'Only that you follow your head and your instincts and usually they're good. Sometimes they're a bit misguided.' He sighs again. 'I have a few things I found out about your young Spook, Dante. I'll email you what I've got. All I ask you is to keep me up to date with everything that's going on. Especially anything he drops about who in Suola's court is feeding the Spooks intel. I'll get our people working on it too.'

'What will the rest of the family say?' I ask him, still sharp, still a bit annoyed at his jab about my mum.

'They'll grumble and think you've gone over to the dark side,' he says, his voice full of humour. 'But I'll assure them you're a Blackhart claimed and trained and know how to handle yourself.'

'You guys are so full of it.'

'Read the stuff I'm sending you on your new friend. Tell Aiden to stick around as much as he can too. I don't want you going at this alone. I'm talking to his dad in a few hours. I'll keep you updated on stuff.'

'Yes, sir!' I snap out smartly and it earns me a laugh. 'I've got to go. My frappe's getting warm.'

'Get some rest, Kit. You look tired.'

Bah, I hate it when he does that. I look around me and spot the CCTV camera above the door pointing at me.

I salute with two fingers to my brow and click my heels like a good soldier and know he's watching me. Kyle didn't get his tech savvy from nowhere. Pocketing my phone I head back into George's to find Dante on the phone. Possibly speaking to one of his bosses.

He rolls his pretty eyes at me in an apology when I sit down and grab my frappe.

'Yes, sir. I understand.' A pause. 'Highly irregular. Yes. Understood.' He nods a few times. 'I'll see you in a few hours and will make my report then.'

He shares my grimace.

'Do you ever feel like a pawn in a much bigger game?' he asks me with a weary sigh.

'All the time. The pawn that gets bashed around and beaten up.'

'Sent on errands that lead nowhere.'

My frappe's melting so I push it aside. 'I was born into this; you chose it,' I tell him. 'You're still young. You can leg it. Go somewhere else, do something else.'

'Huh, not as easy as that. I'm being put through uni by the SDI. Without it I get to sling burgers somewhere if I'm lucky.'

'What about your parents?'

'There's no way they could afford it. Besides, they think I got a scholarship and that I'm going into IT. They don't know anything about the SDI.'

'That must be hard.' It's hard enough not being able to speak to other people about what I do. But at least I have my family, who are all so immersed in all the weirdness that it's not unusual to have long rambling conversations about it at breakfast. For example, on the luxuries of waking up and not having blue hair. All because a nixie got annoyed with you the day before and slammed you with a blue-hair-for-a-month spell.

He shrugs eloquently and the edge of his T-shirt collar moves, revealing a further hint of tattoo. A part of me wonders how big the tattoo is. Something tells me it's not tiny and I wonder how intricate it is. My cousins Marc and Megan each have one on their left wrist, an eternity sigil. I find this quite sweet, as it's a promise they made to always be there for one another, no matter what happens. I realize I've been staring intently at Dante's neck with a dazed expression and I snap my gaze back to his face and pretend not to see his amused expression at being caught staring.

'Your uncle not too impressed with us working together?'

'Not really, but I think he's prepared to let me run with this. I suspect he knows better than to tell me outright that he doesn't want me to do it.'

'Why did you decide to do it? I mean, you'll be working with me. Your family will hate that. You're not going against some kind of religious edict or anything?'

His question, although overly dramatic, stills me and I breathe out quietly. I decide to be as honest as I can.

'I think no one else can help these kids,' I tell him. 'What *she* said is true, if we're dealing with kids younger than Dread Boy and his little crew of Lost Boys, any adults who go in there will be met with animosity. We don't look like the establishment.' I flick my eyes over him again and smirk. 'We're likely to get answers and fast too, before these kids turn up dead.'

Dante's dark eyes watch me intently. 'I think there's more, but I won't pester you. My boss isn't madly keen about me working with you either, but mostly I think he's worried I'll run off and join you in fairyland or something.'

My eyebrows shoot up. 'Or something?'

'Yes, be lured to the Otherwhere and sold into slavery to some bad fairy or something and used as a pleasure toy.'

My eyebrows climb higher. 'That's what the Spooks think the Blackharts do?'

'We have no idea what exactly you do. A lot of the files I've seen are old and yellow and falling apart. A lot of superstition and wild stories.'

I'm actually thrilled by this. The agency apparently doesn't know every single thing about the Blackharts, which pleases me immensely.

'Let's go walk around for a bit,' I say, pushing upright. 'I promise not to sell you to anyone to be used as a – what did you call it? A pleasure toy.' I laugh at his scowl. 'Sorry, I forget that we're not in some swashbuckling Regency drama.'

He mutters something about me not being funny and that it could happen as he shrugs into his jacket.

Chapter Eleven

We wave at the waitress and head out into the night. I lift my jacket off the back of the bike and shrug into it, flipping the collar up. The air's become cooler and fresher, with the breeze coming off the river. We head towards the newly restored *Cutty Sark*. The shape of the eighteenth-century tea clipper is lit by bright lights but it still looks ridiculously exotic, as if it is ready to sail off at a moment's notice for places far more exciting than Greenwich.

'Do you want to go to the Brownie Market?' I ask him after we've walked around for a bit.

'I don't even know what that is.'

'Come, I think you'll like it. It's perfectly safe.' I lead him down a set of steps. 'These are the stairs to the foot tunnel that leads beneath the river to the other side.'

'Pardon?' He stops behind me and looks down the long tunnel. 'I'm not comfortable going down there.'

'Seriously?'

He looks shocked by what he just said but he nods after a few seconds. 'I'm not sure where that came from but, yes, the thought of going into that tunnel is making me feel physically ill and I've never experienced anything like it before.' As if to prove it, he sits down heavily and drops his head between his knees. His breath shudders through him. 'Oh my God, what's going on?'

Okay, so this is really weird and I'm pretty freaked out by his odd behaviour. And I've seen odd behaviour in the past. This is something else and the way he just spoke, with his voice a bit high and rushed, makes me more than a bit worried. I lean forwards so that my knees are on the step beneath him and duck my head so I can look at his face. 'You're sweating and shaking. Are you scared of water? Enclosed spaces?'

'No, not at all. I'm a strong swimmer and I've never had issues with tight spaces.' He looks me in the eye and I'm shocked to see how far his pupils are dilated. Genuine fear, I decide.

'But you can't come down there with me?'

He shakes his head and closes his eyes, obviously trying to get a grip on himself. 'No. I've never embarrassed myself like this before. I'm not sure what's going on.' He sucks in a deep breath of air and looks at me. 'Can we please go somewhere else? It feels like something's sitting on my chest and I can't breathe.'

'Yes, sure, of course.' I help him up and we walk back up the river towards Queen Anne Court.

It's a cold clear night but even so his forehead's beaded in sweat and his skin feels feverish under the back of my hand. I make him sit on the stairs to the chapel and settle down next to him.

'Do you want to go home?' I ask him, watching him carefully to see if any part of this is going to kick off into a proper panic attack. I've never had one, but I've seen a young girl go into one when confronted by a goblin eating her dog, and it had been incredibly scary to see.

'I'm okay, thanks. I already feel better. It's just when I stood at the top of those stairs and looked down, it felt as if the world around me tilted and my knees just went lame.' He presses a hand to his chest and sucks in deep breaths of air.

I give him some space to pull himself together. On the other side of the river the buildings of Canary Wharf stand tall and proud, having grown out of the wreckage of the Second World War and many years of urban neglect. I like looking at the new buildings across the river; they make me realize how London will always rise up from its ancient roots and shows a new face to the world.

'Have you met any of Suola's people before?' I ask him to distract him.

He shakes his dark head and the wind ruffles his hair lightly, making his fringe drop across his forehead. I resist the urge to brush it back. The gesture would be too intimate, too strange coming from me. I hardly know him and I'm not sure how he'd react because personally I'd hate it. I hate being touched by strangers and I always have.

'Not face to face, no.' Dante's hands have steadied somewhat but even so he folds them together in a tight knot, twisting his fingers together. I notice that he has nice hands: with long fingers, the nails neat and well cared for. 'I've only ever heard my superiors talk about meeting one of her people, or getting a contract to work on something.'

'What did you think of her Beast?' The questions are meant to distract him enough so that he can think about something else, not about whatever made him freak out so much.

'He seemed pleasant,' Dante eventually says after some

time, his lips twisting in a way and making the word 'pleasant' sound dirty somehow. 'Isn't that strange?'

'He did, didn't he? Like someone's kindly, slightly eccentric uncle.'

He nods, and his gaze is pulled to the reflection of the lights on the water. I can tell he's trying to equate the man we met earlier with the savage murderer and torturer we know by reputation. I somehow expected the Beast to look exactly like his namesake, something akin to the nightmares he induces in the Unseelie realm. Instead, we were given the well-dressed, cane-carrying, middle-aged professor lookalike.

'What do you think will happen when we find the people who've been taking the kids?'

'The Beast will come and take them. It won't be our problem any more.'

'What if they're human?'

'They probably are human. The Fae are no longer allowed to steal children.'

The bleak look he gives me tells me he doesn't really believe me.

'There are treaties between us now,' I explain. 'And they've been around for several hundreds of years. Humans are safe from the Fae. Mostly. Unless they ask to be taken to the Otherwhere; then there's nothing we can do about it.'

'Some people *ask* to be taken?'

I nod, remembering the young artist we found wandering around Dartmoor, his mind entirely gone.

'Yes. And then we can't stop them, not if they go into it willingly. Once they've signed over their free will to the Fae, the Fae can do anything with them.'

Dante shakes his head and leans forward, watching the black water of the river below.

'Why would anyone do that?'

'Fame,' I say. 'Fortune. Sometimes someone wants something so badly they are prepared to do whatever it takes to get it. Artists, singers, musicians, writers. There are records that go back a long time that are evidence of this type of thing.'

We stand quietly for a few minutes before Dante slants a look at me. 'I think I'm learning more from you in one night than in the time I've been with the SDI.'

I check the BBC website and it tells me when dawn's supposed to arrive. Dante's starting to look a bit hollow-eyed and I worry that he'll fall asleep talking to Melusine or on his way back to the office. We huddle near the *Cutty Sark*, drinking tea from polystyrene cups, the warmth from the previous day now completely gone.

We don't have long to wait for Melusine. She comes out of the water in front of us and changes shape as she moves towards us, her mermaid's tail melting and splitting into two trim long legs encased in what looks like silvery leggings. Her hair's long and loose down her back and her eyes are large and dark as she takes us in.

'You've decided?' She frames it as a question but it's a statement really. I try not to stare below her neck because the shirt she's wearing is diaphanous and it leaves *nothing* to the imagination. And, well, I have my own and it's not necessary to stare at someone else's.

'We have,' Dante says, his eyes rigidly above the neckline.

'We'll take on the job,' I tell her. 'At the usual payment. For both of us.'

Melusine's smile is sharp edged. She produces two wooden tokens on silver chains and hands one to each of us.

'Agreed. But on condition that both of you are present when the creature is either taken by the Beast or killed.'

Dante and I share a look but we both nod, in the end.

'Is this your vow, to hunt the thief of children?' She asks us, her voice suddenly sonorous and official. 'To find him and send him to the Otherwhere for judgement?'

'I so vow,' I say.

'Yes. I vow this.'

As both Dante and I speak the words, we slip the tokens around our necks. The shimmer of the spell implanted in the token sparks in the early morning light and I can't help the shiver that steals through me. I finger the rune-carved wooden pendant – no longer or bigger than my thumb – and wonder who the sorcerer is who can work the magic so finely that a piece of wood stows enough energy to open a gateway between two realms.

'It is done,' Melusine says, turning to go. She hesitates for a second, perhaps about to say something, then she seems to think better of it and walks back towards the river. 'Suola expects you to have the case wrapped up soon,' she throws over her shoulder at us. 'You know better than to disappoint her.'

She dives smoothly into the river, her clothes shedding mid-arc and her legs forming into a shimmery mermaid's tail. I watch her dark head dunk beneath the water and she's gone as the sun's early morning rays hit us.

'What now?' Dante asks after a few seconds of watching the river.

'Now I go home, get some sleep and head back to the

estate to check things out. With luck, we'll get calls from the girl or Dread Boy in the meantime to set something up.' I look at him. There's no sign of his earlier queasiness or weirdness, except maybe in the darkness of his eyes. 'And you? Are you okay? What are you doing now?'

Dante checks his watch and grimaces. 'I'm okay. Thanks for sticking with me. I'm off to work, unfortunately. I'll call you later.'

'You don't have my number,' I point out and he passes me his phone. I quickly type in my number and hand it back to him. He immediately hits dial and my pocket starts ringing. 'Where's the trust?' I ask him, laughing openly now.

'Ah, just being careful,' he says, pocketing the phone. 'Drive safely, Kit. Talk later.'

I watch him wander off to the parking garage as I swing my leg over my bike and pull on my helmet. Maybe he wasn't so bad, I think to myself. He was certainly easy on the eye and didn't look too shabby in that T-shirt of his. I laugh at the thought and shake my head as I start the bike. I have to tell Megan about him, I decide. He's definitely her type.

Chapter Twelve

I get back home fast; there's little enough traffic going through town. I love the Ducati for this but I miss my little car, Lolita, and I hope the ogres are taking care of her. Here's a tip: never agree to play poker against ogres. They are canny and like shiny things, like my Mini Cooper. But at least the agreed three months' lending term is almost done and I'll have her back. Megan is still refusing to talk to me about the mess I got myself in there. But the ogres swore very prettily not to damage it, so here's hoping I get her back in one piece.

Kyle's still sleeping when I get in, so I have a quick shower, crawl into bed and pull the covers over my head. I'm exhausted but sleep decides to play elusive and I sit up in bed after half an hour of tossing and turning. I wonder about checking on Aiden for not showing up at the club last night but decide against it. We're good mates but I really don't want to be the clingy one.

I pull my sketchpad over and flip to a clean page. I twiddle the charcoal between my fingers thinking about last night. My sketch is rough and untidy as I draw Suola's face but I like it. It gives her a wildness that seems apt. I draw Melusine too, only her face. I purposely don't sketch Dante.

I don't think I want to have him in my sketchpad, not yet. I do, however, draw the bits of tattoo I saw peeking from beneath the sleeve and collar of his T-shirt. They have sharp strange edges that I think are definitely part of a larger tattoo. I wonder how old he was when he got it. His parents must have been unimpressed. I get the feeling that they were quite strict with him but that obviously didn't stop him from being a bit of a wild child.

I wonder how often he thinks about who his real parents were and why they gave him up – and if he ever thinks about looking them up.

Although I grew up with my nan, I can count on one hand the stuff I know about my mum and dad. Sometimes I wake up in the night feeling a hollow ache, wanting to know more about them. It was no longer enough to know that my mum was stubborn and single minded, or that my dad was a normal human employed by the Spook Squad.

The things I know about them gives me a tiny keyhole view of who they were, but nothing else. I yearn to have an HD widescreen vision of them. I can only imagine that the way I feel might be the way Dante feels about his own parents.

After finishing a final quick sketch of Melusine I close and drop my sketchpad and scoot underneath the covers again. I find my ear buds and plug myself into my iPod and eventually drift off to the sound of instrumental soundtrack music.

Chapter Thirteen

'We need to talk.'

I eye Kyle dubiously as he watches me down my second coffee. I've just come back from a long run and am gearing myself up to do the paperwork for the warehouse job, so I'm not a hundred per cent keen on seeing his scowling face.

'What now?'

'That wallet you took from the guy at the warehouse. His name is Marko Monroe. He runs with the Jericho Gang.'

I sit down at the dining-room table and drop my head into my hands. 'See? When you say something like that, as if it should mean something to me, and it doesn't? This is my confused expression.'

'The Jericho Gang runs drugs from the borders all through the Midlands.'

'Do we know any of them?'

'No. But Aiden's mate Leo's dad does. I spoke to Leo earlier.' Kyle's fingers dance across the keyboard in front of him. 'Here, look at this.'

I push up from my chair with a sigh and go and stand next to my cousin.

'What am I looking at?'

He points to the map of the UK. 'Here, all of this belongs to the Jericho crew.'

I reluctantly have to admit that it's a huge area. 'I can't take them all on by myself,' I tell him.

He grimaces. 'Glad you know that. No, we're passing this information on to the police directly. We have a few sympathetic ears. Also, Leo's dad said he'll speak to some people. He's seen first hand what Glow does to someone.' When he sees my curious expression he explains further. 'A kid died in one of his clubs in Soho last night. He's pi—. He's very angry. Apparently Aiden was there and helped.'

That would explain Aiden not showing up last night. I don't know Leo very well, having only met him a few times, but he's a good friend of Aiden's and they went to some posh private school together. A werewolf and a gangster's son. Nothing wrong with that picture at all.

'How far are you with figuring out what's in the Glow?'

'Not far. Jilly is struggling to lock down some of the ingredients. She says she's never seen anything like it.'

'We don't want her to marry it, we just need her to figure out what it's made of. If we know that, we can get the labs to manufacture a way to help the little girl lying in a coma.'

'I know, Kit. Bloody hell, give me some credit. Jesus. You're getting meaner by the second. Is this how you're going to be, hanging out with a Spook?'

'Not by choice, Kyle. Remember that. This is not my choice.'

'You didn't seem to fight it really hard,' he mutters under his breath.

'What did you want me to do? Tell the Queen of Air and Darkness to shove the job? That she can ask someone else to do it?' I frown at him. 'These are little kids that need our help. I reckon I stand a better chance figuring out what's going on than anyone else she could ask.'

'Yeah, but the Spook.' He looks unhappy. 'I mean, he's not family. An unknown.'

'He's not a liability,' I tell him, hating that I'm using words that Jamie enjoys throwing around. 'I've got this.'

My pocket starts vibrating and I lift my phone to my ear. 'What?'

'Oh! Hi? This is Diane? From like earlier this morning?'

I scowl at Kyle and walk away from him, towards the living room.

'Hi, Diane, thanks for calling.'

'Are you okay? You sound angry.'

'My cousin is being a pain,' I tell her. 'Thank you for asking.'

'Oh right, no worries.' She laughs nervously. 'So I've been talking to the boys and we've decided that we're going to help you. I'm going to get the scrapbooks my auntie's got in her flat so you can look at them. I'm telling her it's for a school thing.'

'Look at you, being a devious person,' I tease her, the smile showing in my voice. 'Thanks for that.'

'Chem said to help. He's really worried about the block, you know? We all are. These are our friends' little brothers and sisters being taken.'

A trickle of ice drips down my spine. 'Diane, are you guys staking out the estate?'

The brief pause at the other end of the phone tells me all I should know.

'You can't do that, okay? It's not safe. Just go to school, go about your business like usual.'

'Yeah? And what about you?'

'This is my job,' I tell her. 'It's in my blood, okay? It's what I do. Me and my family.'

'And the guy from last night? Is he family?'

I sigh and close my eyes. 'No, he's someone I have to work with on this.'

She sucks her teeth and I can feel her defiance right through the phone.

'So, did you guys get to speak to the little boy's brother? The one who almost got taken a few days ago?'

'Yeah, that's the other reason I called? His mum's working tonight so they're going to be alone at home. He said you can come over then.'

She gives me the boys' names, and we confirm the time and flat number before hanging up. I stomp into the kitchen and dial Dante as I pour myself another mug of coffee.

He answers on the second ring. 'Dante Alexander, how may I help you?'

'Wow,' I say, impressed. 'You sound grown up.'

'It's a ploy,' he assures me. 'It happens every time I put on my suit.'

'Sucks to be you.' I laugh when I hear him draw in a breath at my apparent rudeness. The guy really needed to loosen up a bit. 'Listen, Diane called and tonight we get to meet the little kid, Adam, who said someone tried to break into his room. His older brother, Colin, will be there too. We're seeing them at seven. Wear something that doesn't make you look like a government agent.'

'I like my suit.'

'You are twenty,' I tell him. 'You should be wearing shorts and sandals and hideous T-shirts, glorifying surfing off the coast of Hawaii or something.'

'Is this your way of telling me you don't like me, my clothes or what I do for a living?'

I sigh. Gods, what a diva! 'No, it's my way of telling you to not wear a suit tonight.'

'Do I get to tell you what you should be wearing?'

Oh my giddy aunt. He's flirting with me and I can feel my cheeks flame bright red. 'I'm coming by Monster,' I cut him off. 'Jeans and a leather jacket. That's how I'll be dressed.'

'Cool. I dig chicks in leather who ride bikes.'

He can't see me rolling my eyes but he must sense it because he laughs and he doesn't have the grace to sound even a little bit embarrassed.

'I'll see you later, Blackhart.'

'Try not to get too many paper cuts, office boy,' I advise him, before hanging up. 'It's on, Kyle. We're meeting the little boy who was almost taken the other night.' I'm talking as I round the corner back into the dining room.

Kyle nods and hands me back the folder Suola gave me last night.

'Read this again. I'm running a search to see if anything weird went down in the timeframe these kids got taken.'

'Weird, like how?'

'Anything odd, you know – stuff that happened.' He grimaces at me. 'Shut up and study your file and let me do the computer thing.'

'What about the warehouse paperwork?' I say. 'Aunt Letty's going to go mental if I don't have it back to her soon.'

'She can wait. This is more important.'

The look he gives me is so much like Uncle Andrew's that I shut up, grab the file and head off to sit in the living room. Here I sprawl inelegantly on the sofa and flip open the file.

Five kids. All of them under eight years old. I undo the clips and lay each photo on the ground, grouping their bits of paper beneath them. I pick up the details of the first one that disappeared.

Roberto Santos. Four years old. Mum and dad were watching TV in the next room when he was taken. Dad went in to check on him when he got up to go make coffee. It was 9 p.m.

Rachel Mitchell. Five years old. Rachel was taken from her home two days before her sixth birthday. Both her parents were at home. No sign of an intruder.

Joanie Powell. Seven. Parents woke up to a noise at 3 a.m. and found Joanie gone. No sign of an intruder except for an open window. Their flat was on the sixth floor.

Christopher Singh. Aged six. His mum got up to wake him up for school but when she walked into the room it was in a mess and there was no sign of Christopher.

Jerome King. The oldest at almost eight, taken a week before his birthday. His dad heard a commotion in his room and ran in to find his son's window open and no sign of Jerome. They were on the fourth floor of the building.

The police reports are succinct and brief. No sign of forced entry into any of the flats and the CCTV stayed suspiciously blank. Kyle has shown me how easy it is to mess with CCTV footage, so I don't trust the CCTV. I also know that creatures from the Otherwhere knock the cameras out, so they hardly ever show up on any film, unless they want to be seen. No human could do this, so it was definitely Otherwhere related. I will need to check with the other players in town, the Infernal (demons and angels to us average folk) and the Suckers, our very special slang for vampires. There are other creatures too, but those are the major players.

I check on the children's birthday dates compared to when they were taken.

Roberto and Rachel were taken two years ago. Roberto just before 1 May; Rachel disappeared on 19 July. The next disappearance was Joanie on the night of 30 July.

Then there's a gap and it starts again this year. End of January with Christopher Singh and then just before Easter is Jerome King.

The dates are interesting as they are all just before a major pagan holiday.

Roberto's before May Day or Beltane. Then Rachel at Midsummer. Then Joanie just before Lammas, which is Harvest time.

The gap is interesting and I wonder why he didn't continue last year. Next is Christopher Singh at the end of January, skipping Midwinter but in time for one of the equinoxes in February. The final one to be taken is Jerome King, at Easter or Ostara.

So perhaps he skipped May Day, Midsummer and Lammas this year, because he already had the children somewhere . . . returning to take someone at Halloween, or Samhain, as it's called by most pagans I've met.

I rummage around the living room and come up with a ratty book on the wheel of the pagan year and check out the dates. So our guy's now missed out on Halloween too . . . which has definitely thrown a spanner in the works because the next holiday is Yule, around Christmas time. If he's collecting children for pagan festivals, his timings are out.

No. I write down the names and dates and realize he's missed two months from the calendar – September (Mabon, the autumn equinox) and now Halloween or Samhain. I sit back in my seat and wonder if he'll next appear in December.

But why? Why the staggered way of taking the kids?

If he was planning to do a ritual then it would make sense that he'd take them all in one year. Not stagger them and miss out some significant dates entirely.

I stand up and pace around the living room. It makes no sense at all. The days have to mean something or rather, the times of year they were taken, surely? They aren't even the opposites of the eight points that the calendar forms. Argh, it is frustrating.

I check my watch and pick up my phone. It's time to make a call.

'Professor Thorpe, please. It's Kit Blackhart.'

I pull up outside a smart house near the British Museum. The streets here are lined with trees shedding autumnal leaves on impressive imported German cars. My bike immediately looks more disreputable, like a thug at a white-tie affair, and I grin as I feel all the security cameras twitch my way. Tucking my helmet under my arm, I walk up to the green door with its plain knocker.

I rap it once and it opens almost immediately. A young student stands there, I forget his name, but he's Professor Thorpe's assistant and he recognizes me from my previous visits.

'Your colleague is here already,' he says to me as he shows me in to the entrance hall. I glance around, enjoying the academic ambiance. It is still a little bit dusty, with the bust of some Greek philosopher looking on disapprovingly and a coat-rack laden with coats and umbrellas in the corner.

'Is he?' I ask in surprise, wondering how Dante got here

so fast. I rang him after I made the appointment to meet Professor Thorpe.

'He's waiting for you through here. Can I get you anything?'

'I'm fine, thanks.'

Dante stands up when we walk into the small waiting room. With the three of us the small room, a box room really, feels overcrowded. Add in the bookcase and the assistant's desk, where he now sits tapping at his keyboard, and the room is positively, breathlessly, small.

Dante smiles at me.

'You look fresh,' he says by way of greeting.

'Thanks.' I feel rubbish and suspect I look it. 'Nice tie.'

We sit down next to one another and I fiddle with my bike keys after stowing my helmet beneath my chair.

'You going to talk me through this before we go in?' Dante asks me, keeping his voice low.

'Not much to say really – the dates the kids were taken peripherally look as if they line up with the pagan wheel of the year. There are eight festivals: four major festivals and four slightly less major, but all still important. Whoever is taking the kids seems to be doing it in a very haphazard way. Three between May Day, Midsummer and Lammas, or the first Harvest festival. Those were the first, last year. This year we've got two, Christopher in February and Jerome in March. So Spring and Easter.'

Dante's kept up with my hurried explanation and I'm impressed. He purses his lips and I notice he's missed a bit when he shaved this morning. I lift my eyes to his, distracted. I am so tired. And he smells so nice. 'Are you thinking witches took them?'

'No.' I sigh and try to wake up. 'And don't ask me about

Satanists either. They are far rarer than popular media would have you believe.'

'Then what?'

I shrug. 'That's why we're here, talking to Professor Thorpe.'

'What does he do?'

'*She* is an expert in ancient pagan practices and a well-known historian and anthropologist.'

'And you know her because . . . ?'

'She helped me get rid of a particularly nasty household Roman spirit in St Albans.' At his blank look I explain briefly. 'The god decided that since his shrine was disturbed by some gardeners working on a new development, the owners of the new house should pay him all kinds of respect. He terrorized them, killed their cat, broke stuff in the house. It was petty, dumb stuff.'

'It sounds like you should have called a priest,' Dante says. 'But of course that would have been silly because you handled it. Obviously.'

I sneer at him in an impressive display of insolence that would have Aiden nodding in approval. Just then Professor Thorpe pulls open her door to call us in. She is dressed elegantly in an abstract tunic, leggings and knee-high boots.

'Kit, darling girl. Come inside. And who is this?' She presses a cool cheek against mine in a brief hug.

Imelda Thorpe is one of my favourite people in the world. Eccentric, intelligent and unorthodox, she always makes time for any of us when we need help. I think Jamie may have dated her at some stage, I can't be sure but something has given me that impression.

I introduce Dante by his name only (she has a scholar's

issues with any government agencies) and she smiles at him before inviting us into her office.

Her office is considerably larger than the waiting room. Her walnut desk sits in front of a wide window overlooking a small private park. The office is lined with books, floor to ceiling, crammed higgledy-piggledy onto the shelves. They vie for space with knick-knacks she's picked up from all around the world on various visits to far-flung places. I don't look directly at the weird little owls that were given to her by an archaeologist in San Salvador. They give me the creeps, with their staring eyes and permanently startled expressions. I know – it's weird – don't ask me why, they just do. Owls and rats just freak me out. They are my kryptonite.

I sit in my usual chair, the one to the right and Dante takes the other visitor's seat.

Imelda hovers near us, her various bangles jingling as she clasps her hands to her chest. The way she's standing I'm worried she's going to start singing but, no, she just looks insanely happy.

'Kit. Is he the one?'

'The one what?' I ask her, wondering what she is on about.

'You know, the boy. From the Otherwhere. The prince?'

I look at her in surprise and then at Dante, who manages not to look too worried at being referred to as if he wasn't present.

A jolt of electricity travels through me when I realize what she's asking. I think about the dream I've had of the ruined palace and of Thorn's unexpected appearance, the brief conversation we had, about his hand touching me, pushing me out of harm's way. A yearning I'm not ready to face opens inside me and I turn my attention firmly aside.

I can't control the tremble in my voice and ignore the concerned expression on Dante's face when I speak.

'No. Do you mean Thorn? No. Thorn has gone away, Imelda. I don't think we'll see him again.'

Her mouth forms a little 'oh' of disappointment before she takes her seat. 'Well, it would have been nice to meet him, you know? Just once. Or any of *them*, really.' She moves a few things around on her desk, getting herself back under control. Then she hovers a pen above a notepad again and nods to me. 'Okay, I'm all ears, Kit. What is this about, then?'

Chapter Fourteen

I tell Imelda about the screwed-up pagan calendar and my attempts to figure it out. I show her the dates and explain I initially thought the disappearances have something to do with the cycles of the year. Someone could be sacrificing the children for prosperity or something, but I'm halfway through it when she starts shaking her head.

'No. No, definitely not. Modern-day pagans would never steal children to sacrifice them. Even if they were unhinged, they would have to answer to their communities. Ethically and morally this is wrong on so many levels.' She gestures and her bangles tinkle wildly. 'No. Just no.'

'But what then?' Dante asks her, speaking for the first time. 'If this isn't about witches and things, then what do you think it is?'

'I don't know. I don't know enough about the case at all. Do you have anything else with you?'

To my surprise Dante hands her a USB stick from his pocket. 'What we were given is on there. I scanned everything in this morning when I got to the office.'

Imelda nods in approval. 'He's a clever one, Kit. Keep him around.'

Dante practically squirms in his seat at the approval and

I roll my eyes at him. He's like a puppy that is just aching to have its ears stroked.

She powers up a super sleek-looking laptop and I edge further away, not wanting to be the one to jinx the electronics. She plugs the USB in and spends some time looking through the papers.

'I'm at a loss. If the children were taken in sequence, I would have, like you, thought it was to perform some kind of ritual. But there's nothing here that makes sense at all. No sign left of anyone entering the rooms or anything else taken. A few rooms were disturbed and all of them were high up . . . a cat burglar? Batman? I don't know.'

'Argh!' I sit forward and press the heels of my palms into my eyes so that I see stars in the darkness. 'Prof, I thought you were going to have the magic answers here.'

'Oh, funny, Kit, I never have the magic answers. I have *ideas* and *thoughts* but in this case, I'm not sure what to think.'

She stands up and goes over to her bookcase, running a finger along the various spines. She pulls out a thick paperback and I catch half a glimpse of a title: *Guide to England's Legends*.

She flicks through the pages, going back and forth before shaking her head. 'Nothing in this. I thought maybe it could be related to the area, but nothing's popping here. What do you know about the area?'

'Uhm.' Dante brings out his little notebook and I try to contain my surprise. He seems a bit smug and gives me the side-eye. 'What? I can't have done my own research?' he asks, before addressing us both. 'Well, I did a quick search and Brixton is mentioned in the Domesday Book, called Brixiestan. This guy, a Saxon lord called Brixi, erected a stone to mark the place where the hundred court was held. It was the local district and the court met to administer law and keep the peace.' He snaps his little notebook shut. 'That's what I've got.'

I'm tempted to slow clap but Imelda holds up a finger. 'That's interesting.' She makes a note on a notepad to her left. 'Do you know anything else about this chap?'

Dante reluctantly shakes his head and I flutter my hands. 'Never even heard of the guy till now,' I admit.

She stares at me for a few seconds, her thoughts clearly elsewhere. 'When are you going back?'

'Tonight, at seven.'

She checks her watch. 'Call me in the morning, let me see what I can find out about this guy Brixi. I'll also look into Brixton in general and see if anything pops.'

With that a very unsatisfactory meeting comes to an end but it was worth it for Imelda's company alone. She hugs me fiercely and then her assistant sees us out.

'How did you get here so fast?' I ask Dante as we walk down the stairs. 'Fly?'

'Nope.' He looks around and points. 'Like you. By bike.'

'Seriously? They don't teach you about originality in Spook school?'

He looks exasperated but grins. 'What? I had to BEG to get that baby. Isn't she awesome?'

I cringe a bit at his use of the word *awesome* when I look over at the motorbike. 'It's a Kawasaki. And it's green. Like Kermit green.'

'Hey, don't hate the green thing.'

I shake my head. 'Just, if we're going to travel together

don't make it look like we know one another, okay? My street cred would go down the drain.'

'Oh ha ha, very funny.' He waits for me to zip up my leather jacket and pull on my helmet. 'Straight through to Brixton?'

I nod. 'Go get your bike, let's see if you can ride.'

Damn him, but he can actually ride. Not much better than me, but I give a few motorists near heart attacks and he keeps up for most of it. Now where did a nice boy like him learn to ride a motorbike dirty?

We get to Brixton early and park near the market. I felt my phone vibrate on the way over so I pull it out to check on it while Dante parks his bit of Japanese machine.

The text is from Aiden and, like him, it wasn't very elaborate but it was all spelled correctly. *Sorry about last night. Had to go out with Dad and we're only back now. Want to meet up?*

I work the keypad and write back: *Maybe later. Talking to some people tonight. New case, working with a Spook for Suola. Long story.*

Almost immediately I get a message back that reads: *SPOOK???!?!?!?! WTF???!?!? Be careful. Keep your sword handy. Don't trust them.*

His eloquence makes me laugh and Dante shoots me an enquiring look as he walks up.

'What?'

'Aiden. He seems alarmed.' I flash the screen at him.

'Be careful?' Dante's eyebrows jump up in surprise. 'What? I'm going to chop you up and use you in some kind of stew and offer you to the red queen for dinner?'

'That's disgusting.'

'Tell him that.'

We grab hot drinks from a small cafe and wander around the streets, taking in the vibrant street life. The place feels metropolitan and a bit wild. I hear Arabic, English, Russian and Polish being spoken. We are passing a tiny shop selling all kinds of kitsch toys when a small Asian lady bumps into Dante. He opens his mouth to apologize, but before he can say anything she launches a tirade of words at him and storms off. I watch in shock as he turns back to me and shrugs, looking bemused.

'No idea what that was about,' he says. 'Maybe one of my real parents pissed her off and she recognizes me.'

I shrug and try and catch sight of her among the crowd but she's nowhere to be seen. 'It will forever be a mystery,' I intone in a voice that makes him laugh.

What I like about Brixton is that there is music every-where, blasting from individual radios and speakers in the various shops. Outside a barber's a group of four guys stand, harmonizing. They are dressed like gangsters from the Forties and are crooning something I've never heard before. I throw a bunch of coins from my pocket into the waiting hat and one of the guys does a deep bow as he sees the pound coins. We are about to head away when they change their tune from an upbeat toe-tapping song to something slower, a little bit melancholy. I stop in my tracks as if I've walked into a wall.

'Kit?' Dante pauses at my side. 'Are you okay?'

His words only reach me peripherally as I turn back and look at the four guys. One of them had started the new song, but the group are so attuned to each other that they all pick up the rhythm of the music. The tune is familiar and my mind reels. This is the same lullaby that I heard

Thorn sing in Blackhart Manor when he woke up the scrying mirror. Strains of it were in the song he sang when he helped Istvan open the gateway between our world and the prison where the Elder Gods were trapped.

I turn back and watch them perform; the lullaby, bobbing and weaving through the chorus of something else, which they then segue into without a moment's beat or hesitation.

'Kit?'

Dante's touch on my arm is tentative and it jerks me from my memories.

'Sorry.' I put on a smile but my face feels stiff and awkward. 'I thought I recognized the song.'

'I didn't really pay attention.' He's watching me carefully, as if he's worried I might do something strange. And it's not just him – the performers are watching us too, and I wonder if I look as wild eyed as I feel. To mask my minor mental crisis, I turn away and walk rapidly up the road, towards the flats.

'That was weird. I don't think I've ever seen you look so freaked out.'

'The song, the lullaby.' How do I explain it to him? A boy I cared about deeply sang that song to talk to a magic mirror and then later, the lullaby helped wake up a bunch of ancient banished gods? 'I've not actually heard anyone else sing it before now.'

'Now I want to hear this thing, it sounds pretty special.'

'No, don't go back. Don't talk to them.'

He considers me for a few seconds before nodding. 'Okay, as you wish. Do you want to sit down?'

Do I look that bad? I take a deep breath and calm my nerves. I'm being stupid and overreacting to a bloody song. I run a hand through my hair, straighten my blouse and tug at my leather jacket. I pull my shoulders back, lift my chin and close my eyes for a second, getting my head back into the game.

'I'm good, thanks.' I smile at Dante and this time it's a real smile rather than something twisty and weird. 'Sorry about that.'

'Yeah, I still don't believe you. But we can let it go. For now, as long as you tell me what this is about at some stage.'

I give a quick nod.

We walk a few more metres before I look at him. 'Hey, why are you wearing your suit?'

'I didn't have time to change. I got to work, had a shower and changed into the spare I had in the office. I've not been home yet today.'

'Very dedicated, I'm super impressed. I hope the kids don't think you're too dodgy to talk to.' I laugh at his outraged expression as he tugs at his suit jacket. 'What did your boss say about it all?'

'He gave me a stern lecture. We're understaffed at the moment and don't have any senior agents to oversee this, except for him. He laid down the law: no fraternizing, no jaunts into the Otherwhere, no doing anything illegal.'

'Oh.' A beat, then I ask, 'Does *he* expect *me* to chop you up and sell you to the sluagh for dinner?'

'I think it's fair to say that both our sides' concerned parties seem to have trust issues. With one another.'

'But we're okay?'

'We are,' he assures me.

Chapter Fifteen

Diane is sitting on the low wall near the block of flats, phone in hand. Today she's dressed in a tiny skirt, layered leggings and a pair of genuinely ugly yellow boots. She stands up once we near her and gives us a smile. Her hair is an untidy mess of little round nests and I envy her her style and sense of self.

'Hi. I wasn't sure you'd come.'

I frown at her in surprise. 'We said we'd come.'

'I know that now.'

She gives Dante a slow look and I'm not sure if she approves or disapproves of the suit he's wearing.

'You look like a cop,' she tells him.

'Lose the tie and carry your jacket,' I suggest to him. 'It'll make you look less like a grown-up when we meet the kids.'

'How old are you?' Diane asks as she leads us towards the main building.

'I'm seventeen, almost eighteen and he's, I think . . . twenty?'

Dante nods. 'You?'

'Fifteen.' She watches Dante again and there's a crease between her brows. 'How old were you when you got inked?'

'Sixteen. I lied about my age. I looked older than I was but I got my dad's signature forged to get it done.'

I'm both surprised and appalled at his admission but Diane seems really impressed. 'Is it big?'

'Upper arm, shoulder, part of my back and up into my neck.' He's untied his tie and opens his collar for her to see the black marks that look sharp enough to impale yourself on. 'It was fu— . . . hellishly sore.'

Diane seems taken by it but doesn't say anything else until we're in the building's foyer.

'The lifts aren't working,' she says, pointing at the vandalized doors with their 'OUT OF ORDER' signs, and leads us up several flights of stairs. The stairwell smells like bleach and industrial cleaner and it's clean, despite the graffiti on the walls. 'But the superintendent is obsessed with making sure everything looks okay. He lets the kids scrawl on the walls in here; it prevents them from doing it outside. As long as it's nothing rude or drug related.'

We push through the doors and I'm gratified to see that Dante looks as out of breath as I am, while Diane seems fine. The corridor is long and narrow, with a door every few metres. Diane leads us towards a door near the end of the passage and knocks.

'I'll see you guys when you're finished, yeah? I'm on the fourth floor. 4B.'

With that she leaves us standing while she clatters back along the passage, furiously thumbing her phone's keypad.

The door opens and a boy no older than Diane stands there. He's skinny, all angles and sharp cheekbones with wide intelligent eyes.

Colin's eyes flick between us, but come to rest on my

face. 'Are you Kit?' he asks me, his voice very quiet, as if he's asking me a secret thing.

'Yes. This is Dante.'

Colin hesitates for a second but Dante's smile is patient and he tones down the Spook vibe just enough for Colin to nod briefly before standing aside and letting us in.

The flat isn't very big, but I've stayed in smaller. There's an open-plan lounge and dining room. The furniture is old and worn but good quality. The TV isn't new or a flat screen but it's in one piece and hooked up to an Xbox. There are books all over the place, stacked haphazardly on the floor, there being no space left on the crammed bookcase. There's a school blazer slung over one of the small dining table's chairs and there are school books lying open on the surface.

I take it all in, noticing a few plants in the corners. The place feels warm and friendly. The walls hold photos of Colin and a younger boy, his brother Adam. There's one with their mum. She's a plump woman of mixed race with startlingly green eyes and a wide sunny smile. I like her instantly and, looking at Colin, I can see the hard work she's done in raising a decent kid.

'Can I get you guys anything to drink?' He gestures awkwardly to the door that leads off the lounge. 'We have some Coke or I can make tea.'

'I'm good, thanks,' I say and carefully move a set of books to the side so I can sit down on the couch.

Dante also declines something to drink and instead of sitting next to me, he pulls over one of the dining-room chairs.

'Where's your brother?' I ask Colin, gesturing for him to sit too.

'Adam's sleeping. Or trying to. He's not doing so great.'

'Do you want to tell us what you saw?'

Dante takes out a small reporter's notebook and I send him an angry look. Does the guy really think this kid's going to tell us what we need to know if he sits there and writes everything down like a cop? Dante gives me a complicated eyebrow jiggle before crossly stuffing the notebook back in his pocket when I refuse to stop staring him down.

'What *I* saw?' Colin rubs his face and I realize he must be exhausted. 'I woke up because I heard noises in Adam's room. When he was little he had really bad dreams so I thought it was just that again. And because he'd woken me, I thought I'd go and check on him. I was just by my door when he screamed so loud.' Colin's hands shake visibly at the memory. 'I ran past my mum's room and saw she was just waking up – I knew she was exhausted from working a double shift. I get to Adam's room and I don't see him at all at first. It was dark in there. Darker than it should have been, you know?'

I nod, knowing what he means. Some supernatural creatures use the night and darkness to hide themselves. And some have the ability to become the night itself.

'It happened so fast. I keep going over it in my head, to figure it out, and each time it gets harder to make sense of it.'

Alarm bells go off in my head. His fear will trigger the usual human capacity to try to make sense of the impossible. It means he'll forget what really happened and I won't get the full story. I don't like doing this, but I lean forward, towards Colin, and put my hand on his. The gold band on my finger briefly touches his skin before I drop my hand again. Colin blinks at me and the panic I saw in his face lessens. The smile he gives me is almost one of relief but then he draws a deep breath and continues. 'I saw some*thing* outside the window, just hanging there. I saw it for maybe a second or two and then it was gone. But its face . . .' His voice is low as it peters out. 'That was when I saw Adam lying on the floor, covered in blood. His face was messed up.' He touches his forehead. 'Cut here and his nose is broken and his arm looked burned. The ambulance came, we went to hospital and they took X-rays and things, and kept him overnight. They talked to my mum a lot too. They were asking about other accidents and things. She was so angry by the time we left, she was shaking.'

'They were making sure that Adam wasn't being abused,' Dante says. 'They have to be careful.'

Colin nods, looking resigned. 'I know. The police came and spoke to us and questioned Adam too. But Adam just told them he was playing in his sleep and ran into his wall. I don't think they believed him. He spoke to a social worker and everything. But they eventually just left.'

'Where's your mum now?' Dante asks him.

'At work. She's a nurse. She rang the school and asked if I could stay with Adam, and because I'm only going to school for study periods right now, they let me. As long as I keep up with my homework.'

'Can we see Adam?' I ask him, standing up. I rub my hands down my jeans, hating that I used the ring to clear this kid's mind so that he didn't freak out on us.

'He's sleeping,' Colin warns. 'Or he should be. This way.'

The passage is small and narrow. Four doors lead off it. Bathroom, remarkably tidy. A smaller bedroom, posters of the galaxy and various constellations dotting the wall, along-side pictures of a few rock bands: Colin's room, also neat, even by comparison to my own room. Then a larger room, with a double bed covered by a floral duvet and the faint scent of Chanel in the air. The next room is Adam's.

Adam, it turns out, isn't sleeping. He's sitting in the middle of his bed, with his back to us, staring at the window. He's maybe eight, I judge from his build. He's dressed in a Spider-Man T-shirt and pyjama bottoms. His face is a mess of bruises, but even under all of that I can see he's a sweet-looking kid with the same good features his brother and mother share. His eyes are tired when they turn to look at me.

The force of his gaze takes me by surprise. It's as if I am the only person in the room and he's not noticed Colin or Dante. I kneel next to the bed.

'Hi,' I say. 'I'm Kit. I'm a friend of Colin's.'

Adam nods, silent, and turns those big eyes back to the window. 'Do you think it's still out there?' he asks me, staring at the world outside his window.

'Unfortunately, yes. But I'm here to stop it.' I see Dante making a movement towards me, to stop me from telling the kid the truth, but I silence him with a sharp look.

'How?' There isn't doubt in Adam's voice and I know he is asking a legitimate question. Sometimes dealing with young kids is so easy.

'Magic. I will track it down and either send it back to a place where it can't come back from . . .'

'Or?' he prompts me when I hesitate.

'I hunt it down and kill it.'

'I think you'll need to kill it,' Adam tells me in his serious voice. 'It will be back and then Arvind will be gone, like all the others.'

Colin moves forward. 'Adam, you can't say things like that. You can't know if . . .'

'It's the same monster as before, Colin. You know it is.' Adam sits up so that he's kneeling now and he looks at me, his expression very earnest. 'Something is stealing the children.'

Chapter Sixteen

Dante's solemn expression meets mine over the heads of the two boys and he tilts his head to the side, indicating that he wants to talk to me alone. I stand up and step out into the small passage so that he can follow me.

'Are you insane?' he asks me, his voice low and angry. 'You can't tell this boy you're going to hunt and kill the monster.'

'Why not?' I counter. 'I'm telling him the truth.'

'You can't know if this is a case for someone with your set of special skills.'

The way he says 'special skills' makes it sound as if I'm a small child dabbling with watercolours.

'Can't you feel it?' I ask him, gesturing to the room where I can hear Colin and Adam talking. 'That boy is scared. So is his older brother. They are so scared that they aren't keeping quiet. Do you think, for one second, that Colin would want to lose face in front of adults or Chem and his mates?'

Dante narrows his eyes behind his glasses and frowns at me. 'Do you have to be so honest about what you do?' he counters. 'Telling them about monsters?'

I grimace. 'Monsters are real, Dante. And they are as

happy to eat little kids as they are to eat grown adults. It will do no one any harm to be a little bit more careful.'

'So what do we do now?' he asks me, frustrated, and I'm surprised that he's letting me take the lead again.

'We talk to Adam. We find out exactly what he saw.' I sigh and run my hand through my hair. 'And then we go from there.'

Adam looks relieved when we come back into the room. Colin is sitting on the small chair at the desk and his expression is miserable.

'My mum won't be happy if she knows you guys have been here,' he says. 'The neighbours will talk.'

'Just say we're from school. Well, I can be from school. Dante here can be a teacher or something.' I smile at him and briefly touch his hand again. 'We're here to help, Colin.'

'Can I ask you for a glass of water?' Dante looks at Colin. 'I think it will be easier if Kit chats to Adam alone for a little while.'

Colin hesitates, clearly not keen on the idea of leaving his baby brother alone with me. I give him a reassuring smile and he nods briefly. 'Okay. But not too long. He needs sleep.'

I watch them go, with Dante leaving the door slightly ajar.

Adam turns to me and leans forward. 'You're magic, aren't you?'

I make a show of looking over my shoulder, pretending to make sure we're alone. I press my finger to my lips in a *shhh* gesture. A look of delight crosses Adam's face and he watches in awe as I cup my hands together. A small ball of light forms there, no bigger than a marble. I take my hands away and just let the little sphere rotate there for a few seconds, before I close my hand around it once more and it disappears.

Adam breathes out and his eyes are huge. 'That was amazing!' His smile is sunny and friendly, even if his poor face looks sore and bruised. 'Why is it that when I told the grown-ups about what really happened with the Raggedy Man they didn't believe me? The police think I'm lying. The doctors told my mum that I hit my head so hard I was imagining things.'

I sit down on the floor next to the bed and cross my legs under me. This is going to be an interesting talk.

'I don't know why some grown-ups are like that, Adam. I think some people, when they grow old, forget how to see impossible things.' I tap his forehead. 'They forget to just accept the magic.'

'I never want to be like that,' he says solemnly, watching me with big eyes. 'Why is the Raggedy Man here?'

'I don't know, matey. Can you tell me what you remember?'

I listen without interrupting to Adam telling me about waking up, about seeing the monster hanging onto the outside of the building a few windows down, shifting and trying to get into another apartment before it turned its attention to him. About the thing coming for Adam and reaching for him through the wall. I watch him carefully and everything about his small frame and honest answers convinces me that this boy is telling the truth. Something really did try and pull him out of his room.

'Do you know whose room he was trying to get into?' I ask him as he pauses to order his thoughts. I like the way he talks, slowly and clearly. From what I've seen of Colin and the way they are together, I get the idea that their mum is keen on making sure her kids are brought up clever, for the lack of another word.

'Arvind. He's only little. I mean, he's younger than me. His mum and dad are always working and so his gran lives with them. She looks after him. I like her cos she always has sweets and she's friendly. She doesn't speak English but Arvind does, so whenever we play he will tell me what she's saying.'

'Do you have any idea why the monster would want to steal Arvind?'

Adam looks up and out of the window again. The clouds race across the blue sky and it looks like a perfect autumn day, not the kind of day to be talking about monsters stealing little children.

'I don't know. All the children here know about the Raggedy Man. Mostly he's just around, watching us, making sure we're okay. But why would he want to take Arvind?'

'Where is Arvind now? Do you think we would be able to talk to him?'

'They left. Gone to India for his cousin's wedding.'

'Did you know they were leaving? Or did they leave after the creature tried getting into his room?'

Adam blinks at me and shrugs. 'I don't know.'

I nod and think about what he's said previously. 'You told Colin that it's the same monster as before. What did you mean by that?'

There's a flash of fear in his eyes. 'Before we lived here, other children went missing. All of them little, like under twelve.'

'How do you know this?'

He shrugs, making patterns on his duvet cover with his fingers. 'The other children talk. Everyone knows.'

I lean back, propping my arms behind me. We sit quietly for a few minutes and I take in the room. Everything here is completely ordinary. The toys, the books, the clothes, the posters of famous football players.

'Show me the shoe you used to hurt him.'

Adam scampers towards his bed and digs around on the far side and eventually hands me the shoe. It is a football boot with spikes on the sole. It looks the worse for wear, mangled and twisted.

'What happened to it?' I ask him. Adam leans forward and points at the shoe before answering.

'I grabbed it and just smacked the thing with it. As hard as I could. Over and over. I must have hurt it, don't you think?'

I turn the shoe around and examine the spikes. They look worn away, like melted wax, more than just the normal wear and tear of a football boot.

'It definitely looks like it. What did it do?'

'It spat at the window. Like you see some old men do.'

Standing up, I lean over the desk and examine the window. There's a flaw in the glass. My hand touches the spot and I turn to look at Adam in question. His nod tells me that I'm looking at where the thing's spittle put a flaw in the double glazing. I press my cheek against the glass and look sideways, following the line of the wall. I count six windows, with the window I'm looking out of being the seventh.

'Can you tell me what it looked like?' I ask him, turning away from the window. 'This monster?'

Before he can answer, the door opens wider and Colin and Dante come in carrying mugs and a glass of juice for Adam.

Colin sits down next to Adam and passes a glass of juice to him.

'We've been trying to draw it,' he says. He reaches into his back pocket and hands me a series of folded pieces of paper.

I stand up and walk over to where Dante's standing, making a show of examining Adam's football posters. He looks down at the sketches in my hand and mutters something under his breath.

Whichever of the two brothers drew these, did a decent job. The thing staring back at us from the crumpled notebook pages looks as if it crawled straight out of a nightmare. It has flat features, bulging eyes and a wide nose. An odd line runs down from the nose and upper lip and, when I check the next page, it's clear that this bizarre feature actually split its face open. A shudder roils through me as I look at the rows of shark-like teeth depicted in the picture.

'Any idea?' Dante asks me, taking the pictures from me.

I shake my head. My mind's completely blank. All the research and lore I'd managed to cram into my head over months of intense study seem useless now. But there is one thing I can do.

My magic sizzles under my skin when I reach for it. I close my eyes briefly, letting it settle over me. I need to see this room through my Sight. The creature, whatever it was, would have left a residue. And that might give me a clue as to what it can be and how to hunt it, capture it and sling its ass back to the Otherwhere. Of course, that's assuming it is an illegal escapee from the Otherwhere.

Chapter Seventeen

The room flares into high definition around me. Both Colin and Adam shine with life and vitality. I examine Adam, concentrating on the arm the creature grabbed during their encounter. It looks fine but I detect a discolouration in what some people would call his aura. He lets me touch his arm and I spread my hand to get an idea of the size of the monster's grip. It's far bigger than the span of my hand, taking up Adam's entire forearm. I ruffle his hair and smile at him and get a grin back.

I swing myself around and check the wall and window. The window's badly damaged. Whatever acid it spat at the window has left a definite residue on there. I'll have to try and get a scraping of it to take back for Kyle to check out. The wall where Adam said the creature pressed through is covered in a weird black mould I couldn't see before. I have a small baggie ready and scrape some off with the blade of my small bone-handled knife. I return the knife to my hip pocket, seal the baggie and zip it securely in a jacket pocket.

I pretend not to notice Dante's highly interested expression as I look around the room, touching things. He makes distracted conversation with Colin and Adam, who give equally vague answers while they watch me drift around the tiny room.

Adam's eyes are huge when I turn back to the wall and window. I crouch down in front of him.

'Adam, can I put a protection spell on this window? It won't take long. I want to make sure that this thing can't get back in here again.'

He nods quickly. 'Yes.' He shoots a look at Colin. 'Mum will be okay with it, won't she?'

Colin shifts uncomfortably. 'As long as you're not using blood or anything weird.'

'Why would you say that?' I ask him, wondering what exactly he's read and how he's heard about spells that need blood to be effective.

'I read stuff. You know, on the Internet.'

'Right. You shouldn't always believe what you read on there,' I tell him. I take a small piece of chalk out of my pocket. 'Can I have the room?' I address the question to Dante, who gives a sigh, far too long suffering for someone who's known me for less than forty-eight hours. But he nods, very reluctantly, and ushers both Colin and Adam out. He closes the door behind them with a soft *snick*, but not before he gives me a long slow look, as if he's trying to puzzle something out.

The chalk is not your average blackboard stuff. Before it's compressed it's mixed with salt and a selection of herbs that help with protection. This time I actually know what's in there because I helped my cousin Megan make the stuff. I quickly and expertly sketch a variety of sigils on the windowsills and walls, along the skirting boards and as high as I can reach. The chalk doesn't leave any visible signs and I work with confidence, having had this routine deeply ingrained in me since the Manor was destroyed a few months ago in a magical attack. The Blackharts have learned their lesson: we no longer ask for outside help when it comes to protecting our own homes.

My magic flows steadily from me into the chalk, into the peculiar runes I'm drawing. Instead of tiring me out, as it's done in the past, I feel invigorated and a little bit wild as it zings through me. The basic training I had with Aelfric's sorcerers in the Otherwhere has definitely changed how easily I can access my well of magic. I've been so afraid of it in the past, seeing it as something wholly alien, rather than just one more thing that makes up who I am.

Half an hour later I'm done in the room. I've secured it and double secured it as well as I can. While I did my quick search, I also checked around the room for any fetishes, or the little curse bags that magicians sometimes use. These could have called the creature to Adam, but I find none. The room held only little boy stuff. As an extra bit of caution I drop a spell of protection into the small teddy bear on Adam's bed. If nothing else, it should help Adam sleep.

When I step out of the room and into the lounge area, I stop in my tracks, surprised to see Dante sitting on the floor in front of the TV, jacket off, tie gone, game controller in hand. On the TV, his figure, a small human in crappy armour, is battling against a giant robot creature. From the determination on Adam's face as he sits next to Dante, I can tell Adam is the robot.

Dante catches my movements in the reflection of the TV, fumbles his controls and goes down in a dramatic firefight, being blown to smithereens. Adam crows and high-fives Colin, who is laughing at his brother's antics.

'Guys? I'm done in there. The room should be fine now.

I put some minor spells in place that should stop some nasty things getting back in. It would take me most of the day to do the rest of the flat so I need you guys to be careful.' I hand Colin one of my business cards. 'If you hear or see anything out of the ordinary, call me immediately, okay? I'm going home to research this guy.' I tap my pocket where their sketches are tucked away. 'And then I'm going to come back and hunt him.'

Adam pops around the couch and I lean down to give him a hug. He's a cute kid and I like him. I like both him and Colin but I feel old around them, having long since forgotten what it's like to just hang out with mates, watching DVDs and playing Xbox. Admittedly, I get to do that with my cousins, but there's always shop talk about monsters, the various Courts and rumours about what the Infernal are doing. It's tiring. I sometimes yearn just to be a teen girl again. My life before the Blackharts claimed me seems really simple and uncomplicated.

I shake Colin's hand and I can tell he's worried. 'Do you think this thing will come back?' he asks me, keeping his voice low. 'What if it does? What if it comes for Adam again?'

'It's been about a week since the attack, right? It's either been scared off or is biding its time. I'm going to work hard to get this sorted out so that I can get to it before it comes back.' I pause and look at him. 'I will jump on my bike the second you ring me,' I assure him. 'Believe me.'

'You have my details too,' Dante cuts in. 'Give either one of us a call if you're worried about anything. We'll come running.'

Colin nods, pocketing the business card.

'Thanks. Thanks for coming and for believing us. No one else did.'

We leave the two brothers in the doorway and make our way back to the stairwell.

'You handled that well,' Dante says, holding the door open for me. 'But it's risky, promising them that you'll help them.'

'What do you mean?' I frown at him as I head down the stairs at a much slower pace than going up. I cradle my helmet under my arm.

'You can't know you'll be able to protect them or save Adam if that thing comes for him again.'

'I know that I will do my utmost to find out what it is and to hunt it down. Blackharts do not easily give their word.'

'You're making promises you can't possibly keep. What if it comes back tonight and takes Adam?'

'Then I will hunt it down and find Adam and bring him back.'

Dante grumbles under his breath. 'You're not listening to what I'm saying here.'

'No.' I stop and look at him. He's one step behind me so I have to look up at him. 'I am listening to what you're saying. My word is my bond. That boy is as safe as he can be. I dumped so much magic in that room it will take one of the Sidhe sorcerers a day to work through the layers of spells I put up.' I grimace when I read the disbelief in his face. 'You Spook guys really get my goat. You know magic is real, that monsters exist, but you can't ever accept it, can you? With all your files and all your technology, magic and flying fairies still freak you out.'

'I suppose we have to be the ones that stay level headed

in situations like this,' he counters, shrugging. 'And we believe in all these things, but we just try and find a modern way to fix it.'

'Yeah,' I say, pushing the fire door to the fourth floor open with my shoulder. 'Good luck with that.'

The flat Diane shares with her mum, two sisters and cousin is no bigger than the flat we've just left, and the living room's been transformed into a fourth bedroom. I expected a mess, a bit of chaos, but instead it's like walking into an Aladdin's cave. The flat strongly reflects the personalities of the women who live in it. There are photos of them everywhere, knick-knacks gathered on trips and no doubt bought for birthdays and Christmas.

Diane's room, shared with her cousin, is the same size and on the same side of the block as Adam's, overlooking a small playground that is in even more of a state than the one to the front.

'My auntie let me have these, so you have to bring them back in exactly the same condition, yeah?' She pulls the two scrap books back as I reach for them. 'Promise?'

'I promise. I'll take good care of them, thank you.'

She presses them into my hands. 'My auntie's not been well for a long time. This is how she keeps track of things happening in the area.'

'We'll be careful. I promise.'

Dante's smile would melt the heart of the toughest of people and Diane eventually nods, letting out a bit of a sigh. 'Okay? You promise?'

'Yes,' I say. 'We'll make copies of them and bring them back to you. In tiptop shape.' I hesitate by the door. 'Diane, do you know about the Raggedy Man?'

She grimaces. 'Yeah, it's the local bogeyman. The kids like to freak one another out about him. They dare one another to call him. You know, like Bloody Mary?'

I shudder at the mention of Bloody Mary because if there is one urban legend that is based on a real thing, it's that and it really does freak me out. The mere idea of standing in front of a mirror and repeating her name three times to see if she would manifest is enough to creep me out. I see plenty creepy things, I don't need to add Bloody Mary to that.

'Adam said that the thing that tried to get into his room was the Raggedy Man.'

'Look, the whole Raggedy Man thing is weird. There used to be an old guy who lived here. He always kept an eye on the kids. He dressed in weird clothes, this tattered coat, and so the kids gave him that name. He moved away and they still say he shows up now and again.'

'You don't believe them?'

'I've never seen him myself. It was before we moved here.'

Just then there's a commotion from the front of the flat. The sound of laughter and shopping and the delicious aroma of food.

'My mum's back. You've got to go.'

She ushers us out of the room and down the narrow passage into the extra bedroom and towards the door. A statuesque woman in a colourful and intricately folded turban steps out of the kitchen, hands on her ample hips.

'What have we here den, girl? Who are your friends?' Her accent holds a hint of Jamaican and more than a bit of French too.

'Mami, this is Kit and Dante. They're from school.'

I shake Diane's mum's hand and I like how strong her grip is. She eyes me up and down and I'm not entirely sure if she approves of what she sees.

'You look familiar,' she says.

'You might have seen me around,' I say smiling brightly. I hold up the scrapbooks. 'We've got to run, Mrs . . .' I flounder, realizing that I have no idea what Diane's surname is.

'Call me Julia, girl. And you, boy? Why do you wear a suit?'

Dante looks taken aback by the direct question but only for a second. 'I work after school. In the city. In my uncle's office. I do filing.'

'Eh. Now see, Diane? These are the kinds of friends you should have. Not that boy Chem. He is not good news.'

'Mum, please. They have to go. We've got school tomorrow.' Diane jerks her head towards the door in a flagrant attempt to get rid of us. 'Also, Chem's a good friend. Things have just been hard for him.'

I motion for Dante and we head towards the door. I glimpse two other girls in the kitchen, one of them younger than Diane, the other looks older. They are both built along the same lines as Julia and they look definitely interested in what is happening out here. Suddenly I don't envy Diane the grilling she's about to undergo when we leave.

'It was nice meeting you, Julia.' I nod at her and the girls in the kitchen.

'Come visit soon, we can talk about you being friends with my Diane.'

I'm out in the doorway and as the door swings shut behind Dante I hear one of her sisters say, 'That boy is hot,

Di! He can come back *anytime*.' The statement is followed by peals of laughter and an undignified squeak from Diane.

I start laughing and look up at Dante.

'How do you feel being objectified?' I ask him.

His face has taken on a definite red tint along the cheeks. 'You get used to it,' he mumbles but, to my amusement, he's shrunk into his jacket in embarrassment.

Chapter Eighteen

'You're wearing your thinking face,' Dante tells me as we leave the block of flats.

'I have a thinking face?'

'Yeah, it's like this.' He scrunches up his nose and wrinkles his forehead. As handsome as he is, it makes him look demented. It's not a good look.

'I do not look like that!' But I'm laughing. 'Geez, you really don't believe in giving a girl a break, do you?'

He shrugs and grins at me. 'Out with it: what are you thinking?'

'That I'd like to come back and check out the outside of the building, specifically the wall where Adam's window's located.'

'That's six floors up. Can you fly?'

'No. But I can call in a favour from someone I know.'

'A faerie?'

When I nod he shakes his head. 'No, definitely not. Let's go and check out the back of the flats. I might be able to do something.'

We walk around the side of the buildings. The shadows are deep here because a lot of the lights are out. They've either been broken on purpose to hide dodgy dealings, or they've fused and the council's not bothered to replace them. The play area is a sad little place, half-lit by a weakly flickering overhead spotlight. The swings hang broken and the frame is skewed to one side, while the little rocking rooster thing tilts wildly to the left. I turn to look up at the building and immediately spot Adam's room.

There's a glow from the window that has nothing to do with the light on within and everything to do with the magics I anchored to the room itself.

I point to the window. 'Can you see it?' I ask Dante, wondering if he'll be able to see what I'm seeing.

'I can count so I know which room is Adam's,' he says. 'Is that what you mean?'

I swear softly under my breath. 'No, the place is lit up by the spells I worked into the room. Can you see the light?'

He shifts next to me, following the line of my arm and finger. He stays still for some time but then shakes his head.

'No, nothing.'

'Do you trust me?' I watch his face so close to mine. He really is a very attractive young man. He looks fresh and clean cut, uncomplicated. As I stare at him he looks back at me and from somewhere unbidden I hear the refrain of the lullaby that freaked me out so much earlier this evening. The strains of it are all around me, clinging to me like spider webs and I physically shake my head to clear my mind.

'Yes.' Dante's breath is a whisper across my cheek and I can't help the warm tingle that spreads out from inside of me. My magic really likes this boy.

'Close your eyes.'

He does it without further prompting. I lick my lips, just a little bit, and stand on tiptoe. I press my lips gently, softly, to each of his eyes and as I do, I feed a bit of my magic into him. I hear his breath hitch and I don't know if it's because I'm kissing his eyes or if he's reacting to the magic he can feel working its way through him.

'When you open your eyes, do it carefully,' I warn him. 'Slowly, like you're looking into the sun.'

I watch his face as he follows my instructions.

'Is this what you see?' he asks me after a few moments. 'Everything is clear and bright. You're shining, like you've got a fire inside you.'

'It's the magic. I'm not trying to keep you from seeing me properly. Look up at Adam's room. Can you see what I mean now?'

'Yes.' He steps away from me, his head turned upwards. 'Can you see where the thing climbed the wall? Look, the bricks are discoloured, almost like they've been burned.'

We walk closer until we stand underneath the windows and look straight up. 'I need to get up there and get samples of the burned brick but also the stuff it spat onto Adam's window.' I'm wondering about coming back with some ropes and climbing gear when Dante takes a few steps back from me and does a fast run-up at the wall. The next thing I know, he's up and climbing the wall as if it's something he does every day. I gape up at him as he quickly scales the side of the building, finding finger and toe-holds, whereas to me it looks like a normal wall.

Just beneath Adam's window, he lets his weight drop and hangs by one hand as he struggles to get something out of his pocket. I step back to get a clearer look, my heart thudding in my chest. He shimmies over and his body hides his movements but I think he's managing to scrape something off the wall and then pocket it. Then he moves, carefully, on to Adam's window.

All of this takes both far longer and less time than I expect. I'm okay with heights, I can jump off buildings and free fall, but even I'm a bit awestruck by how easily Dante moves, without any harness or safety equipment on the side of the building.

I'm concentrating so hard, staring upwards, that I don't hear or see the guy walking up to me until it's too late.

The blow takes me across my shoulders, sending me stumbling forward so that I fall to my knees with a grunt. Shock and pain follow, but the instinct to defend myself takes over. I kick backwards and feel the heavy sole of my boot connecting with ribs as the guy lunges towards me. I risk a quick look, noticing that the steel pipe he hit me with the first time is gripped tightly in one hand.

He staggers a few paces and it gives me time to get up and assess the situation. He's bigger than me, wider in the shoulders and also taller. His longer arms and the fact that he has a pipe that extends his reach are definite issues.

'What the hell,' I shout at him. 'What do you want?'

'For you to get off our turf, *devochka*.' He straightens and stalks towards me with menace in every line of his body. I don't try and talk to him because, well, I'm not in the mood and he just whacked me with a big steel rod. In my book that's just plain rude and he obviously needs a lesson or two in how to talk to women. I pull out my knife and let the little light there is play across the blade. I beckon him forward with my other hand and when he hesitates, his eyes widening at the sight of the blade, I resist the urge to rush him.

'You should just go,' he says. 'Take your friend and leave.'

'I can't do that,' I say, walking closer, when everything in me screams to turn tail and run. If this was one of the drug pushers Chem and his friends had pointed out, he could easily be armed with a gun too.

'You want to feel more pain?' he counters, lifting the steel pole. Suddenly he's aiming an elaborate swing at my head. I sway backwards, grunting as the pipe whooshes past my face. He follows up with a fast backhanded swing and I yelp as the blow glances off my ribs. But it doesn't stop me from lunging towards him, coming up inside his guard. He wastes no time landing a fist to my ribs and I stomp on his foot to keep him in place, landing my own fist in his gut. He doubles over with an *oomph* and I grab his long greasy hair and yank him up.

'Kit!'

Dante's voice is somewhere behind me, but I've got the edge of the knife pressing against the guy's taught neck as I'm pulling his head back, exposing his vulnerable jugular. I'm now very keen to kick his face in, because I hurt all over. Anger at being punched and hurt licks at me and I have trouble focusing.

'Drop your weapon,' I hiss at him, wiggling my fingers so they tangle further into his hair. 'Or I'll be forced to cut you.'

I feel him drop the pipe to the ground.

'Who are you?' I ask him. 'What are you doing here?'

His Adam's apple bobs against my wrist and, just to make sure he understands how serious I am, I lean a tiny bit closer against him and the blade digs in, just a fraction harder.

'Jesus, they were right, you are nuts.'

I let out a laugh. 'No, just highly strung. Who are you and why are you attacking me?'

'They told me to come here and give you a message. They don't want you here; you're bad for business.'

'And that involved you hitting me with a steel pipe?'

He's in the process of shrugging but then remembers the blade under his chin and he stops.

'They said you could handle yourself.'

'Who are these *they* you mention?'

This time he does shrug and I press harder. He swears angrily in what sounds like Russian.

'Telling you isn't worth my family's life,' he says in English as he peers at me. 'I'm just the messenger.'

'Kit? What are you doing?'

I startle at Dante's voice.

'The guy attacked me,' I tell him. 'I think he's with the drug dealers from the other night, when we met the estate kids for the first time.'

'That doesn't mean you have to threaten him with your knife, Kit. He's unarmed.'

'He was armed. Before.' I scowl at the man. 'He hit me with a steel pipe, Dante. I made him drop it.'

Dante exhales heavily and moves so I can see him. 'Kit, he's bleeding.'

I open my mouth to deny it but my eyes drop to my attacker's neck and there's definitely something wet and sticky beneath my blade.

I'm so close to the guy that I can feel his heartbeat kick up a notch.

'Please,' he mutters. 'Just let me go, okay? No harm done, *devochka*. I'll tell them you said you'd stay away and wouldn't deal here any more. I'll tell them I beat you up a bit. We both win.'

'They think I'm selling drugs?' I ask him. 'Is that what all this is about?'

'Yes, of course. People like you and your boyfriend don't come round here unless you're recruiting for buyers. Or you're cops.' He gasp-laughs. 'But you're definitely too young and crazy to be cops.' He smirks. 'Besides, the stuff we're selling is *sweet* so no one will want yours anyway.'

There are sirens somewhere in the distance and the guy shifts against me as I try and focus on what he's saying.

'Look, let's just think about this now. I told you what you wanted to know. You threatened me, I got a lucky swing in. Your boyfriend is worried you're going to turn me into fillet and the cops are coming. Someone's definitely called them. Those sirens are for us.' I like that he's sounding panicked and that he's trying to appeal to my better nature.

If he only knew.

Dante's watching me and even in the bad light I can see him evaluate my sanity and the situation we're in. He gives me a slight shake of the head as if saying, *No, this isn't good, Kit*, and I wonder if he can sense the angry buzzing in my head, that this man dared attack me. After a moment to consider options, I lower my knife and step back, kicking the steel pipe further away.

'Go,' I say to him, my knife still held ready. 'Leave before I think this through and decide to hand you to the cops.'

The guy wastes no time running off into the dark. Dante watches me slide the knife out of sight before hurrying me away from the back of the estate. We're near the main road when my stomach protests at how casually I've just attacked another human being. I break away from Dante's grip; the need to be elsewhere is urgent. I make it as far as the nearest shrubs before I'm horrifically sick and throw up everything I have in my stomach.

'Kit? Are you okay?'

Dante's hand is soothing on the small of my back. I try and talk but I just have no air or energy, and the noise that unexpectedly comes out sounds suspiciously like a sob.

'Shit.' Dante's arm goes around my waist and he drapes my other arm around his shoulder. 'You need to straighten up,' he tells me from far away. 'You'll start breathing fine soon.'

I'm shaking now, my mind replaying what it felt like wanting to slide the knife a little bit more tightly across the man's skin, because he'd hurt me and deserved to be hurt in turn.

I've never had a panic attack before. I've been frightened and shaky before and felt trapped, but not this. This is something else.

I feel my knees buckle after a few steps and only the strength in Dante's arms holds me upright.

'Kit, what's going on? You're okay. We're okay.' Dante lets me sit down on a low wall and crouches in front of me, his warm hands wrapped tightly around my ice-cold shaking ones. I open my mouth to tell him that something's wrong with me, that I feel weird *in my head* and that I'd come so close to pressing the knife into the guy, but I can't. My throat locks up and suddenly I'm crying. Huge, ugly fat tears and, God, there are wracking sobs and I can't stop shaking.

Dante pulls me against him and just holds me. I'm aware of people walking by, of someone stopping to ask if everything is okay and of Dante answering them in a low but dismissive voice. I dig my nails into my palms, the pain helping me to focus until my breathing evens out and I don't feel as if I've been scattered throughout the multiverse any more.

Slowly I move away from Dante, and wipe my face. 'I'm fine now,' I say after some time, when I can speak again. I hate that my voice sounds so small, and I clear my throat, trying to find my usual tone. But I know it will take some time before can talk properly again.

He doesn't let go of my elbows. He just keeps watching me for a few minutes longer before nodding and leaning back a little to look at me.

'Are you sure?'

'Yeah.' I press my hand to my ribs and grimace. The ache across my back tells me I'm also going to have a lovely bruise across my shoulders in a few hours. 'It's going to ache like crazy in the morning, but I'm going to be okay.'

He looks sceptical but I have a bad-ass reputation to uphold, so I try to brazen it out.

'I'm a tough girl. I promise.' I draw another deep breath. 'I just really need to shower. I can smell that guy all over me.'

Chapter Nineteen

'What was the Spider-Man stunt you pulled back there?' I ask Dante loudly over the bikes' engines as we idle at a traffic light. 'You could have been seriously hurt.'

He looks at me in surprise. 'I told you I did freerunning, didn't I? Besides, I never fall.'

'What? Freerunning, like parkour? And, no, you've never mentioned it. But that's beside the point. You could have fallen and been killed.'

His eyes crinkle at me. 'I'm fine plus I got the samples you wanted.'

'And what? You always carry baggies with you?' Even in the muted red light of the traffic lights I see a flash of embarrassment across his features. 'That's a bit Boy Scouts, isn't it?'

'Turns out my Spook training was good for something, right?'

'I'm almost impressed.'

The lights are taking a long time to change. I unzip my jacket and ruck my shirt up to check the damage. A bruise is already forming across my ribs and as I press experimentally against them with cool fingers, I hiss at the pain.

'You want to go to hospital?' Dante's watching me curiously as my fingers walk up my ribs. 'It looks sore.'

'No, I'll be fine. I just need sleep.' That almost makes me laugh. Sleep is more rare to me than the fabled golden eggs laid by a fairytale goose. Ideally, I need to be in the Otherwhere, or somewhere here in the Frontier where the leylines are strong. The power coursing through them would help me to heal.

'You need bandaging up. You could have a cracked rib.'

'I've had cracked ribs before,' I assure him. 'This is fine, just bruising.'

The lights change. We move on to the next set, and idle there, waiting for them to change in turn. Two girls stroll past, arm in arm and laughing. They look so terrifically normal; I feel a pang that I'm missing out on something important.

'How long will this last? Seeing all the magic?' Dante asks.

'Until the kiss wears off. Or when you wash your face.'

'And if I don't wash my face?'

I pull my face at him. 'Euch, that's a bit gross.'

'Seriously.'

'It will still go. What I shared with you is a tiny bit of magic, designed – if you can call it that – to let you see magic tonight.'

'Can you do it again?' He gestures to his eyes. 'Can you make it permanent?'

'I don't think so.' The lights change back to green. 'We can talk more later.'

Chapter Twenty

Dante and I decide to call it an early night; both of us have had a tough evening. We're to reconvene over breakfast in Covent Garden, which will give me a chance to read the file on him that Uncle Andrew sent over. It will also give me time to go through the papers I have at home and even, shockingly, get some sleep, I hope.

Kyle's watching a Bruce Lee movie when I get in and he looks surprised to see the state I'm in.

'Are you okay?' He shoves the bowl of popcorn to the side and follows me into the kitchen.

'If you tell me I look bad I'm going to hurt you,' I tell him.

'Okay.' He fills the kettle and moves around me as I throw together the makings of a large cheese, tomato and salad sandwich. 'How was your day?'

Before I can answer, there's a knock on the door. We trade looks. I reach for the large carving knife and follow Kyle to the door. He lifts the cricket bat out of the umbrella stand and lets it casually lean against his leg. We may be the most paranoid set of cousins in the family, but we are also alive and relatively scar free.

He swings the front door open to reveal Dante standing

on the front step, helmet under his arm and a baggie in his other hand.

'Hi,' he says to Kyle. 'I'm Dante. You must be Kyle, I think?' He bends down and leaves his helmet on the step so that he can shake hands. 'Sorry about stopping by unexpectedly. I forgot to give this to Kit.' He hands me the baggie with the scrapings off the window.

I hold it up and peer at it, but honestly, it doesn't look like much. It's just clear *stuff* of some sort.

'Do you want to come in?' Kyle asks, painfully polite, the way his parents raised him, just as I say: 'Thanks for this, I'll see you tomorrow.'

Dante laughs, looking between us. 'Thanks, but I think I'd better get home. It was nice meeting you, and I'll see you tomorrow, Kit.'

I nod and walk back into the kitchen, tossing the baggie onto the table in the dining room.

'You are such a cow sometimes,' Kyle tells me. 'He might be a Spook but he came all the way here to give you that.'

'He did it on purpose. I don't know what that purpose was, but yeah, he did it on . . .'

'Purpose, you said. Why are you suddenly wary of him?'

'Because he's asked me if my magic can let him See permanently.'

'Eh?'

So while Kyle brews us some strong tea and I munch my way through my sandwich and a packet of crisps, I update him with everything that's happened today. One thing about Kyle: he's a superb listener.

'I thought you said Dante joined the Spook Squad after he saw one of their agents fight a monster in an alley. He didn't see the guy fight another guy: he saw the monster with teeth and talons.' When I nod he goes on. 'He also saw the banshee last night, but tonight he couldn't see the magic coming out of the little boy's room.'

'Until I kissed his eyes.'

'Okay, that's weird.'

'Maybe his Sight isn't as strong as I assumed it was.'

'Yeah, it could be. Also, he ran up the wall.' Just to be clear that I meant an actual wall, Kyle patted the surface next to him. 'A wall like this?'

'No, it was a brick wall and it was six storeys high. And he was fast, gecko fast.'

'You think there's something off about Mr Charisma?'

I chuckle at Kyle's nickname, ignoring my twingeing muscles. 'I think there's something going on. Uncle Andrew sent me a file with the info he found on Dante. It may be worthwhile checking it out.'

'Your normal email?' Kyle asks, already heading to his bank of computer screens. 'You can access it through here. The tech on this one isn't as new as the others so you shouldn't be able to fry it so easily.'

He's right and I don't manage to blow the hard drive up as I download the pdf file. I'm not sure what sites Uncle Andrew hacked to get the info on Dante but it looks pretty comprehensive, and there are even photos of Dante and his family.

Dante grew up in an orphanage before going into foster care. He was moved from one family to another for the next couple of years, until his ninth birthday, when he was adopted by a couple: Angela and William Burke.

I examine the pictures. Angela and William Burke look like good people. Both of them are tanned and attractive and look outdoorsy. William has his arm draped around Angela's shoulders and they're both laughing into the camera. Behind them is somewhere with lots of trees and maybe even mountains in the distance. They are both dressed in hiking gear.

In the first photo with Dante, he looks a bit awkward, a bit sulky, and stands to the side of them a little, not quite part of the small family as yet.

Growing up, Dante got into a bit of trouble with some mates – casual vandalism and fighting, nothing too alarming. His grades were good and he excelled at maths and science. He was also a successful athlete. There are pictures of him taking part in martial arts tournaments, with both Angela and William in the audience. There are also photos of a young Dante on a skateboard, cap backwards, smirking at the camera, with his arm around two other boys. Other shots, maybe mobile phone pictures, show Dante and his mate leaping down stairs, doing handstands on railings and the edges of buildings.

He didn't lie, then. He has done freerunning, and some images showing similar stunts are more recent too.

The martial arts training came from William Burke, the file tells me. He's ex-army and set up a martial arts studio in his local area with the help of some loans. Dante joined shortly after he was adopted and excelled at karate, ju-jitsu and capoeira. Even Jamie would be impressed by the mix of styles.

Dante kept having brushes with the law, but never anything serious. It usually had to do with fighting or loitering and getting into scuffles but never went any further. Until he turned fifteen, when everything changed. His grades plummeted. He was charged with assaulting someone while drunk and put this person – a boy from his school – in hospital. I flick around Andrew's notes and suck in my breath. His little sister Emily went missing from a local park. Someone had taken her. It coincided with Dante going off the rails. There were no charges brought against him but he received a caution and he had to do community work.

I flip through the rest of the file, speed-reading. Emily was found in a field a month later, in a grave. The file shows me some follow-up articles about her disappearance, her subsequent discovery and how the police had made no arrests as there were no further leads.

Dante's grades climbed with time, and his community service was to help kids younger than him find ways to keep themselves entertained. He took them to William's dojo and introduced them to martial arts. There is a photo of a group of kids, boys and girls ranging between ten and fourteen, all striking insane martial arts and superhero poses for the camera. The photo was clipped from a newspaper and the title mentions William Burke's dojo and his son Dante's work in the community.

He finished his school career with good grades, but not good enough to get a bursary or scholarship to his chosen university. This was when he was approached by a company called Lawton Limited, which I know is a front for the Spook Squad.

The other photos Uncle Andrew added to the file are of Dante hanging out with some friends, more pictures of him with his family, and especially Emily. Emily looks cute and obviously adored her big brother. It looks as if he doted on her. And although I know they're not blood relatives, they look enough alike to have been taken for brother and sister.

There are photos of Emily opening presents at Christmas and Dante holding her on his lap, laughing, while Angela beams at them both.

There are few photos of Angela and William after Emily's death. In those that do exist, they've lost a bit of their sparkle and Dante looks hollow eyed and sad.

'Has he told you about his baby sister?' Kyle shimmies his chair to the side so he can look at me. 'Well, has he? Do you think that is why he is so interested in this case?'

'He didn't say anything to me about his baby sister being taken. I knew he was adopted. And that he joined the Spooks after leaving school, but really, we've not had much of a heart-to-heart about our personal lives as such.'

'Do you think he'll tell you? Do you think it has anything to do with the case?'

I sit back in my chair and watch Kyle for a few seconds, trying to make up my mind. 'No. I mean, yes. I think he was keen to take on the case to find these missing kids. But no, I don't know if the whole thing with his sister has anything to do with him taking the case. I mean, it might.'

Kyle looks at me as if I'm crazy. 'Imagine if your sister was taken and killed by some psychopath, Kit. You'd want to help out others in the same situation. Right?'

I'm remembering the Unseelie Fae burning down my house and killing my Nan. Yes, I think to myself, I would definitely want to figure out how to get payback. Instead of saying that out loud and making myself sound insane, I grimace and toss a napkin at him. 'I know, Kyle. Why would you think the kids were taken by faeries?'

'Well, it's kinda obvious, isn't it?' He returns my frown with one of his own. 'Isn't it? I mean, it has to be related.'

'Right.' I snap my fingers and do finger-guns at him.

'Now you're going to do some research. Google or sabotage databases you have access to and see what you can find about children going missing under mysterious circumstances. . . in, say, the past five years. Also if any of them have been found subsequent to their disappearance. Let's start with England, Wales, Scotland and Ireland. All of Ireland. See what you can find.'

'That's a big order. It will take me longer than a day to compile all the info.'

I tap an imaginary watch and smile at him. 'Better get a move on, then, hadn't you?'

'And what are you going to be doing?'

'I'm going dancing.'

He puffs an 'of course you are' at me as I head upstairs to find a jacket.

Chapter Twenty-One

I take a taxi to Milton's and Rorke waves me through the barrier – and I'm allowed to enter the fine establishment, but only after Cindy makes sure I'm not carrying anything bigger than my usual concealed knife. She doesn't look happy and I promise her I won't be the one throwing the first punch and she grunts at me, implying she knows better. Cindy stamps my wrist and I head straight upstairs past the twin bodyguards, who nod at me in such a synchronized way that they give me the creeps.

I pause in front of Miron's office and within a few minutes the door swings open and Lisa steps out. She's Miron's bodyguard and a full-blown demon. Lisa looks strangely fragile and fey, yet she is capable of tearing threats to Miron apart with her dainty, bare hands.

'He's expecting you, *cherie*,' she says and steps aside. 'Go on in.' Her accent has a French burr to it, as if she's from New Orleans or somewhere like that, though for all I know she is just a fan of Anne Rice novels.

Miron's office is the business. Spartan with a metal and steel desk the size of a small planet, it is set in front of the one-way glass that shows the heaving dance floor. There's nothing else in his office to distract him from his business.

A wafer-thin laptop is discreetly shut on the far side of his desk, next to a yellow legal notepad.

Miron is not very much taller than me. He's of average height and build and looks utterly mundane and normal, until you get closer and look into his eyes. They're fathomless and engaging but it's his voice that's the kicker. It's warm and deep; you just know the majority of people making deals with him are seduced by the sound of it.

At the moment those dark eyes are sweeping over my leather jacket and jeans and he shakes his head.

'Oh Kit, darling child, when will I see you in a dress? I know you have the legs for it.'

'Uncalled for,' I point out to him, accepting butterfly kisses on both my cheeks. 'But appreciated.'

He chuckles and casually draws me forward so I can take a seat at his desk.

'What can Uncle Miron do for you?'

I roll my eyes and sprawl in the chair.

'Not refer to yourself as Uncle Miron? It's just weird.' I push at my fringe and wince when my ribs protest. 'I've got to know something, Miron, and well, you're the baddest guy I know so I thought I'd come talk to you.'

Miron shucks his shirt cuffs from beneath his jacket as he seats himself again. His pleasant features seem even more benign, if that's possible, as he gestures for me to continue.

'You know I'm not immune to flattery, Kit. What are you after?'

'Do you know of anyone stealing children in London?'

'I almost thought you were asking me if I knew about anyone stealing children.' He watches my face and then blinks slowly. 'Okay, that was not what I was expecting to hear from you.'

'Do you?'

'No, oddly enough.'

So I tell him and while I tell him I watch his face. The thing about Miron is that he's a terrible liar for a demon, so I'd know if he wasn't telling the truth. This time his shock's real, so I give him an abbreviated version of what we know.

'You must understand why I'm asking, Miron. Are any of your Infernal –' I take a breath – 'stealing kids?'

'Honestly, one of the strangest things I've been asked in my long life. Not quite the weirdest thing, but close.'

He taps his fingers absently on the desk, and I watch, wondering if I've managed to annoy him or overstepped my bounds, or both. Possibly both; for sure, both. I try not to flinch when he moves, and if he notices he pretends not to.

'I would like to say that the Infernal have been playing by the rules, Kit, but I can't truthfully say.'

'What? Why not? Aren't you the boss of them?'

An arched brow quirks. 'You are very amusing, Kit.' His chuckle is dry and winsome, making me want to smile. But I think he's actually laughing at me, and I don't appreciate that at all. 'No, I am not the boss of them. I'm what you'd call middle management.'

'So there's someone else I should be talking to?'

He considers this for a very brief second before shaking his head. 'No, I'm the one you need to talk to about this.'

'Can you help me, then? Do you know of any of your demons stealing human children?'

'I will have to ask, but to be quite honest, Kit, I have a feeling that this is not Infernal related.'

'Would you even tell me if it was?'

'I would. Of course.'

As I said, he is a bad liar.

'Oh, Miron. I'm serious.'

'As am I. Look, traditionally speaking, some bad people would sacrifice something precious to them, like a child, in order to bring a demon to this world. The demon would then do his or her summoner a favour, or complete a task. The demon in turn would then be released to go about his or her merry way, as before.'

'You make it sound so simple. Surely people wouldn't have sacrificed their children?'

'Humans have been doing far worse for as long as they've been on this earth.'

It's not my imagination at all. I can hear an inflection of distaste in his voice.

'So what's changed now?' I ask him. 'What's changed since the glory days when demons would be summoned by infant blood?'

'Why, we're right here, Kit. Waiting, watching. All the time. We no longer have to be summoned from the pits of Hell. If you know where to look, all you have to do is ask the right guy for the right favour.'

The way he says it, strangely content, a bit matter of fact, with a bit of underlying menace, makes me feel very young and not at all up to the task of questioning him further.

'How about you just ask around, then? Someone might know something.'

For the longest time he watches me, his gaze inscrutable, but then he nods slowly. 'I will ask.'

'Thank you.' I stand up and catch my breath as my body protests and starts aching all over again.

'Be careful, Kit,' Miron says as he comes away from

behind his desk. 'You are stirring up things that you know very little about.'

I pull open the door as I turn to look at him. Our eyes are level but even so, Miron towers over me, bringing his *otherness* to bear. He allows me to see him for one brief gloriously shining second and I want to open my mouth and scream and never stop. Then his hand cups my elbow, steadying me, and once more he's sweet faced and concerned.

'Make sure you get some rest, girl. You look very tired.'

I nod numbly and walk away, back down the long passage with its dark carpet and many closed doors. I turn deaf walking past those doors, not hearing the deals being made, the soft murmurs of prayers and incantations, and I practically run down the stairs into the nightclub proper. I'm only halfway down them when the lights go out unexpectedly.

I have been in some dark places in the past but here, in Milton's, there is no outside light, no stars to light my way, no secret half-moon to give a hazy glow. A hand in the darkness steadies me, preventing me from stepping forward and falling down the rest of the stairs.

Everyone in the club's gone quiet, the hush anticipatory. An expectant shiver crawls down my spine and I wonder what's going on. A part of me knows that this could be an Unseelie attack, that any second now a starving sluagh could come through the walls or drop from the ceiling above me, tearing everyone in this place apart, but I don't feel fear, just a breathless excitement.

'Watch.' I recognize the voice of one of the twin security guards in my ear and somehow I'm turned so I can see the small stage where the DJ has his kit set up. The single figure is lit by a spotlight's soft glow. He's dressed in black, wearing a black top hat, a black T-shirt and over that a black dinner jacket. The light only illuminates him from the waist up, creating interesting shadows on his face, which is bowed forward as if in contemplation.

He moves, brings a silver flute to his lips and blows a soft breathy note. The note seems to echo for ever through Milton's, now transformed into a cavern in the darkness. A slight breeze from the air-con stirs my fringe and I breathe it in, super aware of the loudness of my heart.

Someone in the audience lets out a low whistle. The DJ raises a hand from the flute and everything stills. He blows another note, and this one stretches out for longer still. It's even more luxurious, inviting listeners forward, beckoning them closer.

The song is something sad, a little bit lonely and intricate. The sound lifts high into the air of the nightclub and, although the strange medieval tone of the flute should feel weird in this modern building more used to techno and dubstep, it doesn't feel out of place. The song he plays meanders gently, its tone pure and silvery. Unbidden, a memory comes, of me sitting with my feet in the little stream behind the Manor. I was chatting to my cousins in the late summer, shortly after I joined them, enjoying a picnic. The sun was hot and the forest seemed so peaceful and still all around us. Everything felt green and vibrant that day. It was one of the few perfect days of my life.

Standing in the darkness, I become aware of another sound. Large drums – forming a heavy ominous counter to the DJ's swift pure notes. Out of the darkness behind him two drummers walk out onto the stage. They are dressed far more colourfully and each carries an instrument I recognize as a bhangra drum. The tone shifts, the flute falls away and the new musicians' compulsive beats elicit a cry from several club-goers. I can actually feel the wave of the crowd's energy pushing back against the drummers as they pound out a sound that reverberates in our very bones. The DJ melts back to his decks and soon the music's back, the bhangra drums giving the rhythm a harder and more percussive presence.

'What was that?' I call into the guard's ear as I step down onto the ground level. 'I love it!'

'That's Torsten. He does that thing with the flute now and again,' he says. 'The crowd seems to like it.'

Everyone is bouncing, moving to the music, carried away by the rhythm. I push my way into the crowd, my tiredness and aches completely and utterly forgotten. I love feeling this elated. I'll stay for an hour before heading home, I decide. For an hour I can just be a girl dancing the night away, be someone with no worries and responsibilities. I throw myself into the crowd, my fist pumping the air in time with the music and lose myself in the anonymity.

Otherwhere, the Tower at the End of the World

Being allowed a rare free afternoon away from the tower, to walk the hunting hounds, felt like a larger reprieve than it should have done.

Thorn tried not to think about his lessons but he felt wrung out and tense. Odalis had become insistent that he share his foreknowledge with her. She also made him study magical theory harder than Istvan ever had. Combining this with the time spent in the crystal room, where he used his magic to keep watch over the realm, he had little concept of how long he'd been at the tower. Day and night flowed into one, as did days and weeks. He was starting to resemble some damsel from a fairy tale, kept prisoner by a jealous aunt.

He laughed at the image, and one of the hounds peered up at him quizzically, before moving off to sniff an interesting grouping of fungi growing on the trunk of an ancient oak.

There'd been no word from the Citadel since he'd left. No messengers had come bearing missives from his mother or his brothers. Even if he saw them seemingly well in visions as he patrolled the Otherwhere, he could sense the distance growing between them.

The loneliness sank into him at the thought of being all alone in this godforsaken place at the end of the worlds. It filled him with a melancholy he'd never known before.

His dreams were dark and unpleasant. He dreamed of worlds destroyed in the wake of the Elder Gods as he looked helplessly on, bound by manacles of iron. He watched his family perish under the boots of giant warriors in steel armour. He felt his powers weaken as the Fae succumbed to a wasting illness. The forests of the Otherwhere withered and died, and with them went the animals.

He also saw the human world of the Frontier tear itself apart, attempting to prevent the disease destroying the Fae take hold in their own realm.

The dreams were so terrifying and real that, during his time in the chamber, he searched endlessly to find the cause of this destruction. He was tireless in hunting for the discordant note he knew should be there. But he couldn't sense it. The event was either too far in the future, or as yet mere possibility among several potential realities.

Amidst all of this, he was aware of a darker danger still,

something stalking the young girl who'd risked her life so many times to save him. He raged then, unable to protect her, because of his inability to find the root of the trouble.

On the nights he found sleep, he dreamed about the dark-haired human girl with the flashing eyes, quick smile and faster blade. When he woke in the morning, he wasn't sure which hurt more – knowing she was in danger from enemies he could barely sense or that he was powerless to help her until her enemies made their first move.

Chapter Twenty-Two

There is not enough caffeine in the world. I slump forward in my chair and wonder about pushing my face into my large mug of cooling coffee and if osmosis works with humans. I don't even look up when Dante scrapes a chair back so that he can sit opposite me.

I eventually straighten up, but barely manage to keep my head from bobbing. Or my eyes from drifting shut.

Dante's face is a mask of disapproval. His gaze rakes my face, resting too long on the dark circles beneath my eyes, on the downturned line of my mouth and on how tightly my hands hold on to the mug.

'Are you wearing the same clothes you did last night, Kit?' he asks me.

'Yes,' I answer dully.

'Have you been home? Have you slept at all?'

I open my mouth to tell him I'll sleep when I'm dead when I realize the flippant comeback may just lead to a fight and I really just can't manage to summon any kind of energy for an argument right now.

'No.'

'Where have you been all night?'

'Milton's.' I sip from my mug. Why is it so heavy? 'I went to speak to Miron.'

'The demon?' Dante leans forward so suddenly I jerk back in fright, but he holds up a hand to calm me. 'Why did you go there, alone?'

'I had to ask him something. I'm okay, really, I just need a few hours' sleep, that's all.'

'Did he do anything to you? Kit?' Dante grabs hold of both my wrists in an attempt to get me to look him in the eye. 'Listen to me. You look really bad. Are you okay?'

I really don't like being touched by people. Even well-meaning people. 'Let go of me. Or you will regret grabbing me.'

I stare at him, letting my magic surface to just below my skin. He should be able to feel the heat building under his hands. He holds on for a few more seconds to make his point while my skin becomes hotter with each moment. Eventually he lets go with a disgusted sigh.

'What can I get you?' The waitress directs her gaze at me and I see sympathy and concern there. She must think I'm having a fight with my boyfriend, because something in her attitude is solicitous towards me and she's cold towards Dante. It makes me feel a tiny bit bad but he's a big boy so I'm sure he'll get over it.

'Can I have the sourdough toast and scrambled eggs, please? Also, really crispy bacon?' I twiddle the plastic-covered menu. 'And more coffee. And orange juice.'

'Tea for me and some scrambled eggs and toast, please.' Dante smiles his chocolate-box smile and for a second she wavers but then smiles back at him.

'What did you have to go and ask Miron that was so

urgent?' he hisses at me as she saunters off to place our order.

'I went to ask him if any of his friends have a taste for human children,' I shoot back, annoyed. 'He said no, of course, but he'll check and get back to us.'

'And you believe him?'

I make an impatient noise in my throat. 'As far as I can, yes. What you must understand is that there are a great many laws that govern the supernatural beings that live on earth. Most of these laws are in place to protect humans. Miron knows that if one of his lot oversteps the line, they will be sent back to the Pit. They know that they walk a fine line and if he suspects any of his Infernal are part of this, he will let me know.'

'And then what?'

'We take care of it.'

'Why did you go there alone?'

'I can't figure this out, Dante. Are you annoyed with me because: a) I went there and spoke to Miron or b) I went there alone or c) I'm an independent person and not answerable to you?'

A tiny muscle jumps in Dante's smoothly shaven jaw. 'You are a brat, Kit Blackhart. Here's why I'm pissed off with you: a) you went there alone when I'm your partner on this and b) you look like shit this morning and will be no good to me for the rest of the day until you've had some rest.'

I open my mouth to argue but I'm interrupted by the waitress as she puts our mugs down along with my glass of orange juice, removing my old cup.

'There you go, loves. Your breakfast will be with you in a jiffy.' She gives me a meaningful look and slants her glance at the bathroom by the counter. I get it: if I want alone time, the bathroom is right there. I give a bleak smile of thanks before reaching for my coffee.

'I get the impression she thinks I'm the bad guy,' Dante says as he adds milk and sugar to his tea.

'You are. You're shouting at me and I'm just feeling a bit delicate.'

'I'm not shouting at you. If anything, I'm speaking a bit softer than usual.'

'Your eyes are shouting,' I tell him and gesture to the offending items in his face.

'And you burned me with your magic, you freak.' The corner of his mouth twitches, as if he's trying not to laugh. 'My *eyes* are shouting? How is that even possible?'

I shrug. 'I don't know; they just are.' I'm surprised that I'm not even angry that he's calling me a freak. Maybe it's because he's now laughing in that cute way he has. Oh my God, what am I thinking? I should punch him in the head and run, right now. No way can I be finding this guy cute. I'm not even over Thorn and whatever we had and now I'm faced with Dante-freaking-Alexander and his boss-level cuteness. There is just no time for it and I have no energy. The thought of Thorn brings back that familiar pang of hurt and uncertainty that I'm not sure how to handle.

Fortunately our breakfasts arrive after a few minutes more and I shovel bacon, egg and toast into my face and sigh contentedly.

'Aren't you supposed to be in school?' Dante asks me after a few mouthfuls. 'Even for someone being privately home schooled I've yet to hear you say anything about cracking open a book.'

'It's not really that kind of schooling,' I tell him. 'It's

more like, what incantation will stop a brownie from stealing honey from your bee hives. Or how to protect your livestock from malignant faeries who you may have upset by not leaving buttered milk out for them.'

'But what about regular school? Maths and history and geography? Stuff like that?'

'We have that too, but less focus is placed on that than you might think. For instance, did you know that in the Battle of Trafalgar, a school of selkies came to Nelson's assistance during a massive storm? They saved a great many British soldiers and sailors from drowning.'

'I did not know that.' He sits back and narrows his dark eyes at me. 'That's rather important, don't you think? That the Fae interfered in a naval battle as big as that and possibly helped turn the tide of the war?'

'Exactly!' I point my buttery knife at him. 'Humans like you know so little about the symbiotic relationship between humans and Fae. Yes, the Blackharts really do the crappy job of sending the bad guys packing, but really, there's far more to it than that. At any given time, there are at least a thousand Fae walking around London. Some work here and live here, others are here for business. And it's the same all over the UK and the rest of the world. We live side by side with them and it's been like that since forever.'

'How is it possible that we don't even know half of it?'

I shrug. 'Humans like not knowing. We're still scared of what the shadows hold, of things that crawl around in the dark. Can you imagine the chaos out there if we woke up one morning and a faerie raid was riding past? The Fae all tall and noble in their silvery and golden finery, with their horses, their armed guards? Followed by their baying hounds, flying creatures and things that shimmer from shadow to shadow? We don't even understand our own world, Dante. How do you expect the world to understand a hidden race of people that use magic?'

He looks a bit disgruntled but nods thoughtfully. 'I'll say it again. You explain things well.'

I chink my mug against his and take a celebratory sip. 'Does this mean you'll stop shouting with your eyes? Because if not, I don't think I can take it and I'll have to go home.'

'I'll tone down the shouting, I promise.'

'Phew.' I wipe my brow dramatically and he laughs. 'Can I ask you something, though? It's personal.'

'Uh oh.' His smile falters but he nods. 'Go on.'

'Why didn't you tell me your little sister was taken when you were younger?'

'I hardly know you and I didn't know if I could trust you.' His gaze meets mine and he looks a little annoyed. 'But I see you managed to do your own research on me anyway. I'm impressed. Your uncle in New York sent you the details?'

Colour flames into my cheeks and I feel ashamed that, yes, I did snoop on his life. But then, I argue to myself, he is a Spook and they have files on us too. Quid pro quo and all that.

'And now?' I ask after I nod briefly. 'Do you trust me?'

'Still not sure. I'm leaning towards you being trustworthy but then you go and do silly reckless things like staying out all night, hanging around with a demon and his mates. I'll be honest, Kit. Sometimes you feel as wild and unpredictable as the creatures you're meant to send back for their sins.'

'Wow.' Wow, how do you come back from that? I stare at Dante and consider just walking away from the table, out of his life. Would it be possible just to ring Uncle Andrew and tell him I don't want to work with Dante any more? To tell Suola that we will handle this ourselves? Force her to let us work the case with no Spook interference? My gut instinct tells me this is not likely to happen – I've taken the vow and it's on me, there's no way of going back now.

Chapter Twenty-Three

'I'm sorry you feel I can't be trusted. But I am good at what I do. I know you're worried that I'm young but I'd like to point out that you're not an OAP either, so maybe less of the doubt and more support?' I turn my coffee mug around between my hands. 'I went to Miron last night, by myself, because I knew he'd play it straight with me. Even his lies are straight lies. With you there things could have become tricky. He doesn't know you but he knows me and he knows my family. Maybe I should have told you what I was planning to do but I didn't stop to think about it. I'm not used to talking to people about what I'm planning, because –' and here I laugh wryly – 'I act on impulse and mostly it works out okay.'

Dante sits quietly for a few seconds, taking in what I've just said before speaking again. 'Are you Fae?'

'Do I look Fae?' I finger the tips of my ears; they're round rather than slightly pointy. 'If I were Fae you'd never see me look tired, my hair would always be immaculate. I'd definitely not be doing this.' I make a sweeping motion towards the cup of caffeine. 'Besides, with no token from my liege, I'd become iron sick.'

'Then why do you have magic? And why do you talk

about humans as if you're not one?' Dante's questions are putting me a little on edge; there's a strange hunger in his voice that makes me uncomfortable.

What is this? A hundred questions before lunch time? 'I don't know why I have magic. One of my ancestors had magic, but no one since then has had power. It turns out I'm a special snowflake and no one really knows what to do with me.' I spread my hands on the table. 'I suppose I tend to talk about other people who aren't Blackharts in a way that pigeon-holes them. It makes it easier than referring to *us* and *them*, you know? Plus, it's not so long ago that I was still one of them.'

'So do you have magic because you have some Fae blood?'

'No. Intermarriage and breeding between Fae and humans and other races is strictly forbidden. The offspring of those unions are usually freaks of nature. Like the cyclops or the minotaur in Crete.' Before he can ask any further questions I hold up my hand. 'Please, can I just finish my food? And drink my coffee? I need a few more minutes to pull myself together.'

We sit in silence and finish our breakfast. As soon as I'm done, I pull out my credit card and do the universal sign for 'bill please' at our waitress. I realize, as she nods and rings up our order, that Dante and I have been on more food-eating dates than most people might go on before moving in together.

I pay for our breakfast, disregarding Dante's protests. The waitress ignores him too and I really quite like that but I don't say anything.

'We have to ring Professor Thorpe,' Dante tells me as we leave the restaurant. 'I thought that maybe we could get you cleaned up a bit before we do that. A shower will help.'

I narrow my eyes at him. 'Are you saying I smell?'

He leans towards me, seriously close and takes a deep obvious sniff of me, his nose very close to the curve of my neck and shoulder.

'No. You definitely don't smell bad. You smell like you.'

'That is not creepy at all,' I tell him, my voice hitching. 'Stop sniffing me. It's weird.'

'Come, my flat's not too far.' He holds open his car door for me and I hesitate. I really dislike being at the mercy of other people for my transport. 'I promise not to ask any further questions. Or hassle you.'

I grunt but get in the car. It's early and the traffic in the City's not too bad. Dante pulls up outside a Georgian town-house near Brick Lane. 'This is it. I share this with two other agents. It's paid for by HMDSDI.'

He unlocks the front door and leads me through the hall, then up two flight of stairs. I see comfortably furnished rooms, a large TV and a pool table. There's lots of open brick, wooden and stone floors. One room seems to be made entirely of glass, with floor-to-ceiling windows and even the roof seems to be made of glass. The place looks huge and completely not what I expected.

'It's pretty flash,' I say, tossing my backpack onto the table in the large kitchen.

Dante looks around and nods. 'It is. My parents think this is part of my university bursary. The other agents are young too, in their early twenties, so they can double as students.'

'Just look at you, lying to your parents.' I say it jokingly but a flash of pain crosses his handsome features. 'So, where's this shower you promised me?'

'Through here. My room is through that door.' He opens a linen cupboard in the passage and hands me fluffy towels. 'I'll even let you borrow a clean T-shirt.'

Biscuits and a pot of freshly brewed tea are waiting for me when I walk back into the kitchen wearing a supersoft long-sleeved Henley T-shirt I'm sure is too small for Dante over my jeans. Dante has a laptop open and a large notepad to the side where he's making notes.

He looks up when I come in and gives a nod of approval.

'At least you look more awake now.'

'I feel better, thanks.' I smile to show him that I harbour no hard feelings. Really, power showers are the best. Although I love the house we have in North London, my en suite is tiny and the shower is more a suggestion of how a shower should work than the real thing.

'Let's give Professor Thorpe a call now. It's past half-nine so she should be in the office already.' He spins his mobile towards me and I dial, hitting the speaker button.

'This is Imelda Thorpe. How may I help you?'

'Prof? It's Kit.'

'And Dante, professor. I hope we're not calling you too early?'

Her laugh is light. 'No, not at all. I have Kit's number here and if she wasn't going to ring me in the next half-hour I was going to ring her myself. I can email the info through to you too, it's not much, but it is interesting.' There's the sound of her shuffling papers around and then she clears her throat. 'So, this Lord Brixi, who gave our modern Brixton its name. He grew up in England in the eleventh century.

176

He and his family had been on the up and up for some years. For his loyalty and steadfastness he was given various pieces of land in the south-east of England. He kept his nose clean and seemed well liked. Basically, he was pretty unremarkable. He fought when he was asked to, sent his men off to war and did all the things a lord was supposed to do for his liege lord.'

'Sounds pretty average to me,' Dante says, making notes.

'It does, doesn't it?' She shuffles more papers. 'But I checked back on who this Brixi chap and his family were before William the Conqueror invaded England. Then I came across something interesting. It seems that Brixi was the second youngest son of a noble lord. He had no prospects at all, with his older brother inheriting his father's lands. Other titles were bestowed on his other much older siblings, due to the various battles they fought in, to reward their valour. No, what makes Brixi interesting is that there were rumours of him being a necromancer.' She pauses for a few seconds, letting this sink in.

'A necromancer? Like raising the dead and turning them into zombies?' Dante's voice rises incredulously. 'No way. I mean, come on, that's just . . .'

She tuts at the interruption. 'Wrong. You're thinking of the Hollywood and Dungeons and Dragons version of what a necromancer is. No, it is said that our friend Brixi could speak to the dead.'

'Why would he want to do that?'

'To find out the future,' I say, pleased that I can lend something to the conversation. 'It's said that the dead can foretell the future.'

Dante's expression veers between disbelief and the need

to keep an open mind. He has seen me do magic, so he should be a bit prepared . . .

'What Kit says is correct.' Imelda's voice holds a hint of approval I can pick up even over the phone. 'The phenomenon is well documented across a range of ancient, medieval and modern scholarly writings. It's even mentioned in the Bible. The Christian bible, that is. Anyway, Brixi is careful in all his dealings with the Crown and manages to retain the lands he won even after William turns up. He goes on to become a moderately successful landholder. But it's his several times great-grandson who interests us, really. That young man, a fine upstanding lad, went on pilgrimage to the Holy Land, throwing in his lot with a bunch of holy knights. But fate had other ideas for young Oswald de Brixi who disappears for years and years and then, one day, reappears back at his family's manor with a crazy story.'

There's the rustling of paper and she mutters to herself. It gives me the chance to take in much of her story. 'Prof, did you even sleep last night?' I ask her, having an inkling how many texts and books she must have read to get even a smidge of this info. Doing research really is long and tiring.

'I caught a nap for a bit. Why? Anyway, this is the really interesting bit. The young lordling said he had been captured during battle and sold to a Bedouin magician and had learned much from the old man during their wanderings around the desert. His own talent for speaking with the dead had saved him from certain death at the hand of the magician's tribe when the old man passed away.'

I bite back a yawn and ignore Dante rolling his eyes at me.

'That's really interesting,' he says, clearly wondering where this is going.

'Isn't it just? I had such fun looking all of this up.'

'So what happens then, to Oswald?' I coax her.

'Oh, he gets married and has some kids. Becomes very staid, buys a position at Court. You know, the usual thing.'

'What does that have to do with our kids disappearing?'

'Ah, so this is the part where we hit the real folklore bit.' She chuckles to herself. 'Legend states that Oswald never grew old. That he never died. There's proof of the village laying a charge against him and his family when the village children started disappearing. Words like witchcraft, necromancy and *vile magics* are used in the tract. The Crown sent an investigator but he found no basis for these accusations, explaining that Oswald's continued good health had to do with his Bedouin learning.'

'Creepy.'

'Very Elizabeth Bathory,' I say. 'Do you think he stole the children and . . . I don't know, performed some kind of magic ritual to steal their youth?' This really was a possibility. And everyone thought that the story of the evil queen in Snow White was *just* a story.

Professor Thorpe sighs heavily. 'Who knows the truth, Kit? It could be that he had some magical ability. It could be that Brixi had some Fae heritage no one knew about.' At my indrawn breath, she hurries on. 'I know we've been told the Fae do not procreate with other races, because it's so horrifically taboo for them, but this was a long time ago. I doubt humans or Fae really abided by the laws as much as we do at present.'

'So what happened to Brixi and his family?'

'There are records of them all moving across to Europe, but that's it for now.'

'Professor, if I give you my email, can you forward your research to us?' Dante asks, watching me with narrowed eyes as I stand and stretch, trying to ease my muscles. Also mostly to wake up.

Dante gives her his Spook email address and I can hear her type it in.

'Professor, do we know if the Brixi family is still around?'

'The surname is no longer in much use. I've found a few in America, but there is one in Germany and another in Poland.'

'Is that unusual? I mean, a surname no longer being used?'

'Not really. A lot of older surnames disappear. I found evidence of another Brixi called Brixi Wolfspear. Can you imagine going around in the modern day and being called Wolfspear?' She laughs. 'I need to head off soon, you two. I have another appointment in a few minutes. I've sent the document I've compiled on to you, Dante, and a copy to you, too, Kit. If you kids need anything else, call me.'

We chorus goodbye to her and she rings off.

'My head hurts with all this stuff,' Dante tells me, pulling his glasses off and rubbing his eyes. 'How do you keep track of everything?'

'Usually my cases are easier than this,' I reluctantly admit. 'I'm told about a Fae transgressing by being here too long or whatever. I follow them around for a few days, then I catch them and send them back.'

'This is definitely not one of those.'

I shake my head. 'No, definitely not. What do you want to do?'

'Not sure. What is Kyle doing with the baggie of creature spit I gave you?'

'Aha, good thinking. He will have dropped it off with his little friend at the lab.' I reach for my phone. 'I'll give him a call while you make me another caffeine-related drink.'

Chapter Twenty-Four

I'm standing in the lounge area looking up at the skylight, watching the rain thunder down, when my phone buzzes. 'Where have you been?' Aiden's voice roars in my ear as I answer on the second ring. I hold the phone a few centimetres away from my head. No need for speakerphone here! 'I've left messages at home and Kyle just kept saying you were out. Are you avoiding me?'

'Don't be stupid, Aiden. Why would I be avoiding you?'

'How would I know? Guilt? Because you're running around with a Spook and Andrew told you to keep me close?'

I'm tempted to tut at him but I know it enrages him stratospherically. Tutting and sucking your teeth at him is like waving a red flag.

'I've really not had much time, Aiden, I'm sorry.'

'Where are you now?'

'At Dante's house. We're going over our notes.'

He makes a noise that's not at all polite. 'Going over notes? Do you fancy this guy, Kit?'

I've been wondering that myself. I like Dante, but do I *like* him, like him? When we accidentally brush against one another or when we talk, why do I find myself thinking of

Thorn? How Thorn would always find my hand to give my fingers a quick squeeze or manage a smile for me even when things were going completely pear-shaped. The thought made me grin and I realize that I've just been standing there, with Aiden's question still hanging unanswered.

'Kit? Oh my God. You can't seriously like this guy! What about Thorn?'

'Aiden, don't shout, please. Dante is cute but that's it and Thorn . . .' My voice hitches on his name. 'Thorn isn't here, and besides, it's none of your business. I'll probably never see him again.' I end and almost curse myself for the way I have to talk past the heaviness in my heart.

There are some choice words Aiden learned from his mum during her stay in Russia which aren't easy to translate. He uses those now as I hear something crash. 'Shit, I dropped this bloody canopic jar.'

'Canopic jar? What are you doing?' I have to yell to be heard over the sound of screeching in the background. 'Where are you?'

'Unclean spirit running amok in a British Museum storeroom.'

Never let it be said Aiden can't be concise.

'Do you need help?'

'No, no. I've got it.' The noise level increases. 'Shit, Kit, I've got to go. The thing is trying to drag Shaun into a sarcophagus. I'll call you later.'

Before I can answer he hangs up, but just as he does I can hear him bellowing at whatever he faced and that bellow held a lot of wolf snarl.

I pocket my phone and head back to the large lounge area where Dante's spread the notes out on the low coffee table.

'You okay?' he asks me as I sit down on the floor opposite him.

I nod and give him a tight smile. 'Kyle's with his friend at the lab today. They're making headway with the baggie of spittle you gave us. So far it looks acidic and has low levels of toxin, but we can't work out if it contains a soporific or not.'

'You don't look surprised.'

'I've been wondering about that thing, let's call it Bob, for now. I've been puzzling over how Bob's been able to get into these kids' rooms, overpower them and drag them out. Without a sound.'

'Magic?'

'I am rolling my eyes at you, in case you can't see,' I tell him, doing just that. 'I'm thinking there must two people involved. So, we say Bob is the guy who does the getting into the kids' rooms because he can somehow get through walls, like a ghost or apparition.' I look up at Dante where he's sprawled on the couch and he nods, waving a hand at me to continue. 'So Bob then somehow be-spells the kids, *or* –' I hold up a finger dramatically – 'he uses his venom on them to make them drowsy and easy to handle. It stops the kids from raising the alarm.'

'Okay.' He does the hand-twirling thing again and I sigh. Obviously I'm doing all the hard work in this partnership.

'After this, he still has to get the children back out again without any alarm being raised. However, I've never come across a creature that can dematerialize a human to drag them through walls. Bob can't have taken them out the same way he came.'

'But we already know none of the CCTV cameras captured anything in the stairwells.'

'Logic sucks, but you're right. We have to assume, regardless of first appearances, that we are indeed dealing with a Fae creature of some sort who must be helping the Bob monster steal the kids once he's managed to get into their homes.'

Dante frowns at me. 'Explain.'

'The Fae do not show up on CCTV or cameras.'

Dante nods thoughtfully. 'So do we think Bob is Fae? As well as the guy that's helping him? Also, how do you know this for sure, that they don't show up on CCTV? They're like vampires?'

I twist my head to peer at him to see if he's joking, as he continues. 'Vampires don't show up in mirrors, isn't that the folklore?' I sigh and he holds up a defensive hand but he's laughing. I don't know if he's laughing at his own stupidity or at me. Possibly at me, so I deepen my scowl. Dante presses on, 'So why doesn't Bob – if he's invisible to CCTV that is – take the kids out of the house too?'

'I've not figured that part out.'

'Maybe he doesn't know where the other guy takes them. So, back to our friend Bob, the child stealer. What's with the face and why does he look like a monster? If I wanted to steal kids I'd be the nicest-looking granny there ever was.'

'Maybe he wasn't going to steal Adam.' I sit up and stare at Dante. '*Maybe* he just wanted to scare him. Hurt him a little. Maybe Bob reacted without thinking. Also, I think Bob isn't the stealer. He's the helper.'

He rolls his eyes at me. 'So, back to *Bob the helper*.'

'Thank you. Yes, so Bob the helper then has to sneak through the apartment and pass the unconscious child along to someone else. A Fae could probably cast a glamour over something as small as a child, to make them invisible too.'

'And this someone else is?'

'I have no idea yet.'

'So you're thinking there are two creatures working together?'

'I think so. At least two.' I give a cracking yawn. 'And think of Bob's spittle – we need to work out exactly what's in it. A small dose of toxin could knock out a small child and make them easier to carry.'

'But why? That's what I don't understand. Why would they steal kids?'

'Money? Love? Hate?' I shrug, which is difficult to do when you're lying on the floor. 'Who knows?'

'Aren't you interested in finding out?'

'I am, but it's difficult to speculate about something you can't possibly know. Until you know. Especially if we're talking about supernatural creatures.' I sit up and stretch. 'I need to hit the books,' I tell him. 'Let me see if my aunt will allow me access to her library.'

Dante looks a bit confused at the statement and I wonder how to explain Aunt Letitia, with her agoraphobia and paranoia. 'She's not keen on visitors, see? So being allowed to visit her is a big deal. Usually takes weeks for her to agree to see anyone.'

'We don't have weeks.'

'I know.' I fiddle with my phone. 'I'm sure she knows what we're facing, as my uncle will've told her about the case. So I'm hoping she'll know where to direct me.'

'Go ahead and call her.'

It occurs to me that I didn't have to explain to Dante who my aunt is and how vast her library is, or the fact that she might only have an inkling of an idea of how to help.

'Right,' I say to him, pressing Aunt Letitia's number. 'Here goes.'

It takes a few long seconds for the call to connect, then it's ringing and I imagine her in the library with its soft golden light, muttering at the call's interference.

'Yes?' Her voice is reminiscent of a Hollywood siren, lush and deep. I suspect that once upon a time she sounded young and girlish, but after smoking all her life and drinking whisky the way I drink coffee, her voice has gone all Lauren Bacall. 'I was wondering when you'd call, girl. What do you need?'

'We've got kids disappearing, Aunt Letty. I need access to the library so I can do research.'

'Will you be coming on your own?'

'Would you allow Dante in the library?' And obviously she would know who I'm talking about because my family and me working with a Spook would be Big News.

'Don't be absurd, child. Of course not. I'd have to fumigate the place and possibly have to redo all my alarm systems if he came here.'

'Then I'll be coming alone.'

'I'll send my driver. Be at home by three this afternoon.'

She hangs up before I can even say another word and I fling the phone onto the couch behind me.

'Dammit, she is so annoying.'

'Your family really don't like us, do they?'

'You are despised,' I say, not worrying about sugar-coating it. 'They utterly dislike you, *utterly*. She's sending her driver.'

'Nice guy?'

'Creepy.'

'Creepy, how?'

'Oh, you know. Friendly. Chatty.'

'And that's creepy?'

'I don't do friendly or chatty.'

His chuckle makes me want to smack him but I restrain myself, especially when he says in a kindly voice, 'You're not that bad.'

'I am. I struggle with people.'

'We all struggle with people. I've seen you be really cool with the little kids.'

'Little kids are easy. They're cool. They believe.'

'You only treated me like I have the plague for a day. Now you actually talk to me. As if I'm a real person.'

I hold up my finger. 'That is yet to be determined. If you're a real person, that is.'

He pulls a face at me and laughs and I do the same.

'I've got to go.' I stand up and stretch again, fighting the fatigue dragging at me. 'I'll call you when I'm done at the library.'

Chapter Twenty-Five

I don't enjoy travelling by Tube, but when it works it works fast, and I'm back at the house by lunch time. Enough time to change and check my emails. Kyle is still out but he's emailed me a list of books to check out at Aunt Letitia's. I print that off and fold it into my messenger bag.

I check the kitchen cupboards and come up with a packet of cookies. Unopened. I definitely miss our brownie, Mrs Evans, and her constant supply of baked goods and sweets. Occasionally she sends stuff back with Marc, if he visits the building site that's now Blackhart Manor, but she's so busy looking after the builders that I think we've been sort of forgotten.

I've been to the site a few times – once was when the foundations were dug and the crucial cornerstone was laid. I spent one sleepless weekend working a heavy protection spell into the foundation of the house. Uncle Andrew had to drive me home to London as I was so high from the pure earth magic I'd accessed from the leyline that runs through our land. I was basically vibrating and unable to sleep for a further two days, followed by three days of deep rejuvenating unconsciousness. The other visits were similar but not as exhausting because I basically just had to bind together the magic I'd already released. It was something like mending a jersey – I had to pick up the stitches and join all the magic together so that it covered what had been built since I'd been there last.

I have no idea how Uncle Andrew or Marc even explained what I did to those builders, but they're from Norway, and don't they believe in faeries there as a matter of course?

Thinking about Marc, who's at Exeter University, feels odd now he isn't here to look out for me any more after nearly two years. My other cousins are studying too, preparing to take on more mature roles within the family. Marc is learning a mix of subjects that probably won't mean much to him in the real world (unless he becomes a farmer by day and a demon-exorcizing mathematician-psychologist by night). Soon, that will be me at uni, if I'm lucky, but I have no idea where I'll go or what on earth I'll study.

I need to get on with the research, so I sit down with my file and read through the info collected so far. I make notes on scraps of paper from what I remember Professor Thorpe telling us and shove them into the file to take along to Aunt Letitia's.

My phone rings; it's Kyle.

'We think we've tracked down the stuff in the spittle,' he says. 'It is venom. Jilly is busy sorting out what snake it belongs to but really, what you need to know is that the venom paralyses the victim.'

'Euch.'

'Exactly, so watch out for this thing if you come face to face with it, okay?'

'I'll do my utmost not to come face to face with it. I'm more than happy to clobber it over its head, I'll be honest.'

'Good girl.' Kyle laughs at me. 'Have fun at Aunt Letty's.'

'Are you sure you can't come?'

'No. I'm here, you know, assisting Jilly.'

'When I get back we're doing unarmed combat training and I'm going to kick your ass.'

'Oh great.' He groans. 'I want my brother and sister back. They never used to torture me.'

'Lies. They left you to the mercy of the dryads in the woods.'

'That wasn't so bad.' His voice goes a bit dreamy. 'They were really nice to me.'

'Inappropriate, Kyle.' I pretend distaste but he just laughs again.

'I can tell you're nervous visiting Aunt Letty, but you'll be fine, really. She's just very focused. None of the digital records I could find held much info about things that enjoyed stealing kids.'

'That's fine. I'm sure I'll find a host of exciting creatures that can eat my face off while I'm doing the research.'

'Yay!' he laughs. 'That's our favourite.'

'Shut up, weirdo, I'll call you later.'

I don't have all that long to wait before I hear Aunt Letitia's car outside. Even if I hadn't heard it, I would be able to feel the vibration of its engine. I heft my bag up over my shoulder and open the front door just as her driver, Isak, touches the front gate. His face breaks into a smile when he sees me. I'm struck by how he embodies the picture of what a chauffeur should look like. Tall, slender, handsome, if slightly effete features, and a great smile that makes you feel that you're the most special person in the world.

As I said: he's just a bit creepy.

'Little Kit Blackhart. A pleasure, as always. Are you ready?'

'Hey, Isak. I'm ready, thanks.'

He holds the gate open and I walk past him towards the giant car that sits idling in the middle of our very suburban road. I can tell from the curtains twitching that our neighbours are getting an eyeful of me, of Isak and of the huge car the size of a steamliner. He opens the door for me and I slide into the luxurious leather interior and lean back with a soft sigh of contentment. There's something about Aunt Letty's car that just makes me feel safe, as if we can drive through anything in our path.

Isak gets in behind the wheel and pulls away smoothly. His dark gaze meets mine in the rear-view mirror.

'I hope you don't mind that I'm a bit early. I was concerned about the traffic.'

'No, not at all.'

He nods and smiles a happy smile.

'Ms Blackhart is very excited that you're coming to visit.'

'She is?' I remember Aunt Letty's voice and she sounded anything but excited, more resigned and possibly a bit annoyed.

'She really does like you, Kit. Your mother was her favourite. She mourned for months after her death.'

This, I did not know. He must see the surprise on my face because he continues talking.

'When you and your grandmother disappeared she urged Andrew to do everything in his power to find you. But of course if Mirabelle didn't want you found, no one would.'

'There's so much I don't know,' I admit. 'Uncle Andrew said we'd talk about it at Christmas.'

Isak's glance towards me is brief. 'I understand why Mirabelle did what she did. I would have done it too.'

I don't know what to say to that, to this unexpected conversation with Isak. I don't know how old he is. He looks maybe twenty-five but is clearly far older. I wonder if he's even human.

'Anyway, just sit back and relax. The heli is waiting for us.'

I do sit back and let my eyes drift shut in the back of the giant Bentley. My thoughts are a tumble. Isak mentioning my nan has made me realize how much I'm missing her. I've not been to the grave for a month and I wonder if Jamie's had the chance to visit, to leave her flowers.

It's a strange situation to be in, knowing that my nan had stolen me from my family in an attempt to keep me safe, away from the world of the Blackharts. There, violence and death was an everyday occurrence, and the strange was not strange at all, but again, an everyday thing. She wanted a different life for me, when she saw her only daughter brought home in a casket, so she resolved to keep me safe for as long as she could. That lasted until I was fifteen and an Unseelie knight recognized her at a country fete where she was selling tinctures and tisanes from her garden. He despised the Blackharts so much, that when he realized she was apart from her family, that the home she lived in had no protection against his kind, he brought a troop of his redcaps with him that night and burned down our home. A neighbour scaled the wall outside my window and got me to safety, but my nan never made it out alive.

That's when I came to live with the Blackharts. My uncle Jamie found me in the hospital and told me who I was. About my heritage. Occasionally I look back at my life before and I miss it – the not knowing, the normality of it all. But only for a short while because I have new friends, new skills and a family who care about me deeply and I care about them. They came into my life when I was at my lowest. They held me close and showed me how to channel the energies that've woken within me to help our world.

The thought and memories lull me to sleep because when I wake up, Isak's at the door, gently shaking me awake.

I grab my bag and accept his hand as he helps me out of the cavernous car. We're parked on the tarmac, just a few metres away from a large helicopter with our family's stag crest painted on the side.

I've never actually been in the helicopter. The last time I got to visit Aunt Letitia's home was by way of speedboat – which you may think is a fun way to travel. But let me just say: I fed all the fishes in the sea. I don't travel well by speedboat or sea, which is possibly why they've decided to see how I would cope travelling by helicopter.

'In you go,' Isak says, handing me into the back. 'Strap in. No, both straps. Like so.' He helps me buckle myself in and hands me a set of earphones with a microphone in front of my mouth. 'Wear these if you want to say anything.' Then he brings out a brown paper bag. 'And this is if you're not feeling a hundred per cent during the flight.'

I open my mouth to say thanks but he turns away and climbs into the pilot seat, whipping his hat off and stowing it underneath his chair. A young woman, dressed similarly in an elegant suit, climbs in the other side next to Isak and shakes my hand.

'I'm Luzette,' she says with a smile.

'Nice to meet you. I'm Kit.'

They both settle down and go through the pre-flight

checks, then the rotors start up. We lift off and I let out a faint yelp of terror when it feels as if I'm falling forward, but my harness keeps me seated. The helicopter levels out soon enough and we speed across the English countryside towards Portsmouth and the coast. I try and enjoy the flight but there's so much noise that I feel completely bombarded by it all. Even so, I fall asleep for a while and when I wake up I have no idea where we are until Isak tells me over his microphone.

We fly over Portsmouth and head for one of the four peculiar buildings in the Solent known as the Palmerston Forts. The forts were built in the nineteenth century, in an attempt to safeguard the Solent against attacks from Napoleon. The place suits Aunt Letitia well. It is literally one of the safest places for her collection of books and for her. For someone who suffers from a fear of the outside world and who just doesn't like people in general, the place is a haven. It is now equipped with living quarters, a pool, a helipad and the family's remaining precious lore books.

Isak keeps the heli low over the waves and I spot a pod of mermaids who rise up from the water and wave to us. They are both beautiful and horrifying in equal measure but I remember my manners and wave back at them. I'm glad of the earphones that block out their voices, which I can feel brush against me in gentle waves of sound.

We come to land on the helipad of the fort with a minimum of fuss. If, that is, a minimum of fuss means that I've not clawed holes in my seat with my short nails. Luzette hops out and comes and helps me with my harness.

Up close Luzette is lovely, with dark lustrous hair and big eyes. I don't recall her from my previous visit at all and

I wonder if she's new. How does Aunt Letitia go about hiring people?

So many questions, none of which I suspect she'll answer.

I follow Luzette down into the building and she leads me without comment to my aunt's study. The room itself isn't large but it is cosy. Her desk looks like something out of Versailles, as do the chairs, and I just hope that the library has better seating.

Aunt Letitia must easily be in her sixties but her figure is trim and she dresses like a fashion icon. Today she looks very Audrey Hepburn in a sleek pair of trousers and small jacket over a black polo-neck sweater. A strand of pearls matches the tiny pearls in her ears. She wears a single signet ring carved out of a ruby on her right hand, and that completes her adornment. Her hair, naturally curly like mine, is more silvery grey than black these days but there's no sign that she's actually ever dyed it.

'Kit, my dear girl.' She moves from behind her desk and inspects me briefly, before folding me into a tight hug. 'Just look at you. So much like your mother, but those eyes – those eyes are definitely your father's. Take a seat and Luzette will bring us some tea.'

'It is so good to see you, Aunt Letty,' I say, sitting down in the world's most uncomfortable chair. 'Thank you for making arrangements to have me brought over so quickly.'

'I understand from Andrew that you're working directly for Suola. If the Queen of Air and Darkness has taken a personal interest in this matter, child, then it's best for us to play her game to the end.'

'It's all very weird,' I say. 'The way she's gone about all of this.'

Aunt Letty takes her seat again. 'Faeries,' she says, as if

it explains everything. 'They always have an agenda, even when they tell us they don't.' She shrugs her elegant shoulders. 'Don't ask me. I sit here on my island and ponder the many ways the world is destroying itself around me.'

Which is a complete lie. My face clearly tells her I don't believe her and she sighs dramatically.

'I think the case of the disappearing children is very curious, though. Why has there not been more of an outcry? The newspapers should be full of it. There's a definite pattern for these disappearances. Even the police should have noticed this. Why aren't the parents making more of a fuss?'

I lean forward, happy to see that she's thinking the same way as I am. 'Exactly. It doesn't make sense. How many people would whoever's doing this have to pay off when it comes to the cops?'

'Not that many, actually. Like all organizations, the police rely on chain of command and hierarchy. It's compartmentalized, so if there's a communication breakdown between two levels, it's unlikely to be spotted higher up or lower down even.' She squints her grey eyes in thought. 'And they're human, Kit. People don't want to make waves or do more work than is necessary to get by.'

I try not to let my anger rise at her words. It makes horrible sense and that fact really makes me itch in anger.

Luzette quietly places a tray with china on the table and pours us each a cup of tea. She's arranged delicate-looking biscuits on a plate and places that between us.

'Anything else, Ms Letitia?' she asks politely.

'Thank you, Luzette. Can I ask you to light the fire in the main library room? The place is colder than Gaia's nose in the middle of winter at the moment. We can't have Kit freezing to death, can we?'

Luzette smiles and moves off, her gait loose and easy.

'Has Luzette been with you for long?' I ask my aunt, wrapping my hands around the delicate china cup.

'Both Luzette and Isak came to me in their early teens. Luzette travels extensively on my behalf. She's got a good eye for curiosities, maps and antique books. Isak was waiting for her to get back from Italy when you rang earlier today. She's brought back some interesting reliquaries that will look great in my *Kunstkammer*.' Aunt Letitia takes another sip of her tea. 'But now, back to your case. It could be that there's magic involved but not the flashy kind you might expect. Also, it will be a powerful kind of magic. An old type of magic.'

I crunch on a biscuit and immediately know it's brownie baked, because omg it is the most gorgeous thing I've tasted in months. I accept the napkin I'm handed without a word and quietly wipe the tears from my eyes, taking a deep breath. Brownie-made food is food for the soul.

'Thank you.' I take a deep breath. 'An old type of magic? Why would you say that?'

'I don't know. It just feels it.' Here she rubs her middle finger and thumb together in a gesture reminiscent of testing fabric. 'There's something that's not modern about this whole thing, I feel.'

'Let me tell you what we've got so far.' I haul my file out of my bag and spread it open carefully so as not to bump my tea or damage the biscuits; really, that would be a disaster from which I might not recover.

Chapter Twenty-Six

The library welcomes me into its golden embrace. I sit behind a large desk complete with a Tiffany lamp that sheds just enough light on the desk to cast the rest of the library in a soft haze of rich colour. To my side stands a statue of Thoth, the Egyptian god of wisdom, who also acted as scribe to the gods. He holds domain here, Aunt Letitia explained when I mentioned the statue – knowledge is power. And power lies in truth, which is why research is an essential part of what the Blackharts do, to enable us to find that truth.

She spoke the words so resolutely that I felt a bit freaked out by the sentiment. Sitting in this library, where I can feel the press of ages on my shoulders from the books and scrolls stored behind their cases, I wonder about doing this alone. I usually do the minimum of research because Kyle loves it, and it allows him to build on his already extensive knowledge of esoteric lore. He therefore always insists on hitting the Internet highway or books to come up with the knowledge. Yet here I am, by myself, in a place that's as foreign to me as any place I've ever been.

Aunt Letitia instructed Luzette to help me with the books. After handing her Kyle's list and explaining to her what I was after, I was installed at the desk, several foreign-language dictionaries to the right of me.

Luzette, now dressed more casually in jeans and a warm jumper, strolls around the large library, pulling books off shelves. Some of the books look old, with bindings of beautiful leather. There are a few scrolls too, in what looks like actual papyrus. The library is in the north side of the fort and covers three floors. It's more as if I'm sitting in Saruman's tower, I decide, as I listen to the instructions Luzette gives me.

'These are studies of faeries and the Otherworld from Victorian times,' she says, heaving three large leather-bound books onto the table. 'Here, we've got some German fables and fairy tales. These are French folklore bits and pieces.' She touches the other books on the carrel. 'Here are some medieval texts, in Latin and French. I also have a book on Egyptian-Arabic lore here. But call me if you need help with these. Start here, first, I think. Find the most recent lore, then we can go back and find the origin tales.' She smiles at me. 'Are you okay? You look a bit nervous.'

'This is not usually what I do,' I admit, gesturing to the books. 'I'm more the go out and clobber someone over the head to get info kinda girl.'

Her laughter rings through the library. 'I understand, trust me, I do. But really, this is where you need to be right now, doing the research yourself. Kyle's emailed to say he's looking into kids disappearing over the past five to ten years. He doesn't have time to help you with this, so it's up to you to do it.'

I'm really aching to hit something and looking at the stacks of books makes me feel trapped.

'I'll do my best,' I say, knowing how forlorn I sound.

'But I don't think I'm going to find much. I don't have the knowledge or the skill Kyle does, or even Megan and Marc.'

'Research is fun. You just open the books and jump in. You'll see.'

I really don't believe her and grimace unhappily. She pats my shoulder sympathetically. 'I'm heading up to my desk to do some tidying up of the catalogue. If you need anything, just shout.'

I watch her climb the stairs to a small desk on the third floor before turning my attention to the books she has put on the desk for me. I creak open the first one and start reading, flipping my notebook open next to me.

Research can be fun. This is what Kyle's told me in the past. As I sit here hours later, my notepad scribbled full of notes, with my nose itching from all the dust and my eyes sore from all the reading, I admit to thinking he's nuts. There is, however, a sense of satisfaction.

I push my chair back and stretch, groaning. Luzette's gone from her desk on the third floor and I don't even remember her leaving me alone in the library. I load the books back onto the carrel and wander out to find a loo and food.

I've lost all track of time and haven't bothered looking at my phone once to check the time, so when I do and see it's almost midnight, I halt in surprise. Aunt Letitia meets me in the passage as I walk out of the bathroom; she smiles at me.

'Did you find something?'

'I found loads of things,' I say to her. 'Can I run a few things past you?'

'Get your notebook and meet me in the kitchen. Luzette's

201

prepared a light dinner. I've not eaten yet as I wanted to wait for you.'

I join her in the kitchen with its futuristic feel and we sit at the chrome, steel and glass table. Dinner is a stunning quiche and a mixed salad followed by a rich dark chocolate torte and fresh cream. I eat every single bit and drink every single lick of chocolate milk I've been given and afterwards I feel both sleepy and replete.

'Right, so talk to me about your list of creatures.'

'Lilith. A nakki from Finnish lore. The Jersey Devil. A kelpie. A Tengu creature.' I count them off on my fingers. 'There's more too.'

Aunt Letitia lights up one of her cigarettes and blows a perfect smoke ring.

'I think you can discount all of them, except for Lilith. None of them is strong enough to steal children consistently, not from modern habitation at least. If we were talking about Victorian times or earlier, then maybe – but not now. What else have you got?'

I flip through my notes. 'Aliens. The Pied Piper of Hamelin,' I say, more flippantly than seriously, and to my consternation Aunt Letitia looks both impressed and interested. She nods.

'Definite possibilities. What else?'

'Just lots of faerie lore about kids being stolen to entertain the faerie queens, with changelings being left behind in the human world. It goes back to Roman times, and the Greeks before then.' I riffle the pages of my notebook. 'I've not even really looked at African, Middle Eastern or any of the Russian folklore. I also have gods and goddesses from various Western pantheons stealing kids. There's this group of creatures called the Faceless that freaks me out a little.

I've not found much about them but they seem tied to the Sidhe somehow.' I rub my eyes tiredly. 'Mostly there's lots of stuff about children across all ages and times wandering off in the middle of the night and being stolen by demons and things.' I sigh and slump in my chair. 'This is hard. Why can't it just be some stupid human?'

'Who is to say it isn't?'

I open my mouth to say something but nothing comes out for a few seconds. 'Excuse me, what?'

'Who is to say a human isn't behind this? Why can't a human be strong and clever enough to engage a supernatural creature to steal the children he or she wants?'

'But what for?'

'Many reasons. Human trafficking. Paedophilia. To trade for something else with someone else.' She lights another cigarette as the other lies dying. 'The world is an ugly place, Kit. Never ever forget that. Bad things happen to the help-less. And no one is more helpless than a small child. Some people are sick and perverted enough to get off on that, on the power they hold over small fragile things.'

My heart lies heavy in my chest as I consider her words. I've not considered a human protagonist in this at all. I've never had to do so.

'If it's a human, I'll have to take the case to the police,' I say. 'How do I even do that? I'm a kid myself. Will they even believe me?'

'You're a Blackhart, girl. We hold some influence with mundane human authority.'

I scrub my eyes and yawn. 'I feel completely lost in the middle of this,' I tell her, surprising myself. 'I feel like I'm treading water.'

She narrows her eyes at me through the smoke and points

with her cigarette. 'Talk to your partner about this. I'm sure he has some insights. Make sure you visit the estate again, talk to those kids. They'll know more than they think. Find the one thing that links the disappeared children. It will be something unexpected, unusual; I bet my next packet of Marlboro's on it.'

'I've spoken to one of the Infernal about the case,' I tell her. 'Miron. Do you think he'd tell me if Lilith's involved in this?'

'If Lilith's involved, the whole world would know. Lilith never ever does anything on a small scale, this restrained. It's not in her nature. And Miron would tell you, I have no doubt, but he will not offer any assistance. No, I do not think it's Lilith, but it's worth keeping an eye on her. She's been quiet for a very long time now and I'm sure we're due some kind of show from her.'

I groan and pretend to sob. 'I'm so tired.'

'Go home, get some rest. The helicopter is ready, so is Isak.'

I dutifully stuff my notes into my bag and give her a hug. She holds on to me for a few seconds before gripping my face between her hands.

'Trust your gut, girl. You're a Blackhart.' Her lips are cool against my forehead. 'You have good instincts: follow them.'

With her words still ringing in my ears I make my way through the dark, dappled interior of her remote fortress of a home, up to the helipad where Isak's waiting patiently for me.

He helps me into the back without a word, passes me my earphones and makes sure my harness is strapped. Despite the noise, I fall asleep before we even lift off.

Chapter Twenty-Seven

I hit the ground running, sword in hand, ignoring all the safety instructions my nan ever gave me about running with sharp objects. The dogs behind me are getting closer and I need to try and get to safety.

They're huge monstrous beasts with slavering red mouths and lolling tongues. They are also sickeningly fast and have fanned out behind me so that I can't slip sideways into the forest.

The forester Crow's lessons on reading the forest are uppermost in my mind. I remember the Fae's tips on how to use it to my advantage as I propel my magic ahead to seek the safest path through the trees. My legs are pumping so fast it feels as if I'm careering heedlessly along and my heart is pounding so hard against my ribs that I can't catch a decent breath.

Behind me the sound of a hunting horn echoes through the early morning dawn air and an involuntary gasp of fear escapes me at how bloody near it sounds, right on my heels.

Fear spikes through me and my magic rockets ahead – it almost feels as though it's pulling me along in its wake and I'm helplessly following along. I'm aware of the ancient forest feeling quite intensely *interested* in me as I race along.

The hunting dogs' masters are closer too, from the horns' sounds; they seem as feral and wild as their hounds.

I desperately wish for Aiden in wolf form by my side. He'd give these dogs something to think about. Then I burst through the undergrowth into a clearing filled with a sea of tall grass the colour of midnight sky. I stumble over my own feet in surprise, the colour so unexpected and yet so beautifully vibrant against the lush green of the surrounding forest, Then the first dog hurls itself towards me from the forest's shadows. I swipe a blow at its side, then there's movement behind me and I'm running again.

In the clearing, perhaps because of the open space, my magic soars high above the grass. I hurl heedlessly along behind it, pumping my arms and thanking Jamie for the level of fitness he expects of us.

The dogs are now further behind, which is peculiar because they should be faster now too. I risk a glance over my shoulder and notice how they're slowing even more until their handlers have caught up. They huddle in a mess of fur and fang on the edge of the clearing and I slow down to a light jog too, wondering what's going on. Of course, it could be a ploy to make me let my guard down, but something has changed. I come to a standstill and watch them mill around in confusion, as if they've lost track of me.

With my magic buzzing in and around me I lift my hand and wave at them. Nothing. The dogs are circling their handlers, whining and growling, while the hunters seem oblivious to my presence a mere two hundred metres or so away from them. Their voices are loud and angry as they discuss where I've gone. I turn and jog deeper into the clearing, keeping a grip on my sword, taking deep steadying breaths.

'You do get into some interesting situations,' a familiar voice tells me and I start with fright.

Thorn's eyes fix on the point of my sword hovering millimetres from his throat, and he lifts an elegant eyebrow. 'This is how you greet me after such a long time?'

'You're not real,' I tell him, my voice definitely not catching on the word *real*.

'But I am real, Kit.' Ignoring the tip of the blade, he presses forward until it dents his skin but even so I don't drop my arm. 'It is important that you believe me.'

'What are you doing here?' My voice isn't even, which I blame on being out of breath, but the thudding of my heart has nothing to do with the run I've just had and everything to do with seeing his stupid beautiful face and impossible eyes. 'Why were they chasing me and how come they can't see me now? What is this place?'

He makes an impatient noise. 'My will is shielding us from them, for now. I don't know how long it will fool them. We have to be quick and get you away from here.' His expression becomes very serious. 'You are facing great peril, Blackhart . . .'

My lips twist because when am I not in danger? Before I can say anything, he continues. 'Much more than you can imagine.' He sighs impatiently and wraps his fingers around my blade, pushing it away and down. He shows me his palms and I'm not surprised by how fast the wounds heal, or by the soft hum of his magic against my skin. These things are as familiar to me as my own face in the mirror. 'Are you paying attention now?'

I nod mutely and sway towards Thorn, all thoughts of self-preservation and things being impossible gone. I feel the steady beating of his heart through his tunic as he folds me against him. He holds me close for a few seconds before kissing me softly on the lips. The kiss is sweet and chaste, but it makes my blood thunder in my ears and I'm grateful he's holding on to me or my knees would have given way.

'Where are we?'

'In our dreams.'

It's cheesy and silly, but I don't care because I want to believe it. A thought occurs to me. '*When* are we?'

He looks surprised, but then seems to understand why I asked the question. 'When? We're now, Kit. Right now. I've been here all along, trying to find you, calling you. I know you heard me. I felt it.' He searches my face. 'You heard me calling you, didn't you?'

I blink at him in confusion. 'I . . . don't . . . Maybe. Thorn, what is going on? Who are they?'

'They've been sent to hunt you down. You know so much already. You are in awful danger, Kit.'

'I am always facing some kind of trouble, Thorn.' My words draw a growl from him and he shifts against me.

'No time for games, Blackhart. Listen.'

His tone is angry and intense; it startles me. Only one person has ever spoken to me in that way – Uncle Jamie, the night he told me about being a Blackhart.

I nod and for a moment there's hesitation in his face, then he presses a finger to my lips and tilts his head to the side. I realize that he actually meant me to *listen*.

For several heartbeats I hear nothing. And then I hear it, the sound I heard in my dream of the ruined palace. A great mass shifting ponderously in a too-tight place; it sounds like metal chains and pain. It's heavy and unhealthy, somehow.

'What is that?'

Thorn opens his mouth and a look of confusion comes over his face. He shakes his head, his hand moving to his throat in alarm. He tries to speak again but there's no sound. Then he's moving a few paces away, his shoulders tense as he tries to take deep breaths. Panic rises in my chest when he turns to look at me. His face is pale and his eyes show fear.

'Can't . . .' He points to his throat. 'Talk to you about, uh . . .' He starts coughing, doubling over with the violence of it.

Geas. The thought whispers through my mind. Not so long ago Thorn and I watched his friend struggle to tell us crucial information. But a spell had been placed on him, and this geas left him unable to speak the words.

'I miss you,' I tell him, staggering myself by just blurting it out while he's having his episode. Never let it be said I can't be appropriate or timely, but if I could distract him, maybe the geas could be bypassed. It was a long shot but in any case, these were things I needed to say. 'I think about you every day.'

'Kit.' My name is a sigh from his lips and he sounds wretched. I can't help the stupid grin on my face, not caring that I have actual tears in my eyes.

'Tell me quickly. We need to figure out how to do this. You must give me a hint about what's going on because I can't guess.'

He tries to smile at my efforts to work this out and makes another attempt. 'Her?' He reaches for me and I move towards him. 'Her . . .' His voice is a growl and he starts shaking. 'Sweet Gaia, what is going *on* with me?'

'You mentioned this mysterious *her* before – the last time we met,' I say, holding his hands and twining my fingers in his. 'Come on, Thorn. Talk to me. See if you can move past this. It has to be a geas. You must be able to break it.'

He bends his head over mine and tilts my face up so that he can look down at me.

'Kit Blackhart, as I live and breathe.' His hand cups my face and he kisses me softly, tentatively. 'Your lips are as soft as I remember.' He traces a finger over my cheek, touches my temple and runs a hand through my hair. 'And you really missed me?'

I laugh and lean into him, locking my arms behind his neck and pressing my lips against his.

'Yes.'

His kiss melts my bones and I cling to him like some Thirties starlet embracing her leading man, drowning in him. He mutters something against my lips and I feel the muscles in his shoulders flex as he brings me closer still so I am held tightly against him. I peer at him through my lashes and I'm happy to see how drunk he looks from the kiss, his eyes unfocused and his handsome face unguarded. He sees my expression and gives a sly grin, seeming to like this game of distraction we're playing, trying to get past the geas.

'She's the one you . . .' And then he starts coughing so violently and gasping for breath that I have to brace him otherwise he'd topple over. As I get my shoulder under his, I catch movement in the corner of my eye and gasp in shock.

The pack of dogs and their handlers are hurtling towards us. Whatever protection we had is now gone, leaving us exposed in the middle of the open clearing with Thorn's weight dragging me down.

'Thorn, come on. Get going. They're coming for us.'

I push him upright and when he dizzily tries to focus on

my face, I feel both concerned and panicky at his sudden frailty. I'm not sure if he wore a glamour earlier or if he's glamoured now, because he looks genuinely ill, with heavy dark circles under his eyes as if he hasn't slept in weeks.

'Thorn, we have to run. Can you run?'

He nods and then we're running. I'm yelling at him to keep up and then he falls and . . .

Lilith is a demon, a relic from biblical times. There are many stories about her – mostly about how evil she was and how she stole human children when her own demon children were hunted down and killed on the instructions of a bunch of angels. Just thinking about it gives me severe creeps and I really hope I never have the opportunity of going up against her – because, really, how do you go up against a creature like her? She would be Mama-Bear-tough and insane. I doubt that my sword and bit of magic would be enough to hold out against her for even two minutes.

I think about what Aunt Letty said: that we would know if it was Lilith. The *world* would know. It puts my mind at ease that whatever we're dealing with here is not Lilith related. It's too quiet, too small, too below the radar.

It's just before dawn and I'm sitting at the desk in my tiny room at the top of the house. As I look out over the rooftops of Camden, I wonder exactly what we're dealing with.

My dream of Thorn had me sitting up in bed, gasping, a scream hovering on my lips, my heart pounding. Unable to get back to sleep, I'm worrying at the edges of my research like an angry but tired terrier. The cup of coffee next to my paperwork has gone cold and I lean back in my chair, stretching and yawning, hearing my shoulders click.

My phone buzzes next to me and I look down to see a text from Dante.

Can't sleep. Worried about you.

Aw, isn't that nice? I text back: *I'm okay. It was a long day yesterday. Go back to bed.*

Why aren't you asleep? He sends back, super fast.

Bad dreams. Also, this Spook called Dante keeps texting me. I think he fancies me or something. I grin as I type it out, knowing it will embarrass him.

Ha, funny girl. I'll pick you up at 7.

Are you going to feed me?

It seems it's all we do. Talk and eat.

I'm not a complicated girl. :-D

There is more to life than . . . no, you're right. I need food. See you at 7.

I put my phone on charge and flick through Andrew Lang's *Red Fairy Book* and reread the Ratcatcher's story. The story of the Pied Piper of Hamelin is so well known: a group of elders reneged on a deal they made with the piper to rid their town of rats; he took his revenge by leading the town's children away, into a mountain, never to be seen again. There were rumours, about a hundred years after the tragic events in Hamelin, that travellers came across German-speaking people living in Transylvania. There was no clear history to explain how they actually came to be living there, and rumours circulated that they were descendants of Hamelin's stolen children.

How that translates into the here and now, I'm not sure.

I set the books aside and stretch again. I need a run and some exercise, I decide. I feel slow and ungainly and I can't remember the last time I had a decent workout. Running from a pack of slavering dogs in your dreams doesn't count.

I pull on my jogging shorts, hoodie and trainers and slink out of the house, after strapping my baton to my forearm.

The streets are deserted, with only the occasional car driving by. The bakery on the corner has its lights off but I can see Carmel and her husband Tony in the back, shaping loaves. They wave as they recognize me and I wave back. There are delivery men dropping off newspapers and milk and some of them banter words back and forth with one another as I run by.

As I run, calmed by the rhythmic slap of my feet on the pavement, my thoughts turn back to the dreams I've been waking from in a tangle of damp sheets. I've never really had vivid dreams before. Or, rather, been someone who remembers them after waking. I have the occasional night-mare that leaves me feeling weird and uncomfortable after-wards. And even, once, a devastatingly sexy dream about my friend Karina's brother, Udo, where my cheeks flamed just remembering it.

But last night's dream felt real, even in the cold light of day, as they say. It had been so vivid, the details so intense. I can still feel the air in the Otherwhere rush against my skin, and hear the sound of dogs racing behind me. I remember the hesitant way Thorn reached out to me at first.

Him kissing me. I close my eyes for a second, relishing how it felt. The taste of him, the feel of him as he pressed me against him. Oh my God, I am becoming insane and falling for a guy in my dreams. He is real – somewhere – but so far out of my reach physically and emotionally. I'd have more luck falling in love with a Hollywood movie star. I open my eyes and see a homeless guy watching me from his warm nook in a shop doorway. He gives me a shaky smile and a thumbs-up and I return the gesture before running past him into the morning.

The path along the canal is deserted. A soft mist rises from above the water and tangles around my feet. It feels great being able to run and being on the move. I pass a few other joggers and we nod at one another. An elderly gentleman is walking his tiny Jack Russell, which clearly is under the impression it's a Great Dane because it bristles at me as I step off the path to make way for them. The sky above me remains grey with no sign of the sun raising its head, apart from a slight lightening in the east. As I near the top of Regent's Park, the traffic's increased enough to make jogging unpleasant. I turn and head back home the way I came, this time on the other side of the canal.

I'm about halfway when I sense movement behind me. Instinct and Jamie's training makes me duck and swerve just in time and someone careers into me. Since my centre of gravity is lower than theirs, I am only knocked a few paces sideways. A muttered curse is followed by a whopping splash, as whoever it is lands in the canal with little grace.

'Idiot!' I hear someone snarl just as a punch takes me in the ribs, close to where the drug dealer's bruise is slowly trying to heal.

I stagger back in shock and spin to face my attacker. He's a big guy, dressed in a tracksuit and sneakers. I passed him and his partner, the guy now swimming in the canal, on the other bank. They'd even smiled at me.

The utter bastards. If they thought I was some kind of victim, they had another thing coming. I flick my wrist and the baton slaps into my palm.

'What the hell?' I say, talking to the big guy. 'What do you want?'

'To smash your pretty little face, love,' he replies, lunging for me again. 'You're sticking your nose in where it don't belong.'

I sway out of his way and bring the baton down against the side of his knee. He lets out a yelp and I spin out of reach, keeping an eye on the other guy, who's trying to climb out of the canal. There's movement in the water behind him as a smooth dark back crests out of the water and I hurriedly move away from the edge, not liking where this is going.

A black shape rises from the canal, water sliding off its steaming flanks. It moves swiftly through the water towards the guy, who must sense something behind him because he turns to look over his shoulder. His mouth opens in shock but no scream comes.

The pookah lunges at him, long white teeth distending from a large strong jaw, clamping firmly down on his shoulder and lifting him away from the edge of the canal where he was trying to clamber back onto the walkway. The man lets out a shriek – cut short as the pookah tosses its head, jerking him up and down like a ragdoll, or as a crocodile would treat its catch. It then sinks beneath the surface, taking the thrashing man with it.

'What the hell?' My guy stares at me in horror, then at the restless water of the canal. 'What—? Did you see?' He runs to stand at the edge, his hands going up to the sides of his head, the universal WTF gesture people display when confronted with the impossible. 'What is a pookah doing here?' He swings back to me. 'All of this is your fault, you stupid girl. Look what you just did!'

'Who sent you?' I ask him warily, keeping my distance.

He is completely distracted by the disappearance of his

friend. I would be too. That pookah is one of the largest I've ever seen and it looked quite pissed off. Also, hungry.

'I'm talking to you, mate. Who sent you?'

'How do *you* command a pookah?' The guy demands of me. 'I have never seen one come to the defence of a human. What did you do? Who did you swear fealty to, Blackhart?'

The way he pronounces 'Blackhart' makes me laugh openly. It sounds like a swear word, and I like it. I'm as shocked as he is by the turn of events but, really, he is just bleating now. And if he thinks I have some kind of control over what that pookah in the canal did, well, that's okay by me.

'I'm running out of time.' I take a step closer and swipe at him with the baton again and he yelps, jumping out of the way. 'Who sent you?'

'No one you'd know, but listen closely. You're being warned to stay away from the children and the estate. This has nothing to do with you, regardless of what *she* made you promise. This is older than even Suola.'

Interesting. So he knows I've been employed by Suola to find the missing kids. That means he has to be working for the person who stole them.

'Why are you even coming to me?' I counter, pursuing him as he keeps backing up. 'If Suola tells me to stop investigating the case, I'll stop. All you need to do is convince her.'

His face twists in a grimace of distaste. 'I don't speak to her kind. But know this, Blackhart, we know where you live, who your friends are.'

My chin lifts. 'You're threatening my friends and my family now? You utter snivelling coward. Tell this to whoever sent you. I vow to do unimaginable damage to anyone who lays a finger on any of my friends or family – because of a job I have been *legally* employed to do.'

The sound of sirens had never been this welcome and I try not to show relief. Maybe someone saw us fighting on the towpath, maybe not, but it makes my attacker less likely to stick around.

The guy's face, already rather red, turns florid and he scowls at me. 'They said you had a mouth on you. Asking too many questions, interfering.' He's focused on me again. 'They want you to stop. This isn't going away and nothing you or your family does will make it go away.'

I keep my arms wide in invitation as I take a few steps back. 'Come on. Teach me a lesson.'

He's fast for a big guy and has obviously had some boxing training. He lands another blow that glances off as I turn at the last minute. It still hurts and I exhale sharply as pain flares through me but it passes quickly and I land my own punch to his throat. Not a move of which Jamie would be proud, because it's not exactly sporting, but this guy is far bigger than me. If he gets hold of me properly, I will land in hospital with broken bones.

He staggers back and I follow him closely, laying in with my baton. The folds of his tracksuit catch many of the blows, as it hangs loosely off him, but enough of them land and hurt. He howls in annoyance, grabbing me around the throat, then starts squeezing.

I'm a strong girl, but even I can't go one on one against an adult man trying to choke the life out of me. I lift my hand and concentrate hard on my magic, forming a small intense white ball of light in my palm. It takes longer than I would like but as soon as I feel the light against my skin

I thrust my hand into the guy's face. He screams in shock at the bright light and drops mc. As he lets go, I drop to my knees and punch him hard on the inside of the leg and he goes down onto his knees, his hands protectively cupping his eyes where my magic's clinging to his face, blinding him. I jump up and deliver a satisfying knee to his jaw, my breath coming fast.

The sirens are closer now, startling me into running, and I leave my injured attacker behind.

Chapter Twenty-Eight

I'm shaking so much that I spill my coffee down my front when I turn away from the counter. Kyle frowns at me over his bowl of Cheerios.

'You okay?' he asks through a mouthful.

'Just angry,' I say, joining him at the table, 'and annoyed. It's the second time now someone's sent people to pounce on me, and this time round I've not even done anything.'

'And you're not hurt? Cut or bleeding?'

I shake my head and lift up my shirt to examine my ribs. Why do people keep punching me in the ribs? I suppose it's better than the face, but still, my poor ribs are a kaleidoscope of sore muscles and bruises. 'Just a bit bruised. Won't be wearing my bikini any time soon.'

Kyle sucks in the air between his teeth when he sees my ribs. 'Jesus, Kit. How big was this guy?'

'Not that big, maybe a bit smaller than Jamie.' I wave my hand. 'I'm okay. Nothing's broken, I swear. I just haven't recovered from the other beating I had, oh, the other night.'

'And it's definitely about the disappearances and not Glow?'

'Warned me to stay away from the estate and the missing

kids investigation, and I was told to stop sticking my nose where it doesn't belong. Definitely about the disappearances.'

'And they were human?'

I shrug. 'They looked human. One was dragged into the canal by a pookah so, you know, things could have gone worse for me.'

'We have to tell my dad,' he says looking worried. 'He might have to talk to Suola about what happened.'

I roll my eyes. 'And what will he say? Please spread the word that whoever it is stealing the kids can't pick on Kit Blackhart, cos she'll cry you a river?'

'Did you cry?'

'Shut up, Kyle.'

He smirks at me and drinks his tea. I lift my cup and grimace at the pull against my ribs. I spot Kyle watching me. 'What?'

'Why are you ignoring Aiden?'

I pull a face. 'Not you too! I spoke to him yesterday. I'm not ignoring him. He's just not been around.'

Kyle picks up his phone, a soft sleek thing that looks as if it could do the dishes, the laundry and arrange for your house to be cleaned at the same time, and waves it at me. 'You can always call him, you know. Keep him up to date with how things are going.'

'When did he become my keeper?' I counter. 'He's a friend, not a partner, or my minder.'

'My dad didn't want you to tackle this case by yourself, Kit. He said to keep Aiden close.'

I push away from the table. 'Look, I'm my own person, Kyle. I understand your dad's worried about the Spook and the case, but I'm sure I can handle the rest of this. I don't need Aiden to babysit me.'

'You really have become such a brat,' Kyle mutters as I stalk out of the kitchen. 'You used to be my favourite!' he calls after me as I climb the stairs to go and have a shower.

The weather outside is one hundred per cent autumn, marching into winter. I choose a pair of skinny jeans, my modified calf-high Docs and various layers of long-sleeved T-shirts to keep me warm. With my leather jacket over this, I should be snug enough. I find a soft fabric scarf I've inherited from Megan and wrap that around my neck. I stuff my fingerless gloves into my pocket and slide my favourite knife into the sheath in my boot. I dither about the baton but decide that today I'm going to try not to get into any fights. I can barely move without wincing and I deserve a day of not being punched and stabbed. My knife will have to do. I suspect that Jamie would be a tiny bit disappointed in me but, you know, he's not around so I'll just have to cope.

I take my time and put on a bit of foundation, sweep mascara over my lashes and some lippy too. I fiddle with the eyeliner a little and manage a thin line just above my lashes. I thank Megan silently for these lessons in girly things because today, after too little sleep and too much fretting, I need a pick-me-up.

I stuff my notes and notebook into my messenger bag and head downstairs, just as Kyle opens the door to Dante.

They both turn to look at me as I jump down the last few steps, momentarily forgetting about my bruised ribs. I wince and mutter under my breath and Kyle wordlessly hands me some ibuprofen from his back pocket.

I take the blister pack from him and smile brightly at Dante, who is looking handsome and well put together in jeans, a long-sleeved T-shirt and leather jacket. Going for the casual bad-boy look, complete with messy hair and stubble.

'Hey, want to come in for a second? I just need to take some painkillers.'

Dante nods and moves forward as Kyle dithers by the door. He spots the grocery bags Dante's holding and frowns.

'Looks like you brought groceries.'

'I'm making you guys breakfast,' he says. 'Pancakes, bacon and maple syrup.'

'Kyle's already eaten,' I point out spitefully, ignoring my surprise that he's decided to make breakfast, rather than us going out somewhere to eat. 'Cheerios.'

There's only a moment of hesitation from Kyle before he speaks. 'Yeah, but Kit, the dude's making pancakes. I mean, pancakes trump Cheerios any time of the day.'

'True.' I swallow two tablets and gesture to the clean kitchen. 'This is where you can play,' I tell Dante.

'Cheers.' He dumps his shopping on the counter and looks around. 'I'll need a mixing bowl, a sieve and two frying pans.'

Kyle hands him the utensils and steps aside, his eyes huge.

'Where did you learn to make pancakes?' he asks.

'My foster parents. They love baking and so it was the first thing they taught me: how to make pancakes and brew proper cowboy coffee. Really, I was forced into child labour so they could sleep in on Sundays.'

'They sound nice,' Kyle says, his tone wistful before he can catch himself. 'Mostly our brownie, Mrs Evans, looked after us at the Manor.'

'Kyle's parents travel a lot,' I put in. 'They've been in New York most often lately.'

Dante looks between us and smiles. 'Look, I'm not here to pass judgement on your family. Or to ask questions about them – let's be clear about that. I'm just here, as a friend, making you breakfast.'

The doorbell rings again and Kyle pales slightly, shooting me a worried look. 'I'll just go and get that,' he says weakly, practically running to answer the door.

'Who?' Dante asks me, nodding towards the empty passage.

'I would guess it's Aiden.'

'Your not-boyfriend?'

I grimace just as Kyle leads Aiden into the kitchen. Aiden's dressed in his trademark black jeans and T-shirt and casual hoodie. I shiver from cold just looking at him but as usual he seems untouched by the weather. Behind him I see Kyle's anxious expression and my heart softens towards him just a little bit. He knows he's screwed up, inviting Aiden over without clearing it with me, and now we're faced with two very large bristling males in our kitchen. The place isn't small but it feels overcrowded with all of us there. Aiden's doing that wolf-thing he does, when he looks taller than his six-foot-one and broader in the chest too. I've seen his dad do it in the past, dominating a room and everyone in it. When Aiden does it, it's sexy and kinda cute, but when his dad does it, I just want to run and hide and pull a duvet over my head and wait for the growling and snarling to end.

'Aiden, this is Dante Alexander. Dante, this is my friend Aiden.' I stand between them and even as a bigger girl, as someone who can handle herself in a fight, I feel overwhelmed by the testosterone in the room.

'I'm the not-boyfriend,' Aiden says, his voice containing a definite growl.

'I'm the partner,' Dante answers not missing a beat, shaking Aiden's offered hand briefly, as he openly assesses Aiden. 'Are you staying for breakfast? I'm making pancakes.'

A look of confusion crosses Aiden's features and he looks at Kyle.

'Sorry, he just showed up,' Kyle says. '*And* he's making pancakes. That's pulling out the big guns, Aiden.'

'He's not lying. I really did force my way into the kitchen. Standard Spook protocol. Conquer those who doubt by cooking them a meal.' Dante is so charming and looks so at home wearing the silly apron, which neither Kyle nor I ever wear, that I can't help the chuckle that escapes me.

'Aiden will stay, for sure. Pancakes are his favourite.'

Aiden's dark eyes meet mine and I plaster a smile on my face. 'It's fine, really. I'm fine, we're fine. Everything's okay.'

'That's not what Kyle said,' he mutters, turning his back on Dante, effectively excluding him from the conversation and crowding into my personal space. 'You got into a fight this morning, jogging?'

'I did. But I'm okay.'

Dante swears as he drops a spatula.

'You were attacked this morning? What were you doing?' His gaze meets mine over Aiden's shoulder and I have the good grace to feel only slightly ashamed by the accusation I see on his face. 'What happened? Are you hurt?'

Three pairs of eyes regard me steadily. Dante's expression looks annoyed and I try and shrug casually but it hurts me to do so I give half a shrug and most of a grimace.

'The guy got a lucky shot at my ribs.'

And then everyone gets to talk at once, except me. I look at their faces, hearing their voices raised at me and I consider just walking out of the door. Admittedly, a part of me likes the fuss, but another part feels angry at how much noise they are making over nothing. I'm fine; I took care of it. One of the attackers is now tucked away in a pookah larder, which isn't the usual thing that happens to people who fight me. However, I'm not about to kick up a fuss and cry about it because it was me or him, and he had it coming.

I watch all three of them trying to out-bellow the others and eventually it just gets tiring and I hold up my hands. Their voices peter out and Kyle looks as relieved as I feel, sagging against the fridge.

'I will tell you what happened once I've got at least one pancake inside me, okay?' When both Dante and Aiden open their mouths I hold up my hand. 'No. Breakfast. Then I will tell you, then there will be no shouting because I dealt with it.'

'Fine.' Aiden turns his back on me and focuses on Dante, pursing his lips. His expression is so done with me. 'So, Spook boy, do you need help?'

Dante hands him the pack of bacon. 'Fry that up, if you'd be so kind.'

'Where'd you learn to cook?'

'My foster parents.'

'Huh, you're adopted?'

'Yeah. You?'

'No, I'm the youngest of four brothers. You got siblings?'

'A baby sister.' There's a beat. 'But she died.'

'Fuck. That sucks. Sorry to hear that.' Aiden cuts open the packet, finds the tongs in the drawer (who even knew we had tongs?) before turning back to the pan. 'My mum's always said she wanted girls but that just never happened for my parents.'

'Are you guys close?'

'My dad and I are very close. My other brothers are all out of the house, working or studying at uni.'

I roll my eyes at Kyle and he looks miserable. Who would have thought it? His plan had backfired badly. Instead of sworn enemies, Aiden and Dante are bonding over making us pancakes. Kyle holds his hand out to me and I grab it and we tiptoe out of the kitchen, back to the dining room.

'That's just weird,' he says. 'I thought Aiden would be like, you know, on our side or something.'

'Your side,' I point out to him. 'Crappy move, by the way, bringing the wolf in. What would have happened if they'd really taken a dislike to one another? Aiden is fond of doing some very stupid stuff.' Like getting into fights in nightclubs and then having to run from the cops.

'How did I know you'd let the Spook come here to cook for you? Geez, it's like you guys are dating or something.'

'Shut up.'

'You shut up.'

'I hate you.'

'I hate you more.'

We scowl at one another over the computer screens. Kyle ducks his head and starts tapping his keyboard loudly and angrily. 'I've been looking at other disappearances, of kids going missing.'

'Did you find anything?'

'Ask a stupid question,' he sighs. 'There have been dis-appearances going back twenty years at least.'

'At that estate?'

226

'No, in the south of England. There are other disappearances too, obviously, but none quite like what we've seen reported recently.'

Something that's been nagging me, at the back of my mind, leaps forward.

'Dammit, I forgot about Diane's auntie's scrapbooks.'

'Who?' Kyle asks me distractedly as he looks up from his screen.

'Dante, do you have the scrapbooks with you?' I yell out to be heard over the clatter in the kitchen.

'Yes, in the boot. The keys.' He steps around the corner and tosses them to me. I quickly run out to the car parked a few doors down. The boot's a mess, I'll be honest, but as I dig through the shirts and the large (and well-equipped) first-aid kit I spot the scrapbooks. When I lift them up I notice a batch of files beneath them. They're all held together with a ribbon.

My curiosity piqued, I lift them up and a sick feeling lodges in my stomach. There's a memo clipped to the topmost file with the Spooks' logo header. The issue date of the internal memo is five days ago. The subject is BLACKHART FAMILY – CURRENT INVESTIGATIONS. They are individual files on my family. All the files look well thumbed, with tabs sticking out of the side. Mine is on top and is the thinnest of them all. I double check the names on them. They are of my immediate family: Uncle Andrew, Aunt Jennifer, Megan, Marc, Kyle, Aunt Letitia and a few of the younger cousins that I don't really know as they're living abroad. There are also ones bearing my parents' names: Samantha Blackhart and David Hoffman-Blackhart. These files are thick, at least an inch each, maybe more. My dad's is the larger of the two, and I recall Jamie's words, that he was a Spook before he met my mum. That they worked together and that's how they fell in love.

I consider stealing the files but there's no way I can smuggle them into the house with everyone there, plus it would be super obvious that I'm the one who took them. I shiver in the cold, grab the scrapbooks and walk back to the flat, wondering how easy it would be to break into the back of Dante's car.

Chapter Twenty-Nine

Breakfast with a Spook, a wolf and two Blackharts turns out to be a noisy affair. As promised, I tell them what happened during my jog and Aiden and Dante posture for a bit about who will accompany me on my other jogs. Kyle looks super amused and I want to throw bacon at him but bacon is sacred so I stuff it in my mouth instead.

'The pancakes are really good,' Aiden grudgingly admits to Dante after a third large stack and gives him a hearty slap on the shoulder. 'You may visit again. But no dating Kit.'

Dante almost chokes on his food and laughingly holds up his hand.

'No, it's okay. I won't be dating Kit, trust me.' When he sees my look of hurt horror he clears his throat. 'I mean, she's too fierce for me.'

'And young.' Aiden glances my way as he says this and I feel murder in my heart.

'What are you doing, Aiden?' I hiss in annoyance. It's hard to keep my voice level and I have to breathe deeply to keep my anger from lighting up the room. 'Why are you being a pest? Are you trying to prove something to someone?'

Aiden watches me from unreadable wolf's eyes and I feel

229

a twinge of fear crawl up my spine. I don't like the way he's gone very quiet, like I've seen him do just before a fight.

'Prove? Nothing. I'm just making sure you look after yourself.'

'By goading me? Insulting me?' I lean forward. 'I am not three years old. I'm not a giggly helpless girl either. I know how to look after myself.'

'You know Andrew's asked me to keep an eye on you, make sure that you don't get into trouble.'

I feel stung by his words and I take a deep breath.

'You're only a little bit older than me,' I point out. 'Why would he ask *you* to "keep an eye" on me? Is it because poor pathetic little Kit can't do anything for herself?'

Kyle and Dante look as if they want to run a mile, but, you know what? Having them there just makes me angrier still. Had they both just played by the rules and not interfered, this wouldn't even be happening – the fight that I'm pretty sure I'm about to have with my best friend.

'I don't know. Maybe Andrew thinks you're prone to walking face-first into fights without thinking about your safety? That maybe you need back-up now and again, like a normal person does?'

'No.' I suck in a breath. 'I don't see anyone running after Marc or Jamie "making sure they're okay". I wonder if anyone's keeping an eye on Megan whilst she's in New York. No? Didn't think so. What makes me the special case, then?' I throw up my hands and stand. 'You know, I think I'll just phone Andrew and ask him what's going on. Because really, with you being a such a complete di— . . .' I growl in frustration. 'Idiot, you've completely damaged my calm. I really don't need this crap in my life.'

'Kit!'

Aiden's standing and he looks almost contrite, but not quite. The way he hesitates sets all my alarm bells ringing.

'What?'

'My dad called me into a meeting this morning. You must know that Andrew's passed the Glow case to the wolves. My dad's having me and Shaun investigate it. The little girl in the coma? She died last night.'

I draw in a shocked breath, taking it in. 'That was . . . is . . . my case,' I say. 'That poor girl. *Andrew* gave you the case? So you guys are now working with us on this?'

Aiden shakes his head. 'No. Just us, no Blackharts this time.' He doesn't say, 'no you this time', but his meaning is clear. 'We're hitting the clubs tonight to see if we can get any further leads.'

I nod, feeling numb. With a last fake smile at them I leave the room, grabbing my jacket. I pull it on, followed by my fingerless gloves, then slam the front door shut behind me – hard enough for the windows to rattle.

A startled crow caws at me and takes off as I stomp past where it sat chilling out on a fence post. I narrow my eyes against the light and watch it fly away, winging south, towards the City. The street isn't busy, with the majority of office workers already on their way to work by Tube or bus. I wonder what day it is, then check my phone. Tomorrow our tutor, Lan, will be coming around for a few hours of hard grafting and I've not even finished the home-work she set me the week before. I can't remember anything about the treaties signed between the Seelie and Unseelie Courts during the Frontier's War of the Roses.

I sigh, unable to feel remotely interested in history, treat-ies or anything. Instead I'm just feeling wiped out, miserable and annoyed at Uncle Andrew for handing the Garretts the

Glow case. I mull this over, pulling my collar up and shoving my hands into my pockets, because guess who stormed out without her scarf? I feel awful for the little girl, Emma, who's died. Her poor family must feel utterly devastated after what they've been through. She's been in a coma for a month and her older sister was a wreck when they realized the Glow had come from the leftover ampoules in her purse.

I keep on walking until I no longer see bright spots in front of my eyes, my anger and mixed-up feelings of betrayal dissipating in the cold air. Then I'm ready to pull out my phone and call Uncle Andrew. And I really don't care that it's the middle of the night in New York.

The phone rings twice before he answers.

'What's wrong?' he asks without preamble. 'Are you okay?'

'I'm not sure. Do you think I'm incapable of looking after myself?'

There's a moment of shocked silence before he sighs. 'You've spoken to Aiden, I take it?'

'Yes.'

'And he's told you . . . ?'

'That the Garretts have now taken control of the Glow thing. I thought you were going to pass it on to someone else in the family.'

'I considered it. I asked a friend of mine from my army days to look into it . . . but, well, I think the Garretts are uniquely placed to take the Glow case for us.'

'Why?' I sigh. 'No, I mean, really, explain it to me. Why was it given to them to look into?'

'Werewolves can't get drunk easily and they can't get high, their metabolism is too fast and they have natural immunity to a variety of poisons that can be fatal to both humans and Fae. That was one of the reasons I approached the pack. The other reason is that Aiden already has ties to one of the largest crime families operating in the UK today.'

I frown. 'You mean *Leo*?'

There's another pause on the transatlantic line and for a second I worry that we've been cut off, but then he speaks again. 'Yes, Leo – whose dad is not the quiet businessman who owns a few nightclubs around town like he'd have you believe.'

I exhale raggedly before grudgingly admitting, 'Okay, well. That makes sense, I suppose. But Aiden's still being an idiot and trying to manage me.'

There's a smothered snort. 'Kit, you came into the family as this perfect package of independence and strong will. I know you're not impressed with me or with Aiden but I've asked the young wolf to keep an eye on you because I don't trust the Spook. You, I trust completely.'

'I'm not sure that Aiden got that message.'

He belly laughs his Uncle Andrew laugh of amusement and it makes me smile, even if anger is still plucking at me like an insistent plucking thing. 'Aiden likes hearing subtext.'

'Can you tell him to back off? He's gone all protective wolf on me and I really don't like it. If we fall out it's going to be ugly and it won't sit well with the Garretts. I don't want to be the cause if the two families get fighting. I'm doing fine working with Dante.'

'Let me see what I can do. You must know that Aiden cares about you, deeply. That boy doesn't give his loyalty easily.' He sighs and I hear the puff of an exhale. 'He's made you part of his pack, Kit, so bear that in mind.'

'But I'm not part of his pack, Uncle Andrew. I'm his

friend – there's a huge difference. Vast!' I'm relieved he can't see me gesturing wildly as I stand on the corner but then there are CCTV cameras everywhere and maybe he can see me after all.

'Why is it so difficult for you to accept that people care about you, Kit?'

The question takes me off-guard and I stare at a mum attempting to wedge her squirming toddler into a buggy as I try to come up with an answer.

'I'd rather just . . . you know, not get involved with people too much, Uncle Andrew. It doesn't work out well for me or them.'

'Oh, Kit, you can't cut yourself off from friends and family. It's no way to live your life.'

I sigh and look over my shoulder. Dante's making his way towards me, his hands stuffed into his jacket pockets and he's carrying my scarf. He looks cold and miserable and I almost feel sorry for him. But not quite.

'I have to go now, Uncle Andrew. Please talk to Aiden and tell him to give me some space. I'm trying to work a case. I'll respect the fact that he'll be working with Shaun to solve the Glow crimes.'

I hang up and walk towards Dante, blocking his path. Instead of handing me my scarf he drapes it around my neck. His smile is a little rueful and apologetic.

'I screwed up, didn't I?' His voice is as miserable as he looks.

'You did. Why didn't you just come and collect me like you said you would?'

He sighs and hunches his shoulders. 'I don't know, I thought it would be a good idea to treat you to a homemade breakfast for a change.'

'You knew my family would freak out.' Subtext: *you knew I'd freak out.*

'I didn't even think about that. I'm sorry.'

Briefly he looks really young and genuinely sorry, but I resolve not to go all mushy because he's giving me piteously cute puppy eyes. I square my shoulders and start back along the street.

'I need my bag. We've got a lot of work to catch up on.'

'Aiden—' He stops when I hold my hand up to stop him from talking.

'No. Nothing about Aiden. If you guys want to hang out, that's fine by me, but just don't include me in your burgeoning bromance. I'm not interested.'

Dante blinks at me and I wonder why he would look that alarmed by what I'd just said, but then he shakes his head.

'I was going to say that Aiden said to tell you he's sorry. His dad called just after you left. Apparently he needs him to run errands. Don't any of you go to school, at all?'

I scowl up at him. 'This again? Why are you so obsessed about school? Do you think me knowing how to put together a business plan will help me fight monsters? The stuff I'm training in with my tutor is what's going to keep me alive.'

'Have you ever been to normal school? Like an average kid?'

'I've been to schools, but not like an average kid. I travelled around Europe with my nan and we stayed all over. We spent a summer in China and wintered in Japan.'

Dante whistles softly and shakes his head. 'That explains a lot.'

I stop walking and narrow my eyes at him. 'What. Does. That. Even. Mean.'

'Just that you're obviously not the girl your family thinks you are. That I thought you were.' He takes a deep breath. 'I look at you, Kit, and I see an attractive girl getting into fights with drug dealers and who beats up monsters. I'm in awe. Your family sees you as the girl they took in when your nan died. Even though Kyle is younger than you, you are the baby, the one to watch at all times because you're the newcomer. They will always worry about you.' He watches me carefully to see how I'm reacting. 'They forget who your grandmother was. That she raised a girl who is very pragmatic, a bit volatile, a bit impatient, a young woman who knows her mind and who is quite capable of taking care of herself.'

Well now, what do you say to that? I turn around and start walking again. Dante falls in beside me.

'I'm being a diva, aren't I?'

'Just a tiny bit, but I can understand why. All the attention they focus on you would drive me crazy. Especially Aiden. He's very intense.'

I wonder at the catch in his voice but he shivers unexpectedly and pulls his collar up as we stride along.

'Aiden's complicated. Yes, he is intense and he forgets that not everyone feels things as keenly as he does. It took me a while to get used to it, but sometimes, like today, he's just a real idiot. Apparently it's a wolf thing. Once he focuses on something he just doesn't let up.'

'And you're sure he's not in love with you?'

I laugh and shake my head as I open our gate. 'No. Definitely not. I'm not Aiden's type. You are, though.' It's a throwaway comment that makes Dante squeak in protest whilst I reach for my keys. Before I can unlock the front door, though, Kyle pulls it open and I stumble into him. His hair's mussed and he looks paler than when I left half an hour ago.

'It's on the news. A little girl's been taken from the estate in Brixton. It happened last night.' He hands me printouts of the online newspaper reports and I follow him back into the house.

I skim-read the articles and pass them on to Dante.

'Why haven't Diane or Chem called us?' Dante edges past me to sit on one of the couches in the living room so he can read the articles. He looks through them quickly and drops them on the coffee table. 'This is unbelievable. I can't believe it's happened again.'

I pull my phone out and find Diane's number. 'I'm phoning Diane, I've got to see what's going on.'

The phone rings once before Diane answers. 'I just found out myself,' she says without even bothering to say hello. 'I'm on my way to school. Chem's over there trying to find out more.'

'Why didn't he call me?'

'His mum confiscated his phone when he stayed out late the other night.'

I sigh, thankful that the only person whining about my nocturnal behaviour is my cousin.

'We're on our way. Does it look bad?'

'Yeah, there are cops everywhere and I'm going to be late for school because they're questioning everyone.'

I wish her luck and hang up. Kyle reappears next to me and hands me my messenger bag and the small compact camera.

'Get photos this time,' he tells me. 'Of everything. The whole flat if you can, including the little girl's bedroom.'

I nod and drop the camera into my bag. 'Anything else?'

'Be careful. And talk to Aiden.'

I roll my eyes and give him a quick hug before dragging Dante out the door to his car.

Chapter Thirty

During the rush-hour drive to Brixton, I update Dante on my research at Aunt Letty's and promise to show him my notes. The villains of our piece don't seem clear at all, not until we can get a decent lead, and I feel panic thrumming through me at the thought of another little child taken from the estate.

We park a couple of blocks away and watch the army of police and onlookers mill about.

'How do we get in?' I ask Dante.

'I'm a Spook, remember? My ID should get us in.'

'Wow. Not just a snappy dresser then?'

'Funny. For a youngling. Get out of my car before I lock you in.'

Outside, the air is blade sharp and clear and my breath plumes. I tie my scarf tighter and dip my fingers into my jacket pockets.

'Are you carrying weapons?' he asks me, as we make our way across the badly kept lawn to where a young police officer is keeping the nosy public at bay.

'Of course.'

I think he sighs but we're in front of the cop by then;

he's spotted us picking our way between the crowd of onlookers and Dante can't ask me what I'm carrying.

'Can I help you folks?' He's got his name sewn on his breast pocket. PC Osborne looks maybe a week older than Dante but there's an authority his uniform lends him that Dante's casual attire doesn't quite pull off.

'I'm with the SDI,' Dante says and shows him the ID from his wallet. 'Dante Alexander. My partner, Kit Blackhart. Can you tell us what happened here?'

Osborne looks from Dante to me, then back to Dante, clearly not sure how to handle this. I can see him mentally going through the alphabet of organizations that work with the police in his head. Eventually, after a few seconds, he realizes who Dante represents and he draws himself up to his full height.

'You guys hunt ghosts, right?' he says and instead of any kind of derision there is definite interest in his voice. 'Do you think there's some kind of woo-woo going on here?'

I bite my lips so as not to laugh but it's difficult because he asks the question without guile, complete with big eyes. I like the guy – I can't help myself.

'What's going on here then, constable?' a female voice asks and we all turn to watch a woman walk towards us. She's dressed in a pair of khaki jeans, hiking boots and a warm-looking peajacket. She looks the business and I can't help but admire her outfit. My kind of lady, dressing sensibly. The boots look as if they can kick up a storm.

'Detective, these two are from the Gho—, I mean, from the SDI. Dante Alexander and Kit Blackhart.'

The detective narrows her dark gaze at us, taking in Dante before swinging back to me. 'Blackhart? Do you know someone called Jamie Blackhart?'

Alarm rushes through me but I nod my head. 'He's my uncle,' I reply, putting on my most winning smile. 'He's not in trouble, is he?'

'No. But when you speak to him again, tell him to collect the motorcycle jacket that he left at my office, along with some of his files.' She holds out an elegant hand with long tapering fingers and neatly trimmed nails. 'I'm Detective Shen.' She shakes both our hands. 'Now, what are a Blackhart and an agent from the SDI doing at what appears to be an utterly normal crime scene?'

'We are investigating other children who've disappeared from this estate,' Dante says, edging us away from PC Osborne and his eager expression. 'We heard another little girl's been taken and so we came straight over.'

'When you say "investigating", are you implying that there's something supernatural going on here?'

'We think so,' I reply, watching the constable ushering other interested people back. 'We need to get inside the flat, to look around. I think we know what to look for.'

Detective Shen's dark eyes rest on my face for a few seconds. 'I'm not sure how I feel about this,' she says. 'You're too young to be part of any kind of investigation. And you?' She nods at Dante. 'What's going on at the SDI that they're sending out people who look like they've just finished college? Don't you have a senior agent?'

Dante shifts uncomfortably under the barrage of questions. 'I can give you my senior officer's details, detective. I'm sure he'll be able to explain his reasoning to you as to why I'm out here "by myself".'

I'm surprised by his tone but keep my expression neutral and interested. My mind is racing. If Detective Shen knows Jamie (and she clearly does), it makes me wonder how many cops know about the Blackharts and what we do. They obviously know about the Spook Squad and even have their own nickname for them – the Ghost-something. The thought makes me feel a bit relieved but I'm not sure what to make of Shen. Is she a believer? Does she know monsters are real and that some might be only occasionally human?

'I think that might be a good idea.' Her smile is cutting as she turns to look over her shoulder. 'We can't have just anyone running around our crime scene.'

Dante takes his business card out and writes his senior officer's information on the back. Shen takes it from him and immediately dials the number, walking away from us so that she can speak privately.

'I like her,' I tell Dante. 'She's badass.'

'She certainly has a presence.' He hunches his shoulders, the same way he did earlier this morning, and I realize he's not wearing a warm coat, just his leather jacket and a T-shirt underneath. There's not much to the leather jacket, no matter how well it's cut to fit his lean frame.

'You should invest in a coat,' I tell him, sounding like a mum. 'It's this new thing that keeps you from shivering to death.'

'I'm not shivering. I'm shaking with anticipation.' He grins. 'Besides, real men don't wear coats. Just look at Aiden.'

I sigh. 'Aiden is dumb. He's also a werewolf and he's never ever cold.'

'So I've spoken to your Captain Francis and he's said to let you in and make sure you get what you need.' Shen doesn't look too happy as she walks back towards us. 'He said he'd clear it with my CO, so, congratulations little Spook: you get to play with the big boys now.'

I feel an unexpected flare of anger from Dante at her words and take a surprised sidestep away from the almost visible electricity that's just come from him. He seems oblivious to it and watches Shen carefully, his expression the unfriendliest I've ever seen it.

'Thank you.' His smile is as cutting as her tone and as falsely grateful. 'For your professionalism, Detective Shen.'

She lets the sarcasm flow over her and jerks her chin at us, a silent invitation to follow. She brushes past Osborne, who looks like a kicked puppy in her wake. I offer him a shrug in apology and hurry to keep up with both Shen and Dante, wondering what exactly it is that I'm missing here and why Dante's acting like a brat. If it's because she referred to him in the diminutive and called him young, he has to know that he does the same thing to me, mentioning it practically every time we meet up. Fair is fair.

She leads us into the second building and up four flights of a graffitied stairs. There are police everywhere, stationed up the stairwell, blocking exits. Shen pushes open the door to the fourth floor and holds up a calming hand as an officer rounds on us, getting ready to ask us our business.

'They're with me,' she says and the young woman steps aside to let us pass.

The layout here is different to the block we visited where Adam and Scott lived. The external walkway is long and narrow, with the flats on one side and a lowish wall looking out over the estate on the other. This is topped with high railings to prevent people from falling down or being pushed off. There are too many people standing around, watching the uniformed officers, who in turn are watching the forensic investigation unit check the flat over.

'This looks like they're taking it seriously,' I mutter to

Dante. 'There already seems to be more action here than at any of the other disappearances.'

He nods. 'I wonder why?'

Shen halts at the open doorway to the flat and passes back cloth booties, gloves and facemasks for us to put on. 'Don't touch anything, don't step on anything,' she says, watching us over her mask. 'If I find out you've somehow interfered with what we're doing here, I will make sure you're never allowed on any crime scene in the future. Clear?'

'Crystal.'

I have trouble with my booties as my shoes are too bulky. Dante sighs dramatically and goes down on one knee to help me before I fall over on my face. I steady myself by gripping his shoulder and when I look up I see Chem. He's standing with a group of teenagers in the doorway of the adjoining flat.

He widens his eyes at me and I shrug. The group that's with him is of a mixture of ages and most look ready to head off to school. I think I recognize some from the other night. Yes, the boy with the yellow eyes is there and he leans in to say something to Chem. Chem taps his watch, flashing me ten fingers, then pointing downstairs.

If my deductions are correct, he wants us to meet him downstairs at ten. I nod and turn back as Dante straightens.

'There, you're sorted.'

'Thanks. Next time I'll wear boots with less tread on them.'

I turn to follow Shen into the flat and walk straight into a wall. I bounce back, letting out a yelp of shock and stumble into Dante, who manages to not trample me.

'What the hell?'

'I don't know what happened,' I reply and walk up to the open doorway where Shen's standing, her expression annoyed. I put my hand forward tentatively and suck in my breath when it makes contact with a clear yet solid wall. I slap the invisible barrier and it makes a soft *zing* noise that sparks against my fingertips. 'It's warded,' I say to Dante. 'Someone warded the flat against me.'

'That's ridiculous.' He moves past me into the flat unhindered. 'Why can I get through if you can't?'

'I don't know.'

'Is there a problem here?' Shen asks, her voice almost bored.

'I can't get into the flat,' I say. 'Look.' I press myself flat against the surface and it's like pressing up against a panel of clear glass. I can see the interior of the flat without a problem and she can obviously see me. 'See?'

'Are you pulling some kind of weird mime crap, Blackhart?'

I roll my eyes at her. 'Seriously?'

Dante exits the flat and frowns at me. 'Can you tell what it is that's stopping you?'

'No clue. It could be a spell reacting to me personally, to my magic. Who knows?' I dig into my bag and hand him the camera. 'Your mission, if you choose to accept it, is to take as many photos of the inside of the flat as you can.'

He takes the small compact digital camera and turns it on, checks the screen and turns it off again.

'Okay, I'll see what I can do.'

'Pay particular attention to anything that's out of place or unusual.' I beckon him closer. 'Just, you've got something on your face.' I lick my thumb and reach up to wipe something from the corner of his eye but he leans back in surprise.

'What are you doing?' His voice sounds breathless and panicked and I stare at him.

'I can't kiss your face, idiot,' I grind out in annoyance. 'Stand still. Let's see if this will work.'

He realizes what I'm doing but it doesn't stop him from sighing in a long-suffering way. He leans closer and I rub my damp finger over both his eyes and as I do, I feed a bit of my magic into my intent to let him See.

'If you two lovebirds are quite finished,' Shen interrupts. 'I've got a job to do here.'

Dante opens his eyes slowly, languidly and gives me a sexy smile that feels far more intimate than it should. As he brushes past me without a word the weird frisson of electricity sparks off him again and I step back, an unexpected wave of dizziness passing over me.

The policewoman standing a few paces away, still keeping an eye on Chem and his group, gives me a brief smile.

'Detective Shen is a bit abrupt, but she's a great cop.'

'My uncle knows her,' I blurt, walking up to her. 'I don't think she likes me.'

'She's like that with everyone she doesn't know.' Her name badge reads S. Peters. 'Your friend, who is he?'

'He's with the SDI,' I say and watch the lively interest in her large blue eyes wane. 'Why do you ask?'

'Nothing, just thought he might be.' She clears her throat. 'Far too pretty to be a cop.'

I laugh and she relaxes a bit. The group behind her mutter among themselves as they notice her scrutiny wavering. Chem quietly slips between them and ducks back down the passage to the doorway.

'He has a certain charm,' I admit. 'Do you need anything? I can do a run for some coffee or something?'

She shakes her head before replying. 'I'm good, thanks. I only just got here.'

Before I head downstairs, I look over my shoulder and see Dante walking down the passage in the flat, taking photos as he goes. He's talking to Shen and I can't hear what they're saying but it doesn't look as if they're planning to be BFFs any time soon.

Chapter Thirty-One

'Yo.'

The parking garage is practically empty of cars, except for a white Corolla on bricks. It looks as if it's hoping to be scrapped and turned into something pretty and not covered in gang graffiti. Chem's hunkered down against one wall, tying his shoelace as he gestures me over.

'Did you find anything out?' he asks me as I walk across to him. 'About Marv's little sister, I mean?'

My face registers my surprise and he continues. 'Yeah, Marv called my house this morning, and he was crying and screaming, saying his little sister got taken last night. We've been trying to find out the whole morning what's going on, but none of us could get near the flat with all the cops hanging about.'

'Oh, Chem, I am so sorry.'

His look is one of wry disbelief. 'You said you'd stop this from happening again.'

'I'm finding out as much as I can, Chem. It's not easy.'

'Riiiight.'

'Listen.' I draw a deep breath. 'Dante's in there right now, checking things out. We're going to find Marv's little sister. What's her name?'

'Tia.'

'How old is Tia?'

'She's five, but she's got a mouth on her. That's how they knew, right? Tia screamed the flat down when that thing came for her.'

'How did he take her, do you know?'

'The guy came through the window. Then they left out of the front door.'

'Shit. How is that possible?' I start pacing. 'I bet you the CCTV cameras in the block don't show anything again. Do you know if anyone heard or saw anything?'

'Not that anyone is saying.' He scrubs his face. 'But Marv swore he saw the guy. He ran after them, leaving his mum to call the police, and he swore he saw the guy jump down the stairs carrying his baby sister.'

I stop in front of him. 'What do you mean, "jump down the stairs"?'

'The guy got to the top of the stairs and then just jumped down between them, into the gap, straight down to the ground floor. Marv said he could swear the guy was wearing a cloak too.'

'So what do we think now? Batman took Tia?'

A grin twists Chem's features. 'Don't be silly, Batman's not real.' Then. 'Is he?'

'Well, my boy cousins are fond of acting like Batman,' I point out reasonably. 'But no, he's not real.'

'What are you going to do next?' He asks me, stifling a yawn without much luck. 'Sorry, that was rude.'

'Next I'm going to see what Dante finds out – and maybe we could speak to Marv. Do you think he'll be okay to do that?'

'Marv's been researching you and your family,' he says

by way of answer. 'Also that guy Dante. I'm pretty sure he wants to talk to you.'

I try not to let my discomfort show and wonder what exactly there is about me to find online and what searches Marv did. I shuffle my feet, suddenly aware of the chill in the garage.

'Great. Let's go and see what Dante's found.'

We round the corner just as Dante leaves the block, looking pale and unwell. We hurry towards him and I'm just in time to push my shoulder under his, preventing him from tripping over his own feet and falling over.

'Dante, what the hell?' I gasp, shocked by how heavy he is.

'Sorry, I can't . . .' He turns away from me just in time and vomits a stream of bile into the straggly bushes growing up against the wall. He leans a hand against the bricks, his body wracked by shivers. Chem and I move to stand in front of him, doing our best to shield him from the curious gazes of the onlookers. 'Shit, what is this?' he mutters before he vomits more.

'Rough night last night?' Chem asks me and I shrug. 'I was up late doing research – no idea what Dante was doing.'

'Sleeping,' comes his voice, sounding utterly wretched. 'I was sleeping. I don't party during the week.'

'Yeah, could have fooled me,' Chem replies with a smirk. 'You look like shit.'

I turn back to Dante as he straightens. He looks older suddenly, the skin tighter across his high cheekbones and his eyes darker.

'Are you okay?'

'I don't know. I was in the flat taking photos when I

suddenly started shaking and feeling really sick. Detective Shen gave me some water to drink but it didn't help.' He shudders and runs a trembling hand through his hair. Possibly one of the first times I've seen him badly rattled. 'I just had to get away from that flat as fast as I could.'

'Look, why don't you guys come to mine?' Chem says. 'It's just around the corner and my nan will be able to mother you. She'd love that.'

'I don't want to be an inconvenience,' Dante starts but I scowl at him and it shuts him up. I hook my arm through his and with Chem leading the way to the opposite block of flats, we head up to the second floor.

Chem's flat is large but made smaller by all the books and knick-knacks that seem to cover every single horizontal surface.

He shows us into the comfortable living room and Dante sits down with a sigh, fishing the camera out of his pocket. Chem goes off to find his nan and soon she's in the room, a tiny wiry woman who takes one look at Dante and immediately goes into mothering mode. She makes us each a large mug of tea; Dante's is served black with enough honey stirred into it to kill a horse. She makes sure he drinks it up before smiling a tight smile that reveals a great set of shiny teeth.

'You children,' she says, although she looks no older than sixty herself. 'Always running around like there is no tomorrow. Just sit here, relax and drink your tea. It will make you feel better.'

'Do you think whatever spell was placed on the flat affected you too? In the end, I mean,' I ask Dante when she heads out of the room to make him some plain toast. Chem's busy plugging his laptop in so we can look at the pictures Dante took; he looks startled at the overheard question.

'I suppose so,' Dante groans, leaning back against the sofa and pressing a hand against his forehead. 'I feel like death.'

'You look it. What happened?'

'I was fine, following Shen around, and then we get to the main living area and, man, it felt like I got hit by a fist to the head. I actually stumbled into a coffee table and then had her shouting at me too. It wasn't my idea of fun.'

'But you got photos?'

He nods and pushes the camera towards Chem. 'Yes. The lighting wasn't too good in there but I did what I could.'

'Did you See anything?' I ask him, touching my eyes to show him what I meant.

'Nothing that jumped out at me, sorry.' He grimaces and rubs his eyes. 'And I'm seeing double too. It feels weird: like somebody put me on a merry-go-round and spun it really fast.'

Wordlessly, I press the back of my hand against his forehead and gasp when I feel how hot his skin is. I wonder if feeding my magic into him made him sick, and if this was somehow my fault. But he was fine the other night when I did it.

Chem slides the SD card into the laptop and clicks a few things before turning it around so I can look through the photos. The flat wasn't as tidy as Chem's but it held a homely quality I liked. Loads of pictures of little Marv, eventually joined by baby Tia. They were cute-looking kids. Marv's room holds a large computer, with books and clothes strewn around. The parents' room is only a bit larger, with a built-in wardrobe and a small dresser by the window.

There's a framed photo on one wall of Mum and Dad, Marv and Tia. It looks pretty recent. The other wall holds a landscape, a generic picture you'd find in IKEA or somewhere like that.

Tia's room reflects her growing interest in everything. There are a lot of pink toys, but I also see some old beat-up cars, a train set and a box of Lego she must have inherited from Marv at some stage. There are no pictures but there is a large mirror, at least three by four foot. The way Dante has taken the picture shows that the mirror is opposite the window.

'Why are you frowning like that?' Dante asks me, stretching forward so he can see what I'm looking at. 'That's Tia's room.'

'Did you feel anything weird when you were in there?' I ask him.

'No, it was just a little girl's room made strange by her not being there.'

I keep flicking through the photos and eventually come back to the lounge area and feel my heart stutter in my chest when I see the tribal African masks lined up on either side of the front door. I tap the screen.

'This?'

Chem's shuffled closer and looks at them. 'I hate those bloody masks. Marv's dad came back from Nigeria with them last year and they just freak me the hell out. If you go there, you can see them following you around with their empty eye sockets. It's creepy, right?'

Dante and I share a look. 'Did he say why he bought them?' I ask Chem.

'No, he said some dude from this village he visited gave

them to him. Said they'd keep him and his family safe against people with magic.'

'Oh.' I twist my lips into a wry smile. 'Well then, that explains it.'

'You mean it actually worked?' Chem's voice rose lightly and he cleared his throat. 'Seriously?'

'Yep, I couldn't get into the flat.'

Chem's eyebrows shot up in shock. 'Wow. Okay.' He watches me for a second before speaking again. 'Do you think they have something to do with Tia being taken?'

'No, if anything it made taking her harder,' I reply. 'This just proves that there must be two of them working together. One to get into her room, another waiting at the front door to take the child.'

'But how, if this other guy is using magic, does he get into the flat if the masks are stopping it from happening?'

'The masks aren't strong enough to protect the whole flat,' I point out. 'Just the main entrance or exit. So it leaves the other guy free to get in through the window. Or wall. Or whatever.'

'Thank you, Mrs . . .' Dante looks blankly at Chem, realizing we don't know his real name or his grandmother's name. She's just come in, carrying more tea and a plate.

'Just call me Auntie May, boy,' she says with a laugh, putting the plate of toast down next to him. 'This will help settle that stomach of yours. Charlie here can eat a whole loaf of bread if you don't watch him so count yourself lucky there's any bread left to give you.'

Chem twitches when she calls him by his real name and I hide a smile. 'Thanks so much for the tea and toast, Auntie May,' I say. 'We'll be out of your hair in a few minutes.'

'Oh, girl, don't be silly. Stay as long as you like. That

boy needs to rest. Something nasty's got hold of him, riding him like a demon.'

'Pardon?'

'Illness, can't you see?' She pressed a firm hand to Dante's shoulder. 'You get home and into bed, boy. You need to rest.' With a last smile she heads off to her room and we hear the TV go on, followed by the dialogue from the news.

'Yeah, sorry about my grandma. She's a bit weird now and again.'

'I think she's perfect,' I tell him and I mean it. Being around Auntie May makes me miss my own nan so much. I like how bright her eyes are and how they twinkle with mischief. I also like the way she trusts Chem and never once stopped to ask him who we are and what we're doing here. I'm sure she has questions but she's too polite to do so in front of strangers.

'I like her too. Looks like she can kick your butt.'

The wry expression at Dante's comment on Chem's face tells us that she can.

'Back to the pictures,' I say, watching as Dante takes a bite of the toast. 'Did you see anything weird, Dante? Anything?'

'Just those masks.'

'Did you start feeling weird after you saw them?'

'No, it was before. Almost as soon as I walked into the flat.'

'Where are Marv and his mum now?' I ask Chem.

'They took them to the police station. His dad's on his way home now. He works shifts.'

'Did Marv tell you anything else that might be useful?'

Chem thought about it and shook his head. 'No, I mean,

the guy jumped down eight flights of stairs with Tia and there's no sign of him or her. I'd say that's pretty unusual.'

'Where's your toilet?' Dante's question interrupts us. Chem points but Dante's already moving towards the doorway; he slams the door shut behind him.

Chapter Thirty-Two

'I'm okay.'

'You are not okay.'

'Maybe I had a bad pancake this morning.'

'Then why aren't I sick? Or Aiden or Kyle?'

'Maybe it was only my pancake.'

'Shut up and lie down.'

I watch him as he tries to get comfortable in the seat. About ten minutes into our drive he starts shivering. I turn the heating on high but it doesn't seem to help. I can hear his teeth clattering as fever grips him.

The sky's grey and overcast and the nip in the air is a definite thing. Traffic's not too bad and we get back to his flat without any further vomiting incidents, although there are a few times when I think he's going to splatter the interior of the car.

I help him into the house and shut the door behind me. The place is as empty as it was yesterday, with no sign that anyone's been there since I left.

'Which is your room again?' I ask him and he points listlessly towards one of the closed doors. He sways against me and I feel a shudder go through his body. 'Are you going to be sick?'

'No, no. I'm just cold. I don't know what's going on.'

I close my eyes in frustration. Just my luck to get saddled with him now that he's going through some kind of flu episode. I push open the door to his room and barely register the huge bed or any of the ruggedly attractive wooden furniture. It's sure bigger than my tiny room.

'Get changed,' I tell him. 'I'll see if I can find any cold and flu medicine.'

'There should be something in the kitchen cupboards, somewhere.' He sits heavily on the bed and pulls off a shoe, letting it drop to the floor with a clunk. 'I can't remember the last time I ever felt this shit.'

'You look it,' I assure him as I walk away. I dump my bag on the table and rummage around the cupboards until I find a medical kit, stocked with all kinds of painkillers and bandages and disinfectant. The kit is even slightly better stocked than the one at home.

I make myself a cup of coffee and stir granules for Dante's Lemsip into the hot water, watching them dissolve. There's a loud *thunk* from Dante's room and a muttered curse followed by another *thunk* again.

I grab his mug and hurry to the room but knock before I open the door, keeping my eyes on the floor. 'Okay for me to come in?' Translation: *Are you naked?*

'Yes, can you help me, please?'

I push into the room to be met by Dante struggling to get up off the floor. He's dressed in a pair of tracksuit bottoms and has a long-sleeved T-shirt gripped in his hand.

'What happened?' I put the mug down and walk over to help him.

'I walked into the bloody wall,' he mutters, taking his

hand away from his face. A bright red line marks his eyebrow and cheek. 'Misjudged the width of the door.'

'And so what? You decided to walk through the wall instead?'

'Something like that.'

My hand makes contact with the smooth skin across the contours of his abs and my pulse climbs as I steady him with my other hand as he sways crazily.

'You often pretend to pass out when you've got a girl in your room?' I ask him, grasping desperately for something to say because really, I am not comfortable being this close to half-naked Dante. He feels as if he's on fire but it's a dry burning fire, with no slick sweatiness to his skin at all. His elaborate tribal tattoo with its wicked edges and weird whorls runs from mid bicep to the curve of his shoulder and then onto his shoulder blade. The intricate pattern draws my gaze and, without realizing it, I run a tentative finger across one of the coils, following its contour, before dropping my hand as if I've been stung. The tattoo felt weird under my touch, as if it had moved; I suppress a shiver of my own.

'You're funny,' he says, shuddering under my touch as I pull him to the side and flip the duvet back. 'My skin is so sensitive, it feels like your hands are on fire.'

'Uhm, no.' I gulp. 'They're not, I promise. Sit down. Give me your shirt.' I take it out of his grip and, making sure I've got it the right way round, I pull it over his head. 'There, put your arms through.' I hover over him and watch him struggle but don't offer to help further, suppressing the memory of how the tattoo felt under my touch. When he eventually drops his arms with a heavy sigh I hand him the mug of Lemsip. 'Here, drink this. Try to keep it down.'

The mug rattles against his teeth and he spills some but he manages to drink most of it, while pulling a face and moaning pathetically.

'That stuff is disgusting. I'd rather be sick.'

'Stop being a baby, and drink it.' I push the proffered mug back. 'Drink it all.'

'So bossy,' he mutters under his breath, taking giant gulps of the stuff before handing me the mug. 'Done.'

'Now lie down. Get some rest.' I push him back against the pillow and drag the duvet over him. 'Sleep.'

I'm halfway to the door when he calls my name and I turn back to look at him. He looks utterly feeble wrapped in his duvet, and I can see him shaking beneath it.

'I know it's unfair, but can you stay?'

I hesitate for a few seconds but then remember the files in the back of his car with my name and those of my family and nod. 'I'll stay till this evening. Your fever should break soon.'

The smile he gives me is sweet. 'Thanks, Kit. I promise to look after you when you get whatever this is.'

'Yeah, not likely,' I tell him, pulling the door shut, but his voice stops me.

'No, don't close the door. It makes me feel closed in. I can't breathe.'

'I'll catch the monsters in your closet,' I tell him, only partly joking. His dry chuckle follows me out of the room as I make my way back to the kitchen.

I pull out my notebook and the files that I have with me and start writing, listing the information gathered so far and trying to link things. I work distractedly for about an hour before getting up to check on Dante. He's asleep on his side but his bedding's all twisted around him. I resist the urge to walk in and readjust the duvet so that it covers him better.

Instead I grab the keys on the entrance hall table and run out to his car. The bound files are where I left them this morning and I carry them back into the flat, locking the door behind me.

Dante's still sleeping, making moaning noises under his breath, twitching uneasily in the grip of whatever dream's got hold of him.

I get the camera out of my bag and hastily take photos of my parents' files, doing my best not to pay attention to them. I don't want to get caught looking through them by anyone and I don't know when Dante's housemates are due back.

I thank my lucky stars that Kyle put a 4Gb memory card in the camera and make sure I take pictures of every single page. It takes about twenty minutes to do both files and I shuffle them back into order, bind them up with their piece of ribbon and take them back out to the car. I replace them in the boot and half-cover them with other bits of debris that I found there.

Back in the house I check on Dante again. This time his duvet's been kicked off completely and he's curled into a tight ball in the middle of the bed, shivering. I lift the duvet off the floor and pull it over him. He makes a strange sound in the back of his throat that almost sounds like a soft growl.

Without thinking, I reach out and brush back the dark curls that cling damply to his forehead and I let my hand rest there for a second or two, registering that he feels hotter than before. My skin tingles where it touches him and I pull back, wondering exactly what's wrong with him and why it came on so quickly and unexpectedly.

My thoughts circle my darkest memory, which, try as I might, keeps surfacing.

It was after my nan had been killed and Jamie had taken me to avenge her death on the Unseelie knight and his redcap cronies. My magic, something I'd not known was part of me, rose to the surface that awful night while I ripped the Unseelie knight and his creatures apart, as the hill outside our village tumbled down on top of them. I remember relishing the wild power as it ran rampant through me, the wind whipping up a storm above us, uprooting trees and damaging homes and cars. But mostly I remember the sound of the knight screaming as he died at my feet.

Afterwards, Jamie carried me away. I was too weak to stand and delirious with a fever that did not abate for almost a week. When I came to, I'd become the only Blackhart in several generations who could wield actual magic. It's been a riot ever since.

With all of this too fresh in my mind I tiptoe out of Dante's room and ring my uncle Jamie's number. As he answers I pull out a chair at the dining-room table and sit down.

'Kit, what's up, kiddo? Having fun?'

'Not so much, Jamie. Can I ask you something?'

'Sure. Just give me a second.' Something metallic screeches and there's a loud bang, followed by another one. 'I was just fiddling around with the Jeep. What's going on?'

'Do you remember when I got so sick, when my magic, uh, you know?' How do I put this? When my magic manifested? When I went psychotic and killed that Sidhe warrior and all his drunken goblin pals?

'When you came into your powers, yes,' Jamie says with a smile in his voice. 'What do you want to know?'

'How long was I sick for? What were my symptoms?'

'You ran a high fever for a couple of days. Not even Mrs Evans could get it to go down. The local doctor wanted to send you to hospital but, before we could, the fever broke. You were really sick, throwing up this clear bile. Pretty gross, actually.'

'Oh great, thanks.' Always good to know you handled yourself really well during a debilitating illness.

'Why do you ask? Kit . . . ?'

'It's just, how do you check if someone is a Fae, Jamie? If you're not sure in the first place?'

'I did it to you. Checking, I mean.' He sounds very serious. 'We weren't sure what was going on with you. Your nan never let any of us near you. So when we returned from the hospital so I could take out that Unseelie knight, and you ripped those redcaps apart all by yourself with your magic . . . Well . . .' He laughs a rueful laugh. 'I was scared senseless. I thought we'd somehow screwed up. That you were a full-blooded Fae who'd been kidnapped by Mirabelle. But afterwards, while you were so sick, Letitia showed us the journals our many times great aunt Helena had written. We couldn't believe you had magic, but I still had to check . . . It was up to me, as the one who brought you to the Manor.'

My pulse thunders at his words. 'Jamie? What did you do?'

'I cut your left arm above your elbow with an iron blade to see if you had any kind of reaction to the iron.'

My mouth opens but no sound comes out. I turn my arm and look at the thin scar there.

'I can't believe it.'

'I'm sorry, Kit. It had to be done. We had to make sure you weren't one of them.'

'What if I had been, Jamie? What then?'

'I don't know. Andrew would have had to make the call. We would probably have sent you to the Otherwhere. Have someone look after you.'

'Just like that?'

'Yes.' His voice is low and I like to think he sounds ashamed. 'The integrity of the Blackharts as a family and organization can't be called into doubt, Kit. Not ever, not when we're all walking such a very fine line between both worlds.'

I stare at my notes and feel suddenly very lost and alone.

'If you have something on you that's iron, Kit, all you have to do is use iron. It doesn't have to break the skin. It will react immediately. You won't miss it. They'll act as if they've just been burned. You'll know you're dealing with a Fae. Possibly a changeling.'

'Changeling? What the hell, Jamie?' My own voice has dropped and is a low whisper.

'Kit, you're not listening to me.'

'I am. But a changeling, Jamie? I mean, that's not even permitted, it's been illegal for the past one hundred years! And if he is a changeling, it's not his fault if his parents decided to dump him in the Frontier.'

'I know, Kit. But the Frontier is not a good place for them – not if they have any kind of magical ability and it's wild. You don't know what this person is or what he's capable of. He won't even know what he is if he's unaware of his heritage.'

I close my eyes and think furiously. He's not prying about

who I'm talking about either and I'm more than grateful to him for it. Neither is he asking further prying questions, trusting me to figure this out and it's flattering to see he thinks I've got a handle on whatever minor crisis it is that I'm facing. I take a deep breath before I speak again.

'What if he doesn't react to the iron?' I ask Jamie. 'What then? What, if like me, he has magical abilities? What then?'

'Then you take him home, and you call Marc for backup. If this person has real magic then we deal with it and we help him if we can. He might not even make it through alive.'

Fear clutches at me. 'What do you mean?'

'He could die, Kit. If the magic burns through him and he can't get a grip on it, he could die.'

Chapter Thirty-Three

The iron nail I have tucked in a side pocket of my messenger bag isn't very big because it doesn't have to be. It's maybe as long as my little finger. I dig it out and walk into Dante's room, holding it flush against my arm and carrying a glass of water in the other. It's ridiculous. I feel as if I'm pretending to be van Helsing trying to slay Dracula with a splinter.

'Kit?' Dante opens heavy eyes and peers at me. 'How did you get here?' He rolls his head and looks around. 'Why am I in bed?'

'You're not doing well,' I tell him. 'Don't you remember getting sick earlier today?' When he nods after a few moments, looking confused, I sigh in relief. 'Can you sit up a bit and drink some water?'

He hefts himself up on one arm but it buckles beneath him and he falls back against the pillow, breathing as if he's just run a mile.

'I feel terrible,' he tells me. His eyes are huge and feverish and there's a flush along his cheeks that makes it look as if he got a bit of sun. 'I can't stop shaking.'

I sit down on the edge of the bed. 'Let me help you.' I grab his arm and pull him forward, towards me, tucking my arm around his waist and steadying him. The iron nail slides along my palm and I press the point up against his skin beneath his shirt. At the touch of the iron he lets out a yelp of pain and grabs hold of my hand and forces it into view.

'What is that? What have you done?'

We both look down at the offending iron nail lying in the palm of my hand. Dante's gaze is confused and worried as he stares back at me.

'What did you do?' There's pain in his eyes, genuine pain but also an expression that makes me feel like I've somehow broken his trust. 'Kit? What is that?'

'It's iron,' I tell him. My voice sounds wrong even to me. 'You're allergic to iron, because you're not human.'

He twists so he can look at his back but grunts when he can't see anything. 'It's still burning. Bloody hell, it hurts.'

Guilt plucks at me and I kneel next to him on the bed, to get a good look at the mark I left on his skin. It's not big but it is bright red, resembling the sort of welt you'd get from touching a pan straight from the oven.

He's shivering but giving off so much heat as I touch his skin that the contact is uncomfortable. I still have the water in my hand and I dip my fingers into the glass and drip water onto the red welt. His breath hisses out but he relaxes marginally before he starts shivering again.

We sit like this for a few seconds, me leaning against him, Dante just shivering and trying to make sense of what I said. When he speaks, his voice is low and raw. 'What does it mean?'

'I think you're a changeling, Dante.' I'm surprised that my voice almost sounds normal and I sit back, moving away from him a little. He was throwing off a lot of heat. There's a hum in the room that I can't place and I'm reminded of

Thorn's magic, how I could feel it thrumming whenever he used it near me.

'That doesn't—' Dante falls back against his pillow. 'I don't understand. How can that be true?' He blinks up at me with fever-bright eyes. 'Kit, I don't think that's right. It can't be true. Can it? I don't understand this.' He rubs a shaking hand over his face. 'My head is pounding. I think I'm dying.'

'You are not dying.' The catch in my voice belies the flippant tone I was going for. 'Look, you're going through something. I think being exposed to my magic has somehow brought your own magic out, maybe broken whatever glamour you had cast over you.' I stand. 'I'm sorry, but I have to tell my family. We need to decide what we're going to do with you.'

'No, Kit . . .' He rolls towards me and grabs my hand, pulling me down towards him so I collapse on my knees next to the bed. 'Please, no. Just stay here, with me. I don't understand what's going on. Let me get through this, then we can talk to your family.'

'I must go,' I whisper, my mind shrinking from the weight of near betrayal. 'I have to tell them.'

'Stay,' he pleads, his voice ragged and not just a tiny bit afraid. 'I can't do this alone.'

I look at him and all I can hear is Jamie's warning voice and my uncle Andrew telling me to keep a level logical mind. But the boy I see before me doesn't look devious or a danger to me or anyone else. Instead I see someone who is scared and confused and, so help me, I know exactly how he feels.

I sit up with a start and groan as all my aches and pains make themselves known. The blow to my ribs from this morning has me hitching my breath in pain and I press my hand beneath my shirt. Yes, it still hurts. I lean forward a bit and the soreness eases slightly. I'm in the process of getting up from the floor where I'd fallen asleep, sitting upright against the bed, when there's movement behind me. I turn to look at Dante, who seems to be fighting demons in his fever dreams. He's moving restlessly beneath the duvet and I can still feel the heat emanating from him, even from where I am on the floor.

A thought wanders into my head and I only have to think it and my magic surfaces. I hold my hand out just above his skin and watch for the answering ebb and flow of his aura. It doesn't take me long to see it. The scarlet lines of energy coursing through him are struck with gold flecks and highlights of a rich vibrant green. My hand remains steady as I watch and see my own magic, a far more muted and controlled red, sink into his energies. I'm carried away briefly by the wild elation that thunders through him. I feel it beckoning me onwards, luring me towards something I'm not sure I want to discover.

Reluctantly, I pull my magic back and stand up, stretching my aching back. The alarm clock on the little side table reads 6 p.m. I need to check in with Kyle and get home.

I wonder if any of Dante's housemates have come home, but from the silence in the house I suspect not. Carefully, so as not to wake him, I walk out of the room and check on the other two rooms down the hallway.

Both rooms are empty, looking like barracks with bare beds, bedding neatly folded at the bottom. I check the wardrobes and there are no clothes or personal items at all. Neither of the two en suites holds any personal toiletries, apart from clean towels and unopened toothpaste and tooth-brushes.

I wander back into the kitchen and make myself some coffee, toying with my phone. Why did he lie and say there were other young agents living here? Maybe there have been others here and they are out on assignment. No, I decide. Those rooms feel as if they've been empty for a long time, not just a few days. This makes me wonder about the SDI. Is he even part of them? But then there are the files in the car, his badge, the business cards. So no, the SDI connection must be real . . .

I call Kyle but there's no answer. I leave a message for him to call me.

In the kitchen I push all thoughts aside apart from food ones and check the fridge and cupboards. Here, I find the makings for a mushroom risotto, possibly the only thing I'm good at making and actually quite like eating.

While I'm stirring the risotto, I lean against the counter and read over my notes, wondering how the masks in little Tia's house blocked me from entering but let Dante in – especially if they were set up to react to magic.

There's so much about this whole job that I don't know. Now with the added complication of Dante being a change-ling creature, it makes me want to cry. I wonder about phoning Jamie to tell him that he reacted to the iron and that we've got a definite situation on our hands. I know he'll get in touch with Zane, the Seelie King's chamberlain and possibly speak to Melusine from the Unseelie Court. He'll want to question them about the possibility of a change-ling child being left in the Frontier as a baby, to be raised by humans – something I thought just couldn't happen these days. But I'm reluctant to talk to Jamie because I know what his advice will be: send Dante into the Otherwhere. He is in our world without permission and a stranger to the magic waking within him. Dante could turn out to be anything and incapable of controlling himself or his magic. But surely changelings shouldn't exist – not any more, that is.

I know from some of the lore books I've read that changelings were often swapped for human children in years gone by, especially in the nineteenth century before the treaties between human and Fae. Sometimes it would happen out of spite, when a faerie decided it liked the look of a human child. Or if a child had been born with a specific gift the Fae thought valuable, they'd take it and leave one of their own. Things never ended well for the Fae child. The human parents would struggle to bring up the changeling left in the place of their own and it has led to a host of lore about witches and possession. All nasty stuff that the Blackhart family had to deal with, to prevent innocent people from being murdered and killed.

But I'm talking at least a hundred or more years ago. The treaties of goodwill, trade and mutual agreement that Fae and humans renew each year are in place to prevent things like this from happening in the 'modern' age. Although, occasionally, it obviously does. Case in point: Dante.

I want to believe that Dante reacted to the iron because it was cold, but the ugly welt it burned into his skin makes it clear that he is highly allergic to the stuff.

The folklore and mythology app that Kyle's been working on for me only functions occasionally, given my temperamental phone. But after a few seconds of prodding, it reluctantly opens and I type in 'changeling'. It comes up with a lot of facts that I know anyway, except for one thing that I've never done in all my time as a Blackhart. I take a breath and square my shoulders. He reacted to the iron, so I'm not sure how he'll react to this.

I turn the stove off and check my risotto, which tastes delicious. Dante's room is now dark and I feel for a light switch next to the bed where I remember seeing a small lamp. Dante's hand grips mine in the dark and I let out a gasp.

'No,' he rasps. 'Don't. I can see you clearly.'

At his touch my magic flares into existence, and I turn my gaze on him where he's sitting up in the middle of the bed, the duvet pushed to one side. He pulses a rich vibrant red in my mind's eye and the air feels thick with unspent magic. I also realize that, instead of being fusty like a sick room, the room smells of wide open spaces, mountains and fresh air.

'What's going on, Kit?' he asks me, his voice ragged and low. 'I can feel *everything*.'

'Your magic is waking up,' I tell him, keeping my own tone low and calm. 'I think you're Fae, Dante.'

'That's not possible.'

He's not let go of my arm yet and I make an impatient gesture, breaking the hold. I do not like being pawed by anyone.

'Can I ask you to do me a favour, Dante?'

'If I can. I feel very weird right now, Kit.' My heart breaks at how tired he sounds.

'I need you to close your eyes until I tell you to open them, then tell me what you can see.'

'Okay.'

He shuts his eyes and I straighten. I shrug off my outer

long-sleeved T-shirt and put it back on, inside out. I feel a weird sensation in the nape of my neck that alerts me to the tiny bit of glamour I've just created by doing this. I keep my own magic steady so that I don't influence how he sees me. I step away from the bed as silently as I can, and go and stand on the far side of the room.

'Open your eyes.'

'I can't see you.' His hands drift up to his eyes in surprise. 'What have you done?'

'Look where my voice is.'

My breath catches for a second when I hear him shift on the bed.

'I can't see you. I can hear you breathing, but I can't see you.'

He faces in my general direction and I can see his eyes scanning the wardrobe and windows and curtains. I do monkey faces at him and squint my eyes but he just shakes his head, looking around the room in confusion.

'Nope, you're invisible to me.'

I creep forward, as quietly as possible, and reach out to touch his shoulder. He jerks back in surprise and gives a startled shake of his head.

'Cut it out. Stop whatever you're doing.' There's a note of panic in his voice. 'Kit?'

I make sure I stand right in front of him as I take my outer top off.

For a long silent moment he stares at me blankly and I shift uncomfortably, suddenly worried that the glamour's not dissipated. 'Can you see me now?'

'What? How did you do that?' He clears his throat and touches me with his fingertips only, as if to make sure I'm real, before dropping his hand.

'An old wives' tale and something I never thought would work. I turned the outer layer of my clothing inside out and put it back on again. It is said to make you invisible to the Fae.'

I let that sink in as I walk around the bed and turn on the bedside light. There is no way the poleaxed expression on Dante's face can be an act. He looks so confused and lost that I'm tempted to try and hug him. But I hold back because I don't know what he is and I don't know if physical contact with me, as egotistical as that sounds, will help him manifest whatever he is becoming faster.

'Now what?' he asks; his voice is flat and miserable. 'You talk to your family and you send me into the Otherwhere?'

He doesn't say 'to meet my fate' but it's implied and I have to look away.

'No. I don't know.' I rub my face and worry at my hair. 'Shit. I don't know. This is all messed up.'

'Why am I this sick?' Dante asks, as he reaches for the glass of water I left there earlier. 'Am I dying?'

'No . . . I don't think so. Does it really feel like you're dying?'

He grimaces. 'How would I know? I just feel weak, dizzy, nauseous and shaky and feverish.'

'Maybe you've just got a cold.'

'Kit. You've done two tests to prove that I'm Fae. You basically turned invisible where before I could see you perfectly fine. In the dark, without using night-vision goggles.' His tone is wry and I like that he's being both scared and strangely pragmatic about this.

I sink down onto my haunches and peer at him.

'We need to talk to your foster parents.'

'No. This is not something they know about.'

'Dante, we have to find out how you came to live with them. How old were you?'

'I remember my life before I went to live there, Kit. There's nothing weird about how I grew up. I was put into an orphanage as a baby. Then foster care. That's it.'

'But how? How did you come to be in the orphanage?'

Dante drops back against his pillows and pushes his hair off his face, pressing the heels of both hands into his eyes. The glass of water hovers in the air next to him, where he let go of it. He doesn't seem to realize what he's done. I take it without comment and put it back on the bedside table.

'I was left. On the steps of a monastery.'

I open my mouth but close it again. I've never heard of that happening, outside of books and movies, so excuse me as I stare at him in disbelief.

'Where?' I sit down on the carpet and watch him narrowly. 'Where was the monastery?'

'Scotland.'

'Near the Cairngorms?'

He raises his head to stare at me. 'How did you know?'

I wave my hand. 'Weird stuff seems to happen in the Cairngorms. Did whoever left you leave you with anything? A note, a blanket, anything?'

A shiver visibly runs down his spine and he hitches his duvet over his shoulders again, wrapping it around him like a cloak.

'Yes. They left a ring.'

Chapter Thirty-Four

Heart racing, I lift the small velvet box from Dante's drawer and carry it back to the bed.

'Here.'

I give it to him and he takes it like a drowning man reaching for a helping hand. He opens the small box and stares down into it for so long that I wonder if he's fallen asleep.

'It's different now,' he says, sounding bemused. 'Bigger than I remember it being.'

I close my eyes at this, my fingers playing with the simple slender gold band around the ring finger on my right hand. I remember putting it on that first time, how the band resized itself to fit my finger. How complete I felt wearing it.

'May I see it?'

A reluctant expression moves across his face but then he nods. I sit on the side of the bed and accept the box from Dante. He shifts forward so we're both sitting on the edge of the mattress. He brings with him a blast of heat and wild magic that hums uncomfortably against me. I don't shift away, not yet.

The band is gold but not engraved like mine. Instead I stare into the moonstone face of a lion, with two very bright rubies for eyes. The workmanship is incredible but that's not what makes my breath stop in my throat. I stare down at the ring and remember, not so long ago, when I sat in front of a scrying mirror and it spoke to me of a man wearing a moonstone ring carved in the shape of a lion's head. The king's brother Eadric, the usurper who tried to take over the High King of Alba's throne, wore a ring similar to this.

I look from the ring to Dante and find him watching me closely.

'You know it?' he asks me and his tone is urgent. 'You know whose emblem this is? Whose ring?'

He's not even stopped speaking yet and I'm already shaking my head. 'No, I don't know for sure, but I've *heard* this ring described to me. Or one similar, at least.'

'Who?'

'It belonged to Eadric of Alba.' I draw in a deep breath and hand the ring box back to him.

'Eadric of Alba.' He rolls the words around his tongue and a shudder passes through him and he hunches deeper into his duvet. 'Is that the High King's . . . brother?' Realization dawns on his face. 'Are you saying I'm related to a traitor to the High King of Alba?'

His agitation makes me uncomfortable and I stand and move towards the doorway.

'I don't know, Dante. I don't know what the ring means. It could be a clever replica. I've never seen it myself so I don't actually know.' I rub my eyes. 'Look, I'm hungry. I've got some food ready. I know you're not well yet but have a shower, get dressed and come and eat something.'

I leave him sitting in a pool of light in the middle of his

bed with the duvet around him, clasping the ring box, looking as if he's been punched in the head.

I'm fiddling with my phone, twirling it between my fingers, wondering what to do, when Dante walks into the kitchen. He's wearing a clean pair of tracksuit bottoms, warm socks and a soft cotton long-sleeved T-shirt. His hair glistens wetly from his shower and there's a brightness to his eyes that I'm not sure is from the fever.

'How're you feeling?' I ask him. I turn to the risotto and serve up two large portions.

'High, I feel high and I can't stop shivering.' He sits down at the small breakfast table and he pulls on a soft grey hoodie. 'Thanks for staying, Kit. It means a lot to me that you did. You're a good friend.'

I smile bleakly and don't admit that I have been arguing with myself for hours about walking to the nearest Tube station and riding the underground home, ringing Jamie and telling him everything. Then crawling into bed and pretending I know nothing of a young changeling called Dante.

'Tell me that after you've had my risotto,' I quip, but my smile feels forced.

He pretends not to notice and falls on his plate of food with gusto. He makes appreciative noises and it makes me laugh when he has to sit back halfway through and mop his brow.

'This is very good.'

'My nan taught me to make it.'

'You miss her.' It wasn't a question, it was a statement. A small silence falls for a few moments before Dante clears his throat. 'My foster parents took me in because they believed everyone should have a family. My mum grew up in a family that fostered children and when doctors told her she couldn't have her own, they decided to foster. My dad's parents were quite old when they had him and he lost them when he was still a teenager. He had a reputation for being wild but then he joined up and the army gave him the stability he needed. When they discovered they couldn't have kids of their own, they adopted me. My baby sister was a miracle when she came along a few years later, but then she was taken and then found dead.' He drew a ragged breath and his voice is now so soft I have to strain to hear it. 'It broke them and me, Kit. My mum still isn't over it and I know my dad worries about her all the time, thinking that she'll do something stupid. It's really hard, coming to grips with something like that. A lot of anger, a lot of hate. Things said and done that can't be taken back. And now this? For them to know *this* about me? It would send my mother into an institution. I can't do this to them. They must never know.'

I watch him carefully, touched by his trust in me and drawn in by his incredibly dark eyes.

'Do you understand what I'm saying, Kit? I don't care who left me here. I have my family. They made me who I am and I would pretty much do anything for them, to keep them safe.'

What can I say to that? How do I even tackle something like this? As much as I admire Dante for being loyal to his foster parents, he has to face the fact that he *isn't human*.

'Why aren't you talking?' he asks, prodding my elbow. 'I don't like it when you're this quiet. I don't think I've ever seen you this quiet. Also, your face is all scrunched up and thinky again. Wait, are you going to punch me?'

'Tempting,' I snap, edging away from his arm. 'I'm trying to eat here, okay? Just let me think for a bit. Eat your food.'

He nods, taking a sip from his glass of water. 'Do you think she knew?' he asks me after a further few mouthfuls of risotto. He rolls his eyes meaningfully, looking into the shadows. 'Her.'

I catch on immediately. Like me, he's reluctant to talk when the shadows are so close. Who knows if Suola has spies nearby who can slip from shadow to shadow and spy on us?

'I don't know. Maybe. Possibly.'

'Wouldn't she have said something?'

'Or this could be a test dreamed up by her to see how the Blackharts react when we realize you are a changeling.'

Dante nods as he eats. 'I'm not really sure. It would imply that she knew who I was all along. Why not just come right out and say it?'

He had a point. But then the Fae are never outright about anything and enjoy the intrigue. I sigh in frustration. 'I'm wondering if we should keep quiet about what's happened,' I say. 'Until we've solved the case. What do you think?'

He doesn't even appear to think about it but just nods his head. 'Yes, I agree. We keep this weirdness quiet and then deal with it when the case is solved.'

'Do you think you'll be able to cope?'

'I've managed thus far, haven't I?' He smiles but his smile isn't very big. 'I'm sure I'll be able to pretend to be human for a little while longer.'

'That's not . . .' I roll my eyes at him. 'You're full of it.'

A shudder passes through him and he grips the table for support.

'Man, that was weird. It felt like the whole building just shook all around me.'

'Finish your food and get back to bed.'

'Yes, miss.'

He dutifully finishes his food but watches me as I push mine around on the plate.

'What are you going to do?'

'I need to get home. And talk to Kyle and see what info he's dug up. He's been looking into other children who have gone missing in the same way these kids have. Then I want to research more about the creatures I found in Aunt Letty's books. Then I'll swing by in the morning and come check up on you.' Which reminds me. 'Dante, why are you the only person living here? I thought you said there were other agents here.'

'Ah, I wondered how long it would take you to spot that.' He sighs, hunching his shoulders. 'I'm the only new agent working for HMDSDI at the moment. They had two other recruits who shared the space with me, but neither did well when they came face to face with a bunch of faeries eating a homeless person. Goblins, you know. Nasty things.'

I curl my lip in distaste. Goblins and redcaps – I really disliked those guys. 'Why did you lie?'

'I didn't want you to feel sorry for me. And my superiors weren't keen to reveal how few of us there were.'

I open my mouth to ask him what he means but then I get it. 'How many are there in the SDI?'

'Five of us, at the moment. Including me. I'm the most junior person.'

Suddenly I understand why Dante's running this case by himself, why he's so new at some things.

'You've not really had much training, have you?'

'I've studied,' he replies defensively. 'We have books. I've been out on a few jobs with the other agents. I've done a few, so I'm not entirely clueless.'

I grin at him. 'I didn't say you were clueless.'

'Your eyes implied.'

'Shut up. Go to bed.'

I hastily clean up the kitchen and load the dishwasher. Stuffing my papers and camera into the bag, I wander into Dante's room. He's propped up against the headboard with two duvets covering him. He holds the ring box in his hands and turns it towards me so I can see the moonstone ring. It gleams impossibly brightly in the soft light of the bedside lamp.

'Do you think it's genuine? I mean, do you think it's the same ring Eadric had?'

'I think it's a similar ring to Eadric's, but I've never seen the real thing so I don't know.'

'Is there a way we can find out?'

I look from him to the box. 'Only way would be to talk to someone in the family.'

'Would that be possible?'

I shrug. 'I'm not sure that's advisable right now.'

He smiles at me but he's shivering so much his teeth click together and he burrows down.

'Thanks for hanging out with me and for not telling anyone about, you know, me.'

I wave my hand.

'I'll call you in the morning. Try not to blow anything up.'

Chapter Thirty-Five

Instead of going home I head to Milton's. Rorke grunts at me from his position at the door and scowls.

'You're early, what's going on?'

'Is Miron here? I need a quick word.'

'If you can get past the twins, you can go up.'

It's not time for the club to be open yet. The staff are all present and in the process of tidying and getting ready for the night as I walk in. There's something very unglamorous about a club when the lights are all on, revealing the sticky floor, the slightly scuffed tables and the ratty chairs. Nothing looks magical at all, not even any of the supernatural creatures doing their chores. It looks a bit sad and I wander past them and return the few nods I get. I spot the DJ on his little stage.

'I love your music,' I call out to him.

He looks up with a smile and edges past his decks.

'Cheers. I've seen you and your friend around. You come here often enough for Philippe to worry when you don't show.' He drops down onto the stage so he can swing his legs off the side.

I smile at him. 'I'm Kit, by the way.'

'I'm Torsten. Really nice to meet you, Kit.' He has a

slight accent, maybe German, maybe French? His smile is friendly as he shakes my hand. His eyes are a vibrant green framed by dark lashes, but I can't decide on his hair colour. It looks red with shocks of gold highlights, as if he spends time in the sun, and I wonder if it's natural or dyed. 'What are you doing here?'

'I'm hoping to find Miron.'

A flash of *something* crosses Torsten's features and he sits back.

'I didn't know you were friends with Miron.'

'Not friends, as such,' I say. 'More like he's a family acquaintance.'

'Ooh, intriguing!' He stands up. 'If you have time before you leave, come back and I'll show you my decks.' He winks at me in an overly exaggerated fashion and laughter bubbles up from me.

'Does that work with all the girls?'

He pretends to be hurt, a hand to his chest. 'I don't know what you mean. It was an honest invite.'

'I'm sure,' I say, turning to walk away but he calls me back.

'No, seriously. I have some new remixes I want to try out. If you have time, before you leave, come by. I'd like to know what you think.'

'We'll see.' I smile at him and walk away towards the staircase where the twins are lounging. Only one of them stands up when I approach.

'Miron's not in,' she says, her gaze sharp.

'Miron is always in,' I reply. 'Ask him if he's got five minutes for me. That's all I ask. Tell him I'm here about Lilith.'

Her twin lifts the weird mobile phone device he carries,

mutters into it, seems to hear something I can't and gives her a nod.

'He says to send her up.'

They do a quick scan to make sure I'm not carrying weapons dangerous enough to hurt Miron. They let me keep the knife because it's a knife and not a *knife*.

Miron is waiting for me in his office. He looks tired, possibly the first actual human frailty I've ever seen on him, and it intrigues me.

'Thank you for seeing me,' I say, meaning it. 'I appreciate that you're busy.'

'You mentioned Lilith?'

'I need to know if you think she can be involved in any of this. I've done more research and the kids going missing feels like it's on a bigger scale than . . .' I move my hand in a circle. 'You know, just an accident. Could it be Lilith or any of her friends, maybe? Someone trying to impress you or her or your bosses?'

He paces to the towering flower arrangement with its slightly too-red blooms and adjusts them until he's happy with it, then turns towards me, shucking the cuffs of his shirt. I guess even demons need their displacement activities.

'Let me explain Lilith. She isn't above being petty and stealing children from humans but she would not do it so haphazardly. She would call a generation of children to be with her across an entire city the size of New York. This? These petty little crimes that you're investigating are as far below her as the Queen of England picking up her own dogs' dirt.' His smile is toothy and a bit hungry and not for the first time I tell myself never to forget that Miron is a fallen angel.

'You could have just said "no", you know.'

His shrug is elegant and his expression weary. 'You would have gone on and on so I had to make sure you understood what I meant. I am a busy man, Kit. Do you have any further questions?'

'What about any of the other Infernal? Would anyone else want to make a name for themselves?'

'Oh, Kit. You are so very human.' His smile is sharp and cutting. I don't turn my back on him, moving as he circles me. 'No, this is not how the Infernal draw attention to themselves. Stealing children is dirty and unpleasant. We look for bigger things, like wars and, if there aren't any, we instigate them.' His eyes slant towards me. 'Happy with my explanation? Did that help?'

'Plenty. Thank you for your time.' I hold myself stiffly as I leave the room, feeling disconcerted and more miserable than before. I've only moved a few steps when I see one of the guards leaning against the wall beside the door. She (he?) pushes away from the wall and leads me back down the passage.

'You got what you needed?'

'I got an answer. I'm sure you're not concerned either way.' I try and bite back the sarcasm but it's there, coating my words.

'But we are concerned, Blackhart, know that.' The warrior's gaze meets mine and she nods, underlining the seriousness of her words. 'There is talk that whoever is behind this is not Fae. Nor are they one of the Infernal.'

'Interesting. So that leaves me with a human who can fly and disappear at will and who likes to steal small children?'

She makes an impatient sound in the back of her throat. 'There are a great many more supernatural creatures than merely the Infernal and the Fae, Blackhart.'

'Are you talking about bloodsuckers?' I sigh when she rolls her eyes at me. 'The shapeshifters?'

'Perhaps. I do not know.'

'You really aren't making this easy.'

An elegant shoulder is lifted, an eyebrow is quirked. 'We are as curious as you about the disappearances. It has become an entertaining diversion.'

We've reached the bottom of the stairs and the other one, maybe her brother(?) joins us. They share a long silent look, which as a complete stranger I can't follow, before the brother turns to look at me.

'Torsten wants to see you before you leave,' he says before turning away and taking his seat at the bottom of the stairs. 'A word, Blackhart?'

I pause next to him and look down into his strange grey eyes that are almost colourless. I have the chilling thought that I'm looking into a strange mist-covered chasm, but then he blinks and I'm fine and he's smiling – it's just my imagination.

'Wrap your case up quickly. Word is She's getting bored waiting.'

'The case takes as long as it takes,' I tell him, annoyed by the implication that I'm dragging my feet. 'Besides, what can she do?'

'She can send her Beast, girl, and we don't want that. None of us does.'

I'm in time to see a shudder visibly shake his sister and a feeling of unease creeps up on me.

'She wouldn't dare,' I say. 'The Beast is not allowed to hunt in the Frontier.'

'There are loopholes. The Beast can do whatever he likes in the Frontier, with or without your sanction. He has –'

he snaps his fingers as he tries to find the right word – 'how do you say it? Diplomatic immunity.'

I look from one to the other. 'Are you guys serious?'

'Like death.'

A bit morbid but I'll take it. I nod goodbye at them and walk past, sidestepping wet patches on the washed floor and head over to the bar.

'Hey, Philippe, can I have something to drink?'

Philippe passes me my bottled water and a can of Coke. 'Give that to Torsten, will you? I've not had a chance to get it to him yet.'

'So he's told you he wants to see me too?' I ask as I move away.

Philippe frowns at me. 'No, he didn't – I just thought I overheard him saying to the twins . . .' He shakes his head. 'Sorry, Kit, I didn't mean to presume . . .'

It's my turn to frown at Philippe. 'Are you okay? You sound off.'

He leans forward against the counter and looks embarrassed. 'Too many late nights. What can I say?'

'I've been coming here a year, dude. I've never seen you tired. Maybe you need a break.'

'That would be nice but things have been tense here recently. Lots of fights and we had to get the cops down to get rid of some guys hanging around dealing.'

I look at him in shock. 'Seriously?'

'Rorke, as you can imagine, went mental. He threw this guy out and almost broke him in two. Then his buddies turned up later and it just got nasty.'

'That would explain Miron.'

Philippe's blond brows rise. 'Oh, yes. He's been in a foul mood ever since.'

'Someone should maybe have pointed it out to me before I went up there to talk to him,' I say.

'Miron loves you, Kit. He knew your parents. He'd never treat you badly.'

I drop my hand, holding the water bottle away from my mouth.

'Seriously?'

Philippe frowns at me. 'You must know, surely? He was really good friends with your mum when she was about your age, maybe a bit older. Yes, the stories are they used to paint the town red.'

'I never knew that.'

He shrugs and smiles. 'Well, now you do.' He checks his watch. 'Gotta get back to work. I'll catch you later.'

I nod wordlessly and lift Torsten's can of Coke. 'I'll pass this on.'

I recross the floor and make my way towards the back of the DJ's box. I recoil briefly when I see something run past my foot and hear the *chitter* of something small that has sharp, mean little teeth. Keeping my gaze trained on the floor, I step carefully over neatly coiled loops of electrical cable. I'm not a squeamish kind of girl, but rodents give me the heebie-jeebies. I can cope with lizards and spiders and moths and other things, but it's the sneaky intelligence in mice and rats that creeps me out.

'Give me your hand.' Torsten leans down and helps me onto the small stage. The space is cosy, made more so by his electrical equipment. 'Ah, thanks for this.' He takes the can out of my hand and pops it open. 'So, you like to dance?'

I nod and look up into his face and I'm struck by how

unusual his features are – a bit sharp and pointy – and I like that he reminds me of a fox, all rich autumn colours.

'When the mood strikes me.'

Torsten laughs and holds a small USB out to me. 'Here. I'd love to hear what you think. I'm at Milton's for another two weeks before I'm travelling back to Spain for the winter.'

I take the memory stick from him and slide it into my hip pocket. 'I'll put it on my iPod and see what I think.'

He smiles, looking pleased, and gives me a sly wink. 'Don't tell Miron I let you have those files. He's very posses-sive over what goes in and out of the club.'

'No one tells me what to do.'

Sharp white teeth flash at me in the hazy dark followed by a low chuckle.

'I like you, Kit Blackhart. You have guts.'

'Why, thank you. I try.'

Chapter Thirty-Six

The Tube ride home is hell. When I eventually exit at Camden I stagger home in a fugue state having stopped by the pizza place to get dinner as I'm pretty sure that Kyle's not bought anything for himself to eat.

The house is in darkness when I let myself in. I turn on the lights and eat a slice of pizza standing in the kitchen. I hear the front door open and then Kyle's standing there looking rough and beaten up. His lip's been cut, his eye is swollen shut and the way he's holding himself tells me everything must hurt.

'What the hell?' I rush towards him and help him sink down into a chair in the dining room.

The look he gives me is one of tired acceptance. 'A bunch of guys waited until I left the lab with Jilly this evening. They threatened us then decided that I didn't look scared enough and decided to beat me up. I lost my glasses and they broke Jilly's phone.'

'How many of them? And is Jilly okay?'

'There were six of them. She's fine. She got a lucky shot in and knocked one guy out.'

'Have you been to hospital?'

He shakes his head, wincing. 'No. I helped Jilly move

all her research to another lab in another part of the building. Then I called a taxi for her and made sure she got home safely. I thought I'd come home and see if you were okay.'

'Were they there to warn you off about the Glow?'

His lips form a wry smile but he shakes his head. 'No, they were goblins – goblins wearing a glamour. They told me that if we didn't stop investigating the children disappearing they'd take things further.'

I swear some choice swears and Kyle tries a laugh but winces in pain.

'Can you move?'

'Yeah, I'm okay. My ribs hurt but they're not broken.'

Taking him on his word, I help him upstairs. It takes some time, but I clean his face carefully and put butterfly plasters over his eyebrow. His ribs, like mine, are bruised but look far worse. They're not cracked either, just painful. I make him down a handful of painkillers and push him into a shower.

One thing I've learned really well in my time as a Blackhart is how to take care of hurts and aches and pains, but I don't really have enough patience with it all. I make Kyle some tea, checking that it's not too hot before carrying it and several slices of pizza upstairs to his room. He's sitting on the side of the bed, his shoulders rounded, and looks so tired and young that my heart suddenly feels heavy.

'I sent Dad a text message when I left Jilly's place,' Kyle says as I walk in. 'He's not replied yet.'

I pull up the chair that lives in front of his desk. 'Why are they so keen to make sure we stay away from this case, Kyle? I've never had this much interference before.'

He tries to shake his head but winces instead 'I don't know. Maybe it's bigger than we think.'

'Did I ever mention before how much I love being part of this family?'

'Every single day.' He wince-laughs at me when I pull a face. 'So what did you find out today?'

'Well, that the little girl who's been taken is called Tia. And her house was warded against me. I couldn't actually get into the flat to check things out for myself, then Dante got sick at the crime scene and I had to drive him home.'

'Wow. Your day sounds as fun as mine. Want to compare notes?'

As he settles himself into his bed, I collect my laptop, the SD card from the camera and all my notes and bring them to him. I find a map of the British Isles and some thumbtacks and bring those too, along with his laptop.

'Okay,' I say. 'Photos from today, first.'

He flicks through the photos, pausing at the masks. 'You think the masks prevented you from getting in?'

'Yes. I also think they made Dante sick.'

'What?'

'Remember I helped Dante See the previous time? I did it again today and I think that whatever's in this flat, which prevented me from getting in, made him sick enough to actually leave.'

'Anything else about the little girl being taken?'

'Her brother, Marvin, ran after the bad guy and saw him jump down the stairwell. Not the stairs,' I clarify, 'but the actual middle bit. They're four storeys up.'

'Even you can't do that.'

I roll my eyes at him. 'I'm not superhuman, Kyle.'

'Whatever. You do some stupid stuff I've not seen any other human do, outside of a Hollywood movie, and you don't die.'

'You're being ridiculous. Pay attention.' I shift uncomfortably. 'So here's a list of all the other kids we've got going missing across Scotland, England, Wales and Ireland. I thought about it and decided we needed to see how they fit together.' I pick up the little box of drawing pins. 'Start reading them out.'

Twenty minutes later I stand back and look at the groups of drawing pins spread around the map of the British Isles. In the past five years, there have been clusters of children disappearing all over the British Isles and somehow no one has thought they were suspicious. Kyle's cursory research found around thirty-eight kids missing, all in small groups of three or four. It started five years ago in Scotland and, if you work chronologically, a pattern emerges of kids disappearing from Inverness, Edinburgh, Glasgow and then Douglas on the Isle of Man. The pins then show kids missing in Ireland – Dublin – then back to England. Here, we logged disappearances in Liverpool, Manchester and now Brixton in London. But the timings are all over the place so I can't definitely link them to any feast days, even as a long shot.

'It's random.'

'But there has to be a connection of some sort.' I think about what the female twin at the club said to me. 'What do all of these have in common?'

Kyle squints at the wall. 'Well, the children are all human. And they're all under eight.' He shrugs. 'No one seems to care about them all that much, in the end. I mean, no one else has linked them together.'

'True. They are from all different races too – so it doesn't seem racially motivated.'

'You're going to hate me saying this,' he says after a few minutes of silence. 'Do you think we should go to the police?'

'I'd like to, trust me. But what do we have?' I gesture to the wall. 'We think there's something there. We need one obvious thing to link all of them together. One thing, that's all.' I jab my forefinger at the map. 'This is frustrating.'

'So, let's think about this. Where were these kids all taken from?'

'Their homes. Usually in the middle of the night.'

'And where are their homes?'

I gesture to the wall. 'All over Britain.'

Kyle moves his plate of now cold pizza aside and stands up. 'No, look at the reports I pulled up, Kit. Look where the majority of these kids are all missing from. Where they lived.'

I frown at him, uncomprehendingly. 'I don't understand.'

'Addresses.' He grabs the files from me. 'Look. The Greenwood Estate. The Lindhoff Estate. The Gate Estate.' He shakes the folder in my face. 'These are all kids from estates.'

I look at him blankly and he grumbles. 'From poorer families or families that are usually in monetary dire straits. Now do you understand?'

'So what, people are selling their kids?' I scowl at him. 'That's not something I think is possible.'

'It happened, Kit. All the time. In less developed parts of the world in olden times. Kids were sold on for money to buy food and to feed others in a large family. I mean, there are records. In some places like India, children are maimed so that they can go out and beg. And that's recent. Nothing stops it from happening here either.'

'No, I refuse to believe that we're talking about people selling their kids. It just makes no sense to me.' I tap my head. 'Come on. These photos don't show any neglect.' I flip through them. 'Look. Toys. Clothes. A bedroom packed full of books, games and pictures. That's not someone who's going to sell their child off so they can feed the rest of their family. Besides, I met this little girl's brother, Marvin. He's a bright kid, no sign of neglect. Apart from maybe a pair of hideous NHS glasses but that's it, really.'

'Then what? How do we explain this?'

'Maybe the kids have some kind of gift, something this person really wants.'

'Do you think it's a paedophile? I mean, you hear about it on the news. Kids being taken, being groomed.'

I inhale deeply. 'We can't be sure. I hope not.'

'Maybe we should talk to the police.'

'Will they listen to us? I don't know. What we've got is a group of kids who have disappeared. They are within roughly the same age group and have vanished in pretty much the same way over the past five years. We don't know why they've disappeared. And until we do, I don't think we'll be able to get anyone to pay us any attention.'

'Dad could talk to someone and make them take us seriously,' Kyle suggests, drinking his tea and pondering the map. 'I hurt too much to sleep. Let me see what I can find tonight. I'll research those families and see if anything stands out.'

'Okay. I've got to have a shower. Just shout if you need anything.'

The few stairs to my tiny room at the top of the house seem to take forever. I have a necessarily long shower and I drag my papers and laptop along with me and crawl onto my bed to work through them. I try not to think about Dante being ill and just why he's so sick.

A part of me feels that I should be there, checking on him, making sure he's okay. I know how badly I hallucinated when my magic settled into me and I can only imagine what it must be like for him. But, a voice tells me, you're not a changeling. You're human who happens to have magic, unlike Dante. Who's not human. But – and this is a big one, and I know Jamie wouldn't be impressed by this because it's about *feelings* – I like Dante and thought we were friends. I like how he listens to me, how he argues, how he tries bossing me around and then attempts to make up for being an idiot. I got to know him as Dante, the SDI agent who is a bit rubbish but who has a great empathy and kindness to him.

I groan and close my eyes, opening them again to focus on the papers spread around me. Torsten's USB stick sits neatly beside my laptop and I plug it in, queuing the music up. I find my headphones and plug myself in.

The music engulfs me in a wall of sound as I bend my will to figuring out why these kids were taken. I also access the folders Kyle had set up on the kids across the UK. I flick through their photos and the brief newspaper articles about them. It's not comfortable reading and I feel strangely as if I'm invading the families' privacy by doing so. When I search the online maps to see where they lived, like the Brixton estate, most locations look run down – in dire need of attention from the councils that run them.

As much as I hate it, I entertain the thought, for only a second, that Kyle could be right. Might whoever is 'taking' these kids be doing it with the help of the parents? Could it be about money?

I grab my phone and send Kyle a text message: *Can you hack these people's bank accounts to see if money's been transferred to them?*

You serious? You now think they could have sold their kids? he replies super fast.

I don't know what to think. Can you do it?

If you make me some coffee.

No.

Make me coffee, and I'll work all night.

Chapter Thirty-Seven

Dawn finds two Blackhart cousins staring blearily at heaps of bank printouts. Kyle's room looks as if a paper mill has exploded across the breadth and width of it. I don't think we'll ever be able to see the floor again, there's that much paper strewn across it – along with coffee cups, biscuit crumbs and empty Coke cans.

Kyle stretches his arms above his head, wincing, and I let out a huge yawn.

'I'm tired.'

'So am I.'

We grin at each other. The all-nighter we just pulled has really paid off. We discovered that in over seventy-five per cent of the cases, the parents had money paid into their bank accounts. And we're not talking corner-shop change here, either. In some instances we found newspaper articles that corresponded with windfalls or lucky finds. The only drawback is that a lot of these windfalls happened *before* the kids went missing, literally a few days before or a week or two before.

'Are we thinking blackmail?'

'Could be.' I yawn again and rub my face. 'That opens

up a whole different kettle of fish. And, to be honest, I can't think any more. I need sleep. And food.'

'Same.' Kyle checks his watch. 'Sleep till ten then I'll take you for breakfast.'

I shake my head. 'I'm okay to have cereal, really. I've been bought so much food recently that if I never look at pancakes or bacon and eggs again, it will be too soon.'

He laughs softly and nods. 'Pass me some aspirin before you go?'

I toss him the box and go to my room. I check my phone. No calls from Dante or text messages. I send him a quick message, asking him how he's doing. I send another one to Chem to see if I can talk to Marvin at some stage.

I crawl into bed and fall asleep in the blink of an eye. Mercifully, there are no dreams. Or if there are, I don't remember them.

'Kit, get up.'

Kyle looms over me and I jerk back in fright. His face is a mess of bruises.

'You really need to practise karate more,' I tell him as I push up against my pillows. 'Especially the blocking the blows to your face part. You look bad.'

'These will go down but you'll still be ugly,' he quips, touching the bruise beneath his eye. 'We forgot about Lan coming today.'

'Crap.'

'No rain check,' Lan says from the door behind Kyle. 'You were away last week and the week before. When do I get to sit and teach you?'

Lan is tiny and fierce. I fear for my life when she kicks off. I eye her warily and wonder how anyone so cute can dress so badly. She's wearing puce leggings, purple DMs and a denim pinafore dress over an acid-green top. So many colours it gives me a headache. I'm not a fashion aficionado but even I know that some colours just don't go.

'We're working a case, Lan,' I tell her, getting up and stretching. 'We don't have time for school right now.'

Lan sucks her teeth at me and jerks a thumb over her shoulder. 'Ten minutes. You have ten minutes to get ready. I'll see you downstairs.'

Kyle shares my look of woe and slumps his shoulders as he clumps down the stairs behind Lan. I suppress my irritation and have a super-quick shower. Then I dress in the previous day's jeans and a stretchy jumper. This one had a hole on the shoulder, marking where Marc's sword flashed past me when I was too slow to duck his attack. Other people have moths, but my clothes face combat training with my cousins.

Downstairs Lan's prepped bowls of cereal for us both and she's got her notebooks ready.

'You eat. I start.' The look she directs us over the frames of her glasses brooks no arguments. 'It's exciting to learn. Remember.'

It's late afternoon when Lan gives up. She was trying to force us to remember the Otherwhere's involvement in the French Revolution. She grumbles about us being distracted and scowls unhappily when my mobile keeps buzzing with text messages – from Chem and Diane, confirming Marvin's okay for us to come by. I hear nothing from Dante all day. I even ring and leave a voicemail during one of my loo breaks.

Lan is merciless and gives us homework to do about the

Fae who sided with the Huguenots during the French rebellion, and the impact that had on the Fae diaspora as they fled France for safer havens such as England and South Africa.

'My brain hurts,' Kyle says, firmly closing the door behind her diminutive form and sinking down onto the couch and collapsing backwards. 'Why is everything so hard when you're beaten up?'

'Shut up, you big girl's blouse. Sit up. Do you want to come with me to meet with Marvin? He also has the whole geek chic thing happening. You guys could maybe bond.'

'No, leave me alone. I want to stay here, cuddle my bruises and order in some Chinese.'

'Can I have some kung pao chicken?'

'What time will you be back?'

I pull on another jumper and yank my leather jacket over it. 'Dunno. Midnight, thereabouts?'

'You've not mentioned Dante the whole day.'

'He's still not doing well. I'm swinging past his place on my way to see Marvin, to see how he is.'

Kyle passes me my helmet. 'Be careful, Kit.'

'I'm always careful,' I answer. 'You get some sleep. Check on Jilly. See how she's doing.'

He gives me a quick hug before I head out to the bike, my messenger bag swung over my shoulder. The traffic's not too bad and only one Volvo driver tries to kill me by jumping a red light. I pull up outside Dante's place just after six and find the place in darkness.

I ring the bell and wait impatiently for him to come to the door. One of his neighbours, a young woman in a business suit, walks past, talking on her mobile. She's carrying groceries and smiles when she sees me.

'You okay over there?'

'Visiting my mate, Dante,' I say. 'When I left last night he was really sick. Have you seen him?'

She gestures me closer. 'We woke up to some really weird noises last night. It sounded like he was fighting with someone. We tried ringing him but he didn't answer and things went quiet again. He's given us a key to look after the place when he goes away so I can let you have that, to check on him. I remember seeing you together before.'

Anxiety thrums through me and I nod mutely, wondering what I'm going to find.

I loiter on the doorstep of her small newly renovated house and she comes out with the key on a green frog fob.

'There you go. Do you want me to come with you?'

It's tempting but I don't know what I'll find so I shake my head.

'I'll bring it back as soon as I've checked on him. He was running a really high fever last night so I bet he was throwing pots at things that weren't there.' I try and smile at her and she looks a bit worried but nods.

I unlock the door and let myself in.

The place is dark and smells musty. I turn lights on as I go and find myself in the kitchen. The place is a mess. There's broken glass everywhere and the leftover risotto I left him lies congealed on the floor.

Without thinking, I flip my wrist and the baton extends into my palm. My knife rests in my other hand and I prowl through the house, moving up towards the empty bedrooms. From a cursory glance they both seem undisturbed and I ghost along the shadowy hallway towards Dante's room.

The door stands ajar and I use the knife to push it further open. Dante's sprawled face down across the bed. His breathing is ragged and the room smells of wild magic and pain.

Before I move towards him, I do a quick check of the room and the adjoining en suite; no one else is there. I push the baton back up my sleeve but I keep my knife handy as I kneel on the bed next to Dante, getting a grip on his shoulder so I can flip him onto his back.

I manage with some difficulty and when I look at his face I swear softly. Two small horn nubs have formed high on Dante's forehead, just inside the hairline. I lean over and turn the bedside light on. When I turn back his eyes are open and I'm startled by how bright they are and how very dark at the same time.

'Kit?' His voice is husky. 'Is it really you? Or am I dreaming you too?'

'It's me, Dante.' I grab hold of his hand. 'What happened? Were you attacked?'

He looks confused for a moment but then shakes his head. 'No, I had nightmares during the night. But I fought them. I won.' The smile he gives me is sickly and weak. 'I showed them who's boss.'

'I tried to get hold of you during the day. I rang and left voice messages.'

'You did? I'm sorry, Kit. I didn't hear.' He sounds so lost that my heart skips a beat.

'It's fine. I'm here now.'

Try as I might I can't stop staring at the nubs poking from beneath his hair.

'Can you see them?' he asks me, his fingers gingerly exploring his hair. 'I wasn't sure if they were real or if I was dreaming them.'

'They're real.' I smile at him. 'They are pretty cool, actually.'

He sits up with a struggle and leans back against the pillows. 'So, I think I'm not human after all.' His voice rasps and I pass him the water by the bedside.

I laugh softly and shake my head. 'I don't think you're human either.'

'Can you see any other changes on me?' he asks me, spreading his arms. 'Do I have a tail? Wings? Scales?'

I'm really laughing now. 'No, you fool. You look fine.'

'I have horns.'

'Nubs. You have nubs.'

'At least it's two horns and not one.'

'There is that. I've never heard of a Fae unicorn before.'

He laughs and winces. 'Why do I feel like I've been fighting with Mike Tyson?'

'I'm surprised you can even speak. When this happened to me I was out for a week and don't remember anything of it.'

He frowns at me. 'You're a changeling?'

'No, but my magic came on me like this, like yours did, unexpectedly. I fell ill for a week.'

'And how do you know you're not a changeling?'

'I can handle iron, I can drink holy water.' I clear my throat. 'It's what I drink when I'm at Milton's, remember. It helps if the Infernal can't snack on me if they feel the need.'

Dante looks at me for a long time, shivers and pulls his blanket up over his shoulders. 'That is just weird. What's going on with our lives?' He draws a deep breath and exhales slowly. 'I really am a faerie.'

Chapter Thirty-Eight

Marvin is waiting for me in Chem's flat. He stands up when I come in and holds his hand out for me to shake but I lean forward and give him a hug. He stiffens for a second, before wrapping his arms round me. His grip is strong and brief and then we're sitting down, looking at one another.

'How are you doing?' I ask him.

'I'm okay, I think. I mean, I know the guy who took Tia is an actual *person*, you know? I could see him and everything.'

'What about the other guy, Marv? The one who came into her room through the window?'

Marv blinks at me. 'What?' His brow wrinkles. 'I don't even . . . oh my God, I forgot about him completely.'

I suppress the urge to mutter under my breath because I am so done with the nasty crap the supernatural creatures pull on humans.

'We'll come back to that. What did the police say when you told them you chased the guy?'

'They told me I was insane because I could have been killed. I told them to fu— . . . piss right off. It's my baby sister. I had to try and save her.'

I grab hold of Marv's hand and will him to be calm,

letting the ring I'm wearing press lightly against his skin, allowing the magic to do its thing. 'I need you to tell me everything you can remember about it. All of it.'

Marvin's voice gains strength as he talks and he answers my questions patiently. He had been up late studying for a test the next day when he heard Tia talking in her room. Used to her dreaming vividly in her sleep, he didn't think anything of it at first, but then she started laughing and giggling so he thought maybe she was awake. As both their parents were asleep, he thought he'd check on his baby sister.

Her room was in darkness but when he walked in and turned on the light, he was pushed aside by someone carrying Tia. The person was bigger and faster than him. He had the impression of a tall form wearing black clothes, before his little sister let out a shriek, loud enough to wake everyone in the flat. Marvin ran after the guy and was hot on his heels when the front door burst open and someone else stood there, waiting to take Tia.

The man in black handed the little girl over to the man outside, before turning around and running for the wall, which he just ran right through, his coat flapping in his wake. Marvin, although angry and scared, took off after the guy who had taken his sister. The guy, the newcomer, held Tia close to his body, her head tucked into the curve of his neck and shoulder. He held a protective hand against her head to prevent it from bumping. She had her legs wrapped around his middle and clung to him like a scared monkey. Marvin's exact words. When the man ran past the lift, Marvin knew he was heading for the stairs and thought he'd be able to catch up with him. But the man swung the door to the stairs shut in Marvin's face, and by the time the boy had wrestled the door to the stairs open, he just saw the guy plunging down the centre of the stairs to the ground floor below, his dark coat flaring out behind him like a cloak. The guy looked up at Marvin, gave him a nod and then exited the building without anyone else even seeing him.

'Is there CCTV in your building?'

'Yes. It showed nothing. Just me, shouting like a crazy person.'

'Nothing from the passage outside your flat?'

'Not a thing.'

I take the proffered glass of Diet Coke from Chem and drink deeply.

'Marvin, do you recall seeing anyone hanging around the flats recently? Anyone new, who doesn't belong?'

'No, just you and that other guy, Dante.'

'No one else weird, or anything?'

He bends forward and rests his head on his forearms. 'No one. I've been talking to the cops about this for hours already. No one at all.'

I catch Chem's eye and he gives me a quick shake of the head. 'We've been talking to loads of people on the estate and no one has seen anything or anyone.'

I lean back on the couch. 'I've been doing this for a little while now,' I tell them. 'And I've never been to a place where no one has seen anything at all. Someone must have seen something.'

Both boys manage to look guilty as I groan in frustration.

'Marvin, this is going to sound weird but do you know if your mum and dad recently got sent money? Or were given money? Or came by money?'

Marvin frowns at me but shrugs. 'My dad got a promotion at work. He's been made a full manager so we'll be moving away from here soon.'

I blink at him. 'He got promoted?'

'Yes. At the stationery supply place he works at. His old manager is retiring and he's been given the job.'

'What will happen now?' Chem asks before I do. 'I mean, with Tia missing?'

'I'm not sure. My dad went to work this morning for a while and my mum's just sitting there, crying. The police are there, they've set up equipment to trace any calls, in case there are ransom demands.'

He looks at me and his eyes are hollow with tiredness and worry.

'Why my sister?' he asks me. 'Why was she taken?'

'I don't know, Marv, but I'm working on finding out.' I take a deep breath. 'Listen, I need a favour. I would like to talk to your mum, if I could? Do you think that's possible?'

'I don't know, man. She's really not doing so good.'

I gently touch his hand. 'I know, Marvin, but maybe only for five minutes?'

I see the conflict in his gaze but he eventually gives a nod, although it's reluctant and wary.

'No longer than five minutes. If you do anything weird, I'm telling the cops.'

I heave a sigh of relief. 'Of course. I won't take up a lot of your time. I promise.'

Chem's frown tells me how unhappy he is but he remains quiet as I follow Marvin out of the door to his flat.

'I need you to do me a favour,' I say to Marvin as we near the door.

'Like what?'

'I need you to invite me in.'

He shoots me a confused look. 'Uh, okay.' He unlocks the door and pushes it open. 'Mum, I've brought a friend of mine from school, is that all right? Kit, don't just stand there, it's okay, come in.'

I take a breath and step up towards the door; as I do, the invisible wall of magic that resisted me the day before gives way. I stumble across the doorstep and have to grab hold of the door to prevent myself from face-planting in the passageway.

Marvin's mum reaches a hand out to me.

'Are you all right?' she asks, her voice thick with unshed tears, but her concern for my lack of coordination is obvious.

'Sorry, yes, just incredibly clumsy. My name is Kit Blackhart, Mrs . . .'

'Please, just call me Alison, Kit. So nice for Marvin to bring someone home from school for a change.' She blows her nose after shaking my hand. 'The place is a bit of a mess at the moment, as you can imagine. Marvin, why don't you make us some tea? Thanks, love.' She shows me to a chair and I nod to the young policewoman sitting stiffly in front of a laptop. 'This is Officer Briggs.'

I nod at her and she gives me a piercing glance before looking away and fiddling with the keyboard. 'Marvin told me what happened, Mrs . . . I mean Alison, I'm really sorry. Have you had any word?'

'Nothing yet, but we're hoping to hear something from someone soon.' She smiles a wan smile as another man walks into the room. 'Steve, this is Kit. She's one of Marvin's friends. From school.'

Steve is obviously Marvin's dad. They look enough alike

to be related and he has the same worried eyes behind similarly framed glasses. I shake his hand and he drops into a seat near the police officer. He seems tired but watches the young policewoman uncomfortably.

'A cup of tea would be good, thanks, son,' he says as Marvin pops his head around the corner.

The awkward silence is broken by Marvin. He edges into the room carrying a large tray laden with mugs, spoons, milk, sugar and biscuits. There are cups for all of us. We each busy ourselves with making our tea the way we like it. Marvin perches on the arm of my couch and looks jittery.

'Are you guys okay if I show Kit my room?'

His mum frowns for a second, looks at me, then at him before nodding. 'Keep the door open.'

A wild blush creeps up Marvin's neck and colours his cheeks but he nods and I follow him down the short passage, past his parents' room to his room. It's tidier than I expected but then I see the elaborate towering computer system and stay on the far side of the room.

'I have bad luck with computers,' I explain, pulling up a chair. 'I go near them and they go boom.'

He looks perplexed but nods. 'What do you need to see?'

'Tia's room. For maybe five minutes, if that.'

He doesn't look happy but nods and beckons me forward and points. The doorway diagonally across from his is obviously his sister's.

'Just hurry, okay.'

I nod and in two strides I'm across the passage and inside the little girl's room. There is a lot of pink, but there are also Lego blocks and stuffed animals alongside a few Ben 10 toys. I draw a breath and as I exhale my magic surfaces. The brightness in the room kicks up a few notches and for a moment I'm staggered by the warmth of feeling that suffuses me. I sense it all around me and it's not just in this room but in the whole of the flat. Here is a close-knit family who truly do love one another.

My examination of the room is swift and I would dearly like to spend more time here, getting a sense of the little girl, but I can hear her parents speaking with the police officer, the clink of mugs and teaspoons.

I've only done what I'm trying to do once before (by accident too) and it knocked me for six, depleting my magic and making me sick. I sit down on Tia's unmade bed and dig my fingers into the bedding, letting myself be sucked into the past, reaching for the images I know I can access if I can sustain my magic for long enough.

There are a few moments of darkness, then it's like a movie playing in reverse.

I see the fingerprint dustings performed on the surfaces and people walking around the room: some in uniform, Detective Shen, Dante looking grey, Marvin, then his parents. And I see the girl curled asleep in her bed. The room smells of talc and a whiff of perfume from her mother. It's dark out and the figure making its way in through the window wears a coat with the collar too high, the panels seemingly stitched together by a blind craftsman. He reminds me of some of the Morris dancers we've had in our village near the Manor in the past. The only thing that's missing is the black top hat and feathers in his hair. There's something about the way he moves and his dress that's peculiar, maybe a bit familiar even, but I can't put my finger on it.

He slips into the room, as softly as a wisp of air. He kneels next to the bed and whispers Tia's name. She turns towards him, murmurs something and he chuckles. She voluntarily sits up and chats to him but the distance is too great and I can't hear what he's saying to her. She laughs and shows him a teddy bear with a squinty button eye. He takes it from her. They chat some more and there is no fear in her at all. When he stands she does too, reaching up to him. He picks her up and she goes willingly, fearlessly. I see her face for a second and there's sadness there, in her eyes, but she's being brave. She holds on to him as he walks out of the room, coming face to face with a sleepy-eyed Marvin.

Shock. Fear. Anger.

There are shouts next, a door banging and Tia's cries of alarm. Marvin screaming now, waking everyone. There's a sense of the world tilting and . . .

Bam, I'm back where I started.

I stand, my legs shaky beneath me, and I walk to the doorway. Marvin's watching me anxiously from his room.

'Bathroom,' I mouth and he points.

'Thanks,' I say out loud and step into the passage, closing the bathroom door behind me with a loud click. I get the tissue to my nose just in time to catch the blood and before I black out.

Chapter Thirty-Nine

'What happened? Are you okay?' Marvin looks worried as I walk back into his room. 'I heard a noise like falling.'

'I'm okay, thanks. I used my magic and it sometimes makes me lightheaded.'

Marvin blinks rapidly behind his glasses but he nods, accepting my words and the use of magic without too much fuss.

'Did you find anything in her room?'

'She knew the guy who came for her.' I hold up my hand to stop further questions. 'She went willingly.'

'But how? I mean, the guy wasn't human. He ran through the wall for fu— . . . heaven's sake. How does my baby sister come to know someone who can do that?'

'That's what we need to figure out. I want to walk back down the passage and stairs and see if I can get a sense of who took her.' I smile at him. 'You're doing great, you know? Your parents are pretty special.'

The smile he gives me is a reluctant one. 'Yeah. It's embarrassing. They hardly ever fight. They always say it's because when they met, they promised one another never to let the bad stuff get to them. They made a vow.'

The words trigger something in my mind. Using the term

'making a vow' isn't your everyday human speak. I promise I'll do my homework. I promise I'll do the chores around the house before I go out. I promise I'll bring you back your favourite book. Promises can be small but vows are pretty big things. Think about wedding vows.

'Where did they meet?' I ask Marvin.

'Some music festival that's been held since the seventies. Up north somewhere.'

'So not Glastonbury?'

'Huh, no. This festival isn't very big but they go every year. It's more of a local thing, with a few folk bands and a few smaller rock bands. Last year they went and said it's become really alternative.'

'What does that mean?'

'That the locals have linked it to some kind of Renaissance fair, with historical re-enactors and things. People pretending to be fairies and creatures. Like they have in the States, apparently. I think it's the same group of people who have taken over running the festival, actually.'

'Do you want to walk me out?' I ask him, my mind whirling. This, I feel sure, is the missing link we need. If we can connect the other people to this festival somehow . . . my mind spins in circles as I wonder if I'm seeing patterns where there aren't any. I'm itching to get hold of Kyle to ask him to check it out.

'Here, you'd better take these.' Marv hands me two science handbooks. 'To make sure my mum and them don't think it's weird you've come by from school and we're not doing schoolwork or something.'

I grin. 'Marv, usually, when a girl visits a boy after school, it's hardly ever about schoolwork.'

'What?' He looks at me blankly for a moment before

realization dawns and another flush spreads up his cheek. 'That's not true. Diane comes round *all* the time after school.'

I raise my eyebrows. 'Really? And she comes to hang out here because?'

'We talk about music and games. Sometimes about school.' He looks as if he wants to run away from me. 'Diane doesn't like me. I mean, she's popular and pretty. She hangs out with Chem and the guys.'

'Does she go to any of their homes?'

His silence gives me the answer. 'She likes you, Marv. Maybe, when all of this is finished, you should ask her out on a date.'

'I don't want to screw things up.'

'You won't. Just say, Hey, would you like to go to the movies with me this Saturday, just the two of us. To see what it's like going out together. By ourselves.'

'As easy as that?'

'Showing a girl you like her needn't be rocket science, Marv.'

His smile is shy and sweet and I grin at him. 'Come on, let's see if I can get an idea who this other guy is.'

I say goodbye to his parents and Officer Briggs, who barely acknowledges my wave with a nod of her head. I take the books from Marv as we step outside.

'Can you walk with me?' I ask him.

'I'm just walking Kit out, Mum,' he calls over his shoulder. 'I'll be back in a minute.'

I hand him back the books. 'This is going to be weird. You may see what I see. Just don't freak out.'

Marvin's eyes behind his glasses are huge but he nods and swallows. I turn to face the passage and take a deep breath, willing my magic upwards. I can't explain how I manage to do this, putting myself in a different time almost, and I hate doing it. It might look as if I'm actually turning back time, which isn't something I can do, unlike trained sorcerers from the Otherwhere. For me, it's more like spooling back a film reel to show what's happened.

There are so many people coming and going, some in police clothes. I hear voices, the sound of sirens; I see curious onlookers. I go back further until I see the figure walk to the door. My sense of him isn't strong and, try as I might, he remains wrapped in darkness. He stands by the door, pressing a gloved hand against it and waits. I see how he listens, tilting his head, seemingly making sense of the movement inside the flat.

There's shouting, then the door is pulled open. The other man stands there, holding Tia. There's a blurriness surrounding them that frustrates me. I can't get a clear view of their faces. The Raggedy Man says something low to the other man, who gives a sharp shake of his head before taking the little girl. She looks up into his face with a half-smile but it changes into the scream that will propel everything into motion again. The Raggedy Man gives a shake of his head and looks over his shoulder, possibly seeing Marvin running towards him. He turns from the door at the same time as his partner and disappears from my view.

The man now running towards me moves with unnatural grace and speed. Marvin, as he rushes past me, has no way of catching up but it doesn't stop him from storming after him.

The door to the stairs bangs open and I watch the man look over his shoulder. For one crucial second, the glamour obscuring his face lifts and I truly See him before he turns and jumps down the stairwell. He crashes out through the lower door with the power of a storm.

I sag against Marvin, who drops the books he's holding so he can grab hold of me. I fumble in my pocket and pull out a wedge of toilet roll and press it against my nose as blood gushes. I'm too heavy for Marvin to hold on to but he slides down the wall with me and we sit there in silence for a few moments.

'I saw him,' Marv says and his voice sounds slow. 'I mean, I saw his face. That can't really be his face, can it?'

I close my eyes in answer and Marvin swears. 'Why would something like that take my sister?'

'Because vows that are made need to be kept,' I say past the tissues. 'And people never remember that. They forget that words have power and so do promises.'

Chapter Forty

I wave at Marvin as I gun the Monster's engine and pull away. I'm exhausted and a headache is pounding between my eyes: the result of using my magic in an unfamiliar way. What I've just seen and experienced was vivid and frightening. But that effect is hugely magnified by the knowledge that Marv saw part of it with me, all over again.

I like Marv and his mum and dad, but then likeable people sometimes do stupid stuff.

The bland, almost blank, features of the second man as he jumped down the stairwell are seared into my brain and I want to get home, sketch him and do research. I don't doubt that he was wearing a mask. He had to be wearing one, or he'd undergone some pretty awful surgery to create a face so featureless and mask-like.

I've never seen anyone with features at all similar but even so, there was something familiar about him that I just couldn't place.

'Kit?'

I look up from the computer screen to find Aiden filling the doorway. I pull my earphones out and pause Torsten's playlist.

'Hey.' I beckon him in and he bends down to drop a kiss on my forehead, as he usually does. I breathe in the fresh scent of him and offer him a smile, my normal response. 'What are you doing here, wolf boy? I thought we were fighting.'

'I've missed you, sparky. I don't like it when we fight. No, I lie, I like it when we fight and it's not for real. What happened with the whole Glow thing and you walking out – that was too real.' He surveys the chaos that is my bed. 'Move your stuff.' He climbs onto my bed and I have to grab wildly at my papers to prevent them from sliding onto the floor. He flops down, stretching himself out lengthways so he can look at me where I sit cross-legged, against the headboard.

'So, solved your case yet?'

'No.' I close the laptop and slide it beneath my bed, out of the way. 'Figured out what's going on with the Glow yet?'

He grimaces and crosses his arms behind his head.

'Don't. Leo and I have been out all night with some of his dad's guys in tow. There is so much crap on the streets, Kit, it makes me sick.'

'When you say crap, do you mean Glow or something else?'

'Just all of it. The stuff kids and people sniff and inject and smear on themselves.' He waves a hand dramatically. 'Is being human such an issue that you have to try and break yourself to be something else? To forget everything you've ever been?'

The question makes me feel sad. 'I don't know, Aiden. I'm talking to a werewolf boy right now whilst trying to figure out what faerie creature is stealing human children for some dodgy reason. My issues aren't normal human issues.'

He snorts a laugh as he scrutinizes me.

'Come on, talk to me. Tell me what you got.'

'Okay, so I'm trying to find more info about a group of people called the Faceless. Have you ever heard of them?'

'No. They sound like the world's crappiest super villains. Who are they?' Aiden leans over me to grab the open packet of biscuits on my nightstand, before lying back again. I'm about to complain about crumbs but then he hands me one too.

'The Faceless worked for the Elder Gods. I know!' I grimace at him as he huffs. 'Them again. According to this crusty old book Aunt Letty's assistant showed me, the Faceless acted as their servants. They went out and found the most delicious morsels of human and Fae to feed their masters. When the Elder Gods had their asses handed to them, the Faceless all but disappeared. But the lore books reckon they still exist, as they are as immortal as the gods they served.'

'Are they our bad guys?'

'I don't know. I've got Kyle trying to find out more about them, but I've done a few of my own searches via the Internet and I can't find anything. Drawing a complete blank.'

'What does Dante say?'

I stare at him blankly and realize that in all of this I've completely forgotten about my partner. Everything about him, including the mess he's pushed us into because he's a bloody changeling.

'I, uh, don't know. I've not had a chance to talk to him yet. He was out at a meeting.'

I sense that Aiden doesn't quite believe me but he lets it drop. 'What else have you got?'

'I also have Kyle checking the possibility that the families of the kidnapped kids all have something to do with a music festival up north.'

'Pagan sacrifices, like in *The Wicker Man*?'

'Aiden, seriously.'

'What? The world is a weird place, Kit Blackhart.'

I roll my eyes and I can't help but laugh.

'Why are you here? It's after midnight.'

'I was in the neighbourhood so I thought I'd stop by to check if you still hated me.'

'Only first thing in the morning, before I've had coffee. Go home, Aiden. I need to get some sleep.' I lean closer and he does the same so our faces are a few centimetres apart. 'You look tired. What's been going on in your life?'

'We have our annual conclave of wolves coming up at the end of the month. I'm running all kinds of errands for my dad and I'm looking into the Glow case. Plus, an assistant in the British Museum woke up an angry spirit, so I was the lucky guy nominated to go help Shaun put it back to sleep.'

'How did that work out for you?'

In answer he pulls up his shirt so I can see four neat claw marks across his muscled abdomen. I reach out and run my fingers across the raised welts without thinking, curious that the cuts look so sore. He hisses and grips my wrist.

'Do you mind not pawing me like some piece of fruit?'

I snatch my hand back and feel colour rush up my cheek at the note of annoyance in his voice.

'Sorry. But that looks sore. Why haven't you healed up yet?'

'I've not had a chance to shift properly,' he says, holding

a protective hand over his stomach. 'Sorry I startled you but you surprised me.' He quirks his lips at me. 'Unless you'd like to do more than touch?' He wiggles his eyebrows suggestively and I laugh at him, relieved that I can breathe again because he was being stupid and himself. I'm not sure I like the serious-eyed boy he'd become.

'No, I'm sorry. I should have been more careful.' I sit back and dig my offending hand into the bedding. 'Do you want me to go for a run with you? Where's Shaun that he's not been around?'

'Busy with stuff for my dad and the conclave. Why are you this jittery?' He takes hold of my trapped hand and spreads my fingers out, pressing his own down on top of it. 'You actually look out of it. What's got you so wild eyed?'

'I don't know. This case. None of it makes sense. I've been having really weird dreams. Every time I close my eyes, I dream I'm being chased by these people and huge dogs. Sometimes Thorn's there and we talk briefly and he tries to tell me to be careful but he can't tell me *why* I have to be careful because there's a geas on him. Then I'm running from wild dogs again and then I eventually wake up.' I shrug. 'And then there's this job. Aiden, I have never felt so clueless as I do on this case, struggling from one place to the next. I really wonder if I'm doing any good.'

'And Dante? How's he been?'

I shrug. 'He's been okay, I suppose. I mean, he's got this job but I worry that he's even more helpless than me really. Did you know the SDI only have a handful of agents? Some of their new recruits walked out on them. Right now there are fewer than ten of them in their department.'

'Do you fancy him?'

'No.' I glanced at him. 'Why do you keep asking that? He keeps asking me the same thing about you.' I watch him for a few seconds, my brain slotting things into place. 'Wait, do you like him?'

Aiden's head comes up in surprise and he blinks at me for a moment. 'No. I mean, sure, he's a nice-looking guy but . . .'

'Aiden. You've dated guys in the past. Plus, you have eyes. He's all kinds of cute.'

A light flush creeps across Aiden's cheeks but then he laughs. 'No, you know what? It's nothing. There's something about him, Kit, that makes me think we're not seeing the whole picture.'

'What do you mean?'

'When I saw him in your kitchen, making those pancakes . . . I had the weirdest feeling that I knew him. Like I knew him really well, you know?'

'Déjà vu?' I make a face, teasing him. 'Did you love him in a previous life, Aiden Garrett?'

'Now you're being ridiculous.' He lies back down. 'I don't know what it is about him. There's something, though.'

I bite my tongue. 'I know what you mean. Dante's not . . .' I clear my throat. 'I think in the next few days I need you to come hang out with us. I think there's something he needs to tell you.'

'Colour me very intrigued,' Aiden replied, giving his most infuriating smile, and I get that familiar feeling of annoyance and fondness. If he ever settled on a serious partner, he or she'd need all the help they could get. Thank God it will never be me.

'So, back to my offer. Do you want to go for a run?'

'I thought you wanted to get some sleep.'

'Running would help tire me out more.'

'Then yes.' He rolls off the bed. 'I'll see you downstairs.'

He closes the door softly behind him and I hear his footsteps go down the short attic staircase. I pull on a pair of shorts and my hoodie and strap my baton to my wrist.

By the time I get downstairs, the front door is open and Aiden in wolf form is sitting on our top step. Kyle's on the sofa in front of the TV, a laptop lighting his face. 'Have a good run. Try not to get in any fights.'

'Ha ha,' I say, closing the door behind me.

The thing I like best about running with Aiden in his wolf form is that I never get hassled. There are no whistles or catcalls or comments. There are people who stop and stare. Usually it's because of Aiden's size and his loping run. There's that primitive part of your brain that tells you the 'dog' that the girl's jogging beside is maybe a bit too feral-looking, a bit too large to be your normal canine companion. We've been stopped and questioned in the past. I've alluded to him being a wolf-hybrid (not wrong), a government experiment, just a big dog made up mostly of mongrel bits, and various other things, much to his annoyance.

Tonight's run takes us through Camden and we pass darkened houses and late-night eateries. Occasionally a house has its windows open and we catch a glimpse of the people inside. In one window a sleepless tousle-haired young woman stands cradling a small baby to her shoulder. Then we're past, my feet hitting the pavement and Aiden's nails clipping the concrete.

We run for over an hour at a steady pace before turning back to the house. Kyle's gone to bed by the time I pull open the front door. Aiden opts to change and have a shower downstairs and just crash out on the sofa for the night. I wait until he's done and make us each a mug of tea. He wraps me in a brief hug and kisses the top of my head.

'Thanks for that. You're a good mate, sparky. I'm all better.' He lifts up his T-shirt – one of Kyle's that he borrowed from the clean washing in the passage. The four claw marks across his abdomen no longer look as deep or as red. By tomorrow they'll be pink lines and possibly gone the day after.

'You just like showing off your abs,' I tease him when I'm halfway up the stairs. 'No wonder your ex-girlfriends and boyfriends stalk me.'

'Mates before dates, yo,' he says, lifting a hand in salute as he settles onto the couch, pulling the spare duvet over him.

'Freak.' But I laugh, feeling relaxed and strangely upbeat. I sleep and I don't dream.

Chapter Forty-One

Dante pulls open the door as I swing my leg off the bike. He's dressed in jeans and a sweater that's seen better days. His dark hair looks glossy in the early morning light. He looks wholesome and there's no sign of the small horns I spied the other day.

'Hey,' I say. 'How're you doing?'

'Better.' His smile is wide, showing off his white teeth against his tanned skin. 'Thanks for asking.'

'How's the . . .' I make circle motions above my head. 'The horn situation?'

'I tried to make them invisible.' He tilts his head forward so I can see. 'What do you think?'

I reach a tentative hand and run my fingers through his hair. I can feel the nubs there but I can't see them. I bring my other hand up and do the same, until it looks like I'm just standing there running my hands through his hair. My thumbs feel the pattern of the swirling horn and I hiss when I feel how sharp the points are.

Dante's gone very quiet beneath my ministrations.

'Yeah, they definitely look gone.' Even to my ears my voice sounds husky and breathless.

He looks up at me from beneath his lashes and I wonder

how I've never noticed how silky they are. His skin is warm beneath my hands and I run my thumbs along his cheek-bones, down towards his mouth.

I sway towards him until we're millimetres apart. I'm mesmerized by the soft darkness in his gaze and I wonder what it would feel like to be kissed by him. I drop my hands to his shoulders, feeling the width of them, the strength of them. I'm peripherally aware of his own hands spanning my waist, hooking into the loops of my jeans, drawing me ever closer. The tips of his fingers graze the skin where my jumper's become untucked beneath my jacket, and my breath hisses out as a jolt of energy goes through me.

And he smells so good. Like rich honey and chocolate with hints of vanilla. The boy is sexy as hell and there is something I should be remembering, possibly some*one*, but right now I really don't want to think about anything except being close to him. Because, really, Dante is the most divine thing ever.

'Kit? What're you doing?'

His voice is dangerously low, and I am so close I can feel the sound vibrate through his chest. I focus on the shape of my hand pressed against the expanse of his chest, feeling the rapid beating of his heart.

He's only a tiny bit taller than me, but even so I lift myself up on my toes until our lips are a hair's breadth apart.

My heart is thundering against my ribcage and I know that when this kiss happens I'll be lost forever and I'm not sure that would be such a bad thing. Would it?

I'm nestled so close to Dante that I have difficulty trying to remember why I've not pressed myself to him like this before, because – God, he feels so good. It takes an eternity for the full implication of the thought to wriggle its way into my brain.

Alarm spikes through me and I gasp, breaking away from Dante. As I do, I instantly mourn the loss of his hands holding me close, of not being near him, breathing him in.

I walk away and my hands are shaking so badly I cross my arms tightly across my chest and clamp my hands under my armpits.

Oh my God, what was that about? A shudder goes through me and I lean against my bike, my knees suddenly too weak to hold me up.

'Kit?' Dante looks bereft, standing in front of his house. He's staring at me as if I've just ripped his heart out and tried to eat it in front of him. 'I'm not sure . . . what just happened?'

I try to inhale but the air is thick with the scent of him, the need to press myself against him. My legs are far cleverer than I am, moving me away from him, and I hold my hand up, stopping his advance.

'Stay,' I say, my voice sounding as if I've just run a marathon and I hate it for its breathless quality. 'Just stay there. Where I can see you.'

He halts and raises his own hands. 'Did I do something wrong?'

'Yes.' My breathing feels almost normal again. 'No. I don't know. Just give me a second.'

My magic flares to life around me, suffusing me with its warmth, steadying me. I sharpen my gaze and look at Dante.

The ring Thorn wore all those months ago, the one his mother gave him and since then passed on to me, lightly influences people to make them feel better inclined towards the bearer. I use it, but not often, because I don't like messing with people's emotions. But occasionally, as with Marvin and the Scott brothers, it helps calm them down. It's a small thing, no great magic, but the whammy Dante just hit me with is something similar. Yet it was altogether more powerful and far more to do with *attraction* and *want* and *need*. Heavy stuff. And from the way he's looking at me, he has no idea what he's doing.

My magic skims him and I can see there's now a golden hue to his magic. It's glowing, like rich amber in sunshine. The scent of his magic reaches me again and I feel myself relenting and wanting to be wrapped in his arms. It would feel so amazing and I'm tired and nothing would be nicer than being held by him.

I clamp down heavily on the feeling, refusing the suggestion that maybe now would be a good time to put my head on his chest and ask him to kiss me a little. I concentrate on my magic, fixing it to my aura like armour, panels overlapping, bolted tight against Dante and whatever it is that he's doing. When I'm clearheaded enough to speak in my own voice I clear my throat and call out to him.

'Dante? What was that?' I look over to where he's standing watching me with hurt and confused eyes and realize that he has no idea what almost just happened and how this was his fault. 'What are you feeling right now?'

He takes a step closer and my fingers curl up my sleeve of their own volition, hovering over the release button of the baton. It gives me some comfort.

'I'm confused. A little bit hurt. I'm not sure what just happened or why you stopped. But I'm glad you did.' He takes a breath and looks horrified at what he just said. 'I mean, that's not what I mean. Oh God, Kit. I don't know what I'm thinking. What was that, even?' He scrubs his hair backwards in a gesture of annoyance. When he speaks again it's as if he's reasoning with himself rather than talking to me. 'I can't like you like that. You're a friend, my partner on this job. I can't screw this up. Besides, you're too young for me to even think about you like that. I don't understand what's going on.'

I watch the conflict of emotions and how his magic responds to it and nod to myself. Okay, he is telling the truth. He genuinely has no idea what is going on.

'Are you wearing the ring you showed me? The moonstone ring?'

Dante shook his head and held up both hands. 'No. I left it on my bedside table.'

'So this is all you.' I gesture at the amber light surrounding him. 'Great. Just great.'

'What are you talking about?'

'You think I *wanted* to act the way I just acted towards you? That's not normal.'

He looks offended for a second but then his brow clears and he looks horrified. 'I did that?' He backs away in horror. 'No way, I didn't do anything weird. I didn't want you to walk up to me and you know . . . try and kiss me.'

'Well, I've definitely not wanted to do it before, either, so this makes me think that this heritage of yours comes with a few extra gifts we're not sure about. Whatever you are, you make people feel attracted to you in quite a primitive way.' I've gone from shocked to scared to amused in such a short space of time, purely because he looks so genuinely taken aback and deeply uncomfortable. 'We need you to, uhm, how do I put this? Get you to tone down the love vibe.'

'Oh my God, don't call it that.'

The horror on his face is classic and I start laughing.

'Don't make me come over there and hug you, Blackhart, because I will and you'll regret it.'

Which only makes me laugh harder and it's good to laugh and feel a tiny bit normal again.

Kyle sounds as taken aback as Dante still looks. 'Okay, so are we saying we think Dante may have some siren genes?'

'Yes.' I'm sitting on the couch in Dante's flat and he's sitting opposite me on the other couch. Dante's phone is on speaker on the coffee table between us. 'Definitely. Or we could go for an incubus but I'm unclear if an incubus is Fae, or a sub-species of the Infernal.'

'Come on, are they even real?' Dante cuts in, looking miserable. 'This sounds so . . .' He shivers and pulls a face. 'So like it's from some medieval monk's nightmare fantasy.'

'Dante, these creatures are as real as you and me. There's recorded proof.' Kyle's voice is huffy. 'Listen, we're not saying you *are* one, okay? We're just trying to figure out *what* you are.'

'But a siren?' Dante says, looking unhappy. 'It sounds so . . . I don't know. Girly?'

'He could possibly be a selkie.' The next suggestion from Kyle has me rolling my eyes but I can hear him frantically paging through books. 'Or anything, basically.'

'Well, he's definitely noble born, a Sidhe first and foremost,' I say. 'We think he may be Eadric's son.'

There's the sound of a bang and Kyle swearing. 'Ha ha, that's funny, Kit. I swear you just said he's Eadric's son.'

'I'm sending you a picture of the ring. Can you check the database?' I sigh and rub my eyes. 'And here I was thinking all I'll have to do today is teach you how to hide your horns.'

'Horns!' Kyle's voice has risen to screeching level. 'He has horns? Kit, you should have said so earlier.'

'What difference does it make?' Dante asks the phone. 'Is that a bad thing?'

'No, but it means it could help me figure out what you are.'

I have to hand it to my cousin. He's handled this call pretty well, considering I've just told him we have a changeling in our midst. And that, oh, I tried to snog Dante's face off because he has some sort of built-in Fae voodoo that makes me fancy him a lot.

'Okay, maybe you can do that once we've rung off,' I say to Kyle. 'And we're not mentioning this to your dad either, right?'

There's a protracted silence from Kyle but he catches on fast enough. 'Yes, of course not. Jamie neither, right?'

I bite my lip, not keen to reveal that Jamie already suspects something. I wonder why he's not called to check on me, but maybe he figures it's something I can handle myself.

'Right.'

'What have your searches shown?' I ask Kyle instead. 'Have you found any connection between the families and the music festival?'

'It was easy enough putting the search parameters into the software,' he says enthusiastically. 'I now have a full database of their financials and social media updates and, no, they don't have that music festival in common. Some of them, yes, but not *all* of them.'

'You're serious?' I lean forward. 'You're sure?'

'As sure as I've been of anything.'

I breathe out. 'Holy smokes. I was counting on this being the thing that ties it up.'

'I know. Now what?' Kyle sounds miserable and I hear a keyboard being hit in frustration.

'It could still mean something, you know. If only some of them go to the same music festival.' Dante frowns at me. 'Usually, if you go to a festival you go with friends, right?'

'Or it's a coincidence and means nothing at all,' Kyle mutters under his breath. 'Kit, this case completely sucks.'

'Give me a few minutes, let me think. If they've got a website up and running I want to check it out.'

'They do, they also have a Facebook account, Tumblr, Twitter – all of it. And a forum.'

Without a word, Dante moves his laptop towards me.

'Some of these people actually worked at the festival, whereas others attended or had something to do with it in some semi-official capacity or other.'

'How do you know?' I ask Kyle.

'Looking at the main website now. There are various picture galleries.'

I hang up and yawn. Keeping my armour in place is tiring and, after spending a few hours with Dante, coaching him on how to dampen down his magic and abilities, I feel as if I've run a bazillion miles. But he's still keeping his distance and looks terrified every time I move.

I'm not sure if I should be amused or ashamed by his reaction. Was it that awful to be near me? I don't grace magazine covers or movie screens but so far no one has run screaming down the road at my approach. Well, not counting the group of goblins I chased down a suburban street that one time, but that was different.

What did he say afterwards? I'm too young for him to

think about me in that way? Did that mean he did think about me like that? I frown at the computer screen as I type in the festival's name and find the website.

There are a lot of picture galleries. I slide down onto the floor in front of the coffee table and turn the computer sideways so that Dante can see the screen too.

'What's it looking like?' he asks me, holding his hands up.

I narrow my eyes at him and scan him with magic. 'You look safe, you sexy beast. Sit down over there and hope I don't try and crawl across the table to snog your face off.'

He barks out a laugh but he relaxes visibly. He sits down cross-legged opposite me and spins the laptop around so he can see the screen. 'You sure you don't have a boyfriend? Your acerbic wit really builds up a guy.'

'Shut up and look at the pretty pictures. Let's see if we can recognize anyone.'

Chapter Forty-Two

'There!'

I jerk with fright as Dante points to something on the screen.

'It's the same guy as before. Can you see him?' I lean on the table so I can peer at the screen. We decided early on that he should take over looking through the photos. Every time I took the laptop the screen juddered or froze completely, yet it was perfectly fine when he used it.

The photo he's pointing at shows a couple laughing together. They're leaning close to one another and the camera's caught them just as they're pulling away from one another. In the background I see the dark figure I recognize from Tia's room. It's definitely the guy who stole into her room to take her away, or it looks as close as dammit. The shape and outline are the same but because the picture is a bit overexposed, focusing on the kissing couple, it makes the rest of it not as clear as I'd like.

'Save it to the folder. Once we've got more pictures, we can decide what we need to do,' I tell Dante.

While he has been checking the website, I've sketched the two figures I saw when I replayed Tia's abduction. The guy in her room had a similar build to the guy I saw in the photos, but nothing conclusive. I shove my notebook aside and mutter in frustration.

We work silently side by side. I'm going through Diane's auntie's scrapbooks again. They contain a mixed bag of local news, focusing heavily on the people she obviously knows. Several pages are devoted to news of the kids who've gone missing over the past few years. They're mostly drawn from the local newspaper and from a police website. Someone, possibly Diane, must have printed them off for her so she could paste them into the scrapbook.

My mind wanders as I read the newspaper accounts and I wonder about the bargain the missing children's parents entered into. Was it for money, fame, fortune? True love? As much as I yearn to believe people wouldn't be stupid enough to strike bargains with supernatural forces, some obviously have. Most likely, none of them, or almost none of them, had believed the bargain was real. Especially not if the bargain was presented in a low-key manner at a time when they were out there having fun, hanging out with their mates, not thinking about the future.

'Here, *have another drink. So, what if I say that five years from now you'll dig up a load of Viking gold and you'll get handsomely rewarded by the government. Would you give me anything I want if I make this come true?'*

'Ha ha, *sure, of course. What would you like? My eldest son? My soul?'*

'No, *no, nothing so ambitious. Your youngest child would do nicely. Deal?'*

'Yeah, *deal.'*

'Here, *sign this IOU. And you need to read the vow out loud too, to make it binding.'*

'Shit, *is this for real?'*

'*Ha ha, no, just a bit of fun, really, don't you think? Helps with the atmosphere. Here, have another shot of this.*'

'*I take this vow, before these witnesses to allow you to come into my house and steal away my youngest child.*'

'*Perfect. Drink up.*'

The thought of it makes me gag but then the likelihood of this type of scenario playing out feels maybe a bit too real.

I stand up and stretch, climbing over Dante's legs to head into the kitchen to make myself a coffee and him some tea.

'Am I no longer allowed to drink coffee?' he asks me when I put the mug down in front of him.

'Did you drink a lot of coffee in the past?'

He looks confused for a second but then shakes his head. 'No, not really. Not that I remember, actually. Mostly tea. Proper strong stuff. Lots of milk and sugar.'

I look at him as I sip my coffee. 'I don't know if I should tell you what happens to the Fae who do imbibe coffee.'

'I don't want to know, do I?'

'Oh, I don't know. It might be interesting.' I can't help the grin as it spreads across my face. 'Coffee is illegal in the Otherwhere and only a few places are allowed to sell it. It's a controlled substance.'

'Does it kill them?'

'No, it makes them . . .' I flap my hand from side to side. 'Amorous.'

'You are kidding me.' How many more times will this poor guy look horrified today, I ask myself as I burst out laughing. 'You're not serious, right? God, you're serious!'

'It's okay, you're safe with tea, I think. Thorn only ever drank the herbal stuff.'

'There's caffeine in tea too, Kit.'

I shrug and drink my coffee, saluting him with my mug. 'I don't make the science,' I tell him. 'I don't know how it works, but that's what I've been told.'

He pushes his mug to the side with a grimace. 'Urgh. I feel sick now. But, on the other hand, I've got a decent set of pictures of our mysterious man in his weird tattered outfit. In a few he's with some other people in the background, but there's never a clear photo of him.'

'That is still great news.' I push myself forward. 'Show me.'

He opens the folder and a range of picture show up, all with our raggedy man on the edges.

'Worst photo-bombing ever,' I say, tapping the screen before hastily drawing my finger back when the laptop makes a weird *urk* sound. 'Put those in the shared folder and I'll call Kyle now.'

I ring Kyle on my mobile. 'Hey, cousin of mine. We've got photos of the man I recognize from Tia's room. Can you see if you can do any magic tricks with photo software and enhance the pictures?'

'I'm on it. Have Dante drop them in the, oh, never mind, they've just showed up. Okay, give me a few, I'll call you back.'

'Cheers,' I say. 'Have you heard from Aiden today?'

'He rang maybe an hour ago to say he's going to some meetings with his dad. And if you wanted him you just needed to call.'

I smile a wide smile. Things were almost back to normal between us. 'Thanks, Kyle, you're a real pal.'

'Whatever. Must your life be this complicated, Kit?'

'Work,' I tell him. 'Work your little fingers to the bone,

Kyle Blackhart, so we can track this bugger and his pal and find those kids and steal them back.'

'You think they're still alive?'

'Think about it – why would you strike a bargain with some stranger so you can take their child . . . and then kill him or her? Seems a bit wasteful, right?'

'Oh, I think I know who you mean.' The voice on the phone belongs to Neville Clarke, one of the main organizers for the Folk and Indie Harvest Festival. 'Don't bother sending the photos through, I'm looking at the site now. The "staff" gallery, right?'

Neville Clarke sounds exactly the way he looks from his photo on the site's website: a large robust man in his sixties, with massive forearms and the kind of craggy face you only get to see on people who spend most of their time outdoors.

'That's the German boy. He comes every year. Stella, what is his name?'

I look at Dante and we share a smile. Stella is the one who answered the phone when we called the number on the website. From the sound of it she's overrun with questions from a lot of children's voices demanding her attention. When Neville answered he excused himself for a few moments to send his granddaughter off to go and play with her siblings.

'Sorry, just bear with me.' Neville's voice becomes muffled as he presses the handset against his chest, no doubt. There's a dog barking somewhere in the background and it sounds like utter madness. 'Hello? Yes, Stella thinks his name is Theodore Pfeiffer. Like I said, he comes every year with his father. His father is Ulrich.'

'Are they an act?' Dante's doing his cop impression and it seems to work fine.

'Yes, they travel with some of the professional Renaissance performers and do odd jobs around the place as required. They are also the core of the musician group. Sorry, who did you say this was?'

'My name is Dante Alexander, sir. I'm with the SDI in London. Would you like the number to ring my superior?'

'You're a policeman?'

'My department is an investigative department within the police.'

'Interesting. Yes, give me your superior's contact information while you're at it. What else do you need to know?'

'Do you know where we can get hold of this Ulrich and Theodore Pfeiffer?' Dante asks him after rattling off his office number and his superior's name.

'One moment.' There is more yelling for Stella in the background. 'I'm giving you to Stella. She'll be able to locate the files.'

'Thank you for your assistance, sir.'

'You're welcome. Can you tell me what this is about?'

'I'm afraid we can't, sir, not until we've completed our investigation.'

'Are they in trouble?'

'I can't say anything about that either, I'm sorry.'

Neville Clarke mutters something and hands the phone over to his out-of-breath wife, Stella, who is all business but as friendly as her husband.

'Theo and his dad travel around the UK and Europe for part of the year. They gave us this address.' She reads it out and I scribble it down on the notepad. 'I know they stay with a relative in Dulwich for some of the time, but I don't have their contact details there. I have Ulrich's mobile number, though.' She gives that to us too.

'Mrs Clarke, you've been very helpful.'

Stella's voice drops and I have the impression she's walked some distance from her husband because the background noise of young voices sounds further away. 'If they've done anything wrong, you will let us know immediately? We can't afford to have any negativity connected with the festival. It would mean the death of us.'

'We'll let you know within the month, Mrs Clarke. I'm really sorry to have bothered you about this.'

'You're more than welcome. Anything else we can do for you, do let us know.'

Dante hangs up and we stare at one another for a few seconds. I've looked up the address on my phone and it's somewhere in the middle of the Black Forest in Germany.

'What do you think?'

'That, unless the Pfeiffers are in Dulwich, we'll have to travel to Germany.' I stifle a yawn and peer at Dante. His magic seems contained and I cautiously let mine drop to see how I react to being around him. He seems pretty stable and I'm impressed that he's not dropped the glamour on his horns the whole day we've been together.

'I really hope they're in Dulwich,' he says, logging into the SDI's database. 'I've never enjoyed flying. I get air-sick.'

I grin at him. 'I really don't want to go to Germany either.' I pick up the phone and ring Kyle and ask him to check if he can find out anything about the two Pfeiffers from our own database. He promises to get right on it.

'Who do you think they're working for?'

I shrug as I stand up and stretch again. I feel achy and cold, sitting on the floor. Why I've been sitting on the floor for most of the afternoon I'm not sure, especially as Dante's couches are so comfortable.

'I don't know, we'll have to figure it out.' I feel my back unkink and turn to find Dante watching me from shadowed eyes. 'What?'

'Just thinking something.'

'Is it bad thinking or good thinking?'

His smile is slow. 'Well, that totally depends on your point of view of good or bad.'

'Are you flirting?'

'Maybe, just a bit.'

I laugh at his jokey evasive tone of voice. 'Okay, well. Just know that, if you try something, I'll be able to take you down.'

'Huh. And that's supposed to not be a challenge?'

My breath hitches when he stands up unexpectedly. He's faster than he was before, I realize. My magic shield slams closed around me but I stand my ground, refusing to give way even if I'm feeling a little scared. I know I can fight Dante if I have to, but I tend not to like beating up my friends. Also, I don't know what his magic abilities are and how they'll manifest here in the Frontier. I've seen a Fae who was pretty average in the Otherwhere lift up a truck, and throw it at a friend when they got into an argument about turning up at a party in the same outfit.

'I'm kidding. Geez, woman, I just want to go and put the heating on in the kitchen. I don't know about you, but I'm actually cold.'

'I'm also hungry,' I tell him, looking at my watch, pretending nonchalance. Breakfast seems a very long time ago. 'What have you got to eat around here?'

'Not sure. We can order something in.' He moves past

me and into the kitchen. He rummages in a drawer and finds take-away menus. 'Choose something.'

While I flick through the leaflets he mutters something darkly about the boiler but seconds later it starts humming happily to itself.

'I don't really care what we eat, as long as we eat a lot of it. I am so hungry I can't think any more.'

I glance to where he's leaning against the oven with his arms crossed. He looks awkward now, I realize, in this place. Before this was where he lived and he liked it. Now he seems to be a stranger here.

'Indian?' I say, holding up a handful of leaflets. 'We're right on the doorstep of Brick Lane. We can't not have Indian food.'

'As you wish,' he says, waving his hand negligently. His wallet, lying next to the microwave, twitches then flies straight at me. I duck, letting out a yelp, and it slams into the back of the couch with a *whump*.

'Shit!' Dante's by my side, checking me over for wounds before looking at his wallet. 'Did I just do that?'

'I'm fine, don't worry, and yes, I think you just tried to knock me unconscious with your wallet.'

'How? Can you explain that?'

I shrug. 'That's not really how my magic works. I can lay down magics, I can See weird things, I can sort of step sideways and see time move past, but I can't animate objects the way you just did.' I prod his shoulder with a finger. 'Try it again.'

'Okay.'

For ages nothing happens but then I feel a shift in the air and the entire couch lifts three feet in the air, moves a foot sideways, knocking into the small table and sending it tumbling over, before crashing back down again.

'Uh.' I look at him doubtfully. 'Were you trying to do that?'

'No. I was trying to move my wallet again.'

'Oops.'

Otherwhere, the Tower at the End of the World

Once more the dream crept up on him. What alarmed him was that it wasn't night and he wasn't asleep. He sat in his study at the top of the tower, overlooking the cascading waterfalls in the distance, a treatise on magic and how the Frontier and Otherwhere were linked open before him.

Kit ducked into the rubble-strewn room and her gaze met his. Her smile lit her face and she breathed his name.

'I've been looking for you,' she said, her tone light, but there were definite signs of worry on her face.

He couldn't help himself. He reached out and drew her to him. She hesitated at first before resting against him, her arms curling around his neck as she hugged him tight.

'I'm glad you found me,' he said and it was the truth. How he missed the clean smell of her, her ever-changing moods reflected in her hazel eyes, how she fitted perfectly against him.

'Thorn, there's danger here.'

'I know.'

'You must be careful.'

'The danger is not aimed at me, but at you.' It was the truth. He could sense the growing menace deep within the abandoned derelict palace. 'You should leave. This is none of your concern.'

'It is.' She made an effort to untangle herself from him and he felt the pang of loss the second she moved. 'They have to be helped. I'm the only one who can help them.'

'Why does it have to be you?'

There's the sound of something heavy moving nearby and Kit edged further away from him, her ever-present sword drawn smoothly and ready for attack.

'Thorn?'

The voice did not belong in his dreams. He shifted, irritated that it dared intrude on this stolen moment.

'What are you doing?'

He blinked slowly, watching Odalis's features swim into view. 'Memorizing,' he said without missing a beat. 'The treatise.' His hand dropped onto the pages before him. 'I didn't realize before how closely the two worlds were connected.'

Odalis gave him a flinty look but nodded. 'The relationship is one of symbiosis. What happens in the Fae Otherwhere affects the human Frontier and vice versa. The witches from the Frontier have a saying: as above, so below. I do not think they realize how apt it truly is.'

'Have you come to ask me something?' he asked, watching how her mouth tightened. She was not an unattractive woman but her stern demeanour and haughty manner made her an unappealing tutor and unpleasant to be around. Not for the first time he wondered if his father deliberately sought out the most miserable person to tutor him in his new role. He knew his thoughts were uncharitable, but thus far she'd not done more than push book upon countless book at him. Then question him for hours and make him practise scrying until headaches debilitated him. Occasionally they would practise magic and he would be required to sense what kind of an attack she was about to launch at him. He got the feeling she was as unimpressed with him as he was with her, but that she was doing this as her duty to Aelfric.

'A messenger came today: there is to be a ball to celebrate the winter solstice. We have been invited.'

'Us? You mean both of us?'

'Correct. Your father has made it clear that your presence will be required. He has the dragon lords from Chin coming and the Empress of the Rus has agreed to travel all that way.'

Thorn raised an eyebrow. 'I'm sure my father knows what he's doing – inviting dignitaries from all over the Otherwhere so soon after his brother's attempt to destroy his kingdom.'

Odalis made an impatient gesture at his disapproving tone. 'Don't be stupid, boy. You know he wants to show you off. You've become a key part of his diplomatic relations with the rulers of the Otherwhere. The Empress is even bringing her granddaughter with a view to you two becoming betrothed.'

Had Thorn not been sitting he would have staggered. As it was, his hands curled into the pages of the book in front of him and he slowly stood up.

'I'm not sure I believe you.'

'Believe what you will. You will hear proof of his plans at the ball, I'm sure.'

Without waiting to be dismissed, Thorn slammed the book shut, tucked it beneath his arm and left the study. He walked to his room, ignoring the surprise of the servant

tidying his quarters, and flung the book against the wall.
The tray with the goblet and silver jug followed suit. Next
he kicked the small table over. In the distance thunder
rumbled and dark clouds scudded across the sun.

'Get my horse,' he snarled at the startled servant, who
watched him with pity rather than fear. 'Now!'

The man fled the room as if the hounds were after him.

Within half an hour Thorn strode into the stables and
accepted the bridle from the worried-looking stable boy.

'Sir, there's a storm brewing.'

'I know.' He swung up onto the horse's back and clicked
his tongue. The stallion surged beneath him and he was
soon lost amid the swaying branches of the forest surrounding
the tower.

Chapter Forty-Three

The drive to Dulwich takes a long time. It's been raining for most of the day and there are snarl-ups along the route. Dante's dressed warmly against the cold but also against the iron and steel in the car and I have the dubious honour of driving us. I've put on the radio to kill the awkward silence that's filled the car.

The way Dante's holding himself, away from the car door and slightly rigid, reminds me of the way Thorn sat when we drove up to London and then Scotland just a few months ago. The unexpected memory leaves a pang in my chest and I swallow against the upswell of emotion. With Thorn, even though we floundered for a bit, we had a clear mission to work towards. We needed to get him home and help his family regain Alba's throne. This involved preventing his uncle Eadric from successfully opening a gateway to another realm to bring about the return of the imprisoned Elder Gods. Easy. (My ass.) But we did it. And then he left. And I stayed behind. And now I've got his long-lost (hidden) cousin working with me as a partner and I have so many questions.

Is Dante really Eadric's son? And if so, why hide him here? Surely he had all the world to hide him in? Why did he choose the UK? Not just that, but where is Dante's mum? Was she okay with her son being taken? And even if she'd died, though I really hoped she hadn't, where was her family? Didn't they have a say when Dante was taken? Or were they part of the conspiracy to hide him? And why hide him, anyway? Was it instigated by Eadric or done without his knowledge? Whatever glamour hid Dante, lasting from when he was a baby to adulthood, must have been cast by someone powerful indeed.

Changelings, as far as my understanding goes, are usually found out as young children because they don't fit in with the humans who are supposed to care for them. I've read Katharine Briggs's books and know how badly children were treated in the past when they were suspected of being left by the faeries. The suspect child would be burned with hot pokers or left out and exposed to the elements. This even happened to normal kids with disabilities and not that long ago either, which makes it sadder still.

'Dante, do you have someone in your life that you see pretty frequently?'

'Apart from my parents?' He shakes his head. 'Not really. I've not seen some of my mates for a few years now. We drifted apart after that night when I saw the SDI guy take down a monster. They all thought I'd lost it, wouldn't believe me when I told them. They thought I was drugged out of my mind. Even my girlfriend left me. She didn't want to hang out with a crazy boy who her mates thought was weird.'

'Seriously? That's awful.'

'I know, poor me, right? But them shutting me out, if you can call it that, didn't come as a big surprise. I mean, I wasn't a nice guy, Kit. I blamed myself for my baby sister being taken. I was supposed to look after her when we went to the park. And I didn't so some evil bastard took her, killed her and left her body for a farmer to find. So, yeah, I drank, and smoked and gave my parents hell. I did martial arts to please my dad and taught those kids because that's what he wanted. And I enjoyed it, but I wasn't nice about doing it. The local cops knew me and would always just happen to find me hanging out with my mates, then pull me aside, giving me warnings. They respected my dad because he was army and good friends with some of them. I had a whole network of people who cared about me and all I wanted to do was see it burn. Until that night. When I saw the monster.' He twists in his seat slightly so he can look at me. 'I knew I had to do something, to stop it. I'd never felt sure of anything like it before. And afterwards, when I tried explaining it to my mates, they thought I'd taken it too far – that the weed we'd smoked earlier that afternoon had fried my brain.'

'What did you do?'

'I shut myself in my room and I researched the HMDSDI. I became obsessed. My grades went through the roof at school and I applied for extra classes to fill the afternoons when I wasn't teaching at the dojo. My dad was so happy, and my mum too. It feels awful to admit it but I loved seeing how they came to love me all over again because I'd been such an awful person to them and myself for so long. They were always proud, so they said, but now I could see it in their faces and in everything they did. And it felt good.'

'So you went from bad boy to swot? Usually it's the other way around.'

'Ha, didn't think about that.'

'Is this when you got your tattoo?'

'It was before. I know I told Diane I was sixteen when I got my tat, but I was younger even. I turned fifteen and couldn't think of any other way to make me feel like *me*. I forged my dad's signature and walked into a tattoo parlour in Bristol and the guy did it in one sitting.'

'I don't know what that means,' I admit.

'Usually, with elaborate tattoos like mine, you have it done over a few sittings. Three, maybe four. Usually it's a time thing, but also a pain thing.'

'And yours was done in one sitting? Did it hurt?'

'Honestly? I think it did, I assume I did, but mostly I can't remember. I remember walking in and talking to the guy about my design. I showed him a few pictures of things I liked. He sat down for a few minutes and sketched something out. It looked amazing, like it was alive. I loved it and handed over the cash. He sat me down, asked me about my pain threshold and I explained that I did martial arts and my dad taught me pain was all in the mind.'

'How long did it take?'

'I don't know. I can't remember. Time went weird while I was there. I walked in when it was dark and I left when it was dark.'

'And it never bothered you? Losing that time?'

'No. I was just so happy with my new ink. I loved it. I walked around Bristol for hours, feeling high, feeling like me for the first time ever.'

'What did your parents say when they saw it?'

'My mum went mental, as you can imagine. She spent a whole afternoon crying. But then she came out and looked at it properly and said she would have been happier with just a I Heart Mum tattoo. My dad looked at it, gave me a beer and grounded me for a month except for working in the dojo. He made me train non-stop that month, then told me the next time I did something that stupid, without talking to him first, he'd put me in traction.'

My eyebrows shoot up my forehead. 'Was he serious?'

'Possibly. But then he got his tats whilst he was in the army when he wasn't much older than me, so he had no real room to talk.'

'Do you miss them?'

'Yes.'

'Do you think they know how different you really are?'

'No.' He laughs. 'If it was a question of either me or Emily being weird, she'd be the one. She was this tiny fragile-looking thing, but, boy, she had a will of steel.' His breath catches. 'I really miss her so much. I miss the possibility of her. She was clever and sweet, but she was also sarcastic and actually a little bit wicked – although you'd never guess.'

'Sounds like my cousin Megan. She looks cute and harmless, you know? No one ever sees how tough she is or spots the grease and dirt under her nails.'

'And what do you think you look like?' he teases. 'All six foot seven of you? All those tattoos and piercings. You scare little children and grannies alike.'

'Oh funny. I know what I look like, I'm not fishing for compliments or complaints. I think people look at me and they see a girl who's capable. No one will rush to my aid if I need help with – I don't know – changing a tyre or something. Not in the same way they'd help Megan. Even if she can strip a car down around a flat tyre, then build it back up again, and somehow it's a better car.'

Dante narrows his dark eyes and looks at me. 'When I look at you, Kit Blackhart, I see a strong, independent, stubborn young woman who intrigues me. You're intelligent, funny and, when you try, you're actually very charming. You don't take crap from anyone. You do what you think is best and have this moral compass that makes me feel safe.' He lifts his hands in surrender when I scowl at him. 'No, seriously. I don't know why. I just know that when you're with me, we can win. Whatever the challenges.'

'You're full of it, Alexander. Get your coat and let's go see if we can talk to Theodore and Ulrich Pfeiffer.'

He smirks and I look away, ridiculously buoyed by his description of me. I feel none of those things he'd just assigned to me. I also feel flattened by the weight of responsibility on my shoulders. What if the Pfeiffers are nothing, and not related to the case in any way, what then? What are our chances of finding these kids alive now and why would I even begin to think I could handle something like this? We should have told Suola no, when she asked us to take this on. Gone to the cops with all our evidence, no matter how tenuous. Detective Shen would have looked into it. Jamie could have badgered her to take our clues seriously.

'Hey, are you okay?'

'Yes, just thinking.' I give him a smile and I hope it's a convincing one.

Chapter Forty-Four

I honestly wish I had my sword with me. I miss the feel of it, but knocking on a stranger's door with a sword sticking up over your shoulder is frowned on in civil society. So instead I have to rely on my baton and my boot knife if help is needed. I leave the sword in the boot of Dante's Lexus.

Dante's carrying his favourite pair of knuckledusters in his jacket pocket, the ones emblazoned with angelic runes (I still feel itchy about him having them, especially now that he has the extra whammy of being Fae). He also has a compact taser attached to his belt in a tidy pouch. I worry that he has no bladed weapons, but then he can run up walls and kick an opponent in the head, so maybe he's better armed than I am.

The house before us is a Georgian in style with a semi-circular driveway. The front garden is neatly kept and presents a facade of well-to-do respectability to the world. I double check the address Kyle confirmed (our database held no further info on the Pfeiffers) before pressing the doorbell. I'm hesitant to use the gargoyle knocker as it might hide a biting spell and its teeth look vicious.

Dante stands next to me and we don't have very long to

wait. The door is opened by a woman of indeterminate age who reminds me a lot of my Aunt Jennifer. She resembles one of those impeccably and effortlessly dressed women who looks as though they are always ready to meet the Queen for high tea.

'May I help you?'

I try not to squirm under her brief examination. Her eyes are an electric blue and the force of their regard is almost physical. She takes me in with one glance before turning her attention to Dante, who's the one that draws her brows together.

'Mrs Taylor? My name is Dante Alexander and this is my partner, Kit Blackhart. I'm with the SDI.' Here he shows her the badge, which she takes from him to look at, before handing it back. 'We're looking for someone whom you may know. Ulrich Pfeiffer and his son, Theodore? We have it on good authority that they may be here at present.'

'Is anything the matter?' she asks. From inside the house I can hear what sounds like the radio. Over her shoulder the place looks immaculate, like something straight out of *Home & Garden* or some other magazine celebrating home interiors.

'I'm afraid we can't say, Mrs Taylor. We do need to speak with Mr Pfeiffer or his son, though. It's quite urgent.'

She purses her lips, considering our request. She looks me over again and I stand tall, hoping that my sturdy jeans, thick-soled biker boots and jumper over a black polo neck T-shirt meets with her approval. I left my biker jacket in the car because I didn't want to look like the poster child for teen rebellion.

'Ulrich is in the back,' she says, beckoning us in. 'He's helping my husband do some DIY.'

'And Theodore?'

She shrugs. 'You'll have to ask his father.'

I let Dante walk ahead of me and follow closely behind. There's no magic here, I decide, as I pass through a small foyer and into a comfortably large sitting room. The furnishings look well cared for but none of it is new. There are a few pieces, like the painting over the fireplace, that look as if they might have been in the family for a fair few years.

I get a sense of a well-off family living here, enjoying a quiet life, as Mrs Taylor leads us towards the back of the house and the garden. We end up in the utility room, where two men are working. They stand up when we near.

'Ulrich, these people are here to talk to you. They say they're from one of the police departments, but I have to say I'm not sure when the police started working with children.'

The younger of the two men stands upright at her words. He's my height but broad across the shoulders and looks like he keeps himself fit. His face is tanned and his eyes are an arresting golden colour.

'Ulrich Pfeiffer,' he says, shaking Dante's hand after wiping his own on a bit of cloth. 'And you are?'

Dante introduces us both and Mr Taylor decides the room is too small, ushering us all back into the kitchen area. Ulrich, I notice, seems to be more at home in this room, with its big windows and expansive garden visible at the back, than the two Taylors are. The place really did look like a show home.

'Mr Pfeiffer, would it be possible to speak to you privately?' Dante looks at the two hovering Taylors seriously. 'The questions are quite personal.'

'We'll go to the lounge, Uli,' Mr Taylor says, nudging his wife. 'Nadine, come along.'

'But Uli is a guest in our house, Philip. We can't just let these children pester him.'

Philip Taylor says something quietly to his wife that shuts her up and I wonder exactly what he said. Ulrich – Uli – Pfeiffer watches us with some interest.

'Please, I'm very interested in why you're here.'

'We are investigating the disappearance of some children. Our research has led us to the Folk and Indie Harvest Festival in Yorkshire. Our information shows that you've been working the festival since it started.'

Mr Pfeiffer nods slowly. 'Yes . . . but then so have Neville, Stella, and a dozen others.'

Dante keeps his face passive yet interested. 'Correct. We are also in the process of talking to others about this. Can you tell me where you were two nights ago, between 10 p.m. and 3 a.m.?'

'Here, I've got notes.' Ulrich gets something from his bag and I move sideways so I can see what he's doing. Here I'm also out of Dante's range if Mr Pfeiffer gets violent and Dante decides to throw a punch. 'I keep a strict record of my comings and goings. It's for accountancy purposes. Two nights ago I was in Cricklewood, at the Molly Malone pub. They were hosting a ceilidh.'

Dante's eyebrows shoot up in surprise. 'I'm not sure I follow?'

'Ceilidh is a Celtic word that means . . . party. If you play an instrument, you're welcome. It's like being part of a super band. You sit around, talk and play music and, of course, you have a drink or two.' He adds the last bit with a cheeky smile.

'And what time did your ceilidh finish?'

'It was a lock-in.' Ulrich Pfeiffer laughs delightedly. 'I love your country and their quirky ways. I got home after 9 a.m. We all went for breakfast first.'

'Can you tell me where your son was at this time, Mr Pfeiffer?'

'I've not seen Torsten for about two months now. It's his holiday time before we head back to Germany to do some of the Christmas markets.'

I twitch at the name 'Torsten' and Dante shoots me a look of interest before I question Mr Pfeiffer again.

'Torsten? I thought your son's name was Theodore.'

'What can I say? The boy hates his name and has been calling himself Torsten for around five years now. To keep him and his mother happy, that's what I call him.'

Dante looks down at his notebook and scribbles something down.

'How old is your son?'

'He's twenty-nine.' A frown draws his brows together. 'Do you think Torsten has anything to do with these children disappearing?'

'We're just following up information, sir. And you're sure you don't know where he is right now?'

'No, I mean, he works in various pubs and clubs.'

'Doing what?'

'He's a DJ and has gigs across London. It's hard keeping track of him.'

I'm grateful that Dante's keeping the attention on himself by asking all the questions now so neither of them notices how the world drops beneath my feet. Torsten? The boy who might be stealing kids is maybe (possibly) the DJ at Milton's? Can't be . . .

Dante asks a few more questions, checks Torsten's mobile number and takes photos of Mr Pfeiffer's diary. He then gives Mr Pfeiffer his business card. Mr Pfeiffer asks a few questions about the investigation that Dante deflects with ease.

Before we turn to leave, I smile at Mr Pfeiffer. 'Do you have a photo of Torsten?' I ask him.

He looks unhappy but opens his wallet and digs a photo out from the billfold. 'This is us in France, at the Balaruc-le-Vieux Medieval Festival. Two years ago, in fact.' He taps his finger against the photo. 'Torsten had a new costume made that year. He looked good.'

He turns the photo over to me to see. I do my best poker face when I realize the DJ I spoke to just the other day is genuinely the same Torsten as in the picture. In the photo, Torsten is dressed in a harlequin's costume – but instead of a motley collection of colours, the costume is black and red. He's striking a pose that I recognize from a CD cover. The lone piper, one leg tilted and resting against his thigh. His arms are up and he's staring straight at the camera, in the process of bringing the flute to his lips. His expression is serious, if a bit challenging.

The costume accentuates his lean build and tawny good looks.

'Would we be able to get a copy of that?' Dante asks Mr Pfeiffer, who just waves it off.

'I have another. Keep that one if you must.'

'Thank you.' Dante shakes Pfeiffer's hand and I give him a nod then follow Dante as we exit the house. The Taylors are behind us, both of them, and they stare at us as if we've just brought the plague to their home.

* * *

'You know who he is, don't you?' He watches me closely as I pull on my seatbelt and fiddle with the keys. 'Why didn't you say anything earlier?'

'I know *now*, yes, but not before Mr Pfeiffer showed us the photo and called his son Torsten.'

'So, what do you know?'

'The DJ at Milton's? His name is Torsten, or that's what he calls himself. The picture we've been shown confirms that it's the same guy.'

He shifts in his seat, leaning away from the door. 'We need to make one hundred per cent sure he's our guy.'

'But don't you think it's weird, that it's all falling into place so . . .?'

'Don't say it,' Dante groans. 'Don't say it's been too easy because it hasn't. And that usually means that there's going to be more trouble.'

I feel a wave of fatigue as Dante yawns and leans back against his seat. I feed a thread of my magic towards him but stop well short of letting it mingle with his. His colour's off and I resist the urge to reach out and press my hand to his forehead because he looks so flushed.

'Are you okay?'

'What? Yes, just hot, weirdly. Aren't you warm? We need to get back to the estate and we need to talk to a few of the parents from the other disappearances to see if they recognize Torsten.'

I start the car and pull into the traffic. We talk as I drive. Even the few minutes we've spent at the Taylors' helped the evening rush hour dissipate and we manage a decent speed.

'But there's two of them,' I point out. 'Who's the other guy?'

'The dad?'

'Nothing magical about Dad Pfeiffer. He is as mundane as . . . tomato soup.'

Dante laughs at that but he nods. 'Do you think it's someone from the club?'

'Who knows? Hopefully if we beat Torsten up a bit he'll reveal all his secrets.'

'Why do you sound personally annoyed by this?'

I click my tongue against my teeth in a gesture of annoyance. 'He just seemed nice, you know? He plays great tunes. He even gave me about five hours of decent new remixes, ones that he'd been working on, to listen to.'

'When did you speak to him?' His voice is sharp and I glance at him guiltily before looking back to the road. 'Kit? I thought you said you wouldn't go back to the club without me. Was Aiden with you? Tell me Aiden was with you.'

'Wow. Can you stop playing the controlling macho dude?' I frown at the car in front of us. 'I went to the club yesterday to check something out with Miron. When I left, Torsten called me up to the DJ box and we chatted. He gave me a USB with some new music to listen to, that's all.'

'So you plugged the USB into your laptop's hard drive . . . ?' He inclines his head at me and raises his eyebrows. 'Kit, seriously? You didn't think to have Kyle check the USB for spyware?'

I immediately dip my fingers into my hip pocket and pass him my phone. 'Call Kyle, right now. Get him to check my laptop. It automatically backs up to our external server. If he gets in there he can wreak havoc.'

The telephone conversation that follows is terse and I can sense Kyle's deep annoyance at my stupidity. I can't even remember why I was last using my laptop. How many of my case notes and thoughts did I transfer onto it?

Definitely the photos from Tia's home. Including the photos I took of my parents' files from Dante's car. While Kyle tries not to have a nervous breakdown about the server being compromised, Dante briefly tells Kyle what we've found out from Mr Pfeiffer, asking him to do a thorough Internet search for Torsten Pfeiffer. He also asks him to check his DJ name and to do searches on that too.

When he's done, I ask him to ring Chem then hold the phone up to my ear. Chem answers within two rings.

"Sup?'

'Chem? It's Kit.'

'I can see your name on the display.' He tuts irritably. 'What do you want? Do you know where Tia is yet? Marv's mum had to go to hospital. She couldn't stop crying.'

'That's the thing, Chem. We have a pretty decent lead. I need you to do me a favour.'

'Yeah?'

'Yes.'

'Go on then, what is it?'

I take a deep breath and explain that we want to show a photo to all the parents on the estate who have missing children.

There's a silence before he speaks. 'This is – what do they call it, serendipity? They're all here, having a meeting because of what's happened to Tia.'

'Where exactly?'

'The community hall, behind the main building of the estate.'

'How long have they been there?'

'Don't know man, how would I know?'

'Can you get there? We're on our way. Can you ring me if they leave or something?'

'You want me to spy on them?'

'Yes.'

His grumbling tells me he's not impressed by the favour but he agrees and hangs up. We're probably about fifteen minutes away.

'I'm just going to close my eyes for a few seconds, okay?' Dante leans his head back against the car seat. 'I feel wiped out right now. Like I'm on the other side of bad flu or something.'

'Yeah, world's worst type of flu. Go to bed, wake up and suddenly you have horns and your friend tells you she thinks you're a faerie.'

He laughs, while giving me a mock-evil look. 'Do you ever stop being full of it?'

'Yes, maybe at about three in the morning when I wake up, my heart pounding and my throat raw from screaming because of a nightmare where I watch all my family die or get taken away from me. Then I can't go back to bed because I can't unsee any of it and my brain is a crazy place anyway and so I lie there and think of ways to keep them safe. Then I get up and pretend everything is okay.' I blink. 'Uh, that was not supposed to come out.'

I feel him watching me as I drive and, instead of feeling awkward, it's okay, not quite as soul-baring as I'd thought. There's a pulse of warmth and I sense that he's resisting the urge to reach out and touch me, for which I'm grateful.

'It never actually occurred to me that you were ever scared,' he says after some time when I'd thought he'd fallen asleep.

'I'm scared all the time.' What is wrong with me? He doesn't need to know this stuff and yet here I am, telling him my feelings. 'I doubt myself all the time. I worry about what people I try to help might be thinking; if they believe they are doomed, if all they have to save them is a teen girl who acts like she has all the answers. If they think that because I'm a girl I can't be as tough as a boy. And I think because I'm young, the fight to get respect is even harder. In the past people haven't taken me seriously until I show up with Uncle Jamie in tow and then it's all, Oh, okay, now we'll do what you tell us to do. It's just the same when I turn up with my cousin Marc. He's big and tall and although he's still young, probably your age, he has this air of confidence that just gets people to believe in him. Maybe it helps because he's male too.'

The smile Dante gives me is slow and I wonder if he's managed to get stoned between us leaving the Taylors and here, because he definitely doesn't look all there.

'You worry too much,' he says. 'You're brimful of confidence and you can sometimes let the fact that you're an attractive girl work in your favour, you know? Don't scowl so much, give people a chance.'

'Are you stoned?'

'No, just really sleepy. I don't know what's going on.' He yawns an impossibly wide yawn and stretches. 'All of me aches.'

'As soon as we're done here tonight, we're getting you back home.'

'Will you nurse me again?'

'Mr Alexander, are you flirting with me?'

'Possibly. I like how it makes you look a little flustered.'

I laugh at him and feel a blush curl up my cheeks. 'Yeah, you freak me out a bit.'

'Is it Aiden? Do you have someone else?'

'I . . .' I look at him. 'It's difficult. There's this other guy.

We went through some bad stuff last year and things were left unresolved . . . I don't know if I'll see him again.' I smile and try to lighten the moment. 'Besides, you need to talk to Aiden, I think. He keeps asking me the same questions about you. I think you can both bond over that.'

'Sucks.' He makes a soft noise in the back of his throat and shifts closer to me. 'About the other guy, I mean. Is that – Thorn?'

'Yes. He's . . . if we're right about who you are, he's your cousin.'

Dante's eyes widen. 'But . . . I thought that Fae can't have relationships with humans?'

'Yes, well, there's that too.'

'There's more?'

Why is he asking all these things? And why am I telling? I suppress a sigh as I bring him up to date on Thorn and my brief history, ending with why he was sent away. 'Turns out there was a prophecy about Thorn. Eadric caught him with the sole purpose of using him to fulfil it, which Eadric interpreted as designed to bring the Elder Gods back.'

'And did he? Succeed, I mean.' Dante's voice still sounds very far off and strange.

'Almost. Eadric came close but we stopped it from happening. And then Thorn went away to become this fabled guardian of the realms.'

'Sounds like Heimdall.'

'What?'

'From Norse mythology. He's the guy who keeps watch at the end of the Bifrost for the start of Ragnarok.'

'How do you even know this?'

'Comics. I can't be a bad boy and not be into comics, can I?' He laughs. 'That's not entirely true. My mum's a teacher and she always had books lying around the house on fairy tales and mythology. So I grew up on a steady stream of the stuff.'

'What else do you know about Heimdall?' I almost don't want to know, as his story makes me feel Thorn's absence all the more keenly.

'Basically that he keeps watch over the nine realms, that he has foreknowledge and is aware of any threats they face.'

I try to swallow down my hurt. 'That definitely sounds like what they're asking of Thorn.'

Dante's hand rests on my shoulder, squeezing lightly before it drops away.

'You can talk to me, you know.'

'Oh, and you know so much about relationships?'

'I'll have you know I had a girlfriend for two years. And a boyfriend for about six months. That worked out less well, so ignore the fact that I said that.'

'And then you saw fairies and she left you and who knows what you did to your poor boyfriend. Yeah, you're the boss of dating.'

'Woah.' He clutches at his heart dramatically. 'That hurt.'

I laugh at his antics. 'Get ready, we're almost there.' And then, because it needs saying, 'Thanks for listening.'

Chapter Forty-Five

Chem's waiting for us as soon as we get out of the car. He nods at Dante but asks me, 'What's wrong with the guy? He looks worse than the other day.'

'He's getting over some flu,' I say, keeping my voice light. 'If he falls over, just make sure he doesn't hit his head.'

Chem grunts in assent and eyes him dubiously.

'I am right here,' Dante points out sourly. 'But feel free to talk about me like I'm not the oldest person here.'

I scoff and exchange an amused look with Chem, then we're at the community hall.

'Right, all the parents are still there. They brought like cake and tea and shit. Like it's a party or something.'

'Is Tia's dad there?'

'Yes. They're all there, and some other people I don't know. Even Diane's auntie is there.'

'Uh. Okay.' I gesture for him. 'Let's go. Show us.'

Chem leads us around the far side of the last block of flats, along a bit of broken paving that was once a walkway, to a low flat-roofed building of the type they were so happy to build in the Seventies. Some of the windows are boarded up and there's graffiti on the walls but the lights are on.

There's a peculiar feeling in the night air, a heaviness I've not felt before. It reminds me of when I accessed the leylines at the Manor – a wild intoxicating experience.

I'm aware of Chem and Dante talking. To me? I can't be sure; I can't hear them properly. As I turn to look at them, they seem to be a long distance away.

I look back towards the abandoned play area and let myself walk into those lines and See.

A group of maybe as many as a hundred men are gathered around a large bonfire. They're talking and laughing, their voices a bit wild in the night air. They're dressed against the cold, heavy cloaks drawn close; a jug of some beverage is being passed around.

They're mature men, bearded and beringed. Affluent with the air of leaders. Slowly, as if by some prearranged signal, the men start falling quiet and a single figure steps forward. He throws the hood of his cloak back to reveal strong features in a darkly tanned face.

He holds up a hand for silence and the men arrange themselves before him in a way that is deferential but not remotely submissive. Annoyingly, I can't hear what's being said – the distance is too great, and the fire is making it difficult for me to concentrate. It flickers in front of my eyes, making the men appear insubstantial. I shift my stance in an attempt to see better, and I can tell he sees me: his gaze widens in shock.

He's talking now, looking right at me and all I can do is stand still as he stalks closer, moving away from the fire. The men behind him are watching this with fear and antici-pation in their upturned faces.

The man is so close now that we lock gazes. I stare into his unfathomable grey eyes as he leans towards me, speaking. I shake my head to show him I can't hear him, so he grabs my arm. Instead of his hand passing through me, he grabs hold of my wrist. Suddenly it's as if the volume's dialled up to eleven, because there's noise and I can hear him. And although his words are a jumble of harsh sounds, I understand that he's trying to reassure me of something. I listen hard, repeating the words out loud, burning them into memory so I can ask Kyle to translate them later.

An arm circles my waist and I start, and the man's face turns pale despite the bonfire's glow. He shows fear for the first time as his gaze finds Dante, who is now behind me. Dante would strike fear into any hardened warrior as he looks now – wild and feral. The horns that were nubs before are now fully grown into impressive antlers that lift proudly from his brow.

The man and his cohorts are shouting. I pull Dante's arm from around my waist, managing to get him away from me long enough to reach out and touch the man. This stills him and I smile as I step away.

'Kit, stop hitting me.' Dante grabs both my wrists as I stop struggling, coming back to the estate and the here and now. 'I see you. There you are, welcome back.'

I stare at him, wondering where the horns went and why he'd looked so different. Then I gasp and remember, pulling free of him to scramble for my phone. I hit dial and as soon as Kyle answers I start talking, repeating the unfamiliar phrases over and over. I hear Kyle swearing and then he tells me to keep talking, he's recording.

I sink to my knees with the phone to my ear, weak from the flow of magic coursing through me. Dante's next to me, close but not touching and I appreciate it. Chem, though – he looks as if he wants to turn tail and run and he's staring at the small play area as if he wants to blow it up.

'What was that?' Chem demands when I hang up. The phone drops from my hands to the grass. 'What did you just do? Who were those people?'

'Chem.' My voice sounds rough, even to my own ears. 'It's okay. I promise. What you just saw wasn't real. It was a memory of what happened here in the past.'

'But how?'

There's an edge of panic to his voice now and I mutely implore Dante to help me out here while I scrabble to pull myself together. I can actually feel Chem relaxing as Dante drops a casual arm around his shoulders, and I wonder if he's using magic to help him out. They move away, Dante talking about magic and the weird shit that Kit does – and how it's actually okay.

I manage to stand and suppress an urge to throw up. My hands are still shaking when they walk back, and Chem looks at me as if I might be in danger of growing another pair of arms or head or who knows? My smile is tight and it takes him a few seconds to respond.

'So, on to the main event of the evening, then?' he asks cautiously and it makes me laugh.

'Definitely.'

Over his head, Dante lifts a questioning brow at me. But because we've not spent enough time together to be able to converse with eyebrows and pursed lips, I just shrug and follow Chem to the side of the building.

'Come and listen first. All of this is screwed up, right?'

We follow him around the side of the building where there's another door. 'It leads to the kitchen and they've left it open so that they can come out here and smoke, and no one from the flats can see them.'

'Do a lot of people use this place?' Dante asks Chem.

'Not really, no. I mean, it used to be used loads when I was little. Then it was a proper community place. People used to come here all the time to drink, play pool, hang out. But things changed. The roof fell in and killed some guy. The council repaired the roof but no one bothered coming here much after that. That was like ten years ago. Sometimes the little kids have birthday parties here and stuff like that but it's not really popular.'

We've reached the back of the building and he brings his finger up to his lips in the universal signal for us to be quiet. We follow him in, keeping low.

'. . . must end some time soon,' someone says, a man with a gruff voice. Definitely a smoker.

'The cycle has come to an end now the girl's been taken.' The voice is mature, decisive. 'Things will quieten down now.'

'What of the boy Arvind? He should have been taken weeks ago.'

'He was bypassed. There was an interference.'

'But what of our quota?'

'It's been filled. The girl, Tia. Her parents knew the chance they took when they signed up for the accommodation.'

'I don't think anyone can prepare for it being their child,' another voice interjects, female this time. She sounds old, her voice whispery.

'What do you want us to say, Georgina? We may be the custodians of the land, but we have all paid.'

'I am saying the practice is archaic and needs reviewing.'

Murmurs now and I can't tell if it's in assent or dissent.

'Who will you speak to about this? Brixi?' The voice is low and scoffing. 'He has not attended our council meetings in years. He only knows us when it's time for the harvesting of the next crop of children.'

'There must be a way to stop this entirely. Surely, after all this time, these sacrifices are no longer required. What has it got to do with modern life, anyway?' There's an impatient shifting of several bodies. 'I say we speak to Brixi and get things changed.'

I turn to stare at Chem and Dante. 'What are they talking about?' I mutter. 'They can't mean *the* Brixi, from like nine hundred years ago, can they?'

Chem looks at me as if I've gone crazy but Dante looks thoughtful. 'They could be. Maybe he was Fae.'

I exhale a low curse then jerk with fright when I recognize the next voice.

'Nice to try and get things stopped now, but what of those who've already had children taken? I bought these juju masks from a witchdoctor in Nigeria and he told me no one with magic could come through the door – and he showed me that they work. Yet this guy Brixi and his friend still came in and took my little girl.' It's Tia's dad; I recognise his voice for sure. Chem nods at my questioning look.

'Magic, is it?' There's a world of bitterness in this new voice. 'There's some ancient pact written into our rental agreement with the lord of the land. It permits some psycho to steal our children by sneaking into our homes – and you call it *magic*?'

'Well I guess that sounds a bit soft, but . . . ?'

'I don't care how they do it. I care that we are victims of something that has nothing to do with us.'

'The police . . .'

'The police don't care. If this was a case of some middle-class or rich kids going missing, they'd care very much. But because it's us, living on an estate, they have other things to be doing.'

'You can't say that, Jimmy. I've seen some of the police investigating this work themselves to the bone trying to get behind all of this.'

'Only for it to go nowhere, for the resources to be re-assigned.'

Someone says something I can't make out, a woman, but I look at Dante.

'Tithe?' I mouth the word at him but he must have been thinking along the same lines because he looks worried but nods his head.

'Could be.'

'What's that?' Chem asks me. 'What are you talking about?'

'A tithe is a really old term, where you pay a percentage of your income to someone you owe loyalty to. They had it in olden times. Like, if I were a king and you were a noble in my court, I'd ask you to pay me say a tenth of the income that you make from your lands and farms. And you would require the same from the people who work on your farms.'

'So basically you're talking about protection money?'

We both look at Chem in surprise. 'You pay me my money and I make sure my bullyboys don't come round and beat up you and your family and trash your shop.'

'Yes, I suppose you can look at it that way,' I admit, not liking that this makes so much sense.

'What the hell is going on, though? Who are they paying the tithe to?'

I shrug at Dante's question. 'I don't know. But it definitely sounds like it has a Fae or magical connection.'

'Why these people?'

'Maybe we should ask them.' I straighten up and gesture for them to do the same. 'We've heard enough to know nothing normal is going on here. Time to play.'

Chem looks panicked for a second. 'I can't be part of this. I don't want them coming after me if something goes wrong.'

'Okay, be our backup then. If things go really south, call the cops.'

He nods mutely and slinks back out. I turn to Dante and nod at him.

'Go on, knock like a cop. I know you get special training to perfect the sound.'

And at my encouraging nod he does exactly that. He raps hard on the door wedged open behind us.

It's followed by the scrape of chairs, and voices raised in alarm.

We walk into the room to face fifteen people, some are the parents of children who've been taken recently; others look older. They wear a mixture of expressions: alarm, concern, guilt and worry.

'Please,' Dante says, holding up his hand and flashing his badge. 'My name is Dante Alexander and this is my associate, Kit Blackhart. We've been asked to investigate the missing children from this estate and, from what we've just overheard, you'll definitely be able to help.'

Never let it be said Dante couldn't string a sentence together.

'This is a private meeting!'

'How did you get in here?'

The voices are loud and four of the larger men surge towards us, indignant and annoyed at our intrusion. Sometimes the best way to stop people from getting hurt is to do something ridiculous. I choose to do that now because I recognize the guy from my early morning jog.

He spots me too, and looks as if he's just seen a ghost. While he hesitates, I flick my wrist and I step forward as the baton slides out.

I lift my other hand and let my magic take shape right in front of all of them. There are startled shouts and a curse or ten, and I look up and away from the flames licking around my hand to smile at them. And it's not a nice smile. It's a smile that Aiden tells me will get me into a lot of trouble one day. He should know: he taught it to me.

'Stop!' I say, addressing Canal Guy. 'We just want to know what's going on. And who we need to talk to, to stop your children being taken.'

He's stopped in his tracks, looking nervous – but I can also see the hostility there and I hope we're not going to have to fight it out again.

'You're too late now,' one of the women says, her eyes heavy with guilt. 'They're gone and there's nothing we can do about it.'

'Do you really believe that?' Another woman looks at her and then turns to us. 'How can you help us? You're still a child yourself. And him? Who does he think he is? King of the fairies?'

I look over my shoulder and see that Dante's dropped his glamour. The nubs of his horns rise from the shocking black of his hair and he looks utterly otherworldly in the bad lighting of the community centre. The scent of high forests and mountains fill the hall and it's such a breath of fresh air in the confines of the room. I inhale deeply before securing a protective magic shield around myself. I'm pretty sure I can cope if Dante's pheromones kick in, but I don't want to be completely open to that risk with so much else going on.

'No, not exactly.' I have a small struggle to look away from him. But I manage and pin the woman with my gaze. 'Look, I know this is hard to accept, but we're here to help. Our ages don't matter; we just want to get your children back and stop whatever is going on here. *So can you help us?*'

'I think we should ask, *will* they help us?' Dante put in. 'Or are you happy with your children being taken as tithe?'

Someone starts sobbing and I shoot Dante a warning glance but he looks fierce. The room's watching us to decide what to do next. I exhale slowly, dropping my hands to my sides, presenting a calmer, less antagonistic, front.

'Look, my family – the Blackharts – hunt monsters that aren't human, and you obviously know there is something supernatural going on here. Dante and I have been asked to help find these missing children. So please, just tell us what you know.'

There are murmurs but then Tia's father speaks up. 'What can you do? How can you help them? Don't you think we've tried to stop this? And now you're here, children yourselves . . .'

I see so much pain and anger in him that I bite back my hasty retort. 'I may be young but at least I'm prepared to help. So is Dante. So are my family and the organization Dante works for. All we're asking is for you to trust us, to tell us why your children are being singled out here.'

Their murmurs die down gradually and the women stare at Dante as if they've just seen their favourite pair of shoes go on sale right before their eyes.

'Please, with your help, we can end this.' He spreads his hands in a gesture of appeal and suddenly everyone is smiling at him – and I mean everyone. 'We will do our utmost and get your children back, but we can only do that if you help us.' I feel a wave of persuasive energy flow from him. It rolls around the room and even the sullen man who's been staring daggers at me shifts his attention and watches Dante tenderly.

Flipping heck, the boy is good, I'll admit that, even if it scares me a little. I edge away and let my flames die down – a wise precaution given my next move is to get my phone out to record the conversation.

'I have a picture here and I'd like to know if you recognize him.' I pass the photo that Ulrich Pfeiffer gave us to the first person, who looks at it, nods in affirmation and passes it to the others, who are murmuring among themselves.

I feel excitement and suppress a smile of relief. Maybe we can win this after all.

Otherwhere, the Tower at the End of the World

The clearing Thorn had been heading for was at the base of a small mountain range; beyond it lay his destination. The palace on the flattened hill ahead was more of a fortress than a playground for courtiers, and between him and it lay a large town. Thorn knew from clandestine research that the entire palace, with its countless rooms and private gardens, lay abandoned – along with the town at its base. It had been unoccupied for over two thousand years, and he doubted anyone had visited it for an age. An air of neglect lay heavily over the whole area, and the forest he'd thundered through felt unnaturally still.

Even without using his newly heightened senses and magical ability, Thorn could sense that he was being watched. He resisted the urge to throw up a masking spell and instead dismounted from his horse, starting the slow walk to the town itself.

It took him almost an hour to cross the clearing, and not once did he hear a bird or see another living thing. It was eerie and gave him too much time to think. Clouds lay low and heavy across the trees and a cold breeze blew down from the mountains, bringing the scent of the first snowfall.

Thorn knew that storming out of the tower was an overreaction, even childish, but Odalis's news was shocking and unexpected. He knew in theory he'd be expected to marry a bride of his family's choosing, but the reality felt very different. And he hadn't expected to meet her so soon – at the Midwinter Ball. He'd felt on edge for weeks, expecting something from his father, and this was it. He knew he was merely a pawn in a bigger game, and it made him bitter and short-tempered. The nightmares and fears filling his dreams in recent weeks had kept him strung out, always on the edge of an outburst. Odalis's announcement was simply the final straw and he'd needed to get away.

The visions he fought so heavily during his lessons found their way into his sleep. He saw a war coming to the Otherwhere and at its centre sat the Blackhart family, besieged from all sides with just a handful of supporters.

The vision twisted him inside, because he knew Kit was

at the heart of the unrest. She was in a world of danger and, try as he might, he just could not make sense of what he saw. She lay unconscious and bleeding on a stone altar, her hair longer than he remembered, streaming out in a ghost wind. She was dressed in unfamiliar armour that looked Fae made and her trusty sword lay broken beside her. The wolf lay in the shadows, its fur thick with blood, and panting with foam at its mouth.

And then the vision burst into flames. From them, a woman emerged, stately and ringed in fire. She looked directly at him and brought her finger to her lips, bidding him be quiet. Then he woke up screaming because he too was consumed in her fire.

It was these dreams that made him search the tower's vast library, looking for answers. He scried, wading deeply into the power of the songlines and singing them awake. He opened doorways to the past and future, always seeking answers to what his dreams meant. Odalis knew nothing of this; he made sure of that.

What he found pointed to the ruins of the ancient fortress before him. So he was damned if he was going back to the tower before he found out its impossible secrets.

Chapter Forty-Six

'So, I heard the shouting,' Chem says as we walk out of the community centre ahead of everyone else. 'Then it got really quiet. Did you hypnotize them or something?'

'Dante did. He made them all fall in love with him.' I grin wickedly. 'Right?'

Dante grumbles under his breath as he tugs his jacket back on. 'It's really hard concentrating when you know you don't look like you.'

Chem looks confused but he holds up both hands. 'Look, I don't care what happened in there. My nan called. I need to get home. You guys okay? You on top of this?'

'We are, yes,' I assure him before he jogs off.

Dante heaves a sigh and his breath plumes in front of his face in the frosty air. 'I feel exhausted,' he says. 'How do the Fae keep their glamour up in the human world?'

'I don't know. But you've been doing a good job. Can you maybe just, I don't know, tone all of it down a bit? You're being super distracting.'

He twists towards me and his lips curve – oh so enticingly. I take a step back from him. 'No, I'm not even joking, Dante. If you come near me I'm going to whack you in the head with my iron stick.'

'So violent,' he says but he looks away, pressing fingers across the bridge of his nose. 'Give me a few minutes to figure this out.'

I turn and watch the handful of people walk back to their homes, their steps slow. A few of the women look out for Dante in the darkness. One of the men, younger than the rest, stops and lights a cigarette in order to stare at him for a minute or two, before clearly coming to some decision and walking off behind the rest.

Once Dante has himself under control (never a good thing when you want to lick your friend's face), we're heading to Milton's to confront Torsten.

At my core I know I shouldn't be surprised at the truth behind the children's disappearances. A logical part of me understands that, although the Blackharts do their utmost to right wrongs, some things slip us by. Especially when they've been carefully hidden under layers of deceit, outright lies and Fae machinations that are centuries old.

At least we've finally discovered the link between the missing children and the estate. The key is the land – or rather who the land belonged to. It all goes back to the Saxon lord Brixi, plus his housecarls and their extensive holdings. They have somehow maintained their centuries-long grip on Brixi's estates, and its inhabitants still owe them a tithe of their own children. Not that we know why – yet. As for the link between the children and the music festival – we're still looking on that one.

I believe Suola knew what she was doing when she decided to interfere here. There are depths to the case that I'm not sure I fully understand.

I shiver in the cold air and dig deeper into my coat,

pulling it more tightly around me and shoot a look at where Dante's pacing and muttering to himself.

The estate isn't quiet, not by a long shot. Music and the sounds of an argument carry on the wind towards us. The music is dub-step with a heavy bass line and I hum it under my breath, drumming my fingers inside my pockets. Then the tune changes to something darker and Thorn's lullaby wraps itself around me. It takes a few bars for me to realize what I'm humming and I stop short in fright, making it Dante's turn to look at me.

'You okay?' he calls out softly.

'No, can we go?' I don't wait for him to answer and instead just walk past him, exerting a great amount of will not to sway towards him. Right now I don't want to appear vulnerable. I need to be tough and in charge of my own mind. Without conscious thought, I tighten the wall of magic between us as I walk back down towards the car. I start it up and wait for Dante to get in.

'Are we ready?' he asks, as he buckles himself in.

'No, but neither is Torsten, I think.'

Vauxhall isn't that far and we make it in a decent amount of time. I park a few blocks away and we walk slowly along the darkened street to the club's main entrance. Rorke's solid presence before the club's large vaulted doors reassures me that some things are still as they should be.

'You here to make trouble, Blackhart?' His voice is a deep rumble but there's humour there. He stands a bit straighter when he sees my serious expression and notices the pommel of my sword over my shoulder. He glances at Dante then back at me. 'I'm half inclined not to let you in.'

'You don't have to,' I say. 'We just need to speak to Torsten. It's business.'

There are about twenty people in the queue waiting for Rorke to notice them and let them into the club, but he's paying them no attention at all. One of the girls in the queue, a pretty blonde girl with incredible legs and huge chocolate-brown eyes leans out to ogle Dante. Her friend grabs her just in time to prevent her from leaning too far and falling on her butt. Dante turns to look at her briefly before turning to look back to Rorke, who's not moved to let us pass.

'Is this Suola's business?' Rorke looks worried now. 'The Beast's been in every night since she came here to see you. He sits upstairs and just waits.'

'Is he here tonight?'

'Not yet. It's too early. After midnight, usually.'

'Do you know what he's waiting for?'

Rorke shakes his head. 'He orders a drink and that's it. He hardly touches it. People come and go, leaving gifts for him to take to Suola and he barely acknowledges them. He's freaking everyone out. Especially Miron.'

'Does he speak to anyone?'

Before Rorke can answer Dante's question, someone from the queue calls out impatiently. 'Hey, come on! It's cold and we want to get in before dawn, mate. Can you chat to your friends after you've let us in?'

The guy who spoke is severely under-dressed, even for Milton's. He blanches as both Rorke and Dante turn to look at him with savage intent.

'I will let you in as and when I like,' Rorke says with a smile that holds far too many teeth to be comfortable viewing. 'And right now? I don't like. So stand there and keep that girl from passing out. What's wrong with her, anyway?' He shakes his head. 'Youth of today. No stamina.'

Dante mutters something I can't hear; his attention is focused on the girl who's being held up by her friends, and I become aware of his magic pressing up against me. It fizzes against my own and I feed more energy into my shield, locking it down, but even so there's a need to do bad things to my partner.

Dante gives me a haunted look before he leaves my side to stalk towards the girl. She looks up and her eyes go wide, her tongue flicking nervously across her lower lip, as if anticipating a kiss. She whimpers as she tries to straighten up and her friend curses roundly as she's pushed away by her. But the girl's not the only one who finds Dante interesting. The guy who spoke up, Mister Tightpants, reaches out a hand and trails it along Dante's arm as he passes, staring after him with a look of longing on his face.

'Is she okay?' Dante asks the blonde's friend, who seems stricken with numb-tongue. 'What's wrong with her?'

The blonde straightens so that she can look up at Dante. Her reaction is immediate – somehow reminiscent of a flower that had grown in darkness, then was exposed to sun for the first time. The smile that curves across her full red lips is both dazzled and hungry. She shakes off her friend and presses herself up against Dante so that there's no light visible between their touching bodies. Her hand curls up around his neck, into his hair, and she stands on tiptoe to reach his lips with hers.

'What the hell?' Rorke asks me, turning to the display of wantonness on his doorstep. 'Is he just kissing some random girl?'

'Dante isn't . . .' I take a deep breath. 'Dante is having a problem controlling this new gift of his,' I finish lamely. 'It's making for interesting times at the moment.'

'Gift?' Rorke's grey eyes flash dangerously. 'When you've finished talking to Torsten, this is a story I want to hear.' He walks over to where Dante has the girl pressed up against the wall, his head bent over hers. I can't be certain, but I'm pretty sure he's not kissing her. Instead it looks as if he's talking to her and she's clinging to him like a drunken sailor would hang on to a last bit of flotsam before being swept into the sea.

Rorke grabs Dante by the collar and literally pulls him off the girl. The girl reaches blindly for him but her friend's there and grabs hold of her instead. Rorke says something and his tone is dark, utterly pissed off. He makes a gesture and one of the black taxis that's always parked nearby drives up. The two girls climb into the back and Rorke speaks to the driver. I see money change hands and the taxi speeds off into the night. Rorke, still holding on to Dante, walks him back towards me with his large hand now pressed between my partner's shoulders.

Dante looks feverish and he's shaking. His eyes are wild and he can't seem to decide what to do with his hands. Static energy is coming off him to which Rorke seems completely oblivious. The few people left in the queue now seem far more interested in watching what we're doing than trying to get into the club.

'Get him under control. I can't let you into the club if he can't act responsibly. That poor girl's going to be sick for days.' He scowls heavily. 'Bloody sirens – you have no business bringing someone who can't control themselves to the club, Kit. What were you thinking?' Rorke turns back to the queue and gestures for the first five people to make their way in. The door opens and the heavy bass escapes into the air before it's shut off again.

'Go around the back and I'll get Torsten sent out to you. We've got two DJs playing tonight. Torsten is due to be on later. Miron is seriously not going to like this.'

I lead Dante to the narrow street next to the club. It's dark and shadowy here but it doesn't smell too bad. There are no overflowing bins or urine aroma, which is a relief. I find a crate and prop Dante on it.

'What the hell?' I ask him, hunkering next to him. 'Dante?'

'I'm so sorry, Kit. I can't think straight.' He turns the full weight of his heavy gaze on me and I feel the incredible pull of his eyes. My magic shifts uncomfortably under my skin and I anchor myself, concentrating on the remnants of Thorn's lullaby still echoing in my mind. It helps, but only slightly, because a part of me is desperate to give in to the urge inside me to just lean in and kiss Dante. The air is thick with his scent – pheromones, I know that now, but it doesn't matter – and I remember how good it felt just being pressed up against him, how hot his hands felt when they came to rest on the bare skin of my back.

'You have to control this, Dante.' I stand up with the utmost reluctance. I even manage to put a step between us. One more. I've got my magic running interference, but what must that poor girl have felt when he had her up against the wall? What did he say to her? I saw the naked want on her face when her friend managed to pull her away, and had felt sympathy but also relief that I didn't have to witness anything further. I wonder why Rorke didn't seem perturbed that Dante no longer seemed human. But then Rorke's been the doorman at Milton's for a long time and has, no doubt, seen a great many things that would still shock little old me.

Chapter Forty-Seven

'I thought I did,' Dante says, watching me with shadowed eyes. 'I thought I had a grip on it. Then I looked at that girl and could read all of her. I knew her deepest longings and needs. It felt as if someone else had taken control and told me I just had to go and talk to her and make her smile. Then she touched me and I felt myself falling into deep water and I couldn't think straight.' He scrubs his hands through his hair. 'It was like I could only breathe when I touched her.'

His voice is raw as he speaks and I feel sorry for him, but only up to a point.

'You felt her *need*?' I can't help the disbelief and annoyance in my voice. 'Seriously? You practically maul a girl who's been influenced by your magic and you say it's because you felt her need? That is seriously screwed up, Dante.'

'Look, I'm trying to explain all of this to you. I'm scared because this is new and it's frightening and I don't know what's going on with me. I walked past those people in the line waiting to get in and I somehow knew what every single one of them wanted the most. It was as if they were whispering into my mind. That girl? She's so lonely in a world that scares her. She wants someone to take care of her. Every night she goes home to an empty flat and sits in the darkness feeling lost and alone. Today is her birthday. She wanted a kiss from a hot boy, something to make her feel alive. It was like she was screaming at the top of her lungs. I had to calm her down somehow because I couldn't think otherwise.' He grimaces at my heavy look of disgust and disbelief. 'What makes it even worse is trying to explain it because I sound psycho. I see you watching me with those big eyes and can see your distaste – I wish there was a way to make you see I'm telling the truth.' He's breathing as if he's just run a marathon. 'Do you think I want this? To know that when I look at you, I feel inappropriate things and remember how great you smell. But mostly I remember how incredible it felt having you pressed up against me – and I have to pretend it didn't happen because you're too young and I'm older and I'm not really me any more.' His smile is savage and the look he gives me is white hot with anger and regret. 'But you want to know what makes all of this even worse? It's knowing you're my friend, that the memory I have of you in my arms is a lie because you would never want me in that way. I listen to you, that part inside you that you don't even want to listen to and, you know who I see there? Thorn, some guy I've never met, and I know that he's the one you really want. So what happened between us really has nothing to do with me but with whatever the thing is I'm becoming. This weird hybrid thing that attracts people but repels you.' He clenches his hands as he slumps on the crate. 'I've never been so conflicted about who I am and what I want in all my life. How could everything be okay one day and so fucked up the next?'

This is a sentiment I can completely relate to, so, before

I over-think it, I step closer and drop a hand on his bowed head.

'Dante? Things are really screwed up right now. I'm worried about you but I need you to keep it together until we've got this thing with Torsten sorted, okay?' I crouch down next to him so I can look into his veiled eyes. 'But to clear the air, let me just say this: I find you seriously hot. I wanted to kiss you even before the fever and you became a faerie sex god.' His lips curve attractively at my words and his breathing slows a little. 'And you're right. I fell for a boy a while ago when things were crazy and, although I think you're cute, you're just not him. But even so, nothing can come of me having feelings for this other boy. It's unnatural and forbidden for us to be together in a romantic way. But he is still my friend and I worry about him a lot. What you and I have . . . I don't know. I'm sorry I'm younger than you but that's not my fault and it's not yours, so maybe we both need to just get over it till after we've got this all wrapped up. I don't want to lose you as a friend and partner in this. You put up with my crap and listen to my mad ideas without too much judgement.' I grin. 'Also, it helps that you can walk into a room and make people tell you stuff just by being cute.'

'Oh, Kit . . .' He tangles his fingers with mine and stands to face me. 'You're possibly one of the best things that's happened to me in a long time.'

The sound of slow applause makes us both turn. A figure stands at the end of the alleyway and I have to squint to make him out.

'What a cute little scene.' Torsten steps towards us until he's in a puddle of light. He's dressed in super-skinny black jeans, combat boots and a T-shirt emblazoned with a burning skull. Something moves at his feet and the sound of scurrying reaches my ears. Rats.

I recoil involuntarily and grimace as I see another three or four of them make an appearance at his feet. I'm happy to face an army of redcaps and hunt down an ogre gone rogue feasting on decomposing cattle carcasses. But rats – man, rats freak me the hell out. It's about how they move, with those god-awful fat tails of theirs, which seem to live as separate entities from the rest of their bodies.

'I would like to nominate you both for Oscars for that outstanding emotional display of true angst,' he says, smiling the smile that I found so pretty just the other day. 'But, you know? I don't really care. I gather you've figured out who I am.'

'You're the child thief,' I say, walking towards him. My hand itches to hold my sword but I resist the urge. Something tells me that Torsten isn't much of a fighter or rather, not a physical I-attack-you-with-my-sword type of fighter.

Torsten's smile fades and his expression is very serious.

'I have been called far worse.' He nods and there's a trace of arrogance in his stance which suggests that he believes he's done nothing wrong. 'You call me a thief, Blackhart, but think on this: if their parents have already signed contracts surrendering their progeny to my kind, am I really stealing them? Whether they thought it unlikely when they signed or whether they were high at a festival. How am I to blame when deals have been struck, sacrifices made and oaths sworn under a full moon? Or has life and time moved on so much for humanity that they are no longer to be taken at their sworn word?' His expression becomes patronizing. 'Well done for figuring it out, though. What gave it away? No! Don't tell me, I don't actually care.' He does a little dance step and moves closer to us; it is such a creepy little move, as if he's showing off, that I step away.

My phone starts buzzing in my pocket right then and I swear under my breath at the distraction, but Dante smoothly takes over with Torsten.

It's Kyle so I answer it without preamble. 'Not a good time.'

'Whatever, listen to me. That phrase you repeated? I got it translated. Say thanks to my Beowulf and Anglo-Saxon obsession, and a misspent year teaching myself the language.'

'*Kyle*.'

'Okay, bad time? Well, the thing you kept repeating is this: *The goddess will have her tithe; I, Brixi, do make this vow*.'

So the bearded warrior I saw at the estate was Brixi himself . . . it was good to have my hunch confirmed.

'Okay, that makes no sense.' Unless Brixi thought I was sent by this goddess when I gatecrashed his bonfire party. But what goddess and what tithe? Did he swear allegiance to a Fae thinking that she was a goddess?

'I'll see what else I can find, but, yeah, it's weird. I'll see what I can dig up about goddesses. It's going to be a nightmare because, well, the bloody Fae have been interfering and pretending to be deities for millennia.'

'I've gotta go, Kyle. We've got someone we think is involved in all of this. Text me if you get something. Also, do me a favour? This is a bit of a long shot, but can you check the land registry? Find the land where that festival is held up north and see who owns it. Also, do the same and check who owns the land where the kids have been going missing. I think we've been focusing on the *who* and *why* too much, and not enough on the *where*.' I listen to him grumble and say goodbye before I pocket my phone and turn back to Dante and Torsten. They are having some kind of little chat and Torsten's probably being mean to Dante, as it looks as if he wants to punch him.

Torsten grins at me as I approach. 'So, what're you going to do next?' He points a finger at Dante. 'You're going to tie me up and take me to jail? Or you, Blackhart, will you summon the Beast and have me dragged off to the Otherwhere?' He holds up both hands and waves them overdramatically. 'What will it be?'

'Where are the children?' I ask him, my voice leaden. I am so tired and just want this to end. Now. And, I'd like the bad guy not to posture, for once. Do they have to turn into Bond villains when cornered?

'Where are the children?' He mimics my voice perfectly but spins a bit of spite into it. 'Serious question though: why would you even care, Blackhart? You've found me now, and they are nothing to you.' He nods at Dante. 'And especially not to you, changeling.' He enjoys the effect of his words. 'Oh yes, I know. I could smell the stink of your pheromones and confusion all the way in the club. I'm surprised Rorke didn't just send you packing. What are you? A siren or something? Can you hear the voices in the club just calling to you? Your kind tend to cause riots, so people like Rorke are trained to deal with you.' Torsten laughs bitterly to himself. 'What is my life worth if a mere human child and bastard Sidhe Fae can hunt me down after all these years of service?'

I react before Dante can get past me. My magic hits Torsten full in the chest, sending him staggering a few paces back. I'm not good at projecting energy in solid bursts like this, but I'm good enough to make a bit of a show. The blow pushes him back into the shadows and, as he straightens, it's a cue for more rats to pour out from the shadows behind him. I don't know where they're coming from but there must easily be thirty of them. They're all around him – one even climbs onto his shoulder and sits there wiggling its nose in my direction.

'Nice trick with the rats, by the way, but we still need your answer. What have you done to the kids? Where are they?'

'If I choose not to tell you, then what?' Torsten's smirk at Dante sets my blood boiling but before I can do anything, Dante's past me.

I'd completely forgotten about Dante's taser, but suddenly he has it, black and ugly. There's a soft *thwap* sound and I watch as Torsten staggers, but he doesn't drop as expected when the electrodes hit him in the chest.

The rodents chitter anxiously as I draw my sword, and let out a little sigh of relief at the feel of it in my hand. With a flick of the blade I slice clean through the rat that leaps from Torsten's shoulder at Dante. As it drops to the ground I shudder and fling it away from me, ignoring the squelching noise it makes as it hits the wall.

More rats are running towards us now and I have a horrible time dancing between them, impaling and flicking them away. Dante seems less squeamish, enjoying just kicking them away from him. One makes it onto his leg and clings on for dear life. He grabs it just behind its neck then tosses it like a cricket ball, sending it flying straight towards Torsten.

Torsten easily sidesteps the flying rodent and produces a slender flute from somewhere with the flourish of a stage magician.

Dante swears under his breath and sprints past me. I follow close behind, jumping over the rats and swiping at them as I go.

The first notes from the flute are discordant and jar through me. Torsten lifts the flute from his lips, shakes his head and tries again. I throw a bolt of energy towards him and he staggers but he doesn't go down. What's with this guy?

Dante reaches him first and grabs for the flute. Torsten moves like water, easily dodging Dante's grabbing hands, and comes up a few feet away from us both, the flute back up at his lips.

This time the notes are clear and bright in the night air. They seem to hang there for a while, almost visible. The night's become very quiet. Even the rats aren't moving or squeaking and instead have turned to watch Torsten with their gross little eyes.

'Stop that,' Dante says, his voice slurring as he holds out his hand. 'Give me the flute.'

'You look tired, Agent Alexander.' Torsten brings his lips back to the flute. 'I think you deserve a nap.' The notes ring out true and crystalline and for a moment I see Dante waver, his knees shaking, and then he drops like a sack of dirty washing.

Chapter Forty-Eight

Torsten's grin is one of triumph. He lifts the flute briefly from his lips and the vermin swarm closer to him. I pack my magic around me, hoping it will protect me from the flute's power. He steps closer and I retreat slowly, my gaze shifting towards Dante where he lies on the ground, out for the count.

'Blackhart, I have nothing against you, believe me.' He lifts the flute once more and I press my hands over my ears and start belting out 'Bohemian Rhapsody' by Queen.

I can't sing. I know that, but I like music and my nan was fond of Queen, so I have an impressive repertoire of their songs which I murder when I do karaoke with my cousins. Nothing gives you the will to kick ass the way Queen does.

Torsten's flute song falters as I yell out the lyrics at the top of my lungs. Perplexed, he brings it to his mouth again. I'm aware of the mice, rats and other vermin now crawling along the walls and ground, gathering around me and swirling towards him. I try not to see the things scuttling all around me as I raise my sword.

'Stop playing the goddamn flute, Torsten,' I grind out.

In answer he strides away from me and his followers

make way for him, flute music ringing in the air. My life is a farce, I decide. I glance at Dante and watch as he stirs and rolls onto his back. I pause briefly to shake his shoulder.

'Get up!' I shout and run towards Torsten but I trip over the crawling things and only just manage not to face-plant at his feet.

Dante struggles up as I fling myself towards Torsten, the blade in my hand swiping towards his hands and flute. Stupidly, I haven't waited to recover my balance from my previous stumble and I go down hard on my knees and hands, my sword skittering off among the rodents.

Torsten lets out a shout of laughter and the song he's playing is no longer alluring but frenzied. It's the signal the rodents and vermin were waiting for and they swarm.

I jump upright, my hands flinging crawling things off me, feeling little teeth, paws and whiskers on my bare skin. My calm is lost, as is the grip on my coiled magic.

A scream of horror tears from my chest at the same time as a huge burst of magic. My terror of the rats is all consuming, even as I watch them sizzle and burn in the magical fire that's flared to dizzying life. It licks out all around me in a tight cone, preventing the rodents from rushing me again. A heavy wind fans the roiling flames across my skin and I lift my head to the dark skies, feeling elated that I'm still alive amid the chaos I'm wreaking.

Torsten's stopped playing the flute now but I can still hear the sound of it in the air. He's watching me with something akin to awe and Dante looks dumbstruck as I stand in the middle of the flames, their heat laying waste to any of the vermin that approach. Dante doesn't come any closer but takes the opportunity to grab Torsten, who allows himself to be pushed up against the wall of the club and frisked for weapons. Dante makes short work of tying his wrists together with a zip-tie handcuff and levers him away from the wall.

It seems about a hundred years until I can make out Dante's voice above the pounding of my heart and the noise of my magic's blue flames. 'Kit? They're all gone now,' he says, his voice low. 'Come back to me.'

It takes another eternity, but the lick of flames eventually dies down around me, seeping back into my pores; the magic creeping back to the darkness inside that I hide from the normal world. I sag slightly where I stand, breathing heavily and almost sobbing. My hands shake badly when I rub my face in an effort to get rid of the ashes on them.

My little display of hysteria cost me, and I feel tired, but nowhere near as much as I would have done in the past. I draw a deep breath and desperately try to unsee the rat and mice carcasses strewn all around me.

I'm too close to the memory of when my magic manifested for the first time, when I tore down that hill, killing the Unseelie knight and all his redcaps. I stumble away and dry heave into the shadows until my stomach aches.

Dante's watching me with far too much concern; Torsten, damn his eyes, just looks thoughtful and maybe a bit sad. I gaze at the devastation around me, as the alleyway now looks as if someone's deployed a flame-thrower.

There are scorch marks on the ground and walls, and someone's graffiti looks like it's seen better days. I don't think my family would be impressed with my mini-meltdown and public display of magic. It's one thing using it to impress kids or frighten suspects, but it's another thing going Terminator in an alleyway.

No, your honour, that was just me. I got really scared of those rats and my magic kinda got out of control.

Dante touches my shoulder but withdraws his hand pretty quickly when I jump with fright. 'How're you doing?'

'I'm okay.' I am so, so not okay, but maybe saying the words will make them true. 'What are we doing with him?' I jerk my head at Torsten. He's still just staring impassively at us, which is weird. But then, he's just called a bunch of rats to attack us, which maybe downgrades the strangeness of his staring.

I find the flute where he's dropped it and pick it up. It feels cold and smooth in my hands and potentially dangerous. It is very much a weapon. Lastly, I collect my sword and slide it into the scabbard between my shoulder blades.

'There's a place we sometimes use. We can take him there.' Dante shrugs out of his jacket and drops it over Torsten's bound hands. He wraps an arm around Torsten's shoulders and walks him back onto the main road and towards the car. 'When we have answers, we can call the Beast. Tell Rorke we're taking their DJ so he can inform Miron.'

I run to the front of the club to speak to the hulking doorman. Rorke looks annoyed that we're taking their DJ for questioning on a case and mutters that Miron will have words. But he lets me go, so I jog back to get on with the main event.

Dante gives me directions and I drive blindly, not paying attention to signs or road names. About forty minutes later, I pull up in front of an abandoned warehouse. I think it's near Greenwich because I can see Canary Wharf's tall buildings.

Torsten's been very quiet during the journey. Whenever my gaze moves to the rear-view mirror, I find him watching me, his strange eyes inscrutable. His silence is unnerving, as is his complete compliance when Dante manhandles him out of the car and makes him walk ahead of us towards the warehouse.

My phone buzzes in my pocket and I check it. A text message from Aiden: *Back in town. Where are you?*

My fingers fly over the keypad as I reply: *Not sure. Near Greenwich. Get Kyle to track me. Please come.*

I slide the phone into my hip pocket and follow the guys into the warehouse.

The place echoes as we rattle the main door open. There are deep pools of darkness, although some light comes from the roof that is part glass and part whatever it is that roofs are made of. There's a soft insistent drip somewhere towards the back and the whole place just seems melancholy and a bit oppressive.

'Sit.'

Dante's produced a chair from out of the shadows and prods Torsten into it.

'Now, tell us. Where are those kids?'

'I don't know.'

'You know. I can tell you're lying. Your heart's just given a little upbeat. There it is again.'

Dante's smile is a razor's edge. How did I never notice that he has the ability to look quite dangerous? He prowls around Torsten before casually grabbing hold of his hair and pulling his head back. The movement is so unexpected that I start a little in surprise, and Dante sends me an icy look.

'Don't look at her. Watch me. I'm the bad guy here.'

There's a sudden wariness in Torsten's eyes. He dutifully focuses on Dante.

'I don't know where the children are taken once I hand them over.' He shifts slightly on the chair.

'I still think you're lying.' Dante lays a gentle hand on Torsten's neck, but as he leans closer his grip under Torsten's jaw tightens cruelly. 'Do you remember now?'

There's a startlingly fast pulse of magic in the air and I feel the jolt of it hum against me. There's a compulsion to yield to Dante, to answer the question myself, even though I'm not his target and have no answers.

Torsten's gaze widens in alarm and he lets out a painful gasp, sucking in a breath of air. A bright red mark shows vividly against his neck, like a brand, when Dante straightens and drops his hand with a low curse.

The air in the warehouse smells of something cloying and sweet: nutmeg, cinnamon and burned sugar. I realize this is the scent of Dante working his magic. And there's something else, a metallic tang that I don't like, which slices sharply through the air. Torsten's eyes follow Dante as he walks towards me, where I stand frozen in a pool of light.

'What are you doing?' I hiss at Dante, grabbing his wrist and pulling him closer. 'I didn't sign up for torture.'

'I'm using the weapon you used against me,' he says, showing me an iron nail resting in the palm of his hand. His own hand looks sore and burned but his eyes are cold, impassive. 'Fae creatures really do not like iron.'

I try to take the nail from him but he slides it into his pocket. I lift my chin and scowl at him. 'Seriously a dick move, dude. We need answers from him, not for him to die from Iron Sickness.'

Dante shrugs. 'He really doesn't look like he's keen to tell us all that much.'

I hate to admit it but Dante's right. I grimace and push him out of my way. 'Torsten? How about you tell us some things before we summon Suola's Beast? We have questions we feel you should be able to answer.'

Torsten's gaze flickers to me but returns to Dante.

'I could try and answer them,' he says cautiously.

'Please, just tell us where the kids are. You must have an idea.'

'I know they're in the Otherwhere,' he says after a few long moments of silence when his heavy breathing is the only sound in the warehouse. 'They're definitely not here in the Frontier.'

'How are you linked to Brixi?'

A sudden fierce grin and a slow nod. 'Ah. You know about him then? Brixi's been one of our employers for a very long time. The contract for the job gets passed on every few years. This year it's my turn.'

Dante drags two more chairs from somewhere and we sit down. Torsten can't stop watching him – it's as if he's drinking in the sight of him; it's disturbing.

'So Brixi, who must have been around for a damn long time, by the way, employed you . . . ?'

'Not me personally, but yes, there's a contract.' He stops, looking as if he's said all he was prepared to say. But Dante just leans forward, his fingers toying suggestively with the iron nail, ignoring the way it blisters his own skin. He drops his glamour a little and wafts some more pheromones Torsten's way, and Torsten suddenly seems eager to please.

'We get paid to find these children and hand them over to someone who can move across to the Otherwhere.'

There's something that doesn't make sense here but before I can ask another question, Dante moves again and Torsten inhales sharply, his eyelids fluttering. Dante pretends not to notice and takes a few seconds to compose his question.

'Are you working with Ulrich Pfeiffer?'

'No. Mr Pfeiffer is a musician and a kind man who thought his son lost to drugs. It wasn't difficult to take over Torsten's life, not when his father wanted his son back.'

'I don't understand.'

A look of surprise crosses Torsten's face. 'You caught me, you know I'm Fae but you don't know *what* I am?' A smile tugs at his mouth. 'So if I were to do this, you'd be surprised.'

The change is subtle and gradual but Torsten shifts into an exact replica of me. He sends me the grin I know drives Jamie nuts, the one he told me would get me beaten up more if I used it outside family meetings. It's not just my face and body he's replicated, but how I'm sitting in my chair and the way I'm blinking at him in confusion.

'That is freaky,' I say.

'That is freaky,' Torsten-me says. 'Mimicry is one of my particular Fae talents, allowing me to take on Theodore Pfeiffer's shape. I took over his life, because his father's connections made it easy to gain access to the music festival.'

'But what exactly did you do at the festival?'

The slow grin that stretches Torsten-me's face gives me the creeps and I look away in discomfort.

'It is not as sordid as you may think, Blackhart.' He flexes, rolling his shoulders forward and cricking his neck before changing back into Torsten. 'Excuse me as I change back. I've never quite felt comfortable being of the female persuasion, although that too can hold some . . .'

Dante leans unbelievably quickly into Torsten's personal space and actually jabs the iron into the exposed skin of his arm. He sits back before I can even react, the offending nail once more between his fingers, the iron singeing his skin.

Torsten hisses in pain and his eyes flash a dangerous black colour. For a moment, so briefly I can almost convince myself I've not seen it, I see the face Adam Scott drew for me – the split face, the sharp teeth. Then it's gone, and he's once more just a fairly ordinary-looking human, tied to a chair in a dodgy London warehouse.

'Can you cut the crap and just tell us what we need to know? Unless, of course, you prefer me using this on you again?' Dante holds up the bit of iron between his fingers and shows it to Torsten. 'Unless you like the pain just a little too much? I find myself intrigued by it. I like how your pain makes me a little *hungry*.' There's a bit too much timbre in his voice as it echoes strangely around the warehouse, making me shiver.

There are some things I don't want to know and the thought that Dante might like inflicting pain on others is one of them.

Torsten watches Dante warily and looks tired; maybe the questioning is starting to wear him down.

'It is simple. Brixi holds the covenant to the land where the festival is held. And it's easy enough to get drunken festival-goers to agree to things they may not remember the next morning, when they leave the festival for their quiet lives.'

Dante purses his lips. 'Still not clear, sorry. Try harder.'

Torsten sighs in annoyance. 'Humans are easily led and tricked into making important vows when inebriated. It is simple really to extract promises should a series of what seem like highly unlikely events come to pass. Especially when they think they are having some kind of religious experience.'

'The leylines,' I say, chilled to the core. 'You drop them into the leylines and they experience magic. Do you know how dangerous that is?'

His expression says, *Duh, yes, I know.*

'Oh my God.' I sit back in my chair. 'You can't do stuff like that. It's irresponsible and stupid. It can drive people over the edge, make them do crazy stuff.'

'Exactly.' He sounds a bit sad but shrugs. 'The earth magic they experience is potent and, maybe ninety per cent of the time, it results in children being born nine months later. We keep watch on them, and if a new tithe is required, we know where to find our crop.'

'So the leylines are pure magic. And you force these people to experience it until they're drunk and high – then you get them to vow to hand over a child that may or may not be born to them sometime in the future,' Dante says, his voice tight.

'In a nutshell.'

'It's disgusting. Illegal and just . . . Euch, how long have you even been doing this?'

Before Torsten can answer me, Dante speaks up again.

'Does the same thing happen in Brixton?'

'With the estate children, it's Brixi's land,' he replies. 'The need to provide a tithe of children is written into the tenants' covenants. They sign it. And they know about the covenant – it's there for them to read.' He grins. 'Of course, no one quite believes it. It's written off as just a quirky clause within the tenancy contracts. And everyone loves the old days, because obviously it can't still be valid, can it? Besides, it might not happen. The clause states that in the eventuality of express need the tithe is required. Years go by when nothing happens and humans forget, so very quickly. But, of course, if a child happens to get taken, there is a monetary recompense.'

I really thought I'd met some seriously vile people in my life, but listening to Torsten explain all of this so casually makes my blood boil. I could only detect the smallest tinge of regret in his voice, which makes me want to punch something hard, and repeatedly.

'Explain to us who you are,' Dante demands. 'In all of this – this sick farce.'

'He's the Pied Piper,' I say, looking at Torsten. 'Look at him – the flute, the rats, the kids. It all fits. Think about it. He can shift the way he did earlier, making the kids think he's their mum or dad when he comes through the window or wall or whatever.'

'What about the pictures we got from Adam Scott and his brother. You looked like a nightmare creature. All fangs and tatters.'

'Meant to scare him,' Torsten admits. 'He threw me off my game and before I could go back for the other boy, they'd left for India. I had to take the little girl instead. Shoddy work, but that's why there's always a plan B. And yes, the Blackhart is right. I am a pied piper. One of several. My tribe and I are in high demand, all over the world. Sometimes we even just hunt the rats we're asked to remove.'

'You break into children's homes and steal them. That is sick.'

He shrugs. 'Just know that this has never been personal. It's a job I've been employed to do. There've been several of us working with Brixi and his people wherever the tithes are still in force.'

'But why . . .' I gather my thoughts. 'Why did you need to set this up with both the festival *and* the estate?'

Torsten looks a bit surprised at this and tilts his head. 'To double our chances, Blackhart. It is prudent animal husbandry.'

My mouth falls open because he's just shown that he really held human lives to be of no higher value than livestock. Dante's burning gaze finds mine and he jerks his head to the side, so I get up and follow him a few paces away.

'Do you believe him?'

'Yes I do; there are a lot of signs that point to this. Including that research I did in my aunt's library. And, you know, there were all those rats,' I point out and don't even bother suppressing the shudder.

Dante nods thoughtfully, then says. 'Let's wrap this up.'

I hunker down next to Torsten and look up at him, shifting the dynamic between us. 'You have to tell me what you know about the kids being held in the Otherwhere.'

'I know I hand them over to Brixi and he takes them away. I don't know what he does with them.'

'It's just a business contract, right?' Dante's voice is bitter. His hands clench at his sides as he turns to look down at Torsten, who shrugs.

'Why are you helping us?'

'Because I want the Beast to know that I cooperated.'

Torsten's smile is fierce and a bit manic as he glances away from me into the darkness. 'He's been in the shadows, listening all this time.'

Both Dante and I swing around at the sound of footsteps behind us. Suola's torturer and enforcer walks out of the shadows, his gait slow and measured. I hardly notice the limp. As before, he's dressed beautifully this time in a severely cut suit, complete with waistcoat and cane. He looks more pressed and properly British than anyone I've ever seen, apart from models in Megan's fashion magazines.

'I am impressed,' he says. 'Only a few instances of minor torture and he gives up the goods.'

'It doesn't matter, though, does it?' I counter, annoyed. 'He knew you were in the shadows. He was saving his own butt by spilling the beans.'

'This is true, but I've seen people relish having power over the weak, regardless of what they're being told.' His strange dark eyes sweep past Torsten and me and come to rest on Dante. 'Boy, you need to make peace with who you are before it gnaws at you and tears you apart.'

Dante looks at him incredulously but the Beast moves towards Torsten.

'Are you sure you've told these children the truth?' he says, bending over him, his face a mere fraction of a millimetre away from Torsten's.

'I have, as much as I have been able.'

The Beast nods slowly, closing his eyes and inhaling deeply. He gestures for Dante. 'Come, tell me what you feel.'

I watch Dante hesitantly move towards him until he's

standing right next to him, closer than most humans would before feeling their private space invaded.

'What I feel?' He asks, looking at the older man.

'Yes, in the alleyway you told young Kit that you could sense, feel, what the people outside that awful nightclub felt. That young woman who called to you with her loneliness. I sensed it too, but not as clearly as you, I think. I want you to tell me what you feel, now.'

Dante shoots me a look of alarm and I know what he's thinking. If Suola's Beast had been in the alleyway, why didn't he interfere, the way he's doing now? Why follow us here? What's his game?

Dante looks down at Torsten, who keeps his gaze set rigidly on the floor between the two men standing in front of him.

'Fear. He's afraid of you.'

'It's natural. I am not quite the Easter Bunny. What else?'

'Relief. He is relieved because he thinks it's over.'

'Excellent. What else?'

'Remorse. He feels remorse for his role in the abduction of the children but there's nothing he could have done. No way he could have gone against the wishes of his employer.'

'You've done really well, young Dante. Your father would have been impressed.' The Beast's smile is one of approval. He reaches out a hand towards Dante to clap him on the shoulder but Dante steps back, out of reach.

'You know? You knew what I was when you gave us this job?'

'No, I *suspected*. Suola acted on her gut feeling and, as usual, she was right.'

'What does that mean?'

'It means, young man, that you are both an asset and a

danger.' The Beast's smile reminds me of the cat that stole the cream. 'You are a full-blooded Fae from a very noble Sidhe house. If your uncle Aelfric dies, you move closer to the throne. Your father worked diligently for years, a great many years, to put a list of allies together who would support him in his quest to overthrow Aelfric – who, as the years have gone by, has become self-indulgent and dangerous to Alba's stability. When you were born to Eadric and his wife, your father knew he had to keep you safe from his brother if he was to attempt the coup. Otherwise he'd be too vulnerable. He used a tremendous amount of power to ensure you stayed hidden, and it mostly paid off.'

'He never contacted me. I never knew him.' Dante shrugs and I see so much anger and defeat in him that my heart hurts for him. 'I'm not sure how I feel about you trying to make me feel better about who I am, when my family never bothered finding me in the first instance.'

The Beast places his cane carefully between his feet, wraps his hands over the worked silver handle and rocks back slightly on his heels to examine Dante.

'Knowing Eadric's thoroughness, I'd be inclined to think that he'd have kept you secret even from family. And he had all the worlds to hide you in as well as any-when.' Suola's enforcer gives me an unreadable look. 'But, of course, no one counted on the Blackharts getting involved.'

I answer with a scowl. I'm really not fond of people disrespecting my family.

'You, my dear, are far too free with your magic in this world. You use spells and fling balls of energy around as if you're some kind of untouchable.' He shakes his head slowly. 'Regardless of what you may think, you aren't invulnerable and you need to be extremely careful. What you did in the

Otherwhere by stopping the Old Ones – that drew a lot of attention and not all of it welcome.' His smile is sharp. 'We can't do with losing you before you've played out the rest of your role, now can we?'

Chapter Forty-Nine

Before I can tell him what I think about his enigmatic advice, he seems to remember himself and the fact that he's here for Torsten. He tucks one hand into his jacket pocket, bringing out a small wooden token. I recognize the sigil inscribed on it: the token is an exact replica of the ones Dante and I were handed by Melusine.

'Enough chatting, I think. I need to get him back to Suola so she can decide what to do with him.' He taps the chair with his cane. 'Get up, Piper.'

I'm used to seeing weird things, but even I'm impressed when Torsten's bindings melt away, allowing him to stand up. He rubs his wrists briefly, before wincing as he touches the burn mark on his neck.

'I'm sorry,' he says, looking at me. 'Sometimes you can't escape the responsibilities placed on you by others.'

I watch the two of them walk away, Torsten looking like a deviant in his ratty black jeans and death metal T-shirt, and the Beast dressed like a lord.

A world of impatience comes crashing down on me.

'So that's it, huh? You take the piper back to Suola and no one cares about the kids?'

The Beast turns to look at me with a raised eyebrow. 'What would you like me to do?'

'Show some compassion. Think about the kids, about their families missing them.'

He taps the cane to his chin and shrugs. 'I'm sorry, they knew what they were agreeing to when they made the compact and they've all been financially compensated, somehow.'

'No.' Dante's voice cuts through the chill air of the warehouse. 'No, they didn't know what they were agreeing to. How can you even say that? I've seen the financial "compensation" that these families have received. And nothing, *nothing*, makes up for the loss of a child from a family.'

That dark eyebrow curves in amusement as Dante speaks. I resist the urge to throw my sword at the Beast's head.

'I agree with you, but, really, what do you want me to do? They are not my concern, nor is it my concern that someone's employing pipers to steal children. Until it is made my concern, I am here for the one who caused unpleasantness for my queen. That is all.'

'So, if Suola instructed you to hunt down Torsten's employer and find the children, you'd do it?'

I don't like the considering look the Beast gives me.

'Perhaps.'

I leave Dante's side and walk towards them. 'I'd like to request an audience with her majesty, the Queen of Air and Darkness.'

'Hmm. Always doing the unexpected, Blackhart. Very well. I will send someone with an answer at dawn tomorrow to your home.'

'We can't go now?' Dante asks, his tone eager.

'No. Tonight I spend with Torsten. He and I will be getting to know one another a little bit better.'

Torsten pales under his tan and he glances towards the door at the far side of the warehouse, but the Beast gives him no opportunity to make a break for it. He lays a gentle hand between his shoulder blades and walks him into the shadows. I watch as they fade from my sight and I hear the fine snap of the token breaking. The magic buffets me lightly and I shake my head to clear it.

'Can we use our tokens to follow them?' Dante asks, opening his hand to show me he still has Suola's token ensuring safe travel to the Otherwhere. I dig mine out from around my neck and stare down at it.

'We can try,' I say.

He gives me a nod and on the count of three, we crack the small wooden tokens to activate their power. I hold my breath, waiting for the *wuff* of magic but nothing happens. With a sigh of disgust Dante tosses the token to the side.

'We're winning, right?' Dante asks me as I walk over and sit down on the chair Torsten's evacuated.

'I suppose so. I'm not sure.' I look at him and feel sad that he looks so serious and freaked out. 'I just want to go to bed after this is all over and sleep for a week. Then! Then, I just need to go somewhere quiet and warm where no one knows who I am, where I don't have to carry iron or my sword and knives.'

'It sounds nice.'

'It does, doesn't it?'

I look at my phone as it buzzes. 'Aiden's on his way. Let's go get food. I'm starving.'

Chapter Fifty

Slightly to my surprise, our request for an audience with Suola is granted. The house we're shown into, shortly after dawn, is just off Park Lane in Mayfair. It's a large affair with tall soaring ceilings and doorways big enough to accommodate giants. The thought of giants makes me uncomfortable because you know anything is possible when dealing with the Fae. The rooms we pass through are mostly empty of furniture; the few pieces left sit under dust covers. There are very few paintings or tapestries and all the mirrors are covered with black cloth. I shudder involuntarily, remembering my past experiences with talking mirrors and scurry past them, following the slender young man who seems to be our guide for today's visit.

Aiden's scowl matches Dante's dark look as they trail me into one of the comfortable waiting rooms. They're really not happy being here and, admittedly, neither am I. If I can get Suola to tell us more about Torsten and his employer, it will give me a chance to figure out where to find the kids and how to bring them back.

The dissonance of the whole morning has been magnified by having to tell Aiden about Dante being a changeling. And, on top of that, that he was most likely related to

Eadric himself by being his son. Aiden stared at Dante with an inscrutable expression for some time but then he nodded, looking less than pleased.

'This sucks, dude. Your dad was a nut job.' Dante looked horrified, but Aiden carried on regardless, oblivious to how his words might actually hurt. 'But it's okay, because if he just dumped you here and you grew up relatively normal, chances are you're not a nut job too.'

'Uh, thanks? I think.'

There have been some frosty silences since then, which I can tell Aiden can't figure out. It makes me want to shake him hard: Dante isn't used to the whole changeling thing himself – never mind being related to a notorious traitor.

Tay, our Fae guard, returns after a few minutes to check if we need anything else. All three of us decline anything to drink. His grey eyes sweep over us and I get the impression that he's not overly keen on us being here, but he gives a short bow before exiting the room.

'I don't like being here,' Aiden says in a low growl. 'And being unarmed? Not my favourite thing in the world.'

I twist my lips into a wry grin. 'Seriously? You're never unarmed, Aiden – get a grip.' And then, when Dante looks at me in surprise, I shrug. 'What? He's a flipping wolf. He can drop his human skin and became a raging tooth-and-claw monster in like ten seconds flat. We're the ones who'll be toast.'

'I know kung fu,' Dante says to Aiden. 'That should help.'

Aiden rolls his eyes and goes to peer out of the window. 'I can't believe this whole block belongs to her. My dad didn't even know.'

'I'm just about coming to terms with the fact that we

don't know all there is to know about any of the Fae,' I reply, seating myself in a chair that looks like it might not hold my weight. 'And that the treaties I've heard Uncle Andrew and Jamie bang on about don't seem to be worth much after all.'

An uncomfortable silence falls on the three of us. Aiden prowls around the room, looking out of the windows, checking the door (locked) and touching the few pieces of furniture. He tosses the dust cloth covering a beautiful piano aside and sits down.

'Any requests?'

I'm too surprised to say anything and Dante clearly thinks he's kidding, so he just shrugs.

'Fine, we'll start with some "Claire de Lune" by Debussy.'

Dante and I share a look of amazement as the familiar bit of music starts.

'Did you know he could play?'

'No idea. Imagine that. A musical wolf.'

'I can hear you, you know.' Aiden's scowl is only half serious. 'Did you know this music is influenced by a poem by the same name? It's by a guy called Paul Verlaine.' He clears his throat and recites in an incredibly clear voice that rises above the music:

'Your soul is a chosen landscape
Where charming masqueraders and bergamaskers go
Playing the lute and dancing and almost
Sad beneath their fanciful disguises.'

I think had Suola walked in at that moment, dressed as Batman, my jaw would not have dropped further.

'Who are you?' I ask Aiden, walking closer to him. 'Why

haven't you ever mentioned you can play the piano? That you know obscure French poetry.'

'My dear Kit, I am deeply mysterious, not to mention incredibly attractive.' His grin is cheeky and I laugh at him. 'Also, my mum loves music and poetry so she made sure her boys knew how to play the piano and could recite poetry.'

'Save us all from this, right now, please,' I joke and turn back to Dante, still laughing, but he's gone very still, his gaze fixed on a small array of pictures in silver frames resting on an ornate marble table.

'What's wrong?'

'Those are photos of Fae?'

'I don't know. Shall we go look?' I stride over and pick up one. 'Yes, this is Aelfric and his sons. See?' The frame seems to weigh a ton as I turn towards him. 'I met them all last year.'

He takes the picture from me and looks down at the picture. 'Which one is Thorn?'

I feels as if he's punched me in the gut. I lean against him so I can see the picture again. 'This is him.'

'He looks a little tense. And young.'

I take it from him and run my thumb across the glass. 'He is. Was. Is.' I take a deep breath and put it back on the small table so I can look at the other framed photos. 'This is Suola and her consort. The Sun King and his wife.' I touch each picture in turn. 'These are other Sidhe nobles I recognize from Aelfric's court but I don't know who they are.'

'None of my father?'

I scan the others and shrug. 'I don't know. I've never met Eadric.'

418

Aiden's piano playing segues into a mournful waltz and when I shoot him a look of annoyance he does a mad rendition of 'Chopsticks' that makes even Dante smile a little. Next up is a lively csardas tune but thankfully the door swings open and Melusine is standing there, her expression mildly irritated.

Her gaze sweeps over the three of us and she sighs. 'Would it kill you people to come here not looking like a band of mercenaries? You are seeing the Queen of the Unseelie, you know. Where's your respect?'

I shrug in my leather jacket, feeling warm and comfortable in my jeans and knee-high biker boots. 'We're not here for a fashion show, Melusine. Will she see us?'

Her hands flutter in a gesture of annoyance and she turns away. 'Come, but hurry. We've got a lot of supplicants to see today and Suola only has a few minutes to spare for you and your little friends.'

Aiden minces up behind Melusine, copying the sway of her hips in her sheath dress that looks more like silk sleepwear. I bite back my laughter because he sashays alarmingly well for a big guy. Melusine leads us into what I can only assume is the largest room in the building of large rooms. There are no curtains on the windows and for a moment I'm disoriented by the light and scale of the place. Heavy chandeliers drip with crystal, reflecting the light. The floor is a wide expanse of white and gold marble. A red strip of carpet runs the length of the room and ends at the foot of a large throne carved from black stone. A heavy throw of black feathers and fur is draped across the back and I shudder to think what creatures died to supply it.

Suola is sitting regally on the throne and she watches us imperiously as we follow Melusine up the length of the carpet. I have never in my life felt more exposed or examined by anyone. Our small intimate meeting when she gave us the job seemed bad enough, until now, in this cavern of an ex-ballroom. We are also under the scrutiny of four heavily armoured bodyguards and a few pale Fae dressed in soft grey robes. I feel hugely unprepared and nervous.

'Blackhart, Dante.' She draws a breath and stands. 'Wolf.'

Both Dante and Aiden stare at her as if they've never seen a woman before and even I'm breathless and bothered by her beauty. She's dressed in a gown straight out of a Goth girl's dream, all tight lace over a stunning silk bodice. Below this, the silk skirt flares sumptuously at the back, the front cut shorter with folds cunningly gathered to just above her knees, revealing long slender legs the colour of dark chocolate. Her feet are bare and as she moves down the little dais towards us I feel like prey.

'What can I do for you today, children?' She walks to a small high table holding two goblets and a carafe of wine. She pours herself a glass and turns back to us, her smile showing a hint of her wildness. 'Do you wish to join my Court?' she asks Dante, who shakes his head mutely. 'Then why are you here? I'm sad to say I do not have too much time for dallying.'

'We've come to ask you about Torsten and Brixi. Do you know where Brixi's taken the children?'

'The children?' Her brows rise in surprise. 'Really? That's why you've risked coming to meet me? How superbly sweet and human of you.' Her laugh is a soft feathery delight and Aiden shivers next to me. I let my fingers creep towards his and squeeze his hand briefly. He grips them tightly, as if thoroughly out of his depth, and the pain helps anchor me against any of Suola's persuasive magics.

'I'd very much like to find them and bring them home to their parents.' The force of her gaze feels almost physical, but I square my shoulders. 'You did say when you asked us to investigate this that we were to find the children and restore them to their parents.'

Suola's dark gaze flickers towards Melusine, who gives a small nod, and she sighs dramatically.

'Very well.' She stalks back to her chair and flings herself into its depths, somehow making it look as if it's the comfiest leather armchair, rather than something carved from black stone. 'You need to go to the forest.'

My breath hitches. 'Pardon?'

'You heard me: you will find Brixi in the forest. The piper gave us that much before he . . .' Her hand makes a motion that implies something rather fatal. '. . . when my Beast finished questioning our guest. Come now, Kit. What did you think was going to happen? That we were going to have high tea and entertain him until he gave up what he knew out of free will?' She sighs as if she can't believe my stupidity. 'You know the place. You've visited it often enough.'

'Did you know about Brixi, that he was the one behind this? That he was one of the Faceless, when you gave us this job?'

'The Faceless are as much a fairy tale to us as we are to your human children, Blackhart. The servants of the Old Gods died away when they were banished. With no masters left, their brand of servitude was no longer required.'

I find it interesting that she's not actually answered the question I asked her. Both Aiden and I start forward to ask more questions, but Suola flicks her fingers towards Melusine. 'They're done now. Have them shown out.'

Melusine walks up to us and herds us away from the throne.

'Excuse me.' Dante, clueless boy, steps past Melusine to face Suola. Her thus-far-immobile guards act immediately, swinging their halberds forwards, the points preventing him from advancing. 'I'm sorry, I just have a question for you.' He falters under her steady gaze. 'Your majesty.'

Melusine reaches back and lays a heavy hand on his arm. 'Come, she is done with you.'

'No, no, Melusine, let's hear what he has to say. Just look how earnest he is, the confused young thing. What is your question?'

'Do you know who my mother is?'

Aiden's grip tightens on my arm and I try to shake it off. What was Dante thinking, asking Suola a question like that? Did he even have anything to pay her with if she decided to answer? I do a mental calculation of the things I have on me but I come up empty. It didn't occur to me, stupidly, to grab any of the baggies of jewels we have at home to use as gifts when dealing with the Fae.

'I do know. What will you give in exchange? Will you join my Court for my answer? Swear allegiance to me?'

Aiden mutters something under his breath and lets go of my arm so he can walk up beside Dante and stop him from making a really big mistake. 'We weren't fully prepared for our visit this morning, your majesty. Dante can only offer you this minor trinket for your favour.'

He drops a small velvet pouch onto the outstretched blade of the halberd that a guard has turned sideways to accept the gift.

Suola nods towards one of her robed Fae courtiers. The

man moves fluidly and palms the velvet pouch. With his back turned, he seems to be examining the contents.

'Well? What is it?'

In answer he holds out a glinting diamond, maybe the size of my thumbnail, between his thumb and forefinger.

Suola makes an impatient gesture that I can't quite read. Is she annoyed because Aiden saved Dante from owing her a favour, or is she merely irritated because we're taking up more of her time?

'Very well, I will answer your question, although I don't think it will serve you greatly. Your mother was a Japanese kami, boy. A Sidhe noble and princess in her own right. She died not long after you were born.'

Dante opens his mouth to ask more but Aiden spins him around and starts walking him out; I hurry to keep up. Our footsteps echo in the large room and I lift the collar of my jacket higher, not liking the chill air I can feel brushing across the nape of my neck.

'Thank you for coming,' Melusine says behind us as we walk into the smaller anteroom. 'Tay here will show you out.'

Our previous Fae escort is waiting for us. His features are impassive as he hands us our weapons and takes us through the house with its echoing empty rooms. It's only when we're standing outside on the pavement, blinking against the early morning brightness, that I catch my breath properly.

'I need coffee,' Aiden says before I can. 'And maybe even whisky.'

I shrug and follow him as he turns, keeping his arm around Dante, who looks as if he's going to be physically ill.

*   *   *

Otherwhere, the Tower at the End of the World

'You were gone for two days.'

It was both an accusation and a statement of fact, in case he wasn't aware of the fact that he had slipped her taloned clutches for a small period of time. Thorn sprawled in his chair and watched his tutor pace.

The frosty facade she'd displayed during all their previous arguments was gone. She was practically pulsing with anger and, yes, possibly even concern. It surprised Thorn, but he watched her struggle to contain her temper.

'Two days!' She spun and scowled at him. 'Where did you go?'

'I went riding.'

'And?'

'And nothing.' He frowned at her. 'I thought you were able to watch me wherever I went. That nothing was hidden from you.'

'You try my patience, Thorn.'

The smile he gave her was a mere twist of his lips. 'What do you want me to say, Odalis? For the first time in months I had complete freedom. I rode, sat out beneath the stars and breathed fresh air.'

She moved things on the table in front of her. The pens and paper. Shuffling them and then spacing them neatly out once more. Small touches, calming herself, bringing order to her universe.

'You must understand, *my prince*, that if anything happened to you it would be on my head.'

'What would happen to me, Odalis? Really? I'd like to know.'

'You could have been taken.'

He rolled his eyes. 'That has failed before.'

'This time they might be more successful. You don't have your little human friend to help you. Who knows if she'd ever find out if something did happen to you.'

He looked coldly at her. 'She would know.'

'Really? And pray tell me, how would she know?'

Thorn rose and stood to his full height and scowled down at the older woman.

'This is a poor way of fishing, Odalis. If you want to know if I am in touch with her, ask me.'

'Are you?'

'Yes. And neither you nor my father can prevent it.'

'You toy with your future and hers. You know your attention puts her in danger, do you not? Your father has plans, Thorn.'

'You have assured me of this. I have seen them too.' He adds as an afterthought: 'Among other things.'

'You saw it?' She looked shocked. 'You never said anything.'

'Why should I? I may still be in training, my lady, but my gifts of foreknowledge and true sight have come some way since I was forced to move here.' He looked bitter. 'I suppose I have to thank you for your tutoring skills.'

She brushed his words aside impatiently. 'What else have you seen or heard?'

Thorn smiled a smile he was sure the wolf boy Aiden would approve. It was one full of self-confidence and no little arrogance.

'You are merely my tutor, Lady Firesky. My visions are mine and mine alone. And of course my father's, if he deigns to remember I'm more than just a pawn in his power play with the other rulers of the Otherwhere.'

Odalis's expression was thoughtful as she watched him. 'You've become a dangerous young man.'

'If I am to be judged by the rulers of the Otherwhere, Lady Firesky, I need to be sure to keep their secrets safe, surely?'

Thorn left without a further word, quietly shutting the study door behind him and leaving her to her thoughts. He had taken a few paces before the sound of something heavy crashing to the floor in the room behind him halted him briefly and he caught the startled gaze of a young page standing nearby, waiting to be called. He shook his head.

'Give her some time,' he advised the girl. 'She's not feeling too well right now.'

A quick satisfied expression flitted across her face before she inclined her head. 'As you say, guardian.'

The formal use of his title startled Thorn and he looked at her more closely.

'You are Lord Belton's . . . ?'

'His youngest granddaughter, guardian. My name is Lonia.' She was well spoken and young, maybe nine or ten. She was wary of him; heaven knew she had cause. Over these past months the increasing pressure of his foreseeing had led to temperamental outbursts, called massive storms which centred on the tower, and led to furious arguments with Odalis. Yet the page was brave enough to show her dislike for Odalis in front of him. He liked that she had that spark of rebellion, and suddenly felt he might have an ally.

Chapter Fifty-One

'How do we get there?'

I look up at Dante's question and shift uncomfortably in my chair. We're in a small coffee shop near Piccadilly Circus, tucked away in a side street. The brownie behind the counter is doing her utmost not to stare at us and I admit that even if I wasn't a Blackhart, accompanied by a changeling and werewolf boy, we would have made quite a group. The boys alone draw a lot of interested looks. They are attractive specimens and where Aiden resembles the bad boy rocker that would love you, break your heart and then leave you, Dante is more the sensitive tortured poet type with his melancholy eyes and strong features. Perhaps likely to compose poems about your heart, before breaking it too and leaving. And me? Me, I look like an extra from Megan's favourite movie, *The Lost Boys*, wearing too much leather, black clothes and eyeliner.

'We go through a gateway.'

'You make it sound so simple,' Dante points out. 'I suspect it isn't, though.'

'Nothing is ever simple when dealing with the Fae,' Aiden replies. 'Cannot believe I lost my diamond to that cow.'

'About that,' Dante says, turning to him. 'I'm sorry, I didn't stop to think. About the cost.'

'Don't worry about it. I'll make you pay it back when we get out of this.' His grin is cheeky and a light flush creeps across Dante's cheeks. I have to bite back a smirk, because trust Aiden to find the most awkward moment to flirt with the hottest person in the room. Then he sobers and turns those blue-green eyes of his to me. 'And we are getting out of this alive, aren't we, Kit?'

My smile is bleak. 'Of course. Just don't get into trouble while we're there.'

'What forest was she talking about?'

Even as Aiden asks me the question I can hear the dread in his voice. Like me he knows exactly what forest Suola meant.

'The Dark Forest.'

A visible shiver shakes him and he closes his eyes and turns away. At Dante's blank look I lean forward and explain. 'The battle against Eadric took place in the Dark Forest. Aiden and his pack fought there with Aelfric's army. They came up against Eadric's beserkers and other chimera-type monsters. These were hybrid monsters, created with dark magic and science to support Eadric's cause.'

'It was not pleasant.' Aiden's features take on a haunted look and I instantly feel bad for not considering what his pack went through in the Otherwhere. But then I was fighting to save Thorn on the island and getting the snot smacked out of me.

I jump when the brownie appears at the table looking nervous. She's carrying a tray of fresh croissants.

'My aunt sends these,' she says, her voice soft, her liquid eyes on Dante. 'She said they will sustain you on your quest.'

'How does she know we're on a quest?' Aiden asks her, flashing one of his knock-out smiles at her. She reluctantly looks away from Dante to him and dimples the cutest smile back at him.

'Oh, everyone knows. The phone rang about ten minutes before you guys came in. My cousin works at a bakery in Mayfair. She heard it from one of the knockers in that big old house the queen likes to hold meetings in.' She drew a breath, slanting another shy look at Dante. 'I've got some fresh coffee brewing so I'll bring that out in a few seconds, along with some tea for you.' With another smile at Dante she's gone in a whirl of strawberry and cupcakes smells.

'She quite seems to fancy you, mate.' Aiden jostles Dante's shoulder. 'Really pretty. Those eyes and dimples. Also, she's a brownie. I've heard that you . . .' He breaks off when I kick him under the table and scowl at him. 'What? I'm just going to say that if you date a brownie you'll never go hungry. Geez, Kit. Get your mind out of the gutter.'

'You were going to be rude about that nice girl, Aiden. You watch your mouth. I predict that one of these days you're going to meet someone and she's going to turn you to pulp. And I want front-row tickets to see that show.'

Dante tears his gaze from the pretty girl, who's blushing wildly under his attention, and frowns at us. 'Can we return to getting to the forest? How do we do that?'

'I talk to Crow,' I say. 'I need to get to a park. It's easier to summon him there.'

'Crow is one of Aelfric's foresters,' Aiden explains. 'He's got a soft spot for our little girl, here.'

'Shut up before I make you shut up,' I tell Aiden but without much anger. I am just so tired, I crave my bed and a stretch of undisturbed sleep with no dramas. 'I need to do this myself, so stay here and I'll call you when I've spoken to Crow.'

'Don't you dare try and do this by yourself, Kit. You need us.' Aiden's voice is low and insistent. 'You know I will come and find you, so don't even think about doing the same thing as last year and leaving us behind.'

I nod guiltily because I know he's right. 'I won't go anywhere without you guys, I promise.'

I stand up and grab one of the croissants from the platter. The brownie looks up as I head towards the doorway. She heads me off with a takeaway cup of coffee in her hand.

'You're brave,' she says, her voice pitched low so that only I can hear. 'But be careful.'

I take the cup from her and smile my thanks before pushing out of the shop. I flag down a taxi and ask him to drop me off at Hyde Park Corner. I could have walked the distance but I am in a hurry and it's cold out; with the skies that incredible blue that hurts your eyes if you stare at it too long.

The driver doesn't bother making conversation and I send Kyle a text to let him know what's happened with Suola, and that our priority now is to get to the Dark Forest. I pay the driver and head into Hyde Park. Even though it's a work day, the park is busy. Mums and nannies with strollers and little dogs in tow crowd the pathways, along with rollerbladers and ambling tourists.

I head towards the Serpentine but on my way there I collect a leaf, possibly a red oak leaf, I can't be sure, and hold on to it gingerly. One of the benches is empty and I sit, removing a piece of chalk from my pocket. I write Crow's name and then my own on the leaf and roll it tightly. It would have to do for now.

At the edge of the man-made lake I hunker next to a little toddler who's tossing bread towards a group of fat ducks. I drop the leaf into the water and watch it bob for a few seconds, before it sinks.

I can't tell how long it will take for my message to reach Crow, so I walk along the side of the Serpentine, enjoying my coffee and relishing the sunshine on my upturned face. I consciously let my magic rise just above my skin. I'm not too worried that anyone will see the weird glow around me. Humans with any kind of second sight or magical ability possibly number about half a percentage of the entire population. Admittedly, that's still a lot if you think about it, but sometimes you have to live on the edge just a bit.

I become aware of someone keeping pace with me but off the main path. I look up and spot a flash of Crow's dark hair as he walks behind one of the trees. I grin and hike over to him.

'That was quick.'

I look up at him and smile. I can't explain how I feel so comfortable with this wild Fae. His features are striking and he makes no attempt to use glamour to tone down his otherworldly looks. A few people actually stop and stare at him but he takes no notice.

He holds onto my shoulders for the longest time, just looking at me, before folding me against his lean chest.

'Kit, what have you been doing to yourself? You look terrible.'

At my annoyed wriggle he chuckles. 'Still pretty, but far too tired for someone as young as you. Come, tell me what's been going on.'

He guides me further into the park, away from curious eyes and settles me on a bench before dropping onto the grass at my feet.

'Tell your Uncle Crow everything.'

I roll my eyes at the phrase 'Uncle Crow' but I do tell him everything, including the part where we have to get to the Dark Forest. I also tell him about the building where I think the children are hidden – the abandoned palace I dream about, where I run into Thorn.

'Let me get this straight: Suola told you where to find the children?'

'Not in so many words. She said we need to get to the forest and then said, *the place you've been visiting.*' I sigh. 'And that's the only place I've been visiting. In my dreams.'

'Do you remember anything about it? About the palace?'

'It's huge, ancient. Beautifully built, long passages. It looks and feels very romantic. It's definitely in the forest because I remember seeing the forest beyond the town at the palace's base.'

'Does the town look inhabited?'

I close my eyes and think back. 'No. Deserted, for sure. No movement and the houses look dilapidated.' I watch his face and wonder how old he is. To my human eye he looks no older than say thirty, Uncle Jamie's age, but I know he is far older than that. His sister implied as much. 'Do you know it?'

'Yes.' His eyes are troubled as he looks at me. 'I do, but it's not a place we visit very often.'

I wait for him to continue talking and after a short while he does. 'There is an abandoned town in the far north of the Dark Forest. It is an old place. Some say it dates from the Time Before Time.'

I blink. 'Do you mean from the time of the Elder Gods?'

He inclines his head. 'Yes, it is where Istvan's many-times-great-grandfather reigned.'

I swear softly. 'And why has no one destroyed it?'

'There was no need. Once the Elder Gods were destroyed and Aelfric's family took the throne for themselves, the village and palace fell into disrepair and no one really bothered with it much.'

'Until now.'

He shrugs and leans forward, running his hands about an inch over the grass. The blades move and I watch in amazement as they grow right before my eyes until they reach his palm.

'Until now. And you want to go there?'

'I need to go there. If that's where they're taking the children.'

'It's going to be dangerous.'

'I know.' I sigh and sit forward so I can peer at his face. 'There are three of us that need to get to the forest. Can you help?'

'Yes, of course I will. It will be fantastic to have you back in the forest. The trees have missed you.'

'You're such a hippy, Crow.'

'I don't know what that means, but I'll take it as a compliment.'

I laugh and hug him awkwardly.

Chapter Fifty-Two

It's after midday when we meet Crow back at the Serpentine. He is easy to spot. He has a troop of little kids around him and he is letting them feed two squirrels that he holds carefully on either hand. When he looks up and sees us he gives us a nod and speaks softly to the squirrels. They chitter at him and scamper off into the trees, their cheeks packed with nuts. The kids complain loudly but their mums and minders sweep in and carry them off, thanking Crow for entertaining them. One woman hesitates and hands something to Crow. He looks down at the thing in his hand in a bemused way and when the woman blushes, he gives a slow smile and I can almost see her knees buckle.

She says something to the little boy by her side and they hurriedly follow the group moving away.

'Look at you, Casanova,' I say. 'Making friends and influencing people. What did she give you?'

He opens his palm and I see a piece of paper there with her name and number. Aiden sees it too and laughs. 'Crow, you old dog.'

'What do the numbers mean?' Crow asks, after he's let himself be thumped on the back.

'She gave you her mobile number. To call her? To make a date.'

The Fae forester shook his head. 'I don't know what that means.'

'She wants to go out with you. Courting? To dinner? To have food?'

'Oh!' He looks at Aiden in surprise and hands him the piece of paper. 'No, you send her a messenger and tell her I can't do that. It wouldn't be proper. Human and Fae do not mingle in that way, not any more.' He notices Dante and takes a step back in surprise. 'This is who you have accompanying you?'

Both Aiden and I look at Dante, who looks pale and worried, shifting under our scrutiny.

'Do you know who he is?' I ask Crow.

'Well, no, but he's not human.' Crow inhales deeply. 'Siren, possibly? And male. Interesting.'

Before Dante can be further mauled by more people being rude about his heritage, I introduce them. 'Dante, this is my friend Crow. He's one of the foresters in the Dark Forest. Crow, this is Dante.'

'There is a story here,' Crow says slowly. 'One I feel I need to hear before I take you to the Otherwhere.'

Dante looks troubled as he explains what we've figured out about his heritage, including the latest on his mother being a Sidhe noble and kami.

'You have the ring? As proof?' Crow demands, and when Dante nods, Crow looks at me. 'And you've seen it for yourself – it's real?'

I nod. 'Oh yes, it's very real. The ring looks exactly as Eadric's ring was described to me.'

'This makes things very interesting indeed. Apart from

you being Eadric's son, the kami are powerful nature spirits,' Crow explains. 'They are what you might call divine spirits and in some instances they are revered as gods. I think that once we've found this Brixi and your missing children, we should look to reunite you with your mother's family.' He claps a hand to Dante's shoulder. 'There is no need for you to look so concerned. They would be proud to welcome you home.'

Aiden jostles Dante. 'Huh, check you out. What do you feel like most? A divine spirit or a revered god?'

'Shut up, Aiden,' Dante says but he's laughing, and it makes me feel so much better. 'I'd like nothing more, Crow,' he says. 'Thank you.'

Crow shakes his head as if he can't quite believe any of it. 'Let's get going.'

Crow gives us a curt nod and walks away from the Serpentine, towards the north of the park where there are more trees. 'We're going through the trees,' he tells us. 'They are easier to navigate. I will take you as far as I can. I warn you now that it's going to be a strange experience.'

'What do you mean we're going *through* the trees?'

'All forests are connected,' Crow explains as we walk. 'Wherever you find a small copse of trees, if you know how, you can travel between places. I'm taking you to the Otherwhere, to the Dark Forest, in this way.'

His smile is sweet and he clearly doesn't understand the panic we feel when he places his palm against one of the large oak trees and just steps into it as if he's opened a door to a house.

The sense of dislocation is tremendous. We pass through a dozen or more trees and I don't know how far we've travelled but my body tells me it's going to break if I don't stop soon. The air around me is rich with the smell of undergrowth and the scent of night-blooming flowers.

Crow rubs my back as I heave into some bushes. Dante looks fine, though a bit wide-eyed, taking in the thick forest around us. Aiden looks completely rattled at being back in the place that holds so many bad memories.

'We are literally on the other side of the world,' Aiden says, taking deep breaths of air. 'I can smell everything.'

Crow chuckles and passes me a canteen that he produces from somewhere. He walks towards the boys and claps them on the shoulders. 'Welcome to my world.' He gestures. 'This is Alba's beating heart, the Dark Forest. The place where mysteries are born.'

I roll my eyes and hand back the half-full canteen. 'You really are a hippy. How far are we from the abandoned palace?'

'Not far, as the crow flies.'

I groan, remembering him using the exact same phrase the last time I was here and how it took ages to get where we were going.

'I have arranged with one of my friends to meet you here. She will be taking you further, as I have reached the borders of my territory.'

As he is speaking, something large moves in the forest behind me and I scurry to his other side. A warning growl grows in Aiden's throat but Crow holds out a calming hand.

I have *never* seen a bear in real life. They are frightening enough on TV, so when a giant bear the size of a truck comes lumbering into the clearing I want to turn and run and never stop. Crow steps forward until he stands in front of the bear.

The bear bellows at him, shaking its enormous head from side to side. Crow speaks rapidly in a language I don't understand. The bear rears up on its hind legs and I am horrified to see how tall it is when it's standing upright. It could eat all four of us and still be hungry. Just as I'm about to shout a warning, the bear starts shrinking and, as it does, it assumes a human shape.

I've seen Aiden change shape before. It was a peculiar and intimate experience and it startled us both. He'd been hurt in a fight and I'd thought his arm had been broken. The pain had been so severe that it triggered his change, much to the horror of the group of animal smugglers we were facing off against, and much to my own shock. One moment he'd been Aiden, howling in rage, the next he was fully wolf and angry. Afterwards he assured me that for him the change took a long time, whereas for me watching it seemed like mere moments.

The woman who stands before us is big, built along broad lines. She accepts Crow's cloak, shaking out her long thick hair, and smiling at him in thanks.

'It will be my honour to travel with you the rest of the way,' she says. Her voice is as rich as honey. 'Please call me Nura.'

Her hand when I shake it is firm. 'I'm Kit, and these are my friends, Dante and Aiden.'

The boys each shake her hand as Crow ducks out of the clearing and comes back with a bundle of clothes in his hands.

'As promised,' he says, handing it to her.

'Thank you.' She drops the cloak once more and I can actually hear Aiden swallow at the sight of so much perfect skin and voluptuous curves. 'We don't have far to go, fortunately. I made good time in my bear aspect.'

I walk up to both boys and lead them some distance away so that Nura can get changed without them ogling her as if she's the last bit of glazed doughnut in the shop. Crow watches us, puzzled, but then grins wickedly at me when he realizes that human and Fae modesty mean very different things.

Chapter Fifty-Three

Nura's pace through the forest is faster than Crow's. She has no qualms about using her skill to clear a path for us and bends the forest to her will. Crow works with the forest, listening and taking care. He coasts, like his bird namesake, whereas Nura makes her own way.

I'm grateful for the amount of running I've been doing and I do my utmost to keep up with the statuesque Fae forester. Aiden has that look in his eye that tells me he's smitten once more. He wears that same expression around Megan whenever she's home, not that she ever actually notices. Dante's incredibly quiet as he follows closely behind. His eyes are wide and I can tell he has a million questions about everything around him: about Crow, about Nura, about the forest. For almost the first time since I've known him, he looks dishevelled and not entirely in control. It's a good look on him, as is the healthy flush that's crept back into his face.

Nura took one look at him before we set off and with one hand on her heart she executed a small bow.

'Your mother was a great lady, young Dante. She did not deserve the death that came for her.' Dante tried asking questions but Nura shook her head. 'Afterwards, there'll be time for talking. Now, I have to lead you to the palace.'

We walk at a punishing pace but Nura ensures that we take regular breaks, drinking water and snacking on the fruits and nuts she scavenges. I watch Dante as he becomes aware of the residual power of the forest. He drops his glamour gradually and I grin at him when the small horns rise from his forehead once more. He spends a lot of time talking quietly to Aiden when we walk, and he seems to have shrugged off Aiden's artless remarks about his father. There are real smiles there now, an easiness between them that makes me feel I'm seeing the start of true friendship.

The forest is verdant and teeming with wildlife, some of which I'm pretty sure has never been featured on National Geographic's nature programmes. We stop briefly near midnight for a few hours' sleep and Nura stands guard before hustling us on again.

When dawn comes round, we step out into a clearing and I let out a gasp as I look up – on the rise ahead, I see the edifice that's been in my dreams for weeks now. It's bigger than I'd imagined. It looks more like a fortress from down here than a palace, with a sturdy outer wall. Built of gold-coloured stone, the place looks warm and inviting and yet lonely. For all its solidness, its lines are elegant and beautiful, and I release a breath of relief that we've finally arrived. The town at its base, with its winding roads, is deserted. The buildings look a little Middle Eastern, a little Mediterranean.

'What happened here?' Dante asks as he draws level with us. 'Where are all the people?'

'They were all put to death for supporting the murder of their fellow Fae,' Nura replies. 'Those who weren't killed were left behind to bury the dead. Most eventually died too, overcome with illnesses from handling the thousands of bodies of their dead. Few survived that, and those that did were shunned by Fae trying to rebuild their lives – after the destruction the Elder Gods and their followers had wrought. This place has been cursed ever since.'

'No one comes here?'

Nura hesitates. 'Those who come here are usually people who do not want to be found.'

'Oh great.' Aiden sighs. 'So we have to fight them too?'

'Maybe, it depends on this Faceless you seek. If he's keeping the children up at the palace, he might have secured the town first.'

'Let's go,' I say and motion for her to lead the way but she shakes her glossy head.

'No, Lady Blackhart, this is as far as I go. My jurisdiction is the forest. I have no powers in the town. I will wait here for you as Crow asked me to. If you aren't back by tomorrow night, sunset, I will leave.' She turns and walks towards the forest and as she does she morphs back into her bear shape. Although I've seen her do it the other way around, a shiver still passes over me.

'That does not stop being the sexiest thing I've ever seen,' Aiden says, shaking his head. 'Do you think that when we come back she'll be naked again?'

I shove him hard and he staggers dramatically, falling over his own feet, and is helped up by Dante, who looks both amused and horrified. 'Stop being an idiot. Let's get going.'

We climb through the town's deserted streets. An eerie feeling that we're being watched settled over me when we walked through the gate almost an hour ago, and I can't shake it. I carry my sword and still feel exposed and uncomfortable. The town is much larger than I expected from the clearing. Probably several thousand people lived here before they were killed. As we pass the empty houses I'm struck by the personal items I see left behind. Pots and pans, a vase, someone's loom.

It's like a fairytale village caught in a hundred-year sleep. I almost expect to see heavy rose vines keeping us out of the palace, but the doors and windows are all gone and the only vines belong to thick growths of ivy. I gingerly step through the doorway and a weird sense of déjà vu overcomes me.

Here's the palace I've dreamed of so often. It feels odd being here in reality when I've been here so often in my dreams, exploring its abandoned rooms and meeting with Thorn. I remember the presence I felt whenever we met up here and how he kept urging me to 'keep her safe', whoever 'she' was.

'If you were a bad guy hiding kids, where would you hide them?' Dante asks me.

He's carrying his taser and I wonder if it will even work here. I consider passing him one of my knives but think he probably has a few of his own. Even so, he looks uncomfortably under-armed. Aiden, by comparison, is carrying a kukri and I am a bit jealous at how prettily the curved blade reflects the light.

'Dungeon,' Aiden and I answer at the same time.

Aiden grimaces. 'The guy who lived here wasn't exactly Prince Charming, was he? I mean, I expected more ugliness than this from him.' He points to the still vivid murals of pastoral landscapes. 'Seeing as this was the guy who supported the crazy Elder Gods, and we all know they were more about eating their followers than ruling them.'

A shiver tracks down my spine and I step into a shaft of sunlight to counter it, but even that doesn't warm me.

I frown at him. 'Okay, smarty pants, let's go find ourselves some stairs that go down.'

He takes the lead and I bring up the rear with Dante between us. We move cautiously. In some places the roof's fallen in completely and we have to skirt rubble. There are some rooms that are utterly untouched by time and it's as if the occupants have only just left. Tapestries hang on the walls, defying age and time. Some floor tiles crumble to dust beneath our feet. My blade brushes a stone set in an archway as we pass through and gouges a chunk from it. I hurriedly step forward, concerned that the whole arch will crumble, but it miraculously stays up, keeping the remnants of the ceiling above us where they belong.

What I find strange about the whole place is how there are no birds or any other creatures to be seen or heard. After the living forest we walked through during the night, the absence of animals feels peculiar.

'Is it just me or does it feel like we're going to stumble into Sleeping Beauty's bower any second now?' Aiden asks over his shoulder. 'Also, can this place be any creepier?'

'There could be zombies,' Dante says apparently without thinking. Then: 'Zombies aren't real, are they?'

Aiden shrugs. 'Well, I've seen some ugly things crawl out of Milton's some nights, so I can't be sure.'

He catches my eye and I point with my sword. Surprise registers on his face when he sees what I've spotted. We've come to a passage and there are sets of stairs going up and down. He gives me a thumbs-up and starts heading downwards. Dante and I follow him closely. There is so much light that it's not necessary to bring my magic out to play just yet.

We wind down the stairs and, whereas the floors above still seemed in good, although derelict, order, the places we pass as we descend are less well kept. It's as if whatever keeps the palace standing has no hold here in the dark musty depths.

The palace had been built on a rocky outcrop, not unlike the main city of Alba, the Citadel. The further we descend, the more it feels that we're descending into the hill itself, and I wonder uncomfortably if we'll be facing trolls again.

The last time I faced trolls in a cavern things had gone badly wrong and someone had lost their life. My thoughts are interrupted by Aiden coming to a halt.

'I think we're here.'

I edge past Aiden and spot the heavy iron gate blocking our way. Once upon a time it had been locked with a thick iron chain. Now that chain lies in brittle pieces on the floor.

'What are the chances,' I say, 'that we're walking into a trap?'

'Of course we're walking into a trap. We've not exactly been subtle about walking through the palace or about our intention to come here.'

I shrug. Aiden's right. 'Okay then, let's go.'

Dante uses a piece of wood from the corner and pushes the gate open until it swings wide enough for us to pass through. Aiden and I follow him along the passage.

It's darker here, more damp. I call my magic, creating two balls of softly glowing light. I tether one above and to the right of Aiden's shoulder and do the same above me. That way they are giving light but not blinding us.

We move on, and once we've checked the first floor of cells (gross damp places full of rubble and glowing fungi), we move further down still.

I've lost count of how many floors we check over, cautiously stepping into each cell, expecting the worst, but there's nothing. The fact that there's nothing to fight or hurt is more tiring than I can actually explain. My nerves, already on edge, are drawn tight – so when we come to a halt, within what feels like the very basement of the palace, my hand holding the sword is sweaty and I'm breathing fast.

I dry my hands on my jeans. 'I'll take point,' I say to Aiden, aware that I'm falling into Jamie's military speak. 'You bring up the rear. Keep Dante safe.'

It looks for a moment as if he wants to argue, also remembering a time when we had a third party to our duo and how we were instructed to keep him safe. The memory of Thorn makes me realize how much I miss him. The ache is unexpected and sharp but I push it aside, knowing that now is not the time for a mini-breakdown.

I hold back a sigh and gesture. Onwards.

There are no cells here. The passage is narrow and the ceiling is high. My light glints off thousands upon thousands of gems stuck into the basalt stone. I remember seeing similar stone in the trolls' cave and wonder if we've somehow slipped between worlds again, and if the next door we're going to find will lead us to London.

Aiden hears it before I do. He makes a barely audible clicking sound at the back of his throat and I stop. He brings a finger to his lips and taps his ear.

Above the sound of water dripping somewhere, is the sound of something moving. The sound is laborious and slow. I close my eyes and imagine scales and possibly a chain.

A dragon? Could the palace be built on top of a dragon? I shudder. A giant snake, like in Conan? Or, my imagination reaches, the world serpent from Norse mythology?

Dante touches my arm lightly and shows me the palm of his hand. I frown in surprise. Ink-black marks have crept along his arm, winding their way around his wrist and onto his hand. I recognize sharp points as looking like the ivy we passed earlier.

'My tattoo seems to be growing,' he says, lifting his shirt and turning sideways so I can see the rest of it. I'm not even distracted by his abs because the tattoo is so absorbing, and I don't remember it stretching over this much of his skin before.

Aiden mutters something and grabs Dante, turning him so he can look at the marks. 'Bloody hell, Dante, what's that?'

'I have absolutely no idea. It doesn't hurt at all, but I can feel it shifting and growing.' Dante presses his hand against the almost imperceptibly moving ink. 'It almost tickles.'

'I don't like this,' I say, looking at Aiden. 'Maybe we should get Dante out of here. We don't know if his magic is reacting to this place or to whatever's down here.'

'Don't be stupid, Kit. I'm your partner – we're seeing this through together.' Dante's grumbling makes Aiden grin and he nods towards the changeling.

'The man has a point.'

I give Aiden a filthy look before I turn to look back at Dante. 'Don't come crying to me if you turn into a hideous beast monster or something, okay?'

Dante rolls his eyes. 'Lead the way, Blackhart.'

Chapter Fifty-Four

The passage narrows considerably for about a hundred metres before widening again. The steady sound of dripping is closer now and I wonder if we're going to find another cavern at the end of this tunnel. What might there be in such a cavern?

'I really don't like being underground,' Aiden admits unexpectedly. 'It makes me think about weight of the earth above me. I can't breathe properly.'

'We'll be out of here soon. Can you feel it? The path is going uphill now.'

Dante's right and the gradient's increasing too. I'm already puffing and out of breath when the passage opens wide and we spill out into a large room held up by stone arches and solid columns. I stop to catch my breath and turn to check that Dante and Aiden are okay. As I do, I spot the man sitting casually on a small chair, watching us with interest.

His features are pleasantly bland, almost unremarkable, and he's dressed in boots, a tunic and comfortable-looking trousers. He watches us without alarm and seems unsurprised by our presence, but even so I can almost feel the weight of his regard. The guys notice him too and Dante murmurs something ugly but I grab hold of his arm before he can run at the guy.

'You actually found us,' the man says, sounding impressed. 'I wondered when you would. I have been waiting to see you for a very long time.' He nods at me and I know he has to be Brixi; I recognize him from my weird little time-slip adventure at the estate. 'I didn't think you had it in you, but then you sent my men packing and I had to reassess your abilities.'

I glance around as casually as I can as I move towards him. 'What have you done with the kids?'

'They are here, sleeping, of course.'

'We are here to take them back.'

At my words both Aiden and Dante walk forward so that they flank me. It's a neat move but it doesn't seem to impress Brixi at all.

'You can try, but I don't think you'll be able to.' He stands up from the small chair. 'Come, let me show you. I know you're dying to see what this is all about.'

Both Aiden and Dante shoot a glance at me and I can practically hear them telling me it's a trap. But I nod anyway and we follow him.

Brixi makes sure his hands stay visible as he walks ahead. We soon come to another room, smaller than before, but we don't stop. It's a labyrinth down here and all the rooms look alike, with vaulted ceilings and archways.

However, the atmosphere is fresh rather than musty, which means that there's enough air getting in here from somewhere. This cheers me up because it means that if air can come in, we have a way out.

We don't go far at all, even if the journey is a confusing one. Brixi pushes open a massive wooden door banded with silver and beckons us in. He enters the room without waiting to see if we're following. Aiden puts his shoulder to the door and pushes it all the way open while Dante blocks the door from shutting on us with a small boulder.

The room looks like the outer chamber to a wealthy noblewoman's room, but everything is on a larger scale. When I say larger scale, I mean very big. Gossamer curtains stir in the air and flutter towards us in the softest of breezes. Brixi puts his finger to his lips and leads us through the curtains into the chamber beyond.

It isn't possible to miss the sleeping giant dozing in the middle of the room. Nor is it possible not to notice the thirteen beds spaced around her, each one holding a sleeping child. A soft haze hangs over the scene and there's a silence to this place that reminds me of being alone in a large cathedral.

The figure at the centre of the room is female and draped with soft cloths. I can't see her features because the slab she's lying on is raised too high, so all I can make out is her sleeping form. There are steps that lead up to the dais; if I could climb these, I'd be able to look down on her.

Aiden nudges me and frowns questioningly at the scene. *How would I know what's going on here?* I mime back in annoyance before moving forwards. A soft pressure prevents me from getting too close, no matter how much I try to push through. The haze looks like watery mist but it doesn't feel damp or unpleasant against my skin. My magic buzzes happily, not at all alarmed by the shield in place. The way it pushes me back reminds me of when I tried to gain access to little Tia's apartment but couldn't. Dante's next to me and he presses his hand into the barrier before pulling back.

'Is this what you felt back on the estate at Tia's parents'

flat?' he asks me, looking surprised. 'So, it was you, all along?' His gaze finds Brixi, who's watching us with a watchful expression. 'Then it was you who prevented Kit from gaining access to Tia's home . . . Were you also responsible for making me sick?'

'I might have been overzealous with my offensive spell, but look how that turned out,' Brixi said, gesturing at him. 'Although you were waking up to who you were already. Lady Blackhart had already triggered the demise of your glamour. It was interesting to watch, but then kisses from maidens always carried the utmost power and intent.'

Dante's clearly burning to have a throwdown with Brixi, so I jump in with questions of my own. I'm not really flushing at the implication of maidens and kissing, not at all.

'What is going on here? Who is she?' I ask him, turning back to the sleeping figure and mentally ticking off the names of the kids lying like satellites around her. 'What are the children doing here?'

'Step away, please.' Brixi's eyes drift anxiously towards the figure in the middle of the haze and he reaches for my arm but I jerk back. Annoyance shifts across his features and as it does, they change. For a moment his face looks different, and I recognize someone else: Officer Briggs, the policewoman in little Tia's parents' lounge, her electronic equipment hooked up to the telephone as she waits for the kidnapper to call.

My mind is quick to make sense of it. Brixi had impersonated a police officer and had been in Tia's and her mother's home all along. He'd set up the spell so that I couldn't enter; only when Marvin invited me in could I walk freely into the flat.

'Who is she, Brixi?'

'She is a living goddess,' he answers after a beat, tracking Dante and Aiden as they prowl around the room, peering at the sleeping children. 'We have been looking after her for an age, making sure she stays alive.'

'By stealing children whose parents you trick into god knows what?' I can't help the revulsion in my voice or finish the accusation, because – really, does it need acknowledging again? 'What about their families, the people who care for them? How can you do this to them?'

Brixi shakes his head, pressing a finger to his lips. 'No, no. You don't understand. The children want to be here, they need to be here, to look after their mother.'

Actual waves of crazy are coming off Brixi now. There's something about the way he's staring at the sleeping figure in the centre of the room that makes me want to run and hide. How can the word 'mother' be even remotely appropriate here? Both Dante and Aiden are standing closer to me now. They look worried and Aiden's pale beneath his tan. Dante's rubbing at his hands; the tattoo markings are far more vivid than before.

'Those children need to go home. Their parents are waiting for them.' Dante's voice is harsh. 'This is so incredibly morally wrong.'

'There is no way the children can be moved without killing them,' Brixi says, his tone soft and almost apologetic. 'They have completely bonded with the goddess. They are now her sources of power, keeping her strong.'

'Excuse me, but did you say this sleeping giant is a goddess?' Aiden shoots a look at the prone figure. 'Are you sure? She doesn't look very powerful to me.'

'And the children are her sources of power?' Dante chimes in. 'This situation is wrong.'

Brixi gestures elegantly. 'It is what it is. Every few generations the children need to be replaced. It is our job as her keepers to find those children and bring them here.'

'Wait,' I say, holding up my hand to prevent both boys from asking questions. 'Why don't we just let Brixi tell us the story from the beginning?'

Dante and Aiden share disgruntled looks and it's cute how they try to gang up against me, but I give them an aggressive stare that shuts them up. Brixi watches the quiet struggle for power before he nods. 'Very well. It has been some time since I told the story in its entirety. The last time was to your parents,' he says, nodding at me. 'How long ago was that? Sixteen years? Time moves differently here.'

I don't even have a second to process that he's just mentioned my parents before he starts his story.

'In the beginning, four of the five Elder Gods rampaged through villages and towns, laying waste to entire tribes. The fifth chose to dedicate her life to the people who loved her. She brought them fire, taught them how to tell futures, and how to use the natural magics of the world. She showed the men animal husbandry and she showed the women how to hunt and gather. She was strong and capable but her brothers raged across the face of the world in a wave of destruction. She decided that they had to be stopped. She spoke with the strongest sorcerers she had trained, and together they devised a way to banish her brothers, when it became clear they were bent on the total annihilation of the people who worshipped them.' Brixi breathes deeply before plunging ahead. 'The ritual was performed by Fae and human sorcerers. One Fae warrior, one of the dragon-born, swore to become the Elder Gods' keeper and watch over them for all eternity. The success of the ritual caused what became the Sundering of the human and Fae worlds. The goddess wept at the loss of her brothers but she knew she had betrayed them for the good of the people, whom she'd come to love. She went into mourning, falling into a deep sleep. Shortly after the Sundering it became clear that the Otherwhere wasn't stable and that its magics were leaking into the human world. This was incredibly dangerous and lethal to both Fae and human. The sorcerers realized it was the presence of the Elder Gods that stabilized the realms. The Fae lords discussed matters at length and they instructed their sorcerors to weave thousands of spells to create one all-encompassing binding spell, the strongest spell ever to have been worked on since the beginning of our time. The spell would ensure that she would never wake, and with her magical presence in the Otherwhere, the Fae realm remained stable. The songlines burned with power and the sorcerers once more grew strong and feared. As time passed, the goddess's powers have ebbed and flowed in the way of all things. More recently, it became obvious that she was weakening. A thousand years ago, a great congregation of sorcerers and rulers met and it was decided to try whatever it took to stabilize her and enhance her power.'

'And so you found that children could be used as batteries to feed your sleeping goddess?' I stare at Brixi in horror. 'That's awful. Not just for the kids but for the poor woman you've kept prisoner here for I don't know how long.'

Brixi looks deeply unhappy. 'You must understand that I love her more than life itself. A few of us look after her needs but I am her caretaker. However, I am not the one who put her here. I care deeply for her and it's because of me and the sacrifices I've made that she survives.'

'Yeah, you might not have put her here but you are definitely keeping her here.' Aiden scowls and advances on him, bulking up and towering over the smaller man, who doesn't look at all scared, just wary. 'How would you feel if you were trapped in there by someone else? Especially if you were a little kid and you were stolen from your family to come here, to this weird place, to become food for something that shouldn't even exist any more?'

Brixi seems very conflicted as he regards us. 'You don't understand. She will die if her power gives out entirely. And if she dies, the Otherwhere dies. The Veil that separates the Frontier and the Otherwhere will be shredded. Creatures will storm your world, and humanity will not survive. In turn, humans will fight and try and invade the Otherwhere with their weapons, because humans are ever on the lookout for things they don't understand so that they can destroy them.'

I take this in and see both Aiden and Dante hesitate. I walk back towards the prone figure and the surrounding tiny beds. I can't get further than a few feet from them before I'm gently pressed back, insistently.

'How many people know about this?' Aiden asks him. 'The wolves have never heard this legend.'

'I'm pretty sure I would have heard this from someone in my family,' I pipe up, walking around the periphery of the barrier. I trail my fingertips along, liking the buzzing feel of it against my sensitive skin. 'But then last year, the whole Elder Gods thing seemed a bit of a shock to all of them too.'

'Aelfric knows. He's always known. It was his many-times-great-grandfather who worked with the sorcerers to put her under the spell. Istvan knew, as his family ruled during the time the Elder Gods walked the earth.' Brixi's gaze rests on me as I complete my examination. 'Our new guardian, Aelfric's youngest son, knows. But other than that, it's me and whoever has enough determination to wade through ancient histories in rotting libraries.'

I draw a ragged breath, taking it all in. 'You said my parents knew? Did you tell them?'

'They already seemed to know so much when they came looking for her.' Brixi's voice is apologetic. 'I liked them. You remind me of your mother: she had something fierce about her too. I am sorry for your loss, Blackhart.'

The need to sit down is nearly overwhelming as my legs suddenly feel weak. Could my parents' death perhaps be linked to their finding out about the goddess? The thought and its implications nearly flatten me and I cross my arms protectively over my chest and turn away from Brixi. There is stuff going on here, secrets that don't sit well with me. The urge to be alone so I can figure this out is overwhelming, but I know this isn't the time. Both Dante and Aiden are watching me closely for clues as to what to do next.

'Has she ever woken up?' Dante asks.

'Once, when the bombs of your second great war shook the Frontier, it threatened to tear the Veil between the worlds. She woke up then and caused a lot of upset. She killed all her guards and tried to escape her chambers.'

'But they put her back under?'

'Istvan did. He spent a long time here, locked away with her, working on the spells that kept her safe.' Brixi peers down at his charge's face. 'She is so beautiful.'

'How did you become her custodian?' I ask him, curious against my will.

'I'm one of the Faceless. It is my family's obligation; we were her guards and handmaidens in the old days. We continue to serve her still, even if I am one of only a handful of us left.'

'You have no right to make yourself sound noble. You steal children to keep her alive,' Dante bites out as he stalks towards Brixi but Aiden bars his advance with an arm across his chest.

'Dante, dude. Come on, all of this is different now,' he rumbles warningly. 'None of this is what we thought it would be. Lines are blurred although there's still so much wrong here. We need to think this through.'

I'm so confused by everything I've heard, that I don't even realize I've sat down until I register my back leaning against the smooth stone wall.

'I don't know what to think.' I hate how small my voice sounds. 'How do we even begin to fix this?'

Maybe Brixi looks ashamed for a second, but maybe I'm wrong.

'There are some things that are better left undisturbed, Blackhart. For everyone's safety,' he says.

Chapter Fifty-Five

I allow myself to wallow in misery for a few more minutes before deciding we need to head back and talk to Uncle Andrew. And Aiden needs to put this to the wolves. Basically, the whole scenario needs looking after by adults because there is just no way I can handle it myself. I'm about to suggest this when Aiden's head comes up sharply and his whole posture becomes super alert.

'What?' I call out to him, worry thrumming through me.

'There's someone coming.' He holds up his hand and turns his head, listening. 'Only one. But there are others too, further back.'

'How do we stop them? Can we shut the doors to this room?' I'm back on my feet, looking out into the smaller chamber beyond.

'Let's see who we've got first,' Dante says. 'It could be someone Suola sent.'

'I'm not sure if that's better or worse,' I reply, already moving for the doorway. There are fast-running footsteps now too and baying hounds in the distance. Because the large rooms echo so well, it sounds as if there are hundreds of people rushing towards us.

'Does anyone else feel very last stand in Moria right now?' Dante asks, an expectantly savage grin on his face.

I shake my head. 'Really? A Tolkien reference? Now?'

His grin widens. 'Sorry, when I get nervous I randomly refer to Tolkien and think WWSD.'

'WWSD?'

'What would Strider do?'

'I can't believe you,' I retort but I can't help giving a laugh, even though it's slightly hysterical. I turn as Brixi nears me. He's carrying two fighting knives with blades as long as his forearms. They look boss-level mean. 'Are you expecting anyone?' I ask him. He mutely shakes his head before moving past me into the small antechamber and I follow him, my sword ready.

You know when things slow down in movies and you think that never actually happens in real life? I can testify that it does happen.

The figure running towards us is dressed in light armour. I see the glint of a familiar cuirass and overlong blond hair. My heart stutters from shock when I recognize Thorn – and this time it's real and it's not a dream.

'Holy shit, is that Thorn?' Aiden breathes next to me and I have to lean against him because my knees feel week. He wraps an arm around me and pulls me back into the large chamber, just as Thorn arrives at a run.

'Brixi,' Thorn gasps, still unaware of us as he reaches for the Faceless. A hand is pressed to his side, where blood's dripping from a wound. 'What have you done? There are guards all over the forest. Hundreds of them.'

'We have guests,' Brixi says and pulls him around to face us.

Seeing the person you think you're in love with in your dreams, then seeing them in real life when your world is crumbling – it's not ideal, but you take what you can get.

Thorn looks shocked to see me but then he's reaching blindly for me, and I let myself be pulled into his arms. I can hear him talking to Aiden and feel Aiden reaching around me to hug him fiercely.

'You stupid bloody faerie, what trouble are you in now? You look like crap.'

'Wolf, I'd say I missed you but that would be a lie.' Thorn's voice is deep and still holds that cute hint of the exotic. Even through the strain in his voice I can hear his amusement at Aiden's snort of annoyance. 'And Kit. This is now, isn't it? And real?'

I grin up at him. 'Of course it's real. You're bleeding and running away from people. This is how it usually goes, isn't it?'

'True. And who . . .' Thorn goes dangerously still. 'You're him, aren't you? Eadric's son.'

I have enough self-preservation instinct – unbelievably – to step away from Thorn as he looks at Dante. The telltale hum of his magic washes over me, and Aiden must sense something too. He pulls me behind him protectively, then pushes Thorn back and away from Dante.

'Dude, Dante's nothing like his father, okay? Take it easy.'

'I'm fine, Aiden,' Dante says. 'I can handle this.'

Thorn calms and the tension breaks as he holds out a hand out to Dante. 'I knew you were out there somewhere; I'm sorry I overreacted. I didn't expect to see you here, but it's a relief to meet you finally. I should have known Kit would find you. She attracts trouble like . . .' He shrugs. 'She's just a trouble magnet.'

Dante's smile is wary but amused. 'It's good to meet you too. I've heard some interesting stuff about you.'

They look at one another and it's a frank and assessing moment and not at all hostile. Thorn seems to come to some sort of decision. 'A whole army of wild Fae followed me into this place – on my father's instructions. We need to get you to safety.' He turns to look at Aiden. 'Wolf, listen to me. We have to move, and quickly.'

Brixi's fighting knives flash in the light as he moves forward. 'You know the way through the back tunnels, guardian. I suggest you start running.'

'Why would your father send people to chase you?' Aiden asks him in surprise.

'Not me, specifically. Just anyone who approaches the fortress without one of the foresters as a guide.'

'But, surely, if they knew who you are . . . ?' Dante hesitates, looking blank. 'I mean, he'd have his people attack his own son?'

'Let's just say that I'm not exactly here with anyone's blessing. And from what I've found out, my father is not particularly keen to have others knowing about the palace or what it houses.' Thorn looks grim as he says this, and before I can move or Dante can question him further, a dog the size of a Great Dane, but more muscular and the colour of smoke at night, bursts into the room. Brixi spins into a deadly tornado of blades, catching the dog as it leaps at him. I turn away in horror as the dog falls in a heap on the floor. But even as I try not to see it, its body melts to goo and muck on the floor, leaving behind a gross mixture of intestines and bones.

'What the actual hell,' shouts Aiden, looking at the mess, shock clearly etched on his face.

'Kit, come.' Dante's grip is firm on my arm as he tries to pull me away from my position right in front of the doorway. More people are hurtling towards us, wild Fae dressed in leather and furs, their dogs barely restrained by leashes. 'Move away.'

I dig my heels in and scowl at him. 'No, we fight. I do not run away. Not ever.'

He doesn't have time to argue because chaos erupts in the room as we're crowded by howling Fae and barking dogs. I catch a glimpse of Thorn blasting pure energy into one of the Fae attacking him before ducking the blow of another and running him through. Aiden throws back his head and, with a wolf howl that startles the newcomers near him, he launches an attack of his own that looks devastating.

Dante tosses the taser to the side before punching one of the Fae in the head. Brixi's laying into the group with his blades and I keep a watchful eye on him as my own sword parries a blow from a mean-looking Fae. I catch a glimpse of his fanged necklace, and wildness rolls in his amber eyes. His sword is beautifully made, similar to a Japanese katana, but the blade's pitted and looks as if he's been using it to fry skewered meat over an open fire. I concentrate harder on blocking his thrusts and launch my own attacks. I notice that the Fae favours his left leg and I spring towards him. I pretend to stagger and overreach, putting myself inside his circle of defence.

'Hello, Blackhart. Didn't think we'd find you here. Thought you'd been scared away.'

'I don't kiss,' I say, swiping for his legs. 'On the first date, no matter what you've been told.'

He hit the floor with a bounce and as he does I launch

another kick to the side of his head and he lies still. A blow to my shoulder sends me staggering. My new opponent looks only a little less like a wild man from Wild Town. He doesn't bother engaging me in any kind of conversation and instead we have a friendly bit of banter by blade. Which is refreshing, because it's always hard coming up with one-liners when you're fighting for your life.

My opponent, after managing to bash the back of my sword hand with the pommel of his, stumbles into Brixi as he straightens from skewering one of his colleagues. Brixi pushes him back towards me and I spin, using his own momentum against him, then draw my blade across his throat.

There's no real chance to recover and get freaked out by the blood because the opponents keep coming. I fall back to the cuts and stances I've practised endlessly with Jamie and Marc. My movements stay fluid and I do my best to stay out of my friends' way as we battle the newcomers.

Dante's fighting with a large knife he's picked up from someone's body and he's bloody good at it. From the glimpses I get I recognize a mixture of capoeira, with other martial arts thrown into the mix. It seems rather effective in laying waste to the wild Fae rushing him. I have no idea what style of fighting Aiden's managing but it looks more like ripping, clawing and growling – and that's okay too because he's got a circle of prone and bleeding bodies scattered around him. The dogs have formed an outer ring and seem intent on watching him fight. It is one of the strangest things I've seen in my life.

Thorn is deadly and efficient in his fighting style. Blast of energy, followed by a cut to the abdomen or throat, then maybe a kick to complete the target passing on into unconsciousness. He looks so intense that I hardly recognize him or the way he moves. I've seen him fight before, but now he's less stylized and more fluid in his attacks. I sense his magic and the potential for it to rage within the limited space of the cave, and I feel my own magic hovering in response, ready to be called. I hold back, concerned that I might lose control of it and screw things up. What happened with Torsten and the rats in that alleyway is too fresh in my mind.

Because I'm worrying about other things, rather than the small wiry Fae dancing in front of me, with his two sharp knives, he gets past my guard. I feel the bite of his blade on the back of my arm, My blood slicks his blade and I gasp in surprise as pain flares in its wake. I lash out a kick and take him full in the chest because he's so much shorter than me and he goes flying. I run to corner him where he's collapsed in a bundle, gasping for breath. But Brixi grips my shoulder and pulls me away.

'No,' he heaves. 'We're done.'

He's right. I've lost count of how many of them we fought, but there must be at least twenty, not counting the dogs. The dogs! My gaze widens when I find Aiden kneeling beside one of them. The dog makes soft growling noises in its chest before collapsing to the floor and rolling on its back.

'That is just weird.' Dante says to him, wiping his blade on his jeans. 'You the dog whisperer too?'

'It's a wolf thing,' Aiden answers with a grin before straightening with a grimace.

Brixi walks towards Thorn and sinks into a low, if shaky bow. 'Thank you.' He casts a look over his shoulder towards the goddess and the children. 'But you really need to go now. Before more of them come. I need to secure these rooms and I can't do that with you here.'

Thorn turns to me and for the longest time, I just watch him watching me. I worry about the gore on me, about the mess my hair is in, the fact that I look like a thug. But he smiles and I grin back and then I'm in his arms and he's holding on to me as if he's never letting me go again. I lean against him for a long time, not liking the fact that I'm pressed up against that stupid cuirass he's wearing and it's not the most comfortable thing to be squashed against. But I love how his arms are hugging me tight as he drops a kiss on my forehead.

'Kit Blackhart, always in the middle of trouble,' he says as he pulls away, pushing strands of unruly hair from my face. 'This time I got to play at being the rescuer. How does it feel?'

I push him a little, laughing. 'Not sure I'll get used to it,' I say and I mean it. 'What are you doing here, Thorn?' I ask him. 'How do you know about Brixi and *her*?'

He grimaces. 'It's a long story.'

Chapter Fifty-Six

After going through their pockets, we move the bodies to one side of the room and those who've been injured to the other side. Aiden sets the dogs to guard the Fae, who seem completely taken aback by the change of events, especially the fact that their own dogs are being used against them. One tried luring his dog towards him, but was rewarded with a sharp snarl a mere hair's breadth from his vulnerable neck. He sat back in a hurry, looking queasier than warranted by a broken nose alone.

Aiden shows Thorn something they've taken from one of the bodies and they form a small huddle to discuss it. I consider joining them but my arm's hurting too much to bother.

I move to the side to see what I can do to stem the bleeding. I shrug out of my leather jacket and, after wrestling fruitlessly with my long-sleeved thermal vest, decide just to take it off. I am wearing a sports bra anyway so, even though there'll be a bit of pale belly skin showing, it won't mean the end of modesty as we know it.

Brixi's touch on my shoulder makes me jerk with fright but he offers a smile. 'I can help.'

He produces a large first-aid kit from a cunningly hidden

crevice and makes me sit down so he can check my arm. The cut is wide but not deep. He disinfects it quickly and expertly. I hiss in pain. His breath is warm as he blows lightly across the wound.

'If you open yourself to the songlines it will help you heal,' he says. 'Look, Thorn's cut has stopped bleeding and even the wolf boy looks fine.'

I glance over to them both and, yes, Thorn's cut is already healing and he's no longer bleeding from the wound in his side. Aiden's shaking his arms out, flexing his fingers and chatting as if he's not just been a devastating dervish of destruction. Dante doesn't look to be doing too well. He's standing to the side, staring at the heap of bodies and swallowing repeatedly. Even from where I'm sitting I can see how pale he's looking.

'Dante doesn't look good,' I say and he glances over briefly.

'A lot has happened for him today,' he says. 'Be kind to him.'

I grimace, feeling chastised. 'Are the kids okay? Is *she* okay?' I ask and nod towards the sleeping goddess, with the attendant small bodies lying on their tiny beds.

'Yes, they are all unharmed. The spell reacts to the intentions of those who approach. Had any of the other Fae run into the wardings, they would have been turned to dust.'

I gulp and look over at the soft haze. 'And you let me prod it and walk around touching it? I could have been killed.'

'Yes. But it was interesting seeing how it reacted to you. You were curious, not malicious.'

'Yes, but I could have been killed,' I repeat for emphasis,

letting my true horror show. 'You really could have warned me.'

Brixi's shrug is far more casual and *whatever* than I would have liked and I feel like punching him. But then Thorn walks over, just as Brixi finishes placing a series of small butterfly plasters across the cut on my arm.

'Kit,' he says and then seems unable to say anything else. He looks down at me, before dropping to crouch next to Brixi. 'We have to go. You have to leave the Otherwhere as soon as you can. You can't ever tell anyone what you've found here.'

'What?' I hiss. 'Are you crazy? What about those children? We have to figure out a way to get them away from here.'

He shakes his head. 'There is no way.'

Brixi excuses himself to go and check on Dante. We wait until he's out of earshot before I question Thorn further.

'How do you know about her, the goddess and the kids, anyway? Does everyone know?'

He shakes his head. 'I only know because Istvan told me during one of his crazy rambles, when he held me captive on the island. The geas he cast effectively prevented me from talking about it to anyone, including you, even in my dreams.' He touches my wrist lightly. 'I have tried for so long to tell you about her, to make you aware of her. I was terrified of the danger you'd be in if you continued your search for the children.'

'This? You knew what I was going through? Knew it would lead me here?' I ask him incredulously. 'How?'

The look he levels at me expresses so many things – annoyance, tenderness and amusement. 'Kit. It's what I do. I am pretty much aware of all the threats aimed at our realms.'

'And me? I was a threat?'

'You are a threat. The biggest threat this realm has seen since Istvan.'

My breath catches because he's not even joking. 'Okay. Now what do I do?'

'We get you to safety. You walk away from this, all of this, and we wait for it to die down.'

'Why must it die down?' I ask him. 'Those children belong with their parents, Thorn. This isn't fair on them.'

'You realize that if the children are taken from her, both our worlds will shake themselves apart?' His eyes are very serious. 'I can't allow that to happen.'

His fingers find mine as he talks and I have a really diffi-cult time concentrating on what he's saying. I seriously have to get over this boy or I'll be ruined forever more, I quietly vow to myself, before leaning closer to hear his hushed tones.

'I spent months researching her and I hardly slept. Kit, the library where I'm studying is vast. It makes my father's library look understocked. One day, I must take you there and show you the ancient treaties that were signed by the Fae – you can actually see how they divided the Otherwhere up into territories. It's incredible.' He sees the expression of disbelief on my face and laughs. He's obviously remembering that I'm more a smacking and stabbing kind of girl than a hiding in a library kind of girl. 'Anyway, I stumbled across a spell to wake the spirit of one of the old librarians. I asked for help to find more on the goddess, and she took me to the right shelves without a moment's hesitation. I smuggled the books to my room and hid them. Then, whenever I knew I'd be left alone, I'd study them. I've lived with knowing that she was real and not just a madman's dream for about two months.'

'The dream,' I say, leaning towards him. 'I started dreaming about this place months ago. You were always here, or on your way here. Sometimes those men and their dogs too.'

'I threw all my magic into pulling you into my dreams. I had to see you, tell you to be careful.'

'I thought I was, you know . . . dreaming about you because I missed you so much.' My hand claps over my mouth. That was so not what I meant to blurt out, yet I just did, much to my horror. Thorn's eyes soften and he brushes his lips across the knuckles of my bruised hand.

'I dreamed about you every night.'

Who has lashes like this in real life? They're thick and heavy against his cheeks as he leans even closer to press his lips against mine. It's a small chaste kiss, really, barely a whisper of a thing, but so full of promise that I feel like passing out. Oh my soul. He has to hear the sound of my heart thudding against my ribs. A flush has crept up my neck and I feel my ears blaze and my cheeks radiate heat.

'You need to breathe, Kit,' he says, his lips against my burning ear. 'Don't pass out.'

I find my brain, scoop it back into my head and lean back a bit to look at him. 'I can't think with you this close to me. You're very distracting.'

'I can barely keep my hands off you, Blackhart. You're the one who's only partially dressed.'

His grin is brazen and far more Aiden than I like. It jolts me a bit and I burst out laughing.

'Cheeky. Help me up. Let's go talk to the others.'

Aiden wraps an arm around both Thorn and me and hugs us hard. 'Look at us, back together again. Like the old days.'

I fight free of his grip and scowl at him. 'Less celebrating the "old days" and more figuring out what we're doing now,' I say to him.

'Kit's right. All of you, including Dante, need to leave here immediately. It's not safe here.' Thorn nods to the remaining handful of Fae who've been tied up. 'I need to figure out what to do with them sooner rather than later. My father will be expecting reports of goings on around the fortress, as he will have already heard about the three of you entering the Otherwhere.'

'What will you do?' Dante asks him curiously. 'He'll know that you've been here too, that you've been talking to Brixi. It's obvious that you've been here before and Brixi isn't much of a liar, I'll be honest.'

Thorn grins at his cousin and claps him on the shoulder. 'My father does well when confronted with truth, Dante. He ignores it and makes up a version of events that suits him better.'

I'm surprised by Thorn's cynical tone; it's very different to his deferential behaviour towards his father in the past.

'You need to be leaving,' Brixi says.' I've not scried for them but I know more are coming.'

Thorn nods brusquely and stands up to go and speak to Brixi. They seem to be talking about the captives.

'I don't want to leave the kids,' I say to Aiden and Dante. 'We promised we'd bring them home.'

'Kit, you heard what both Brixi and Dante said. If we move the kids, the Veil tears. This is bigger than us rescuing some kids. Far bigger. This is crazy business.' Aiden's face is serious as he looks over the sleeping children and the immobile goddess. 'Besides, I'm sure you thought about this yourself, but what if your parents died because of what they found out about her?' His voice dropped even lower. 'You have to admit it makes sense, Kit. We've seen how screwed up things get when the Fae are involved.'

I curse and nod at him, missing Thorn to lean against. 'I know. This is an even bigger mess than I'd first thought. I'd like to resign from this job now. I'm tired. I'm tired of the mess, the fuss, the blood, the fighting, the getting hurt.' I'm whining and I just don't care. 'All of it, really.'

Aiden gives me a quick hug. 'Sorry, matey. This isn't just a job. It's family.'

I rest my forehead briefly against his shoulder before nodding.

I push away from him and find the bloody shirt I'd discarded. Using my knife, I cut the right arm off at the elbow, so the fabric won't touch my wound. Next I shrug into my jacket, wincing as it scratches against the cut. But as it's the only warm thing I have, it will have to do.

Chapter Fifty-Seven

Brixi looks stoic as we leave him standing in the doorway to the goddess's chamber. I keep checking over my shoulder until he's completely out of sight. Thorn rests a comforting hand on my shoulder as we move as silently as possible back through the tunnels. There are echoes of voices from somewhere and dogs barking but Thorn moves swiftly and surely, leading us further into the fortress.

'This doesn't feel right,' I say for the umpteenth time. 'We can't just leave the goddess and those kids behind.'

Thorn catches hold of my hand and pushes me ahead of him. 'Come on, this is bad enough, don't make it worse.'

'How are you going to keep this hidden from your father?' This comes from Dante. He's less pale now we've left the cave. I think the fact that we're all armed probably helps too. I know I feel better for it. Holding onto a sword, even if you can't really use it, goes a long way to giving you courage.

'I'm not going to bother keeping it from him, I've decided.' Thorn's expression is dark. 'It's time my father admitted some of his secrets.' He takes out a gold coin that's maybe the size of a fifty-pence piece. 'The Fae who attacked us all had these coins in their possession. They're from my father's personal treasury.'

I roll my eyes because of course Aelfric of Alba would have his own personal treasury *and* coins – why not?

'Will the coins be proof enough to confront him about the goddess and the children?' Aiden asks. 'He can always say they were taken without his say-so.'

'I doubt it.' Thorn flips the coin in the air, catches it and hides it away on his person. 'Even the king is not above being questioned by his ministers if they find out that one of the Faceless has been breaking covenants to supply an Elder God with children. An Elder God everyone thinks was banished . . .' He grimaces. 'Imagine the outcry. And if it's revealed that my father was guarding the fortress in which the goddess was housed . . . there would be a lot of questions.'

'What would it mean for your family, though?' Aiden asks him. 'Won't there be problems?'

Thorn shrugs. 'Yes. My father would rage and he'd be forced to deal with the repercussions of lying to allies. It would be a good look on him. The outrage levelled against him would be considerable.'

'You sound dangerously like you're looking forward to this,' Dante points out. 'It could all go very badly wrong for you.'

Thorn's expression is resolute. 'I'm prepared to take the chance. There has to be another way to keep the Otherwhere safe and the Veil protected. We can't rely on a goddess that's been trapped against her will and whose magic might fail anyway.'

We fall silent for a while, Aiden and Dante leading the way while Thorn and I hang back a little.

'What do we do when we leave here?' I ask Thorn, feeling a bit forlorn.

'We stay in touch,' he replies without a moment's hesitation. His voice is low, keeping our conversation private. 'I can't not talk to you. Or hear what you're doing. Sometimes, when I scry, I sense you and wonder if you're sad. I want nothing more than to make you smile.'

He's so honest about this it makes my heart ache.

'Thorn, we can't do this,' I say, lagging behind so the others pull ahead of us even more. 'Things are going to get bad in the next few weeks when we try and figure out where to go next with these secrets. We can't have this, this *thing* we have.' *What the hell am I doing?* 'You know it's not allowed, us being together. It's your law.'

His expression is haunted but he nods, slowly, reluctantly. 'I know. I'm sorry.'

'We have to abide by the rules, right?' I watch his handsome face. 'Sometimes.'

'I don't want to. They are laws made by old and frightened lords keen to protect the purity of ancient bloodlines.' He looks pained but forces a smile. 'If only we'd been dealt different fates.'

'I'm human and you're a Sidhe prince fulfilling some grand prophecy. Nothing about us would ever not be complicated.' *Why am I saying these things? Why am I pointing out to him all the nos?*

He pulls me to a standstill and I turn to face him. 'I need you to know something. Those rules made years ago are not my rules. Never mine.' He moves closer until it's up to me to take half a step forward but I hesitate, fear making me a coward. He reaches up and tucks a curl behind my ear. 'But I know what you're saying. I hear it here.' He touches his head. 'And I hear it here.' He touches his heart. 'But here's the thing: something tells me that you and I have something very special, Kit. It makes me reject these out-of-date values and rules. I don't care about them or what my father would say. Or for that matter the objections from any of the Courts in Alba, or the other noble families across the Otherwhere. I grew to know you over a few days when the world was upside down, Kit. You showed me that you are someone very special indeed, someone who is smart, kind and loyal. Strangely, I can't get enough of your smile and, since I said goodbye to you, you are all I think about, and every night I pray to the gods to keep you safe.' His smile is embarrassed and cute. 'I sound ridiculous. I'm sorry, I'm not good with words.'

I bite my lip. 'You're fine with words,' I say. 'But we have to figure this out, Thorn. Sooner, rather than later, because you are a distraction and danger to my mental health.' I try to joke but it sounds horribly as if I'm about to cry.

His hand cups my cheek and he leans breathlessly close.

'Can I kiss you, Kit Blackhart? Before we figure things out and it turns out not the way I want it to be?'

In answer, I sway towards him but don't close the distance between us. His lips are warm and soft on mine and I sigh, feeling my eyes flutter shut. I shiver at the sensations drowning me, as I suddenly feel warm all over. Then his arm tugs me towards him and I let him pull me against him.

The kiss is even more devastating than the first time we kissed. My traitorous hands creep up, across his shoulders and tangle in the mess of hair at the back of his neck. I feel him rather than hear him murmur something against my mouth.

His one hand curls around my hip in a gesture of pure ownership and the other wraps itself in my own hair. I give in to my utterly female need to be held and kissed by this gloriously beautiful boy and open my mouth against his.

I lose track of time and I'm sure we stand there kissing for an eternity, but even so, when he lifts his head from mine and his eyes open to look down at me, it feels too soon.

'You are a drug, Kit Blackhart. The more I'm around you, the more I want to hold you.'

I mean, come on. Any girl in her right mind would want to hear something like this, from someone as incredible as him. I'm certainly not immune to his words or the heat in his gaze. I wrap my hand around his, duck my head as if I'm twelve and smile a secret smile that must tell him everything I can't quite say out loud.

'Are you guys done?' Aiden calls back towards us. His voice is impatient but his expression holds too much devilry. 'We're almost out.'

We turn and walk the rest of the way in silence, Thorn and I walk along the passage, our fingers linked.

Aiden and Dante are waiting for us at the top of the stairs and Thorn takes point, easily leading us out of the ruined palace. It looks to be late morning and I wonder how long we've been down in the caves. He guides us back through the village and across the clearing towards the forest.

I draw back in fright when I see the pale hounds sitting just within the treeline. They look *other* with their pink-red eyes and Anubis-like postures. They're all sitting at Nura's feet, so can't be a threat, but they're so motionless that it's freaky. Nura acknowledges us with a wave and gives Thorn a nod.

'My prince.' Her smile is brief and a bit stiff. 'I thought the hounds belonged to Odalis so I was surprised to see them roaming the forest. Then I remembered you were her guest.'

'Nura.' Thorn inclines his head respectfully. 'They are hers and she allows them to accompany me on my rambles. I stumbled across your charges while exploring the ruins of the old palace.' He turns to look at us and his gaze lingers on my face before he turns back to her. 'I think you should make sure they journey back to the Frontier from here. The forest isn't safe. Not even for the likes of us.'

'Crow is nearby. I think it's best if we start immediately.'

Thorn turns to shake hands with Aiden but Aiden pulls him into a hug instead. 'Stay in touch, Thorn. Don't leave it so long next time. We miss you, dude.'

'It was good meeting you,' Dante says to Thorn, gripping his hand firmly. 'I look forward to talking to you. Soon.'

Thorn keeps hold of his hand but looks at me. 'Get him to the Free Fae. They will look after him and introduce him to his kami family when he's ready.' Then he's speaking to Dante and there's urgency in his voice. 'You're not your father's son. Don't ever think that, no matter what others may try to make you believe.' He hesitates and I see the formality of his upbringing war within for just a second before he draws Dante into a hug. 'We have fought together and I am proud to call you friend and family.'

'Thank you. For everything.' Dante's voice is sincere, but I see his pain at the mention of his family. Aiden drapes an arm around Dante's shoulder and my heart is heavy for him.

The poor guy's been through so much in such a short period of time, it makes me feel so bad. For both of them.

Thorn fiddles with something around his neck before he pulls me towards him and presses it into my hand.

'I've been carrying this around for a little while now. I made it for you.'

I take the object from him. For a second the pendant makes no sense but then I realize what it is. It's a small scrying mirror, made of black obsidian set in a circle of silver, suspended from a silver chain.

'Do you remember my lullaby? I worked on this for months, so it should find me wherever I am. Give us a chance, Kit. We deserve it.'

He closes my hand over the little mirror and kisses my forehead.

A roar from somewhere in the forest dumps me straight back into reality and I jerk with fright. There's the sound of something big crashing through the forest and loud voices and dogs barking.

'Odalis's guards have found me,' Thorn says quickly. 'I didn't even think we'd get the chance to say goodbye. At least we got that. Now, go quickly and don't look back.'

Aiden's by my side before I can even react to Thorn's words. He grabs my hand and we start running, with Nura guiding us, just as the treeline explodes to the left and three ogres, the size of trucks, charge towards Thorn. There's the tell-tale feel of Thorn tapping into his magic, the familiar buzz and hum of it against my skin. We reach the far side of the glade and Nura and Dante are sprinting ahead, but I pull back against Aiden's guiding arm and look back. As I do, I see Thorn throw one last look at me over his shoulder before he shifts shape and lights up the clearing in a blaze of fire.

Even in daylight, the light from the exploding fire is so bright I have to throw my hand up to cover my eyes, but I still catch most of Thorn's transformation into a burning golden dragon.

It's something that will be forever imprinted in my mind as Thorn's bloodline reveals its other true form. Aiden yells something, but I can't make it out as he locks his arm around my waist and drags me with him. We retreat further into the coolness of the forest, while behind us there's just the incredible noise of roaring and flames.

extracts reading groups

books

competitions

discounts extracts

books new

extracts

competitions

books

discounts

new

events

extracts

reading groups

books

reading groups

events

extracts

discounts

books

extracts

new

titles

reading groups

new

interviews

books

events extracts

events

new

discounts

books

new books events

interviews

events

new books

www.panmacmillan.com

books

extracts events reading groups

competitions books extracts new